W9-BXU-603

0 1197 0781814 0

TRUST NO ONE

THE X FILES™

EDITED BY

Jonathan Maberry

IDW

PUBLISHING

DEDICATION

The authors of *X-Files Vol 1: Trust No One*
wish to thank the legion of fans
who have supported Scully and Mulder
since the beginning.

We know that you want to believe.
So do we.

Become our fan on Facebook **facebook.com/idwpublishing**
Follow us on Twitter **@idwpublishing**
Check us out on YouTube **youtube.com/idwpublishing**
Instagram **instagram.com/idwpublishing**
deviantART **idwpublishing.deviantart.com**
Pinterest **pinterest.com/idwpublishing/idw-staff-faves**

978-1-63140-278-4 **18 17 16 15   1 2 3 4**

COVER TREATMENT BY
WES DRIVER

EDITED BY
JUSTIN EISINGER

EDITORIAL ASSISTANCE BY
LAUREN GENNAWEY

COLLECTION DESIGN BY
RICHARD SHEINAUS/
GOTHAM

Ted Adams, CEO & Publisher
Greg Goldstein, President & COO
Robbie Robbins, EVP/Sr. Graphic Artist
Chris Ryall, Chief Creative Officer/Editor-in-Chief
Matthew Ruzicka, CPA, Chief Financial Officer
Alan Payne, VP of Sales
Dirk Wood, VP of Marketing
Lorelei Bunjes, VP of Digital Services

IDW founded by Ted Adams, Alex Garner, Kris Oprisko, and Robbie Robbins

The X-Files created by Chris Carter.

TABLE OF CONTENTS

INTRODUCTION

By Jonathan Maberry

The X-Files.

Every time I hear that name I have two immediate and conflicting thoughts.

Trust no one.

I want to believe.

Always. Bang, bang. Together but different like two sides of a coin.

Trust no one because, hey, no one is trustworthy. In a world (yes, pause and say it in that actor's voice) where there are shape-shifting alien bounty hunters, gender-swapping fundamentalist aliens, vampires, double and triple agents, government conspiracies, aliens among us, mind control, and a slew of other proofs positive that observation is fault and certain knowledge is either a joke or a suicidal tactical flaw.

Trust no one.

Sage advice from a government mole who lay dying on the street, a man almost certainly gunned down by his own people.

Trust no one.

And yet.

I want to believe.

I do. I really do.

Not just in the possibility of extraterrestrial life, but in all of it. The Jersey Devil, dybbuks, Native American medicine men, groups of savvy conspiracy theory gunslingers, astronauts who had seen things, small town sheriffs who have seen lots of things, sewer workers, and everyone else. There is something out there and I am willing to believe in it. Eager to believe.

On the whole, I am more like Mulder. I want to find those things that are probably there. The things that are hidden because no one has been brave enough to shine a flashlight into the darkness. Things that cruise the edges of our culture, relying on our civilized blind indifference. Things that are so radically different from us that we haven't even learned how to interact.

Oh, and the bad guys. The ones who hide and obfuscate and outright lie. The ones in black suits that are willing to pull a trigger to silence a voice. I want them dragged out into the light, too.

I want all of that.

And if I have my skeptical Scully moments, too, then so be it. Maybe I want to do more than believe. Maybe I want to see it. Test it. Weigh and measure it. Prove it beyond doubt.

This is *The X-Files*.

This wasn't a show Chris Carter popped out of nowhere. It's ground-breaking but the ground it breaks is common to many. There are a lot of skeptics out there, a lot of paranoid types. But shoulder-to-shoulder with them are the curious skeptics. The ones who don't believe but would be willing to crawl through the underbrush, or hide in a crypt, or slog through the storm drains to find out. Not to disprove, not really. They are secretly like Mulder. They want to believe.

So many of us do.

The X-Files opened up that secret door in our heads and let our doubt and paranoia and rationalization and restless curiosity all come out to play. We watched through shows with the nit-picking intensity of a crowd sitting through an important documentary.

We want to believe.

We want to know.

Watching a show as intelligent as *The X-Files* allows us to be partners in the conversation between those who want to know and those who are trying to keep that knowledge secret. And we let the relentlessness of Scully and Mulder drive us forward for nine seasons, two movies, comics, games, novels…

We still want to believe.

And with that, we still don't anyone worth a damn.

Which is the kind of reality check that keeps us from becoming the aluminum foil hat-wearing crowd.

Which brings us to this anthology. Not the aluminum foil hats, though a case can be made.

No, it's the lifelong love of *The X-Files* that allowed me to reach out to so many notable writers of mystery, thriller, horror, fantasy and science fiction. Every author here has been hand-picked for their love of the show, their understanding of how *X-Files* ticks, and for the quality of their storytelling. You don't have to wade through anything lukewarm in order to find a real boiler. Every single writer in *The X-Files: Trust No One* brought serious game.

They brought passion, too.

As if they all believed.

And they brought their natural skepticism and clinical attention to the details of federal investigation. They don't trust anyone.

But they all want to believe.

So will you.

Here are fifteen tales of darkness. The darkness from beyond our shared human experience to the far more personal darkness that hides beneath our clothes. These are not tales to pass a casual afternoon. These are tales with teeth. And claws. And...

Well you'll have to discover that for yourself.

You wouldn't be reading this if you weren't already caught up in the magic that was *The X-Files*. But even if you were a casual watcher of the show or a fan dedicated enough to be able to give the full names of each member of the Lone Gunmen, there is something new to discover here. Something new to make you lock your door, check to see if the phone lines are working, and keep the lights on.

I want to believe, I really do.

Because the truth is out there.

Let's go find it...

— Jonathan Maberry, *Editor*

CATATONIA

By Tim Lebbon

LYNOTT SOUND, MASSACHUSETTS
12th OCTOBER, 1994, 3 a.m.

"**D**id I wake you?"

"Mulder? Urgh… no, I had to get up to answer the phone. Damn, it's three in the morning, don't you ever sleep?"

"Why?"

"You get tired. Your eyes get heavy. You sleep."

"Oh, that. Sometimes. But not right now."

"Why not?"

"I need your help."

"Really? At three in the morning?"

"It *could* wait 'til tomorrow, I guess."

"What exactly is 'it'?"

"Lynott Sound. Little town in Massachusetts. Four kids vanished from home two nights ago, and yesterday morning they were all found in the local woods. Catatonic. They were brought home, and they're healthy but completely non-responsive. Sound intriguing?"

"Sounds like a bunch of kids on drugs."

"No drugs found in their systems, Scully."

"Mass hypnotism. They love playing around with that stuff. The less susceptible ones ran home because they were scared, leaving their friends out in the woods. Kids are cruel."

"They all vanished separately, and none of them are close friends. They'd never have been hanging out with each other. Scully, are you really doing this?"

"Doing what? Maybe they're just copy-catting. Happens a lot. One has a rare form of sleep apnea, the others think it's cool and gets them atten-tion, so they do the same. Classic teenage angst."

"Doing what you always do. Trying to rationalize it away."

"Look, *you're* the one who rang *me* for help!"

"You sound sexy when you're angry."

"I'm not angry, I'm tired."

"Then you sound sexy when you're tired."

"Damn it, why aren't you asleep? And anyway, we don't work together anymore."

"Officially."

"Right. So why do you want me along on this one?"

"Same reason as always. It wouldn't be the same without you."

"And because I'm the voice of reason."

"The reason is what we're looking for. See you midday tomorrow?"

"Lynott Sound, right?"

"A diner called Marshall's, just outside town. I knew you couldn't resist."

"I'm going back to sleep, Mulder."

"Sweet dreams, Scully."

As diner's went, it wasn't the most salubrious Mulder had ever visited. Two trucks stood on blocks at the edge of its graveled car park, wheels gone, windscreens smashed, seats ripped and spewing foam guts. A ditch that ran along the other side of the narrow road smelled like something dead. The building had once been a gas station, and though the pumps were gone, the tattered canopy remained, as did the stench of spilled fuel. It hung in the air as he slammed his car door and walked across the lot, and he felt faintly queasy as the tang of petrol fumes merged with the scent of hot fat and sizzling bacon. Mulder hadn't eaten for almost twenty-four hours, but this place did little to perk his appetite.

Paint peeled from walls, the door stuck in the frame, and the sign across the front—'Marshall's Diner'—had been hand-painted in uneven and dribbled paint. It looked like a place that wanted to be loved but made do with being needed.

But once inside, a huge woman behind the counter smiled and welcomed him with a friendly wave. There didn't seem to be any other customers. That didn't bode well, but the place seemed well-used and clean, on the surface at least. And Mulder was suddenly, surprisingly hungry.

"Now there's a man who needs a mug of coffee," she said, and she poured without waiting for a reply.

"Is it good?" Mulder asked, taking a stool at the counter. Still pouring, the woman looked up at him through wild eyebrows. She was ruddy-faced and round, the clichéd cheery chef.

"He asks if the coffee's good, Patton!"

"Good? Best coffee in the east." The old man was crouched in a window seat, so small, wizened and hairless that Mulder wondered whether he'd merit a file of his own. The mug on his table was almost as big as him.

"Patton?" Mulder asked. The old man waved a hand around his head, as if shooing away a fly.

"My mother didn't like me, my father never knew me."

"First name or last?"

"Depends on which side I get out of bed."

Mulder smiled, then shook his head when the woman—Marshall, he surmised, though he couldn't guess whether it was her first name or last——offered him cream and sugar. He picked up his hot mug and took a careful sip, and damned if Patton wasn't right. It was the best coffee he'd tasted in ages.

Still sipping, he glanced at the menu chalked clumsily on a wide board on the wall above the counter. It offered typical diner fare in an array of delightfully original, and occasionally worrying, forms. Bacon and pancakes with nut-warmingly sweet syrup, triple-death burgers, meatloaf with Heavenly mash fit for the Lord Himself, a variety of pastries baked with Wonder and Love. Cautious, he caught Marshall's eye where she worked stacking washed plates.

"So is the food as good as the coffee?"

"You judge by appearances, Hon?"

Mulder thought of the stink of gas, the ravaged trucks, and the coffee, and shook his head.

"I'll do you my breakfast special." She smiled and disappeared through a wide doorway into the kitchen beyond.

"First brewed that coffee myself, almost forty years back," Patton said. "Sourced the beans, measured the grind, stored them in a way only I knew how. Passed down what I knew to my daughter." He nodded in the direction of the kitchens, smiling warmly. "Now she's making coffee just as good as I ever did. People ask, strangers and regulars alike, they ask how we do it, what we do, when we grind and mix and pour, how long we let it stand, whether we use special water from a particular creek or well. They ask, but I don't tell 'em." The old man tapped his nose with a twig-like finger. "'Cos it's a secret."

Mulder sat at a table across the aisle from Patton. He couldn't help liking the man, and knowing that he was Marshall's father made the diner seem an even warmer, friendlier place.

"Yeah, well, I won't ask," he said, sipping at the divine coffee once more. "I like a good mystery."

"But mysteries are there to be solved, eh?" Patton asked. He looked Mulder up and down, his wrinkled smile not quite as open as it had been. "By people like you, I mean."

"People like me?" Mulder asked.

"Cops."

"I'm not a cop."

"Feds, then."

Mulder looked away and drank some more. He'd need a new cup soon, and he wondered whether the second would taste as good as the first. Some mysteries had a way of growing stale.

"I'm not your usual kind of Fed," he said softly. He didn't want to alienate this old guy. In small places like Lynott Sound, old characters like Patton might know things that most other people did not. Me might be shriveled and ancient and barely able to move, but Mulder guessed he had his finger on the pulse of the town. It was often people like this that possessed nuggets of information that could make or break a case.

Patton laughed, a brittle sound like a newspaper being crumpled. "You'll be here for the sleepers, then."

Mulder nodded.

"Buncha' kids. Drunk or drugged up, most likely."

"You really think that?"

"Sure." But Patton wasn't looking at Mulder any more. He was staring at his own hands, clasping the edge of the table before him as if terrified to let go. His knuckles were bony nubs, nails blackened scabs.

"There's something else," Mulder said.

"Angels' songs," the old man muttered.

"What's that?"

"Here ya go, hon," Marshall said, then whispered, "Oh, don't mind him, mad old coot." She slid a plate before Mulder, glancing back and forth between him and Patton. She didn't look quite so welcoming anymore. "You okay, Pop?"

"Can I get another coffee?" Mulder asked. "And one for my partner, too. She'll take cream, but no sugar."

"Partner?" the woman asked.

Mulder shrugged. "She's late."

Marshall disappeared back behind the counter, and while he dug into the breakfast of pancakes, eggs and crispy bacon, he glanced at Patton every few seconds, noticing how the tension slowly went out of the old man as he relaxed even more into the shiny leather seat. It could have been his age, diffusing the knowledge of what they'd been discussing. But Mulder thought it was a slow easing of anticipation. Patton had been expecting Mulder to ask some more, to delve deeper, and he was terrified at the prospect.

He knew to ease back, for now. Simply knowing that there were depths to plumb was enough.

"You'll get fat," a voice said behind him, and Mulder felt a rush of affection. He'd missed Scully. It had been almost two months since they'd seen each other, and although they spoke on the phone—and although she sometimes feigned frustration, he knew that she liked talking with him—nothing could trump meeting face to face.

"I have a fast metabolism," he said.

"Yeah, still full of bullshit."

Mulder stood to greet Scully. Her hair was longer, and perhaps she was a little leaner, but other than that she was the Scully he knew. Sharp suit, sharper wit, and a tongue that could cut a man in half from ten paces.

"Thanks for coming," he said. "It's good to see you."

She looked around, smiling briefly at Patton. "You bring me to the nicest places," she said quietly, so that only Mulder could hear.

"Yeah, but you've gotta try their coffee."

She smiled, and this time it touched her eyes. "So where's your new friend?"

"Krycek? Still running surveillance on a third-rate gang boss in Boston, and expecting me to relieve him..." He glanced at his watch. "... about an hour ago."

"You'll get into trouble with Skinner."

"Again?"

"Coffee's here," Marshall said, emerging from the kitchen. "Oh, so this is your partner. Very pretty, too."

"I hadn't noticed," Mulder said. "Can we get those coffees to go?"

"I've been driving for six hours!" Scully protested.

"All the more reason not to sit and relax," he said. "Come on, Scully. Places to go, sleeping people to see." He sensed movement behind him, and glancing back he saw Patton huddling down deeper into his seat. Perhaps he never moved from there at all. He was watching Mulder, barely acknowledging Scully's presence. Staring at him with those old, rheumy eyes.

Mulder dropped some cash onto the table, accepted the coffee cartons from Marshall, and nodded his thanks.

Outside, breathing in the fresh country air and stale fuel fumes, Scully yawned.

"I really need to sleep."

"You know the saying. You can sleep when you're dead."

"Oh, thanks Mulder, that's really nice and cheery."

"Come on. We'll take my car."

"Her name's Laura Connolly," Mulder said. "Thirteen, doing well at school, comfortable family."

"And why is she the one we're visiting?" Scully asked.

"Because her's is the first house we come to." Mulder offered her his charming smile, but she really wasn't in the mood. She was tired, and she'd slipped away from the Academy under the pretense of having a sick relative. She was running out of excuses. Mulder drew her on his wild goose chases, and she went along every time, drawn perhaps by the simple fact that he needed her, and perhaps...

Well, she was too tired to think about this now. Too exhausted to dwell on shadows and wraiths, and things that should not be. Her scientist's mind was never comfortable in that place, even when she was well rested.

"So what's her story?" she asked.

"Like the other three, she disappeared from home two days ago. Parents attest that she's a happy kid, not prone to running off. No boyfriend that they know of. No reason for her to skip school, not come home." They were approaching the outskirts of Lynott Sound, and it looked like a hundred towns Scully had visited. Normal, ordered, entirely forgettable.

"No parent knows their thirteen-year-old girl," she said.

"Speaking from experience?" Mulder asked. He was always smiling, always offering a joke.

"That's for me to know," she said, and she couldn't help smiling. Sometimes he just made her want to do that. "So where'd you get this information?" she asked. "Local police?"

"As far as I'm aware, they're no longer involved. The girl came home. Case solved."

"Hospitals, then? Local doctors? She must have been checked over, at least."

"Must have," Mulder said, but it was dismissive.

"So?" she asked. *Maybe I don't want to know*, she thought. Mulder had a shadowy side and often dubious sources, she'd already seen that, and she'd also seen what the Bureau thought of it.

"Just a guy I know," he said. "We're here."

"What guy?"

But Mulder was already out of the car and approaching the small, neat house. All she could do was follow. She got out of the car and brushed herself down, ran a hand through her hair, trying to forget how tired she was and how much trouble she'd be in if she wasn't back at the Academy by morning.

"Someone who wants us both to know," Mulder called back at her, before knocking on the front door.

A short, bald man answered. He seemed nervous, glancing past Mulder at her and back again.

"Morning, Sir. FBI." Mulder flashed his badge. The man became even more nervous, if that were possible.

"What do *you* want?" he asked.

As Scully drew level with Mulder she looked past the man into the house. Curtains were drawn and it was shady inside, but she smelled breakfast cooking, fresh coffee, and a couple of kids were running back and forth in the open living area, laughing and shouting.

"We're here to ask you about Laura," Scully said. She smiled, trying to put him at ease. But the man's gaze didn't settle. *Drugs?* she wondered, but only briefly. He wasn't high. He was scared. "She hasn't done anything wrong, Sir," she continued.

"Why are the FBI interested in her?" the man asked.

"Sorry, Mr. Connolly," Mulder said. "I should have explained. We're a very specialized part of the Bureau, just looking into ... very special cases. And your Laura appears to be special." If he was appealing to the man's pride in his child, it didn't seem to work.

"Don't you need a warrant, or something?"

"No," Scully said.

"We've only just got up, and—"

"Laura's awake?" Scully asked.

The man stared at her for the first time, and she could see the fear, deep and real. Fear for his child. "No," he said.

"I'm a doctor. I'd be happy to look her over. I'm sure you've already had her examined, and I'm surprised she isn't in hospital."

"There's nothing wrong with her, that's why!"

"I'm sure." She let that hang for a while.

"Come in," the man said at last, stepping back from the door. "I'll show you to... Just follow me and..."

"Who's that?" A woman appeared from the kitchen doorway, carrying a tray of plated pancakes. "Oh." She was short, thin and pretty, and Scully took an instant dislike to her. She couldn't really make out why, but she had learned to trust her instincts.

"We're just here to check on Laura," Scully said.

"Who's 'we'?"

"FBI," the man said.

The woman seemed to verge on panic, then quickly calmed herself.

"Kids. Breakfast." The two rug rats reduced speed to merely fast, snatching a plate each from the tray and retreating to a corner of the room to protect their feasts.

"I'll show you through," the man said. His wife put down the tray to follow.

"Any chance of some of that coffee you've got brewing in there?" Scully asked sweetly.

"Yeah, we've been travelling for hours," Mulder added. Good. He could see the trouble behind the mother's eyes, too. Scully felt a pang of regret that they didn't officially work together anymore. She missed that casual chemistry.

Hesitant, the woman nodded and slipped back into the kitchen, while the nervous man headed out into a hallway from the rear of the open-plan living area. Scully took a moment to size the place up—well-stocked bookshelves, a couple of nice prints on the walls, board games piled on one corner shelf. She moved closer to one of the prints, noticed it was an original painting, and then saw the signature Betty Connolly. They were an intelligent, creative family, and the place was clean and well kept. Yet they still had something to hide.

Maybe they were just troubled because they hadn't taken their catatonic daughter to hospital. Which was weird in itself.

"In there," the father whispered, standing back against the wall and gesturing towards an open door.

Scully experienced a shiver of doubt. She watched the man, not the room, but he was sad and lost, not alert and scheming. Mulder entered the bedroom and Scully followed.

"I'll bring the coffee," the man said as she passed.

"Thanks."

"If you can help her?"

Scully wasn't sure whether it was a condition or a request, so she simply did not reply. She couldn't. She still had no idea what she was about to face.

Unlike in the rest of the house, the bedroom curtains were open, and morning sunlight fell across the bed. It was a typical teenager's room—posters on the wall, books and albums in disarray on a couple of shelves, stereo silent on a corner table. Clothes were piled on a chair and in a washing basket in another corner, and a wardrobe stood open, displaying a splash of colorful attire. A dressing table mirror held a scatter of photographs around its edge, all of them showing smiling, happy teenagers accompanying the girl in the bed.

She looked nothing like she did in the photos. She looked dead.

Scully heard Mulder's sharp intake of breath. "Scully..." he said, and she knew what he was thinking. The girl was dead, and the parents were keeping her here, unable to accept the fact of their daughter's demise. A horrific idea, but she'd heard about it happening before.

Crossing quickly to the bed, she took up Laura's hand where it lay outside the sheets. It was warm. Her pulse was slow and strong. Scully's shoulder relaxed, and she breathed a sigh of relief.

"She's alive," she said.

"Phew," Mulder said. "Well, they're hiding something else, then."

"For sure."

While Mulder looked around the room, Scully began examining the girl. She was deeply asleep. Her eyes did not seem to be moving, and her breathing was slow and even. Her skin was warm to the touch, but the blankets used to cover her were probably too thick for the time of year. She touched her beneath the nose, pinched her ear lobe, then lifted the covers at the bottom of the bed and scratched the underside of her foot. Laura emitted a low groan, but nothing else.

"How is she?" Mulder asked. He was pacing the room, opening drawers, touching objects, doing what he did. He had an eye for things out of place. If a hint about whatever the family was hiding was in this room, he'd find it.

"She seems fine, physically," she said. "At least from a cursory examination. I could do some sensory tests, given time, but I'm not sure Mommy will want me sticking needles in her girl."

"Nothing obviously amiss?"

Scully looked again, checking the girl's relaxed face, lifting her long hair away from her ears. She glanced up at Mulder and nodded towards the bookcase in the corner.

"Oh, sure," he said.

Scully lifted the covers and popped open the buttons on the girls night dress. Without moving her, a full check over was impossible. But she seemed like a normal teenager in good health. Just sleeping.

Deeply asleep.

Scully held Laura's hand again. Turned it over, scratched at her palm. No response. Then she examined her fingers.

"Look here," Scully said.

"Cut on her knuckles."

"Yeah. Scratches, really. Might have bled a little, but not much. But look under her nails."

"Dirt. She was found out in the woods, with the three others who disappeared."

"She's clean everywhere else. Even the bottom of her feet. She's been bathed and changed more than once since she was found, and what mother wouldn't do that? This is more recent. And I don't think it's mud."

Mulder glanced back at the open bedroom door, suddenly more alert and serious. He drew a penknife from his pocket and opened a small blade. While Scully held the girl's hand steady, Mulder scraped the tip of the blade beneath the nail of her index finger, careful to retain the matter that crumbled out.

He held it up at eye level, and they both drew close.

"That's blood," Scully said.

Mulder touched his fingertip to the blade, picked up a speck of the dark detritus, and rubbed it between his fingers. Then he showed Scully. Both fingertips displayed a gritty red smear.

"And not that old," he said.

"Can you help her?" the father asked. He stood at the doorway, his wife behind him. The man held coffee cups. They steamed. To Scully, it didn't smell very good.

"Has Laura moved since you found her in the woods?" Mulder asked.

"No!" they both said at the same time. "No, not at all," Mr. Connolly continued. "When they were found, the first thing we did was bring her home." He nodded past them at his daughter, tears in his eyes.

"She's asleep, and dreaming," her mother said. She never quite met Scully's eyes.

"What do you mean?" Mulder asked.

"She makes noises. In her sleep. As if she's being…" Her face crumpled, and Scully felt regretful about her earlier assessment of the woman. "Being hurt," the girl's mother said.

"She really needs to be in a hospital," Scully said. "She's catatonic, similar to a low level coma. Does she suffer from any mental illness? Take drugs? Is she on any new medicines?" Her parents shook their heads. "Well, she needs looking after by—"

"No!" The father came forward quickly, coffee cups slipping and spilling hot fluid down his stomach and legs. He dropped the cups, Mulder backed up, hand lifting to his belt, and Scully held her breath.

The man gasped and clasped at his clothes, pulling them away from his body as the coffee quickly cooled.

"Once they have her, they might never let her go," the woman said. "She'll be an oddity."

"Why do you say that?" Mulder asked. The couple, obviously troubled and deeply disturbed, offered no reply. The woman stepped back, gesturing for them to leave.

I should ask about the blood, Scully thought. But Mulder spared her a quick glance, and in that look she saw that he shared her own concern. Something was going on, and they had to be delicate getting to the bottom of it.

They passed back through the living area and out the front door. Scully looked back at the woman following them, recognizing her fear, wanting to help. But she also saw the haze of secrecy, and the blood beneath the girl's fingernails was troubling.

She and Mulder had to ask around. And after that they'd come back.

"She's a good girl," the mother whispered.

"I'm sure she is, Mrs. Connolly. But you need to help her."

Back in the car, Mulder started the engine and pulled them away from the house.

"That could have gone better," he said.

"They're terrified," Scully replied. "The girl's the center of that house, did you feel that? They're just orbiting around her, and something's scaring them more than the condition she's in."

"And what condition is that?" Mulder asked.

"Catatonia is traditionally recognized as a symptom of schizophrenia. But it's an effect that can be found in drug users or alcoholics, especially when they're going through withdrawal."

"She didn't strike me as an alcoholic or junkie."

"No, nor me."

"And the same effect on four people?"

That was what confused Scully. If the others were similar to Connolly, then they were looking for an outside cause. And that made things so much more complicated.

"There's a human-jaguar hybrid in the Amazon," Mulder said. "It's a legend leftover from the Aztecs. It breathes its victims to sleep and sets them hunting for it."

Scully rolled her eyes, hoping that Mulder saw.

"Border control isn't what it used to be," he continued. She could hear the subtle tone of self-mockery in his voice, but she usually assumed it was a defense mechanism rather than self-deprecation. She still wasn't sure how much of the tall stories Mulder came out with he actually believed, but she knew for sure that he *wanted* to believe.

"Really?"

"Just an option, Scully. These stories come from somewhere. Maybe the people who came up with that one knew of a plant extract, a drug, something that put people to sleep like this. And maybe that plant has somehow appeared in these local woods."

"Or maybe a jaguar monster put them to sleep and is using them to hunt, eh, Mulder?"

"What else caused what's happened? And why is it not only her?"

"We haven't seen the other cases yet."

"Way ahead of you."

As they drove through the little town, Scully remained alert. Her tiredness still burned behind her eyes, but since seeing Laura Connolly and witnessing how flighty her parents were, she already knew this was not a normal case.

If there ever *was* a normal case involving Mulder. She'd seen strange things with him, experienced some phenomena that could not easily be rationalized away. She tried. She had to try, because she was a scientist and a realist. But sometimes logical explanations were not so easy to find. The difference between her and Mulder was that she actively looked for them, while he consciously willed them aside.

"You think her parents just missed that blood under her fingernails?" Mulder asked.

"Not when they brought her home, cleaned her, and put her to bed, no."

"Which means it got there later."

"That's what I figure."

"When she was supposedly asleep."

"Right." Scully nodded, frowning. *Hunting for the jaguar beast*, she thought. *But hunting what?*

They drove through the town square and into another street, a wide road with houses spread a comfortable distance apart, mature trees shading them, and four-wheel-drives on driveways. It was the classic image of an affluent neighborhood.

Mulder drew up in front of a big, light blue house, checking out a slip of paper in his hand.

"Here we are. The home of—"

"Oh, shit," Scully said. "Look who's come to the party."

A familiar man leaned against a car already parked across the street.

"And I didn't even send him an invite," Mulder said.

He didn't trust Krycek. Introduced as a partner, Mulder thought of him more as a watcher, a guard, someone to keep track of him and his more arcane beliefs and concerns. What the purpose behind this observation was, he was not yet sure. But he was determined to find out.

They got on well enough, even though their surface bonhomie hid a deeper suspicion and mistrust. Mulder saw it in Krycek, and he made no effort to hide it himself. That was why he'd slipped away from their meaningless stakeout to come here, leaving Krycek behind.

At least, that was his intent.

As Mulder and Scully crossed the road towards him, Krycek yawned and stretched his arms to the sky. He interlaced his fingers, clicking them. He was fit and strong, and if this display was intended to intimidate Mulder, it failed. He'd seen enough to know that real strength was mostly hidden away.

"How's our friend Morrissey?" Mulder asked, referring to the two-bit gangster they'd been watching back in Boston.

Krycek shrugged but said nothing.

"Did he make you?"

Krycek's face darkened, but only for an instant. "He'll still be there tomorrow."

"Maybe I still won't."

Mulder's partner sighed heavily as if already bored with the conversation, then turned to Scully. "Dana. Radiant as ever."

"Surprised to see you here, Krycek," she said.

"Likewise."

"Just helping Mulder on a new investigation."

"Authorized?"

A loaded silence. Then Krycek laughed.

"Not that I give a shit about that, really, guys. Give me a break. I've come a long way, and only because I know Mulder's got a nose for an interesting case."

"And how did you follow me?" Mulder asked.

"We have mutual friends."

It must have been X, Mulder thought. He knew the man by no other name, knew nothing about him, no clue as to his intentions or allegiances. But X provided good intel on cases that might be classed as an X-File, even though the X-Files no longer officially existed. Mulder supposed it was arrogant to assume that he was the only one X chose to talk to.

"There's a guy at a diner out of town, place called Marshall's. Old guy, Patton. I'm pretty sure he knows something he's not telling. He already knows me and Scully and why we're here, so maybe you'd have a better chance of getting something from him."

"Sending me on an errand, Spooky?" Krycek asked. "And I've only just arrived."

"You want to investigate?" Mulder asked, perhaps harshly. "I guess you already know the basics. Scully and I are checking in on the victims, but that guy Patton knows more. Ask him about the angels singing. Weird thing he said to me. Then perhaps between us we can clear up the bigger picture."

"Yeah, perhaps." Krycek yawned again and took a long, slow look around them. "Pretty little place. Sort of place you'd never remember visiting."

"Let's hope it stays that way," Scully said.

But Mulder thought not.

"He got here quickly," Scully said. They were standing on the front deck of the big blue house, waiting for their knock to be answered.

"He's got a nose for an interesting case."

"I don't believe that for a minute," she said.

The door opened. A young black man answered, dressed in shorts and a tight tee shirt. Good looking, fit, exuding arrogance.

"We're looking for Walter Russell," Scully said.

"Yeah."

"Is he home?"

The man pointed at himself with his thumb.

"You?"

No reply.

"Is this the home of Rosie Russell?"

The man's face softened a little, but he only nodded.

"Can we see her?" Mulder asked.

"You Feds?"

Scully reached for her badge, but the man waved them in. Mulder had told her that Rosie Russell, another one of those who'd vanished and turned up catatonic, was almost eight years old, so she'd been expecting someone in their early thirties, at least. This man looked barely old enough to be out of college.

The house was large, well-appointed, and as attractive as its owners. Inside they were met by Walter Russell's wife, equally young and fit and pretty, and she showed them upstairs to their little girl's bedroom.

It was mostly the same. Scully examined the girl while Mulder prowled the bedroom, opening books, looking inside wardrobes, running his fingers along shelves. He grunted softly a couple of times, but said nothing. The mother remained in the doorway. They asked her questions and she answered through tears, and Scully could see that she had been crying a lot. None of the answers seemed evasive, and the parents displayed only a deep concern for their daughter. She'd been examined by the town's doctor and pronounced in good health, other than the strange sleep that held her low.

Scully checked the girl's hands and nails. They were clean. But she wasn't clean all over.

Outside, standing by their car with the sun warming her skin, Scully closed her eyes and looked to the sky.

"Well?" Mulder asked.

"She had dried blood at the corners of her mouth and in a couple of creases in her lower lip."

"Her own?"

"Not sure." She felt strange even saying it, because the implications seemed too heavy. She kept her eyes closed, sensing Mulder's expectant silence. "But I don't think so. No sign of wounds, no damage inside her mouth." She opened her eyes. The glare of the sun hurt them, and she squinted and turned her head away. It hurt to look too closely.

"We should visit the other victims," Mulder said.

"Maybe they don't need us," she replied. "Maybe they need psychologists. Therapy. There's nothing apparently wrong with Connolly or Marshall, and I'm guessing the other two will be the same."

"Apart from the blood."

"That's jumping out just because we're looking for something amiss."

"Scully, that doesn't sound a bit like you."

"What, you think we should go jaguar hunting?"

A police car approached quickly along the street, nose dipping as it braked. "No need," he said.

Krycek jumped from the passenger seat. The cop who climbed awkwardly from the driver's side was huge, tall and round, his uniform stained with sweat marks and dried food. He looked grim.

"Agents," he said, touching the brim of his hat as if he welcomed FBI into his small town every day.

"So you didn't get to the diner," Mulder said.

"Sheriff Meloy picked me up before I could," Krycek said. "He needs us to go with him to the doctor's surgery."

"Why?" Scully asked.

"Because that's where the bodies are."

Bodies, thought Mulder. *There are always bodies.* This time he'd been hoping that they were sleeping one, but it seemed they weren't that lucky.

He remained by the door of the examination room. They were waiting for an ambulance to come and take them to the nearby hospital, but meanwhile Scully was checking them over, much to the Sheriff's chagrin. But he did not try to intervene. He stood in the corner, breathing like a landed walrus and whispering with the old doctor who'd probably been treating the town for half a century.

Krycek had remained in the reception area, saying he had to use the phone. Mulder suspected he was checking in, perhaps with Skinner. Trouble was brewing. But with three dead people laid out before him, he was hardly concerned.

They had died badly.

"I'm done here," Scully said to the Sheriff and doctor. "I agree, looks like animal attacks. Could be black bear or coyote."

Mulder raised an eyebrow in surprise, but refrained from making any comment. Even from where he stood he could see obvious signs that she had pretended to ignore, and she'd have a reason for that. Looking at the sheriff and doctor, seeing an apparent relaxing of tension in them, he thought he knew what that was.

"Okay, we're all done here," Krycek said from behind Mulder. He'd approached quietly. Mulder would have to watch that.

"What does that mean?"

"It means Skinner's ordered us back to Boston, and Scully's been missed from the Academy. We're all in trouble. Thanks, Mulder."

"I'm used to it."

"Yeah, but I'm not." The big man couldn't keep the smile from his eyes, and Mulder sensed something deeper. There was excitement there, not fear over being reprimanded.

"You should make sure you get some specialists in, hunt down whatever did this," Scully said.

"Oh, we will, we will," the sheriff said. "So you'll be leaving?" He'd heard Krycek and directed the question to him.

"Tomorrow," Mulder said. "We're all tired, and it's a long way back. Is there a good place to stay in town?"

If there was a good place, the sheriff certainly didn't seem keen on telling them.

"If not, we can just hang around town for the evening, asking questions."

"Deakin's Hotel out on 12th is pretty decent," the sheriff said. "Tell them I sent you."

"Will that get us a discount?" Mulder asked.

The sheriff didn't answer. He was talking to the doctor again as the little man covered the bodies.

"I guess we are done here," Mulder said.

"We should get back now," Krycek said when they were outside. "It's not that late. We can make the journey before midnight and be back where we're supposed to be tomorrow."

"I think I'm supposed to be here," Mulder said. He surveyed the little town square, trying to see it with fresh eyes, not filtered through the knowledge of what had happened here. Four people in a deep slumber, three more dead.

"Animal attack," Scully said as if weighing the words. "And all three victims were from out of town."

"Coincidence," Krycek said.

"I don't believe in coincidences," Mulder said.

Krycek laughed out loud, attracting the attention of a group of kids on their way home from school. "Really? You believe in everything else."

"I'm tired and hungry," Mulder said. He wanted Krycek away from them, wanted to be closer to Scully so they could talk, bounce ideas off each other, and do the thing they did best. He hadn't known her for long, but already it felt like forever. They worked well together. They were a team, and even though they'd been pulled apart, the draw between them felt stronger than ever. That's why he'd called her down here.

"You're really staying at this town's crummy hotel?"

"Sure. See you there." Mulder and Scully walked towards her car.

"My car's halfway across town!" Krycek protested.

"Enjoy your walk," Mulder said.

"Animals, Scully?"

She started the engine and pulled away, glancing in her rearview mirror. Krycek was watching them go, and there was something about his stance that scared her. He watched intently, wound like a spring. She pressed on the gas and got them away from there as fast as she could. The guy spooked the hell out of her.

"I'd say they were beaten, clawed, and bitten to death by other people," she said. "Some of the bite marks looked like they were done by human teeth. Scratches were done by nails, not claws. Brutal. Horribly violent."

"I really don't like the way this is going."

"I don't think it's going. I think it's here already."

"Is that little Russell kid really capable of—"

"What's that?" Mulder was pointing ahead, and above a huddle of houses a dull blue light glowed high in the sky. It pulsed, as bright as the sun and then brighter, seeming to grow and shrink with each beat.

Several cars skidded to a halt, drivers leaving them and dashing towards the closest buildings. Pedestrians ran. In moments the street was deserted.

"Not good," Mulder said. Scully gripped the steering wheel hard.

The sound smashed in. Loud, sudden, sharp and clear, the ululating call might have been a scream or a song, all in a language she did not know. It came from outside and rang within, reverberating inside her skull like fantastical hymns in a cathedral's dome. It hurt, and it was beautiful. It caused pain, and ecstasy.

Scully gasped, pressing her hands to her ears, and for a moment she lost herself, forgetting where she was and what she was doing. She had the presence of mind to slip her foot from the gas, but the car drifted to the right and its wheels struck the high curb, rocking them in their seat, before nudging the back end of a parked truck and stalling. She leaned back in her seat, pushing harder against her ears but then relaxing. She wanted to shut out the noise altogether, and welcome it completely into her head. *It's the song of forever*, she thought, and she would have been happy to accompany it.

A shadow flickered before her, a shape distorted in her blurred vision. The shadow moved quickly and her head flipped to one side.

She saw across the road, and the previously busy street was deserted.

"Scully!" The voice cut in over the song, crass and clumsy and so much less than the beauty and horror of what she was hearing. She tried to ignore it but was struck across the face again, and when she turned her head back she saw Mulder. He was saying something, holding both hands out to her and clasping something between his fingers. Small, silvery shapes. She couldn't hear him. She didn't want to hear him. Bucking, trying to shake him off, she raised her hands and—

Mulder pressed against her and she felt pressure in her ears. Cold pressure, heavy and harsh.

"No!" she shouted, because the song was all but gone. Her own voice was muffled.

Mulder held her face in his hands and stared at her. He held up one finger, picked up his gun's magazine with the other hand, and slipped out a shell. Then he turned his head and touched his own ear, and she saw the tip of another shell pushed deep into his ear canal.

"What the hell..." she said, but realized he couldn't hear her. She could barely hear herself.

Mulder waved both hands around, then froze as he looked past her towards the rear of the vehicle.

Scully twisted in her seat to follow his gaze.

Along the street, back the way they had come, Krycek was struggling with two shapes. One of them was a tall youth she didn't know, dressed in shorts and nothing else. The other was Laura Connolly.

Scully tumbled from her door, fell to the ground, scrabbled upright and pulled her gun. Mulder was already running across the quiet street. Several cars sat badly parked, doors open and occupants missing. She saw no one else.

Krycek was pushing the boy back, one hand held flat in front of him, the other raised in a threatening fist. He looked terrified, distracted and in pain, as if he was struggling to fight against something inside. But while he fended off the tall boy, Laura Connolly was scratching at his clothing and biting at his hip and stomach. Gnawing, Scully saw as she drew close. And there was blood.

A whisper came in, an insinuation of the strange song she had heard. She wanted to dig the shells from her ears and hear again, but she saw Mulder power into the boy, shoving him away from Krycek and against the glass window of a bookstore. The glass rattled but held.

Scully went for Laura Connolly, grabbing her beneath the arms and pulling her aside. She had her teeth well into the minimal flab around Krycek's waist, and as Scully pulled a shred of clothing and skin stretched, splitting and spitting blood.

Krycek screamed, distant and strange. His eyes were still wide and he appeared not to have seen Mulder and Scully. He was looking for something else.

Scully threw the girl. She bounced from a parked car and sprang upright again, attacking with hands outstretched and an expression that was completely neutral and vacant.

Scully raised her gun but the girl took no notice.

She could not fire. Instead, she stepped aside, tripped the girl, and shoved her in the back as she fell. Laura hit the pavement, her head ricocheting from the concrete. She lay still. Scully was glad she hadn't heard the impact, and she took a moment to feel for the girl's pulse. It was slow, gentle, as if she still slept.

Mulder had fought off the tall boy and punched him to the ground, securing him to a bike rack with his handcuffs. He wiped blood from his face and nodded at Scully, then looked past her at Krycek.

He was wandering across the road, stumbling and aimless, looking up at the sky with his hands held out as if praying for rain.

Scully ran at him, slipping the magazine from her gun as she went. Her heavy breathing echoed in her head, and she was glad, because it cut out any errant whispers of that weird song. She pushed a couple of shells from the magazine, thrust it and the gun into her pocket, then paused behind Krycek.

What if he's now as bad as them? she thought.

But then Mulder was with her. He snatched one shell from her and pressed it firmly into Krycek's left ear. Scully did the same to the right, and the man slumped before them, going to his knees and then lying flat out on the pavement. He had his head to one side, and Scully could see his wide, fearful eyes.

She and Mulder stood staring at each other, taking comfort. Then they looked around. She saw blinds flicker along the street, and spinning around she caught sight of a curtain falling back into place. The boy was struggling against his handcuffs, and Laura Connolly was stirring, lifting herself up and ignoring the ugly, bloody bruise on her forehead.

And then they both fell again and grew completely still, and a pressure Scully had barely even noticed lifted from her skin. It was as if a heavy, cloying atmosphere had suddenly been sucked away. She gasped, probed a fingernail into her right ear, and flicked out the shell.

Cool air rushed in, and silence. A deeper silence than she had ever heard. Until Mulder said, "Holy shit."

"That way," Scully said, pointing away over a row of shops.

"Yeah," Mulder said. "Where that weird glow was."

"Like a beacon."

"What was it?"

Scully shook her head. "I've no idea. But it did something to the sleepers, the town was ready for it, and it was horrible."

Mulder walked back to the fallen boy and girl. They were motionless. "Were they even awake?"

"We need to find out," Scully said. "I think if we hadn't been here, if you hadn't thought of that bullet thing, Krycek might be dead now."

"Yeah. And looks like the locals are taking an interest again."

Mulder was right. Doors were opening, townsfolk emerging. Many of them were slack-jawed and dribbling, some wandering almost aimlessly. A few looked their way, but none of them seemed particularly threatening. Some appeared drunk. A few simply stood there and smiled.

"Why was Krycek so scared?" she asked.

"Because he knows more than he's letting on," Mulder said. "Come on. I should have put it together before, but I think I've got an idea where that sound was coming from."

"And where's that?"

"That old guy Patton talked about the angels' song, and when X passed me the tip about this place, he mentioned that the sleepers were all found in a clearing in a woodland outside of town. Nephilim Woods."

"Him?" Scully asked, nodding down at Krycek.

Mulder grabbed her arm and pulled her towards the car. "He can thank me later."

It felt good driving from town and out into the countryside. The sun was dipping down into the hills to their left, and ahead of them were swathes of woodland. It was beautiful.

Scully had asked him to drive, saying she still felt dizzy and disconcerted. So did he. But he didn't need to tell her that.

Something weird was happening here. The townsfolk were involved, and he was sure that Krycek had an inkling as well. But Mulder wanted the whole picture. Both of them had dropped the two shells they'd used into their jacket pockets. The shells remaining in the guns themselves were protection of a more aggressive manner.

The road wound across the hillside, then veered off down to the right and towards a spread of woodland, signposted Nephilim Woods. He drove between the trees, and the road quickly narrowed, shaded by the tall pine and birch and lined with shallow ditches on both sides.

"We should be calling this in," Scully said.

"You see a phone booth anywhere close?"

"But we left them on the road, that boy and girl."

"Krycek's with them."

"Is he?"

He knew what she meant. His suspicions about Krycek were hers as well, and neither really knew where his true loyalties lay.

"Something's using them, Scully. Whatever drew them out here and put them to sleep, it has some sort of a hold on them. Did you see their faces?"

"Blank."

"*Empty.* While they're like that they're not eating, or drinking, and they're wasting away."

"And killing," she said. "Let's not forget that."

"Right. So we help them best by breaking the hold."

"So what is this, Mulder? Military? Some sort of experiment?"

He didn't answer because he did not know, and flashes of memory were making him nauseous. The sound of those voices. The joy their song promised, and their harmonious hum of despair.

"What did you come here expecting to find?" Scully asked.

"I don't know. That's what draws me."

The going was getting harder, road surface broken and crumbled by successive years of heat and frost and negligible maintenance. Weeds sprouted between the cracks. Whatever was out here, not many people bothered paying it a visit.

"Looks like we're going the right way," he said, slowing the car and pointing at a painted wooden angel shape nailed to a fir tree's trunk.

"Seems it used to be a popular place," Scully said.

Mulder drove on. And he was so intent on what lay ahead that he didn't see what came from behind until it was too late.

At the last instant he glanced in the rearview mirror and saw the bright bulge of headlights on full, then the car struck. Scully cried out and braced herself against the dashboard, and Mulder gripped the wheel as it jumped in his hand, trying to hold on as the car slewed to the left. He slammed on the brakes and heard the straining engine of the vehicle behind them, shoving them towards the ditch on the left and using their momentum to drive them over. The car lurched, hard, knocking the wind from them, and the tree loomed large before them.

Mulder had a chance to lean across and meet Scully where she leaned towards him, and they hugged as the impact smashed through the car.

Seat belts tugged tight, cutting into his stomach and the side of his neck. Glass smashed and shattered. A weight drove back against his legs, the steering wheel crumpled and crushed against his side. The stink of heat and spilled petrol filled his nose as he gasped in the next breath. Scully's hair tickled his face and nose, and her hands gripped the back of his jacket, holding him tight.

The car rocked back on broken axles and settled, creaking and clicking. And dripping.

Mulder breathed in deeper and held his breath.

"Scully?"

"Yeah." She pulled back and tugged the gun from its holster on her belt.

"Gas is leaking."

She nodded, and they both kept hunkered down, looking past the back seat towards the other car. But the rear window had smashed and remained in place, misting opaque. A few areas fell away, affording them a limited view of the ditch and road behind them. Just enough to see tires spinning, dust rising, and to hear the other vehicle speeding away back towards town.

"Let's get outta here," Mulder said. He noticed blood on Scully's face, but that would have to wait.

They scrambled from the car, falling into scratching and prickling bushes.

"Into the trees!" Scully said. Mulder knew she was right—the attacker might easily have left someone behind with a rifle. Crouching, both now clasping their guns, they pushed past the wrecked car and sought the shelter of deeper woodland.

Moving felt good. Moving away from the wreck felt better. The car was a write-off, but Mulder knew that they were close. Nephilim Woods called, silent but just as powerful as that strange song. Someone didn't want them out here, and that was more reason than any to continue. He was shaken from the crash, but the adrenalin rush had sharpened his senses. He scanned the forest ahead of them for movement, and every few steps he glanced back towards the car and road. Already the vehicle was a vague shape behind trees and undergrowth, steam hissing from the ruptured radiator and clouding the scene. Beyond, the road was nothing but an open space. There was no sign of anyone watching them, and no evidence of pursuit.

Whoever had run them from the road had not stayed behind to finish the job.

For a few minutes they moved quickly, silently, heading slightly downhill and crossing several old, overgrown paths. Poison ivy brushed subtly against the backs of their hands and brambles pricked their skin. Then Scully said, "Mulder, here." She had paused ahead next to a large fallen tree, leaning on the downed trunk and holding her gun by her side. She was breathing hard, but he sensed the same excitement in her. The scent of a mystery. She wasn't so open about the allure of the unknown as him, but he knew she felt it.

He joined her by the tree and looked into the clearing beyond.

"Just an old quarry," he said.

"Maybe."

"What do you mean?" But Scully didn't answer. She was looking, frowning, and Mulder did the same.

The clearing was maybe fifty meters across, totally denuded of trees and stripped of all grasses and undergrowth. A few errant shrubs and weeds grew here and there, but they were lackluster, colors muted by layers of dust. The far edge of the clearing dropped away into a much wider open area—the quarry. In the clearing stood several items of old equipment, probably used for excavation or above-ground movement of materials. Mulder saw a broken conveyor belt tangled with rusted framing, several huge wheels piled together bearing deflated tires, a small vehicle of some kind with decayed cabin and smashed windows.

"There," Scully said, pointing. "And there."

And Mulder saw. Not every piece of equipment was old and decayed. The newer items of machinery looked different. Their style was wrong, the shapes too fluid, no right angles or sharp edges. The dropping sun glowed from slick surfaces, shimmering, wet. They seemed to flex, almost as if alive, but Mulder thought it might have been his heartbeat pulsing behind his eyes.

"Hiding in plain sight," he said.

"But what's hiding?"

"Let's go and see, Scully." She glanced at him, unsettled. "Hey, we're here now." He smiled and climbed over the fallen tree, and the song sang in again.

Mulder screamed. He felt the scream in his throat and skull, but he didn't hear it, because the dreadful song was too loud. As he slipped from the tree, still gripping his gun, he saw Scully drop to her knees, then roll onto her side. She fumbled in her pocket for the spare bullets, but he didn't think it would do any good. They were too close to the source, the strange sound pounding through the ground and air. It penetrated their skulls. His eyes throbbed, his teeth ached, his ears felt as if a wasp had crawled into each one and was now buzzing its wings and stabbing its sting as it tried to get back out.

Mulder rested his arms on the trunk, leveled his gun, and tried to fire at one of the objects. His fingers didn't work. He had no strength. As he tried to summon the will to shoot, the world began to recede.

The strange mechanical items began to glow, a heavy blue light that thickened the air. It hurt to look at it, but Mulder could not look away. He reached down for Scully and caught her beneath the arms, lifting her so that she could see too.

She saw. Then she fell against Mulder, pressing her arms across his face and tripping him back so that they both fell behind the tumbled tree. She held his face and started at him, trying to say something. He hugged her tight.

As they buried their faces against each other's neck, an almighty thud pounded through the ground and knocked the breath from them.

When Mulder finally gasped in his next breath, silence had fallen.

They sat for a while on the fallen tree, trying to gather themselves and wondering what had happened. What they had seen. And more importantly, what they had not.

The several items of strange machinery had vanished, leaving only scorched soil behind. The scent of burning hung in the air, gradually being dispersed by the gentle evening breeze. The clearing looked strangely empty, even though the rusted, decaying mining machinery was still there. Something was missing, and Scully's heart almost ached.

"What happened, Mulder?"

"I don't know. But whatever it was, we scared it away."

"It?"

He shrugged, gesturing out across the clearing.

"Ball lightning," she said. "That's what we saw. I've seen evidence of it before, it leaves behind burn marks like those. We got here just as it was forming. Several instances of it. That's what we saw."

"Believe that if you want, Scully."

She did not reply, but neither did she believe it.

"We should get back to town," Mulder said after a few silent minutes.

"Long walk in the dark," Scully said.

"You'd rather wait here til dawn?"

Scully thought of that song reverberating in her skull and through her body, how strange and intimate it had been, how alluring and suggestive.

"Hell, no," she said.

They held hands as they walked back through the woods. When they finally reached their ruined car the moon was out, and it lit the road all the way back to Lynott Sound.

They went the wrong way a couple of times, and by the time they saw the lights of the town in the distance, it was almost 4 a.m. Mulder was surprised to see so much illumination, not only streetlights but inside houses, and he also saw the shifting glares of several hidden vehicles moving around the town. By the time they reached the first building the vehicles had gone, but lights remained on behind many curtained windows.

"More murders?" Scully wondered.

"Hope not. Maybe something different. I think we shook things up."

"So we should go to Laura Connolly's place."

"You're a mind reader, Scully."

"There's no such thing."

Tired now, muddy and scratched, aching from the car crash and with ears still throbbing from the intensity of that eldritch song, they walked across the town square. Mulder felt no eyes on them. They were alone, and whatever this town had been through, it was coming to terms with it behind closed doors.

"Well, I suppose I should have guessed," Scully said. She nodded across the square. Close to the war memorial was the car they'd seen Krycek arrive in. Its front fender was missing, bonnet crumpled, offside wheel arch torn and ragged. Of Krycek, there was no sign.

"Thanks, partner," Mulder muttered.

"You know he's not your partner, right?" Scully said. "You know he's something more than that?"

Mulder nodded but said nothing.

As they approached Laura Connolly's house they saw her mother on a chair on the front deck. She was motionless, sitting in shadows, the only sign of life a haze of steam from the coffee cup in her hands. Street lights caught the steam as it drifted from beneath the canopy, soon lost to the night.

"They took her," she said as Mulder and Scully approached.

"Who took her?" Scully asked.

"Men and women in uniforms. Army, or something. In trucks. Her and the other three sleepers. There were doctors and nurses too, and they said it was for the best. She'll be treated and brought back home." Mulder caught the glimmer of tears. "But they never said when." Laura's mother's voice broke, and Scully went to comfort her. The woman—previously unwelcoming and evasive—stood to embrace the agent.

"Can I see her room one more time?" Mulder asked. He saw no nod, heard no agreement, but neither did he hear a no. So he went inside.

They were waiting for a hire car to arrive. The Bureau would have to be told about the wrecked car out in the woods. But Scully had a feeling they already knew.

She'd been hoping that the old man Patton would be there, but they were alone in Marshall's Diner. The coffee was really good.

Mulder was uncharacteristically quiet.

After Scully had finished her second mug, and the caffeine was battling the exhaustion that threatened to drag her down, she asked him, "Well?"

He looked up, startled. He'd been somewhere else.

"Neither of the Connolly parents smoked?"

"Don't think so," Scully said. She frowned, concentrated, recalled the interior of their house. "No ashtrays, no smoke stains on the ceilings. House smelled nice."

"It doesn't anymore," Mulder said. "It stank of cigarettes. So did the curtains of Laura's room."

Scully's blood ran cold. She remembered him—a wrinkled, weathered face, drawing deeply on a cigarette, hidden by veils of smoke and shadow.

"I'll bet it's a brand we both know," she said. They sat in silence until the Marshall woman brought their breakfast, because right then there was little more to say.

Twenty minutes later a car pulled up outside. A young man got out and stood by the driver's door, waiting with the hire contract in his hand.

Mulder sighed. "Let's get back to work."

THE END

THE BEAST OF LITTLE HILL

By Peter Clines

S cully looked out the window as the blue sedan rolled through the center of town. The town, she noticed, didn't seem to be much more than a few blocks of one- and two-story buildings. Most of them were brick, but a few wooden ones stood out. On a guess, the newest one had been built sometime in the '50s. The streets were gray concrete marked with a few thin lines of green weeds.

"So, Mulder," she asked the driver, "what's so amazing here that we had to drive four hours out from Kansas City?"

He looked at her, and his lips made the curved line she'd come to recognize as his smile. "Isn't it enough that they have the best cheeseburger in the state and the best apple pie in the world?" he asked, gesturing at the signs in the diner window.

"I don't think Skinner will think so."

"You know, I've wanted to come here for almost ten years and never had a chance. There was always something more pressing, from the bureau or my own investigations."

She waited.

"We're in Hill County," said Mulder. "The town's called Little Hill."

"Is there a Big Hill?"

"I don't believe so, no."

"And you've brought us here because...?"

"Back in 1969 there was an incident here. A hundred and eight people called state and local authorities to report a UFO crash in the woods outside of town."

"That'd be, what," Scully said with a straight face, "right over there?"

"Before authorities could even get on the scene, though," he continued, ignoring her, "the craft and all wreckage vanished. Several large military trucks were reported in the area at the time. The popular theory is that the craft was actually shot down and retrieval teams were already standing by to collect it."

"Isn't it possible that it was just a plane crash? The Air Force always has some prototype or another. It would explain the retrieval teams, too."

"It's been discussed," said Mulder. "There are no records of any military or private sector trials that week within six hundred miles of here."

"Six hundred miles isn't that far for a jet."

"Try not to laugh," he said, "but the closest test was a weather balloon system."

She smiled.

He gestured to the north. "Even more interesting is that there were seven more UFO sightings in the months afterwards that were also never explained. The last one was in February of 1970. They were some of the first cases MUFON ever investigated, which is ironic because the crash itself was one of the final ten cases examined by Project Blue Book before that study was terminated."

"Well," said Scully, "that's not surprising. It's a perfect example of collective hysteria. People under stress all coming to share the same delusion, regardless of actual evidence."

Mulder nodded. "That's what everyone concluded about Little Hill," he said. "A few people even theorized that it might have been influenced by the name, connecting the events here to the abduction of Betty and Barney Hill seven and a half years earlier in New Hampshire."

"Seven and a half years is a long time for that level of hysteria."

"I agree," said Mulder, "and so do a few other people. Still, interest in this location has dwindled over the years and it's dropping off most lists. The last serious investigation was back in 1987, although there have been a few amateurs who come by to suggest new theories."

"So you've been here before?"

He shook his head. "Never. But we were more or less in the area and I heard that rates have gone down on a lot of the exhibits."

Scully looked around the town. "Exhibits?"

COPE FARM
2:54 p.m.

The barn, Scully had to admit, was cleaner than most of the ones she'd seen in her career with the FBI. It was swept and spacious, more of a showroom than a storage area. The corners were free of the usual clutter of old straw, dirt, and rat traps.

Granted, the near-overpowering smell of cat urine probably explained the lack of rat traps.

Abraham Cope didn't seem to notice the smell. She wasn't sure if he was used to it or just too deep into his spiel to notice. He stood before them in his tucked-in plaid shirt, gesturing with all the force and conviction of a Sunday sermon. By her practiced estimate, he was in his late forties to early fifties. He had white hair and leathery skin from years in the sun. He was clean-shaven, despite what looked like severe arthritis in his dominant right hand.

Scully and Mulder stood before an upright freezer chest that had been white once but yellowed with age. A bright orange extension cord fed it electricity. A teenage boy stood with them. In theory he was part of the audience, but he looked too bored and too much like Cope for Scully to believe he was here by chance.

"After it killed fourteen sheep in one night," said Cope, "the local men said enough was enough. The old sheriff weren't doing nothing, so they decided to track down the creature themselves. My Pop and the rest of them spent two days hunting this monster before they cornered it not far from here. It'd just torn up two more cows and left their innards spread across a field.

"Pop drew down on the monster with that very shotgun," Cope said, waving his arm up at a cobweb-covered weapon on one of the beams. "Gave it both barrels, right in the face, and it dropped like a stone. After a bit of debate, they decided to drag the body back for a trophy, or maybe to sell it to a science college or something. Pop was never clear on that part of the story. But he was very clear about what happened next."

Cope took a step closer. He looked Scully in the eye, then Mulder, and then his gaze slid back to Scully. He ignored the teenager. His voice dropped into a conspiratorial stage-whisper.

"Y'see, two shotgun shells to the face hadn't killed the Beast of Little Hill, just knocked it out. Skull like an elephant." He tapped his own forehead for emphasis. "They were just coming in through those very barn doors when it started to wake up. Flexing its claws. Twitching its tail. Pop, he knew they had seconds. He ran over here with one of his friends, Kip Witness, and they dumped everything out of the freezer."

Scully glanced at Mulder and mouthed the words "Kip Witness". She punctuated it with a skeptical eyebrow.

"The men dragged the monster over and forced it in this very freezer before it could wake up all the way. It took all five of them to hold it shut, and the creature fought the whole time. Pop said it was like trying to keep a grizzly bear in an outhouse. They would've lost if they hadn't got the tow chain wrapped around it."

Cope gestured across the barn to a rusted set of links that hung from another beam. A hand-painted sign next to it read THE CHAIN.

"The creature fought for another twenty minutes or so, but it was getting weaker the whole time." He placed his hand on the freezer. "Airtight, y'see," he said with a sage nod.

Mulder returned the nod. Scully bit her tongue. The teenager scratched his ear.

"Pop wasn't going to risk it not being dead again, though. They took the chain off, lay the freezer down, and started pouring water over the thing. It took him the better part of six weeks, doing a bucket a day, but when he was done the Beast was frozen in a block of ice almost a foot thick on every side."

He took in a deep breath and placed his hand on the freezer's handle. "Ladies and gentlemen," he said, "I give you... the Beast of Little Hill!"

Cope pulled on the handle and lurched forward as the door refused to budge. He tugged again. Then he gave the door a kick, slamming his heel into the edge. The door scraped forward and sprayed flecks of ice across the barn floor. A second kick knocked it loose. The door swung wide and banged open on its hinges.

A few wisps of cold air rolled out. Scully and Mulder stepped forward. The teenager yawned and glanced out at the yard.

A block of cloudy ice filled every inch of the freezer. It had cracked some of the plastic panels. One corner was a few dozen shards held in place by the frozen water.

The thing inside the block was the size of a large dog, a German Shepard or a Great Dane. Scully put its weight at about ninety to a hundred pounds. It seemed hairless, but it was hard to tell through the layers of ice. The dark eyes looked oversized for its skull, but it was possible she was just seeing empty sockets.

The front limbs were longer, at the very least straighter than the back legs. It gave the figure a somewhat simian stature, but she couldn't say anything for sure. The ice blurred the creature so much it almost looked like one of Mulder's Bigfoot pictures.

"Is your father around?" Mulder asked the farmer. "Is there any chance we could ask him a few questions about that night?"

"Regrettably, sir," said Cope, "the good Lord called my father home seven years ago this summer."

"I'm sorry to hear that."

Scully wondered if the thing in the ice was a goat or maybe a small calf that had been the victim of an over-creative taxidermist. The second leg on her side was close to the surface, and there she could see what looked like small talons.

She blinked, took a step back, then leaned in again. The ice blurred lines, but if those were the forelegs and *those* were the hindquarters...

"It has six legs," she said.

"Yes, ma'am," said Cope. "And each one's got a set of claws like one of those *Jurassic Park* dinosaurs, the velocirippers."

Behind them, the teenager shuffled toward the doors. A glare from Cope stopped him.

Scully tilted her head to try to get a better view through the ice. "What about the... Mr. Witness?"

"Most of the Witness family moved away when I was in high school," said Cope. He smiled. "I was sweet on their daughter, Sally, at the time and it broke my heart. I believe they ended up in San Diego."

"California?"

Cope snorted. "Texas. They've still got some cousins in town."

Mulder's shoulders perked up inside his coat. "Were any of them part of these events?"

"Naw. Most of them were just younguns like me at the time."

Scully straightened up and took a step back. "Thank you," she said to Mr. Cope.

Mulder pulled a business card from his coat. "If you remember anything else about the story, or anyone else does, please give me a call."

Cope studied the card. Then his face lit up. "Oh, I getcha. Here to fetch the last of it away, eh?"

Scully shook her head. "Just passing through," she said.

"Y'know," said the farmer, "I'd be willing to let it go for a couple hundred bucks. In the name of science and all that."

The teen craned his head to see the card.

"Like she said," Mulder told him, "we're just passing through."

They left Cope and the teen kicking the door shut on the freezer. Mulder gave Scully a hopeful look. "What do you think?"

She raised an eyebrow. "Seriously, Mulder?"

"Of course."

"It's a fake."

"Yeah, that's what Frohike said, too. He was on the 1987 team."

"So if even he thinks it's a fake, what are we doing here?"

Their feet crunched through the leaves in the driveway and Mulder glanced up at the afternoon sky. "The interesting thing is," he said, "there was a series of cattle mutilations in this area back in the fall of 1969."

"Mulder..."

"Not the usual kind, either. These weren't possible dissections, they were actual mutilations. The sheep and cows were torn apart, like they'd been savaged by wolves or a bear. What do you think could've done that?"

"Do I really need to answer that?"

"There hasn't been a wolf sighting in these parts in years, Scully. And even so, wouldn't the men in the hunting party be able to differentiate between a wolf and 'something else?'"

"I suppose that'd depend on how much drinking they'd done that night." She shook her head. "Mulder, even considering that it's obscured by over a foot of ice, I'd say that thing looks more like a large dog wearing a Halloween costume than an alien."

"You did see that it had an extra set of legs, yes?"

"And the Fiji mermaid had a tail and scales. It didn't make it a real mermaid."

"Just because we had one case where it wasn't the Fiji mermaid does not disprove the existence of—"

"It was a fake, Mulder."

He gave her another tight smile. A momentary concession. "Okay," he said, "but wait until you see the other one."

She paused with her fingers on the door handle. "There's another one?"

MARSH RESIDENCE
4:23 p.m.

Their car rolled to a stop where the long dirt driveway opened up into a small field of gravel. A weather beaten sign offered a chance to SEE THE ALIEN in six inch tall letters that hadn't been white for years. A farmhouse with a double garage stood on the other side of the gravel circle.

A large man set down a wheelbarrow filled with melons and lumbered toward their car. A half-breed beagle stood by the wheelbarrow and barked three or four times before he turned back and hushed it. He came to a halt a few yards away and eyed Mulder and Scully through the windshield.

They stepped out of the car and the man glared at them for a moment. Then he took a few more steps closer and called out to them. "Younses wanna gander at Marvin?"

"Marvin?"

"The alien?" The man's hair was darker than Mulder's, as black as Cope's had been white. He had broad shoulders and a broader belly, barely contained by his overalls. Scully noticed he favored his left leg as he walked toward them.

"Yes, we would," said Mulder, closing the car door. "Are you Mr. Marsh?"

"Yessir."

"We're looking into the UFO crash from nineteen-sixty—"

"Five bucks for five minutes," Marsh said.

They waited for a moment. The farmer said nothing else and moved no closer. Mulder glanced at Scully, shrugged, and pulled out his wallet. He thumbed through until he found a five dollar bill and held it out. "Can you tell us how—"

"Five bucks each," said Marsh.

Mulder stared at him for a moment, then glanced over at Scully. She gave a small shake of her head. He sighed and rifled through his wallet for another bill. He held up two fives.

Marsh lurched forward and snatched them away. "S'way," he muttered. He spun on his good leg and headed toward the house.

Mulder looked at Scully and shrugged. They followed him. The dog barked one more time and Marsh silenced it with a wave of his hand.

The farmer veered off and headed for the garage door farthest from the house. He fumbled in his pocket for a set of keys, twisted the handle, and rolled the door up and away. He glanced over his shoulder at the two FBI agents and lumbered into the garage.

Two cars filled the other side of the garage, one whole, the other in pieces, both covered with dust. There were shelves stuffed full of boxes and jars. A nearby tool bench displayed components of what might've been a lawnmower at one point.

A freezer chest sat on the floor, its hinges toward the door. It had been ivory to start. Now it was almost yellow. A latch had been bolted onto it, and a heavy padlock over that. On the side facing the door, someone had written ALIEN in what looked like magic marker.

Marsh fiddled with his key ring, the padlock popped open, and he pushed the lid up. It made Scully think of someone throwing back the lid of a coffin. "Five minutes," the farmer said. "Startin' now."

Mulder and Scully exchanged another glance and stepped forward.

The lid cast a shadow over the inside of the freezer chest, but they could see it was as yellowed as the outside. There wasn't any ice, but it was cold enough that the warm air from outside had filled it with steam. They batted their hands at the clouds until the small space cleared out.

At first glance the thing at the bottom looked to be the same size as a child. After a moment, Scully realized it was just the slim limbs and fetal pose that gave that impression. Straightened out and standing up, the figure in the chest would've been close to seven feet tall.

It had a large head and long fingers. She couldn't see any hair on the body anywhere. Its wrinkled skin was driftwood gray.

It was also, Scully was quite sure, made of plastic.

"How long have you had it for?" asked Mulder.

Marsh shrugged. "Uncle Rom found Marvin in the woods after the crash. Said he was plumb near dead."

Mulder glanced down into the chest. "It... he was alive?"

"So he told me."

Scully slipped a latex glove from her pocket and snapped it over her hand. She reached down and pressed her fingers against the creature's shoulder.

"Hey," said Marsh. "Youns wanna touch it, s'another five bucks."

Mulder sighed and pulled his wallet back out. "Can you make change for a twenty?"

Marsh pulled two small wads of bills from his pocket and nodded.

Scully worked her way down the arm, watching how the skin bent and flexed as she pushed against it. Smooth and firm with a slight yield when she pushed hardest. The tiny fingernails felt just like the skin. So did the eyes.

Mulder took his change. "Did it speak to your uncle before it died?"

"Naw. Jess hid in the corner of the garage all skeered, made some clicky noise. Coupla days later he curled up an went to sleep. That's when his skin got all risen-like."

"Sorry?" asked Scully. She pushed herself up off the rim of the freezer chest.

"Risen," said Marsh. "Uncle Rom said the little guy jess leaked it out. He got all kivvered with wet, then it got all hard."

"Would it be possible to speak to your uncle?" asked Mulder. "Maybe ask him a few questions about that night?"

"Y'can try," said Marsh. "He remarried, moved t'Florida, and now he's in a home." Marsh twirled his finger by his ear. "Ain't been right in the head for ten years now."

Mulder reached into his coat for a card but Scully caught his arm. "Thank you," she said to Marsh.

"Younses got another minute an a half," he said with a glance at his watch.

"That's okay," she said. She walked out of the garage.

Mulder glanced after her, handed Marsh a card, and took a few quick steps. He caught up with her just outside. "What did you think?"

"If it's possible, I think it's more fake than the last one. The whole thing's made of plastic."

"Or resin."

She smiled. "You think it sweated out resin to protect itself like some sort of, what, cocoon?"

"Good thinking, Scully," he said with a smile.

"Even if that were true Mulder, he's keeping it in a freezer. The cold would've done irreparable damage on a cellular level."

"You're assuming it has a cell structure similar to terrestrial life."

"Actually, I'm assuming it's a plastic Halloween decoration."

The beagle barked at them as they passed it. It bounced back and forth, its tail wagging as it barked again. It sounded more playful than angry.

"You have to admit, though, it's interesting that two unrelated people in the same town would both claim to have dead aliens in their freezers."

"It's no different than two different shops at Loch Ness both selling stuffed Nessies or similar coffee mugs. It's a tourist trap."

"But when you go to Loch Ness, one of the striking things is how similar all the designs are," said Mulder. He unlocked the car. "There isn't anyone claiming the monster has wings or ten flippers or anything."

She pulled open the passenger door. "Because they're all based off the same urban myths that have been passed down over the years, that the monster is a plesiosaur or similar dinosaur that's survived into the modern age."

"So shouldn't the same thing hold here? Why don't they have at least two that are very similar?"

"Maybe that's all Cope could find. It could be another reason his is buried in ice, to help hide how different it is."

Mulder slid into the driver's seat. "I just find it interesting that after twenty-five years, both of these men are still insisting they have alien bodies, even though they look nothing alike. I'm surprised so many people at MUFON lost interest in this place."

"Well, Mulder," she said, "unless you've got a third alien to show me, I'm ready to go."

"I was hoping to ask around, see if anyone can point out the original crash site."

Scully started to talk, then pressed her lips together. "Okay," she said. "How long do you think you'll need?"

He glanced up at the sky. "Well, we've only got about ninety minutes of daylight left. And maybe a quick check in with the local historical society after that..."

LITTLE HILL MOTEL, ROOM #15
9:42 p.m.

Mulder was watching *Silk Stalkings* and lamenting the motel's limited cable package when his phone rang. He glanced at the adjoining door to Scully's room before answering. "Mulder."

"This the FBI agent?" asked a voice on the other end. It sounded young.

"It is. Who am I speaking with?"

"You gotta come quick. It got my dad."

He muted the television. "Who is this?"

"It's See-see," said the voice.

"Who?"

"Cecil Cope. You were out in our barn looking at the Beast."

The bored teen flashed through Mulder's mind.

"It got out," continued the boy. "It got out and it got my dad."

Mulder felt a faint prickle on the back of his neck. He walked over to Scully's door and tapped twice on it. "Is it still there, Cecil? Are you okay?"

"My dad, he's bleeding a lot. He's out in the barn. His leg's all messed up."

"Is it still there?"

"I don't know. I think it ran into the woods. I don't know."

Scully opened the door. She was barefoot and her shirt was untucked. She raised a questioning eyebrow at the phone.

"Cecil, take care of your dad, but be careful. Stay safe."

"Okay."

He looked at Scully. "My partner and I can be out there in about twenty minutes."

"Thank you."

"We'll see you soon." He hung up the phone.

"What's going on?"

"It sounds like one of the Halloween decorations got loose and tried to kill Abraham Cope."

COPE FARM
10:03 p.m.

Mulder eased the rental between the two squad cars. They were gold Impalas, but the rack of lights that topped each car was different. A battered ambulance sat closer to the barn. Cope's pickup truck was still parked near the house. Rays of light sprayed out between the planks of the barn.

An officer stood a few yards away, sweeping the ground with a flashlight that wasn't much brighter than the moonlight. His attention shifted to Mulder and Scully as they walked up. He was tall and lanky, with wide eyes and a prominent Adam's Apple. "Hey," he called out. "Crime scene. Younses cain't be here."

Mulder flipped open his badge. "Special agent Mulder. This is my partner, special agent Scully. The sheriff asked us to join him out here."

"FBI?" The deputy's shoulders relaxed. "God, it's good to see younses." He gestured them toward the barn with his flashlight.

Puddles spread out across the floor of the barn. The upright freezer sat on its side. The walls were battered and bent. The yellowed plastic was shattered. Chunks of ice ranging from soccer balls down to frosted gravel formed a path from the freezer to its door a few yards away. The door had been buckled into an arch that looked like a smoker's smile.

There was no sign of the Beast of Little Hill.

Cope lay on a gurney with a tweed jacket balled up behind his head and his pants around his ankles. He flinched and moaned as an older woman wrapped his bloody leg with a gauze bandage. "Stop whining," she muttered.

The teenager who'd stood with them, Cecil, stood near Cope's head. His eyes flitted from Mulder and Scully to his father and then to the back door of the barn. He kept his arms crossed over his chest.

A skinny man stepped out from behind the freezer and cleared his throat. "You must be Agent Mulder," he said. He held up Mulder's business card and glanced over at Cecil. His voice had an odd pace to it. He held out his other hand and they shook.

"My partner, Dana Scully."

"Ma'am. Sheriff Will Ryker."

"Will Ryker?" echoed Scully.

"Yeah, I've heard 'em all before," said the sheriff. "How'd you two get here so fast?"

"We were staying in town."

"Passing through?"

"Sightseeing."

Scully glanced over at Cope. The doctor taped one last gauze pad over his leg. "So what's the story here, sheriff?"

"His boy called us an hour and a half ago. Heard something banging around out in the barn. Abe went to check it out, the boy heard some yelling and screaming, came out here and found his dad with leg liketa torn off. Sorry, near torn off."

The odd pace to Ryker's words became clear.

The doctor looked back at them. "He's lucky," she said. "Tore up, but it missed all the big arteries. Doesn't even look like much tissue loss."

"He'll recover?"

"Should. Prolly limp for a spell."

Scully took a few steps and stared at the gashes still visible on Cope's leg. "What do you think did this?"

"Got to be honest," Ryker said, dropping his voice a few decibels. "My first thought when the boy called was this was some kind of insurance put on. Y'know, like when people fake a robbery or something."

"The Beast of Little Hill was insured?" said Scully.

Ryker nodded at Cope. "He's got a citified cousin up in St. Louis, does insurance policies. Don't know it, but it wouldn't surprise me. Then I got here and saw how bad Abe was tore up."

"People have done a lot more for an insurance policy," said Mulder.

"I've known Abe Cope for thirty years," said Ryker. "He's greedy, but he's also a coward and a wimp. Ain't no way he'd cut his leg up like that. And then I found out Cecil called you before he called me." He held up the card again. "Said you gave it to Abe."

"They're gonna buy the Beast," spat Cecil. "Pa said so."

Cope winced at the loud words and muttered something.

"We're not here to buy it," Mulder said. "We just wanted to see it."

"Pa knew the gov'ment come back and buy up the Beast," said the teen.

Scully tapped her foot two or three times in a puddle. "So, Sheriff, if it's not insurance fraud what are you thinking now?"

"Wild dog, maybe. Been a few years since we've seen a cougar in these parts, but not that many. One mighta wandered into the barn and caused a ruckus."

"What about the Beast?" Mulder pointed at the empty freezer. "Any sign of it?"

Ryker shrugged. "Drug..." He coughed. "Dragged off by whatever attacked Abe."

"You think a cougar beat up the freezer, too?"

Scully walked across the barn, tapping her feet. "I think we're looking at two different events here," she said. "The attack on the freezer and the attack on Mr. Cope."

"Why do you say that, Scully?"

She waved her arm at the puddles. "It's not that warm out. This is a lot of melted ice for just ninety minutes. I'd guess this is at least three or four hours worth."

Mulder followed the orange extension cord back toward the wall. He reached down into a messy coil and came up with two ends. "This cord's been cut with a blade."

Scully glanced at the back door, then at the far wall. "Have your men looked out back yet, sheriff?"

"We've only got here about ten minutes before you. Deputy Witness took a quick look out there but he didn't see anything."

Scully stepped through the door. She glanced back. The barn blocked her view of the house. She pulled out her own flashlight and lit up the ground. The beam panned back and forth three times before she saw it. "Mulder," she called out, stepping back toward the barn. "Sheriff. Check this out."

He joined her, with Ryker a step behind. "Find some monster tracks, Scully?"

"Better.

He and Ryker added their flashlight beams to hers.

"I'm guessing these belong to your deputy," Scully said. She used her flashlight to circle a pair of narrow shoe-prints in the mud by the door. They went off to either side.

"Probably," said Ryker. "Looks about his size."

"Now look at those over there." Scully flipped the beam of light a few yards out from the door. A second set of prints led to and from the tree line.

They stepped around the trail and lit up the footprints. "Very distinct, even with the hard ground," said Mulder. "Someone heavy."

"With a limp," added Scully, panning the beam over the scuffed right print. She glanced back toward the road and then aimed the flashlight out at the trees. "Sheriff, would I be wrong in guessing the Marsh place is off in that direction?"

Ryker scowled. "Yes, ma'am," he said. "It's about seven miles by roads with a couple of the switchbacks, but less'n three as the crow flies. There's even an old path between them."

"What do you think, Mulder?"

She looked over her shoulder. Mulder had wandered back inside.

Scully stepped back through the door. The doctor wheeled the gurney out the front door toward the ambulance. Cecil went with them, helping on the rough ground of the driveway.

"I think we're done here, Mulder," said Scully. "Sheriff Ryker has a solid lead, we don't have any real jurisdiction..." She glanced at her watch. "And Skinner's expecting us back in about fifteen hours."

"Scully, we've received an official request for help from local law enforcement."

"Technically, no we—"

"Not to mention the likely involvement of an extraterrestrial life form."

"It's not an X-File, Mulder," she sighed. "It's a case of petty sabotage between two rival tourist trap sideshows. Marsh thought you were here to buy an alien and tried to make sure he had the only one."

"And what happened to Cope? Was that petty sabotage, too?"

"No, just like the sheriff said, it was probably a cougar or a coyote or something. The freezer gets sabotaged. The ice melts enough that the smell of whatever was in there attracts animals. Cope wanders out to investigate, spooks the animal, and gets his leg slashed up."

Mulder tipped his head after the gurney. "Did that look like a coyote attack to you?"

She shrugged. "I didn't get a good look at it. The doctor didn't seem too bothered by it."

"She was barely looking at it. She was just packing the wound so he could be transported." He shook his head. "What if it has a taste for people now? It killed cattle before, but what if it's the same way lots of large predators will start considering humans a food source once they've wounded one."

"Mulder, if it really was some kind of extraterrestrial creature, it probably wouldn't be trying to eat him."

"Why do you say that?"

"It'd be from a separate ecosystem. Different planet, different evolutionary paths, different biological makeups. There's a good chance eating Cope wouldn't give it any nourishment at all, and it probably would've known that just off his scent. Humans might even be poisonous to it."

"So you're saying..."

"It was just trying to kill him."

"Oh." Mulder watched as they heaved the gurney into the ambulance. "You know, I find that oddly comforting, personally."

"Pardon me, Agent Scully, Agent Mulder." Deputy Witness touched the brim of his hat. "The sheriff wanted to know if younses will be coming out to the Marsh place with us?"

Mulder straightened his shoulders. "Is that an official request, detective?"

Scully rolled her eyes.

"Ummm... I s'pose so. Yes."

"Then please tell the sheriff we'll follow in our car."

Witness nodded and stepped outside.

"You get to explain this to Skinner," said Scully, shaking her head.

MARSH RESIDENCE
11:14 p.m.

The half-breed beagle barked and barked as the cars pulled up. It bounced back and forth across the lawn, its tail beating the air. When the cars stopped, it scampered forward a few feet, then raced back and continued to bark.

Sheriff Ryker took the lead with Mulder and Scully a few steps behind him. Witness stayed behind. His car was a few yards back, angled to block the driveway.

The front door opened before they reached the porch steps. Marsh stood behind the screen in a dirty wife-beater. He kept his right hand out of sight, just beyond the door frame. "Evenin', sheriff," he muttered. He didn't open the screen door. Or move his hand.

"Hiram," said Ryker, touching the brim of his hat. "Hopin' I could speak with you for a few minutes. Ask a few questions."

Marsh stared at Mulder and Scully. "What's they doing here?"

Scully slid her badge out. "Special agents Scully and Mulder, FBI."

"You got a badge?" he grunted at Mulder.

Mulder slid his wallet out and held it open near his head.

Ryker cleared his throat. "Were you out at the Cope farm earlier this evening, Hiram?"

"Why, 'm I suspect?"

Mulder raised an eyebrow. "Suspect of what, Mr. Marsh?"

The man glowered behind his screen door. "Shuddup, Roswell ," he bellowed at the dog.

The beagle stopped barking but continued to dart back and forth across the lawn.

"I need to know, Hiram," said the sheriff. "Did you head over to the Cope farm earlier this evening?"

"Why you askin'?"

Ryker straightened up and squared off his shoulders. "A few hours ago someone sabotaged Cope's freezer and then attacked him."

Marsh took in a sharp breath, ready to argue, and then bit down on it. His mouth vanished into his beard. "I don't know nothing about Abe Cope gettin' attacked," he said a moment later.

"But you know about the freezer being sabotaged," Mulder said.

Marsh slapped his lips shut again.

"Hi," said Ryker, "if you knows something, tell me now. The Feds are involved, and there ain't no way I can protect you if they take over."

"I didn't do nothing to Abe Cope," muttered the bearded man.

"What *did* you do, Mr. Marsh?" Scully asked.

He glared at her, but his eyes softened and his gaze fell to the mat outside the screen door. His hands dropped to his sides. "Heard the talk in town, that the two of you were lookin' to buy his Beast. Got mad. So I snuck over there on the ol' mule path and snipped the cord. Figgered the ice'd melt and everyone'd see the Beast was fake."

Ryker tapped his fingers against the screen door's frame. "When was this? What time were you there?"

Marsh shrugged. "Six-thirty. Maybe seven."

"You sure about that time?"

"Yeah. Got home in time for Final Jeopardy."

Mulder cleared his throat. "What did you use to cut the power cord?"

The bearded man patted his side. "Pocket knife. Weren't that hard."

"And what did you smash up the freezer with? Did you bring something for that or did you use something there?"

Marsh blinked twice. "I used my knife. I just toldja that."

Mulder nodded and took a few steps back away from the porch. The dog barked at him again. Scully glanced back and joined him. "What are you thinking, Mulder?" "I don't think he did it. It's clear he's got some resentment against Cope, but it's not personal."

"If he didn't attack Cope, who did? The son?"

"Not who, Scully. What."

She shook her head.

"Just look at the evidence. The timeframe, supported by the melting ice. The freezer that was damaged from the inside and the remaining ice scattered outward. It all points to the Beast."

"What was that?" Ryker glanced back from the porch.

"Sheriff, I think we're looking at something much bigger than a neighborhood rivalry. I think Mr. Marsh has set the Beast of Little Hill loose."

Scully sighed.

Marsh smirked.

Ryker bit his lip. "Agent Mulder," he said, "I 'preciate that you've taken a shine to our local legends, but I'm in the middle of—"

The radio squawked in his cruiser. It echoed further back and Deputy Witness looked down at his own vehicle. They all looked at him, and he glanced from the radio to the group on the porch. "Troy's calling for youns, sheriff."

Ryker closed his eyes, just for a moment. "Stay right where you are," he said. Then he marched off the porch, past the FBI agents, and leaned in to pull the microphone from his car. "Go for Ryker."

The voice on the other end spat out a double handful of muffled words.

Ryker shot a glance over at Witness, then at the two FBI agents. "Troy, slow down," he said. "Count to five and give it to me again."

Troy counted to three and the radio spewed more sounds. Mulder was too far to hear anything other than the tone. "Something wrong, sheriff?"

Ryker shook his head. "Small town problems."

"How so?"

"People calling in about an animal loose in town. Scared a bunch of folks."

"What kind of animal?" asked Mulder.

"Everyone's kind of hysterical," the sheriff said. "That's all. S'just a cougar or something. No one's gotten a good look at it so they're imagining things."

"What kind of things?"

Ryker stared at Mulder.

"Sheriff, what's loose in your town?"

He tossed the microphone into the car. "They're saying it's some kind of dinosaur."

"You mean it's the Beast."

"Mr. Mulder, I seen that thing for the first time when I was eleven. It's been frozen the whole time and it was frozen for years 'fore that. Right now it's out in the woods somewhere gettin' gnawed on by a coyote."

"Or it's in the middle of town gnawing on one of the people there."

Ryker stepped away from his car. "You think this is some kind of a joke?"

"Not at all, sheriff. But I do think there may be something loose in your town that's a lot more dangerous than a cougar or a coyote. Even if I'm wrong, shouldn't that take priority over an act of petty vandalism?"

The beagle barked three more times. Marsh snapped at it. It ran up to Mulder, stopped a few feet away, then darted back.

"Hiram," called Ryker. "Until this gets sorted out I'm takin' you into custody."

"What?" bellowed the farmer. "I ain't done nothin."

"You destroyed a man's property. Said so yourself. Now get in the damned car or I'll throw the cuffs on you and drag you." He pointed at the back door of his cruiser.

Marsh glared at the sheriff for a moment. He stepped away from the door, vanished, and then reappeared with a thick plaid hunting coat. "Roswell," he yelled, holding the screen open, "get in the house."

The beagle leaped onto the porch and skidded to a stop inside. It looked up at Marsh and wagged its tail. He gave it a rough pat on the head and closed the door behind him. The dog barked twice inside the house.

"Gonna get me a lawyer and sue all younses asses," he muttered as he limped to the car.

LITTLE HILL, MISSOURI
11:58 p.m.

Ryker stopped his car in the middle of the street. Mulder and Scully stopped behind him. Witness crept by, looking left and right. He and Ryker traded a few quick words and the deputy sped off.

Mulder and Scully stepped out and looked around. A trashcan had been tipped and its contents spread across the road. One car parked along the street had a shattered window on the driver's side and what looked to Mulder like a buckshot pattern in the door. The nearby bar was dark, as was the open all-night diner. The sound of the deputy's car had faded away. There were no distant engines or muffled televisions.

There weren't even crickets.

Scully stepped closer to Ryker. "Is this normal, sheriff?"

He shook his head. "S'a quiet town," he said, "but this is downright eerie."

"Where was the last report of it?" asked Mulder. "Do you know?"

"Right here," said Ryker. "I got a call just before we turned on the street, said it was running around out here."

They walked down the street. Mulder glanced back at the car, parked in the middle of the road.

Scully lifted her head. Mulder glanced at her, then tilted his own head. The sheriff closed his eyes, just for a moment. The sound's rise had been so smooth none of them had registered it.

Ryker looked up and down the street. "What is that?"

"It sounds like... tap shoes," said Mulder.

Scully's head went side to side. "No," she said. "It sounds like nails."

"Nails?" Mulder had his hand on his Sig Sauer.

"Toenails," she said. She drew her weapon. "Like a dog on a floor."

The clicking noise echoed between the buildings and the parked cars. Mulder saw a glimpse of something through a car window. "There!" He pointed with his pistol. The shape flickered between the car and the pickup behind it and then he lost track of it.

"Where'd it go?" Ryker had his pistol out, a huge .45 six-shooter. The barrel swept back and forth across the street.

The clicking nails echoed across the concrete road. The sound shifted. Scully turned and the tip of a tail vanished behind a primer-colored

Volkswagen van across the street.

Mulder glanced at Scully. "What was it?"

"I'm not sure."

Ryker spun. "There," he said. He lined up his pistol.

"Wait," said Mulder. "We should see if it's—"

The .45 roared and a chunk of brick turned to red dust. Something cried out and the sound of retreating tap shoes filled the air. A stop sign clanged and shook at the end of the street and a low shadow raced away. Ryker fired another shot after it.

"Sheriff, please," said Mulder. "That could be a living example of extraterrestrial life. It could—"

Ryker slammed his pistol back into its holster. "S'just a mangy old wolf," he said. "D'you see that tail? Picked clean down to the skin."

"You don't know that."

"I do know that, Agent Mulder. And now that we know it, I don't think you need to be here anymore, do you?"

The two men stared at each other for a moment.

"Come on, Mulder," said Scully. "He's got jurisdiction and he's probably right."

He turned to her. "Scully, you saw it. Did it look like a wolf to you?"

"It looked," she said, "like a tail with no hair."

"I'll round up a couple boys tomorrow, hunt it down, put it out of its misery. I can get some pictures for you if you like?"

Mulder took in a breath. His body tensed. Scully set a hand on his arm. "Let it go," she said. "If we leave now, we could be at the airport by three. Maybe there's an earlier flight back to DC."

He stared at Ryker for a few more moments, then turned and marched back to their car.

OLD COUNTY ROAD
12:47 a.m.

Mulder bit his tongue for almost fifteen minutes after they left the motel. "Such a waste," he said. "An actual, living creature from another planet and it's going to get blown apart by a bunch of hillbilly hunters."

A large, pale tree loomed in the headlights and vanished into the dark behind them. Scully turned her head to watch it. "I think it was all a hoax," she said.

He took his eyes off the road and gaped at her. "What?"

She nodded. "Think about it, Mulder. It was all a ploy to drum up new interest in their town. It's all too convenient."

He looked back at the strip of concrete in the headlights. "Kind of inconvenient if you ask me."

"You said yourself the town's been dropping off people's radar. Then we show up just as the fight between Cope and Marsh reaches a boiling point."

"It was because of us," said Mulder.

"Yes," she said, "that's my point. The sabotaged freezer. The phone call. The 'beast' getting loose. It finding us the moment we get back to town. And at no point do we get a good look at it. It's a perfect con."

Mulder shook his head. "How could they know we'd spend the night?"

"They didn't. They saw a chance and they took it. They might've had this planned for ages and they've just been waiting for the right patsies to show up."

"Patsies?"

"Can you think of a better word? Marks? Rubes?"

He smiled. "Maybe." They drove on in silence for a few moments. The turnoff that led down to Marsh's home approached, slid alongside them, and disappeared. "You mind if I ask you a personal question, Scully?"

"Depends."

"Did you take a shower back at the hotel?"

"What?"

"At the hotel. Did you take a shower? When was the last time you washed your hands?"

"I'm not sure. I think at the diner. Why?"

"I was thinking about why there are two kinds of aliens here. And then I thought about Roswell."

"The town?"

"The dog. Back at Hiram Marsh's house." He adjusted his hands on the steering wheel. "Did you know the modern dog is completely man-made?"

"Ten thousand years of selective breeding," she said.

Mulder nodded. "All to create a creature that fills so many roles for us. It's a companion, a protector, a hunter, a fellow warrior. They love us

THE BEAST OF LITTLE HILL

unconditionally and we love them back. Anywhere on this planet that you can find humans, you'll find some kind of dog. We take them with us everywhere. And someday we're going to take them with us out there." He looked up through the windshield. It was a clear night and the stars were clear in the sky. "And maybe they did, too."

She smiled. "You think the Beast of Little Hill is some kind of guard dog?"

"Maybe not even that. Maybe it's just a pet."

"A pet?"

"It explains why there'd be two different life forms at the crash site." He tapped his fingers on the steering wheel. "What if the Beast didn't just happen to find us in town, Scully? What if it came looking for us? Looking for you?"

"Me?"

"You touched the other alien," he said. "Its scent is on you. On your skin or the cuff of your jacket. Maybe some kind of powerful pheromones that set off a specific reaction. You're the only thing that smells familiar to the Beast."

She looked at her hands. "What are you saying?"

"I think we need to go back. We get Ryker to call off the hunting parties, maybe get Frohike and the others down here, and then we can..."

His voice trailed off as he saw the movement out of the corner of his eye. He turned his head and saw the shadow charging out of the woods. It filled the driver's side window with teeth and eyes and claws.

The impact shattered the window and spun the car. Glass filled the air. Scully cried out, and Mulder realized he had, too. Then his training kicked in and he twisted the wheel hard, turning into the skid. The whirling forest steadied, the tires grabbed at the concrete, and the car lurched off the road into a ditch. He heard several thumps and the hiss of shifting dirt and a crack. His arms went up in time to cushion his head as it bounced against the steering wheel. "Scully?!"

"Mulder, are you okay?"

"Yeah. Yeah, no broken bones. You?"

"Shaken up a bit, but I'm okay," said Scully. "What was that? Did we hit a deer?"

Mulder glanced over his shoulder. "I think it was just a mangy old wolf." He fought with his seatbelt until it popped loose.

"Is it still out there?"

"I hope not, but I'm guessing yes." He wiggled his body in the seat until he could pull his pistol free. "Sure you're okay?"

She nodded and drew her own weapon.

They pushed the doors open and climbed out of the car. A driftwood-dry log sat under the front passenger tire, cracked in three places. One of the headlights had exploded and spread powdery glass over the leaves and moss. The tail lights gave everything a red glow. The descent into the ditch had been gentle, but there was no way the car was getting back on the road without a tow truck.

Their weapons led them back up onto the road. The moon cast a few shafts of light through the trees. The road was an expanse of charcoal broken by puddles of shining silver.

They kept their shoulders close. Mulder stumbled once at the edge of the ditch. Scully froze and waited for him to get back to his feet.

On the far side of the road, something rumbled. It was a wet, throaty sound, the sound of something drowning in blood. It echoed across the empty concrete strip.

"Do you have your flashlight?" murmured Mulder.

"It's in my bag," said Scully. "You?"

"I think it's back in the car by the brake pedal." He risked closing his eyes for a few seconds and tried to adjust them to the moonlight.

Something like tap shoes clicked on the concrete. They spun and faced up the road. The sound stopped.

"I can't see anything," she said.

A shape moved in the darkness. It was smaller than a deer, larger than a dog. Mulder tried to count its legs but couldn't make out enough details. It skirted the puddles of moonlight, little more than a shadow.

Scully aimed her weapon.

"Hang on," he murmured.

"Why?"

"It could be an alien life form, Scully."

"Or it could be a dangerous animal."

"Can we risk that?"

It circled around to the far side of the road. Mulder and Scully took a few steps back, leaving the open road behind them. It moved them away from the car.

The thing at the other end of the road took a few steps forward. The click-clack of claws rang out on the road. A few damp breaths heaved in the shadows.

"I have an idea," said Mulder.

"I'd love to hear it."

Mulder fired at the ground. The rounds banged off the concrete road as the reports crashed back and forth between the trees. In the muzzle flashes, Scully saw something lean and hairless turn and race back into the forest. The clatter of talons retreated into the darkness.

"Run!" He grabbed her arm and dragged her in the other direction.

"That's your plan?" Scully threw her legs forward. "Run?"

"Come on."

They ran down the road into the dark.

"Where are we going?"

"Marsh's place," Mulder said between strides. "He's still got the other alien. The one the Beast wants."

MARSH RESIDENCE
1:09 a.m.

The mailbox appeared out of the dark. They stopped running for a moment. "I don't hear the tapping noise," gasped Mulder.

"I don't hear anything," said Scully. "No crickets, no tree frogs, nothing."

They looked around them, took a few more breaths, and headed up the long driveway. Her eyes were more adjusted to the dark now. She could see the shape of trees in the moonlight.

Something roared out of the darkness. It lunged at Mulder and he spun away. Scully fired off three rounds. The beast continued across the dirt driveway and crashed off into the woods.

She kept her gun up until the sound of leaves and breaking branches faded. "You okay, Mulder?"

"Just swell." He pushed himself up. In the dim light they could both see the gashes in his sleeve. "I think I'm bleeding a little, but nothing major." He moved his arm and winced. "Won't be doing any curls at the gym this week, though."

"We need to get you cleaned up."

"Scully, I think if that thing comes back, infection's going to be the least of our worries."

They headed up the driveway to the house. It was a dark hill against the night sky. The garage was a low cliff alongside it.

The garage door was locked. Mulder kicked the handle once, twice, and the door panels rattled with every blow. On the fourth hit the handle turned and he felt the garage door shift. He grabbed it, turned it the rest of the way, and pulled. The door slid up. He and Scully got their hands under it and heaved.

Something crunched and rustled its way out of the forest and onto the dirt driveway.

They ran into the darkened garage.

"Light switch?"

"No time," said Mulder with a glance over his shoulder.

The freezer chest sat in the same place, humming with power. Mulder smashed the lock with the butt of his pistol. The impact knocked the Sig out of his hand to clatter on the floor.

Scully stepped forward and delivered two strikes with her own pistol. "Damn it," she said. She flipped the weapon in her hand and delivered two shots into the clasp above the padlock. The metal twisted and shredded.

He looked over the freezer. The sounds had driven the creature back a few yards, but it was already loping forward again.

Scully threw the lid back and leaned into the case. "It's frozen to the bottom," she said. "I can't get it out."

"Come on." He crouched and heaved at the edge of the freezer.

They rammed their shoulders against the top of the case. Scully stepped past and pulled the lid back like a lever. Decades of grime and dust and mildew resisted for a moment, keeping the freezer sealed to the floor. Then it peeled itself off the floor and lurched up. A second shove tipped it over. The lid fell open against the floor.

There was a crack of frost and Marvin the alien tumbled out onto the garage floor.

Mulder and Scully stumbled back against the far wall of the garage. She had her pistol out. He glanced at his, a few feet away.

The dim moonlight silhouetted the form at the garage entrance. Nails clacked against the floor. It took another step. And another. Its legs shifted up, forward, and down, one after the other.

Its stance shifted and air hissed around its muzzle.

Scully's finger tightened on her Sig's trigger.

"Wait," whispered Mulder. "Just wait."

The Beast drew in another breath. Its head shifted. Light gleamed off an eye the size of a chicken egg. It let the air out in a snort, then sucked in more.

Then it sank low on its limbs and growled.

Scully's arm tensed.

"Don't," Mulder said.

The growl faded into a low rumble that stretched out and echoed in the garage. The creature crawled forward. Its belly dragged on the floor. It sniffed at the frozen body and let out another rumble.

Scully's aim wavered. "Is it... purring?"

"Maybe," said Mulder. "I think so."

The Beast shuffled forward a few more feet and nuzzled Marvin. Its front paw reached forward and pushed at the alien. The frozen body rocked back and forth on the floor.

The garage turned white. Light blasted in through the windows. Mulder and Scully threw their arms up. The Beast roared and Scully tried to line up on it again.

Figures appeared at the garage door. They marched forward. Two stood on either side of the Beast. They had long poles with snares that looped over the creature's wide head.

A third figure stepped in front of Mulder, blocking his view. It was a man in a clean suit. Inside his helmet a rebreather hid most of his face. "Sir," he said in a muffled voice, "are you okay? Did it injure you?"

"What? Who are you? What are you doing here?"

Another man took Scully by the arm. He was guiding her out of the garage, staying between her and the Beast. She looked back. "Mulder?"

"Scully!" He looked at the figure in front of him. "Where are you taking her?"

The Beast howled again as they dragged it away from Marvin. Two more men charged in with restraint poles. Mulder saw a glimpse of huge eyes and multiple legs and a hide that looked like gray snakeskin.

"Leave it alone," he shouted. Another clean-suited figure appeared at his side and grabbed his arm. "It just wants to be with him. Leave it alone!"

They dragged him out of the garage.

MARSH RESIDENCE
6:23 a.m.

Mulder stared at the garage in the dawn light. It had been gutted, every object in it removed, every particle of dust swept up and taken away. The whole thing was wrapped in clear plastic while they finished sterilizing it. Most of the larger vans and trucks had left hours ago.

He shook his head and winced as it pulled on his bandages. Once the endorphins faded, it was clear the Beast had hurt him more than he'd thought. The medics had cleaned and disinfected the wound, removing any possible trace of contaminants. Now there were half a dozen butterflies on his arm and enough gauze for a halfway-decent Invisible Man costume.

Scully walked up. "How's the arm?"

"Annoyed. Frustrated."

"You have a very expressive arm."

"What did they tell you?"

She held out a card with a government crest on it. "Department of Fish and Game. Called in because of a large wolf possibly carrying a dangerous new strain of rabies."

He looked at the card and sighed. "Well, that's a new one."

"Sorry, Mulder."

"You saw it, didn't you? You saw how it was acting toward the alien."

"I saw something. It wasn't a wolf—not a normal one anyway—but I couldn't swear it was something extraterrestrial."

"It had six legs."

She shook her head. "I never got a good look at it in the light."

He sighed again.

"Come on. Deputy Witness called a tow truck. They should be done pulling our car out of the ditch by now."

He stood up. "Well," he said, "maybe something good came out of this."

"What's that, Mulder?"

He glanced back at the house. "Maybe they're together again."

THE END

OVERSIGHT

By Aaron Rosenberg

J. EDGAR HOOVER BUILDING
WASHINGTON, D.C.
12th DECEMBER, 1994, 4:01 p.m

"This is a waste of my time," Walter Skinner declared as he stormed into the room. Closing the door behind him in not quite a slam but certainly hard enough to elicit a resounding click, he stomped across to the desk and leaned over it, both hands flat on its surface. "I've got a division to run," he declared, glaring down at the desk's owner, "which is a hell of a lot more important than putting up with this bullshit."

"Assistant Director Skinner, how good of you to finally join us." Tracy Malloy smiled up at him, the petite ash-blonde's taut expression every bit as sharp-edged as his glare. "Please, have a seat." Her tone sharpened like that of a schoolteacher finally past patience. "We'll try not to take up too much of your time."

Skinner bit back an angry retort. It wouldn't do any good. Though technically he outranked Malloy, who was only a Section Chief, when she was in pursuit of her duties she could compel obedience from anyone up to a Deputy Director. And right now, here in her office at Quantico, he was in her bailiwick, not his own. If he refused, or even put up too much of a fight, she would simply go over his head to his superior, who would then order Skinner to do as he was told.

It was ironic, Skinner admitted to himself as he sank onto the stiff-backed wooden chair across from Malloy. Most people didn't much like the FBI. Most FBI agents didn't much like their ADs and DDs. And those same Assistant Directors and Deputy Directors, in turn, didn't much like Accounting. Especially during the annual budget reviews. Did that mean

Accounting was as necessary in its way as the Bureau's active field agents? Or was it just another case of "everyone has someone they're afraid of?"

"All right, Section Chief Malloy," Skinner drawled, leaning back and making himself as comfortable as he could on the stiff furniture, deliberately dragging out her title to remind her of the difference in their ranks. "You got me here. What do you want?"

Malloy studied him closely, not looking at all phased by his antics. "You know what I want, Assistant Director," she replied. "A balanced budget, for the Bureau if nothing else. And I've come across a few things I'd like to discuss with you, if I might. Areas where I believe we can save substantial funds, freeing up that money for other, more vital programs and services." There was a folder on her desk in front of her, right beside the coffee cup from some civilian accounting firm she had presumably worked at before joining the Bureau, and as Skinner watched she flicked it open and thumbed through the pages there, scanning them with a practiced eye as if speed-reading them. Skinner wasn't fooled, however. He occasionally engaged in such theatrics himself, pretending to study a file in order to fluster an agent or look like he knew more than he did or simply to stall for time. In this case, he was absolutely certain Malloy already knew everything she wanted from this file. He also suspected, with a sinking feeling, that he knew exactly which file she was perusing.

Sure enough, when she finally closed the file and glanced up at him again, she evoked the one name he had really hoped not to hear from her lips: "The X-Files. AD Skinner, this program has been running for several years now, with at best questionable results. Surely you'd agree that it is a waste of our time and resources, both of which are needed in dealing with actual cases?"

Inwardly Skinner fumed, but outwardly he struggled to remain calm. "I disagree," he declared, the words grating from between clenched teeth as he fought to keep his voice level. "That program is important, and needs to remain active." Who put her up to this, he wondered as he studied the Section Chief. Was it the Cigarette-smoking Man? One of the others? They had always seemed content to let Mulder and Scully poke their noses into various cases around the country, presumably because none of those cases threatened them directly. Had something changed? Were the pair onto something that threatened one of those shadowy figures?

"I see. Perhaps you can explain how it is important?" Malloy's acerbic comment brought Skinner's thoughts back to the present. She was watching him closely, gray eyes narrowed, and when she smiled after a moment the expression failed to soften her gaze. "I thought not." She tapped the folder with a fingernail, which Skinner noticed was badly chewed. "In that case, we'll expect the program to be shut down within the week and its assets reallocated."

What? No! Malloy was already turning to a different file, apparently considering the matter closed, when Skinner finally found his voice again. "I object," he rasped out. "You can't simply decide to close one of my projects just because you don't see its worth."

Malloy glanced back up, frowning. "Actually, I can," she corrected. "That's my job." She studied him a second longer, however, before sighing. "But if you feel strongly about it, I suppose you can argue for its continuance. I'll need your explanation of its value, in writing. First thing in the morning." Once again she glanced away to the stack of files waiting off to one side, and Skinner knew he'd just been dismissed as abruptly as any schoolboy. He rose to his feet, gave her a stiff nod, and turned toward the door, his mind already searching for ways to attack this new problem—and to deal with the secondary conflict it was sure to cause. It was already nearing the end of the day, the sky beginning to darken toward dusk. If he was going to come up with some sort of defense of the X-Files by tomorrow morning, he was going to be here very late indeed. And that wouldn't make Sharon very happy.

However, he knew there wasn't much to be done about it—not if he wanted to protect the program and keep it running. And, although initially Skinner had considered the X-Files a strange, largely pointless but also mostly harmless way to keep Mulder occupied, his opinion toward it had changed over the past few years. Now he recognized its value and its importance.

The question was, how was he going to demonstrate those to Section Chief Malloy?

<hr/>

KENSINGTON, MARYLAND
THURSDAY, 7:53 p.m.

Always the same, Malloy thought as she twisted to slip through the elevator's still-opening doors while maintaining her grip on the stack of folders clutched in her arms. Buy an umbrella so you don't get rained on, and the one time you forget to bring it is the time it pours. Buy a new briefcase because the old one's handle finally fell to pieces, and the day you forget it at home is the day you've got to haul a metric assload of paperwork out of the office.

She could have stayed and gone through everything at her desk, she knew. But then she'd have been here even later, with nothing to eat but another one of the granola bars she kept squirreled away in her desk. And, chances were, she'd have fallen asleep at her desk yet again, too, waking in the morning with a stiff neck and an aching back and the imprint of folders against her cheek. No, far better to bring the work home, where at least she could go through the files over Chinese take-out and a glass of wine, and then get a decent night's sleep in her own bed before doing this all over again tomorrow.

It was late enough that the roads were mostly empty, but Malloy kept her eyes open anyway, forcing herself to stay alert despite her fatigue as she pulled out of the Quantico lot, onto the highway, and toward Kensington. The Maryland suburb was quiet as she finally pulled onto her street and eased into her driveway, and the second she shut off her car, her surroundings went pitch dark. *I really need to put in a light above the garage*, she reminded herself again as she unbuckled, shoved the door open, hoisted the files, and began to lever herself out of the car. It was one of many things she'd wanted to do since she'd bought the house eight years ago, back when she was still at Rice & Sloan, but there just never seemed to be enough time to get around to it. Besides, at this point she was used to the dark.

She'd hip-checked the car door shut again and was feeling her way along the short brick path to her front door when she felt the air around her change. "Hello?" she called out, trying to peer into the shadows. "Is somebody there?" No one answered, and of course she couldn't see anything, but she couldn't shake the feeling that she was no longer alone. It was as if the night itself had taken on shape, and that shape was a decidedly menacing one. She shivered despite the thick new leather jacket that had been an early holiday present from her sister, and tried to tell herself it was just from the cold.

Trying to hurry, Malloy cursed as the tip of one shoe caught on a brick, twisting her ankle and sending a shock of pain up her leg. She wobbled a second, almost losing her balance, but managed to stay upright and keep hold of the folders despite the pain. *I'll ice it once I get inside,* she told herself. *And now I'm definitely going to need that glass of wine.*

She was almost to the door when the darkness shifted again. It grew thicker, almost cloying, its impenetrability weighing her down. There was a sound somewhere nearby, echoing oddly through the shadows, a staccato of noise like a burst of rain hitting all at once—

—and then the darkness came alive, a flash of light splitting it wide as pain lanced through Malloy again, this time not from her ankle but from her arm—

—again she heard the rain, though she didn't notice getting wet, and again there was pain, in her arm again but lower down, as she cried out and dropped the files, raising her hands to protect her face and neck from this strange, dark onslaught—

—once more she heard the noise, the quick pattering all around her now, and this time the pain was across her chest, almost blinding in its intensity, and now Malloy did stumble, crashing to the ground with a scream that shattered against the hard bricks, to tumble weakly about her as she lay there, writhing and moaning, delirious in her agony—

—and she thought the darkness leaned in and whispered in her ear, "in the kingdom of the blind, there are no kings" before it lashed out, its anger a palpable force that caught her at the temple and cheek and sent her consciousness winging away further into the dark, where the rest of her could not follow.

Sharon is going to kill me, Skinner thought as he finally slid into his car. By the time he'd gotten back to his own office in the Hoover building it had been nearly noon, and then he'd had to deal with the usual sorts of problems—a judge threatening to veto a wiretap and needing to be cajoled, flattered, and intimidated; a pair of agents whose bickering had come to blows and required disciplinary action but who were both too good to have their careers stalled over one incident; an inter-agency operation that required additional logistical details, some very firm rules for

his people, and a few pointed reminders to the leaders of the other units
so they didn't try treating his agents like errand boys; and of course the
usual update for his Deputy Director, which would then be compiled
into the daily brief for the Director himself. Just the standard minutiae of
running an FBI division, but the sun had already set before Skinner had
cleared his plate of those tasks and could turn his attention to his latest
crisis—finding a way to justify the X-Files.

And the problem was, even after he'd retrieved some junk food and
more coffee from the vending machine down the hall and sat back down at
his desk, now fully ready to focus on this question, he was drawing a blank.

It wasn't that the X-Files didn't have merit. He'd come to see that—
though he still questioned Mulder's methods, and even Scully's at times,
and didn't always buy their fantastical explanations, he couldn't argue that
they often caught or at least stopped someone who had been responsible
for multiple bizarre deaths. That made the program a good thing. But
how did he go about explaining that? Especially to someone as numbers-
driven as Section Chief Tracy Malloy? All she saw were the figures on a
spreadsheet, and those figures told her that the actual number of arrests
made by the X-Files unit was depressingly, almost laughably small. The
spreadsheet couldn't show that part of the reason for such a low number
was that a startlingly large percentage of X-Files suspects wound up disin-
tegrating or turning to solid stone or liquefying or being torn to pieces by
wild animals or any of a thousand other bizarre deaths. And even if it had,
Malloy would have laughed and told him she didn't believe in fairy tales.

No, to convince her that the X-Files should retain its funding he'd
need to show her clear proof that it produced results.

But proof was the one thing the X-Files never seemed to have.

After beating his head against the proverbial wall for a few hours,
Skinner had finally decided he'd had enough. He could be frustrated at
home just as easily as at work, and the sooner he went home the less
angry Sharon would be—it wasn't a question of whether she'd be furious
with him at this point, but just of how much of the potential eruption he
could stave off. So he'd packed it in. Maybe the drive would give him a
chance to come up with some miraculous solution.

The ring of his cell phone interrupted his thoughts, however. "AD
Skinner," he answered, gripping the phone between chin and shoulder

while he backed the car out of its parking space.

"Sir, it's Agent Hanson," a vaguely familiar voice replied. "I'm night shift in Signals. Sorry to bother you so late, sir, but we just picked up a call from a local dispatch and thought you'd want to know. It's Section Chief Malloy, sir. There's been an... incident."

"What?" Skinner hit the brakes so he could focus on the conversation properly. "What happened? Where is she?"

"George Washington, sir," Hanson replied. "Ambulance just picked her up following a neighbor's 911 call."

"Right. I'm en route," Skinner barked, dropping the phone into his lap as he peeled out of the lot. He could be at George Washington in twenty minutes, maybe less. He had no idea what'd happened, but he planned to find out. Whether he liked Malloy or not, whether he was happy about what she was doing to his programs, she was still one of his.

GEORGE WASHINGTON UNIVERSITY HOSPITAL
WASHINGTON, D.C.
THURSDAY, 8:54 p.m.

"She's in bad shape," the doctor, a frighteningly young East Indian named Raj Palur, told Skinner a half hour later. "But she's stable."

It had taken only fifteen minutes to reach the hospital, thanks to the lack of traffic, but Skinner had then been forced to spend another ten arguing with the hospital staff before they finally recognized his authority and let him up to see her. The good doctor had intercepted him on his way into her room, but that was fine because this way Skinner knew he was getting a full brief on her condition, direct from the expert.

"What happened, exactly?" he demanded, trying not to loom over the doctor. Whatever it was, it wasn't this man's fault. He was the one trying to help. Unfortunately, he was also the only available outlet for Skinner's rage at the moment, and so he had to resist the urge to grab the man and shake him to get answers more quickly.

If Dr. Palur felt threatened at all, he didn't show it. He was probably used to dealing with irate loved ones, Skinner realized. "She was beaten," the doctor explained now. "Badly. With some kind of club or pipe, I would guess—the impacts were narrow but far too hard to be from flesh and blood." He consulted the chart in his hands, though Skinner suspected that was just a prop—he was struck by the similarity to earlier today, when it had been Malloy pretending to read a file. Now it was her file that was being read. "Her right arm was fractured in two places, her rotator cuff torn in the process, and several ligaments torn or sprained as well. She took at least one blow to the chest, shattering two ribs and collapsing a lung, and a blow to the head that crushed part of her cheekbone." He sighed and glanced up to meet Skinner's glare. "She was lucky, however. Her coat was thick leather and helped absorb some of the impact. The broken ribs did not pierce any organs, and we were able to reinflate the lung. And the blow to the head did not fracture the skull or cause any damage to her brain, nor did it touch the eye socket or the eye itself. With time, rest, recuperation, and proper physical therapy, she should recover fully."

Skinner nodded. He could see Malloy in her room past the doctor, tubes snaking in and out of her, bandages wrapping her head, arm, and chest. He wasn't sure if she was conscious or not. There was a uniformed cop sitting just outside the door, but no one in the room with her. "Has her family been notified yet?"

"We left a message for her sister, who's listed as her next of kin," Dr. Palur confirmed. "No word from her yet, I believe." He frowned up at Skinner. "If I may ask, how did you know she was here?"

"We monitor calls for agents in distress," Skinner replied absently, scanning the area. Everything seemed quiet. "When her name came up on the 911 call, they called me." He held out his hand. "Thank you, doctor. I may have more questions for you later, but right now I'd like to speak to the officer over there, and then to Ms. Malloy herself, if she's up to it."

"She may be a little disconnected," Palur warned, still frowning. "We have her on some fairly strong pain medication. But she's mostly coherent, so I don't see any reason you can't speak to her." He nodded and turned away, no doubt off to check on other patients, while Skinner made a beeline for the cop.

"AD Skinner, FBI," he introduced himself, displaying his badge and ID. "I'm her boss." Which was close enough to being true—Malloy didn't report to him, of course, but he did outrank her in the Bureau. "What can you tell me about what happened?"

The cop, whose nametag revealed him to be Officer Severen, straightened in his chair at the sight of Skinner's credentials. Heavyset and middle-aged, he had no doubt wanted to be a secret agent when he was younger. "Looks like a mugging gone bad," he answered, his voice just as thick and rundown as the rest of him. "Neighbor heard her screams and called it in. By the time I was on the scene, she was out cold and nobody was around." He shook his head. "Purse was right next to her, didn't look like it'd been rifled, she still had her watch and earrings and necklace on, so most likely she got jumped but then something spooked the perp and he took off before he could get the goods. Either that or it was a failed home invasion, same thing—she showed up unexpectedly, startled the guy in the act of breaking in, he beat her down and then ran."

Skinner scowled and was pleased to see the cop's face pale at the sight of it. A mugging gone bad? In quiet little Kensington? At her own front door? What kind of mugger was stupid enough to go after someone in their own driveway rather than targeting people coming out of the train station or walking to the store? And a home invasion? Really? If she'd startled a burglar on his way out there'd have been signs of a break-in. If she'd interrupted the thief on the way in, any halfway-intelligent crook would've just split before being seen. Why stay and beat her? It made no sense.

He didn't say any of that, though. Severen wasn't one of his, after all. Any agent who'd presented him with such sloppy guesswork would've gotten torn a new one, but this guy was just a sleepy local cop, completely overwhelmed by the violence of the situation. So all Skinner said to him was, "Thanks. I'll want to see the scene myself, soon as the sun's up." Which would be in just a few hours, at this point. There was already a hint of lightening to the sky along the horizon.

Barely acknowledging the officer's nod, Skinner sidestepped and knocked on the door to the room, then slid it open and stepped inside. "Malloy?" he said softly as he approached the hospital bed. "Can you hear me?"

That provoked a raspy laugh in response. "Hello, AD Skinner." Her voice was thinner than it had been that morning, with a noticeable tremor, but still clear. "How lovely to see you again. I'm afraid I won't be able to consider your defense just now. I'm a little preoccupied."

At least she still has her sense of humor, Skinner thought, moving in a little closer. "Don't worry about that right now," he assured her. "We can talk about that later. Right now I want to hear exactly what happened."

"Trying to figure out who to thank?" Malloy asked, and laughed again.

Her laugh was a bit fluttery, and Skinner suspected part of her good mood came from the drugs they were giving her.

But he answered seriously: "No, trying to figure out who to come down on like a ton of bricks for putting the hurt on one of my people. Can you tell me what you remember?"

She frowned, her eyes slightly unfocused, but after a second she nodded. "I was at work late," she started slowly. "I got home, got out of my car, and headed to the front door." The frown deepened, casting new lines across her face. "It started raining. Something—somebody—hit me. On the arm. Then again. Then across my chest. I fell down. Then something hit me in the head. That's all I remember."

"Did you see who did it?" But he wasn't surprised when she shook her head. She'd have mentioned that already, if she had.

"No, it was pitch black," she confirmed. "I never saw a thing." Her gaze skittered toward the door, and the cop stationed outside. "The officer told me he thought it was a mugger. Or a burglar. Something like that."

Skinner balled his hands into fists. "Yes, well, while Officer Severen might be adept at handing out speeding tickets and terrorizing truant schoolchildren," he drawled, "I think I'll decide for myself who might have done this to you and why." He leaned in a little. "Trust me, though, Malloy. I will get whoever's behind this. You have my word."

That earned him a faint, sleepy smile as her eyes drooped shut. "Thank you, AD Skinner. And just for that, you can have a short extension on your defense. Shall we say Monday instead?" Then her chin slid down to rest against her collarbone, and her breathing slowed and deepened. She was out.

Monday, Skinner thought as he turned to go. Apparently Malloy was an optimist. Who knew? But he certainly intended to have some information for her by then, even if it wasn't about the project they'd been discussing a few short hours ago. He was already compiling a list of questions in his head as he strode down the hospital corridor, heading for the elevator that would take him back down to the parking garage and to his car. He had Malloy's address already—he'd see what answers he could find there. First thing in the morning, though. Because if he was any later getting home, Malloy wouldn't be the only FBI agent sporting bruises.

KENSINGTON, MARYLAND
FRIDAY, 8:20 a.m.

"Unreliable witness." That was the first thing to pop into Skinner's head as he surveyed the scene. For all her icy calm and her sharp gaze, Malloy was an unreliable witness. Then again, she was the victim rather than a bystander, so she could hardly be blamed for her memory being muddled. It did mean he had to question everything she'd said, though.

Because there wasn't any rain. Nor had there been. He looked down at the files scattered across the space between her car and her front door, which had clearly fallen when she'd been attacked. Not a single one of them was wet. And the grass beyond was damp, so it had rained at some point earlier, enough for the blades to retain droplets, but the papers were crumpled yet dry.

And curiously unmarked, was the second thing he noticed as he squatted down to examine them. A few were scuffed by what looked to be a woman's shoe, and judging by the angle and the distance between those marks they were from Malloy as she flailed backward and then fell. But he didn't see any other marks. Not one.

Which meant whoever'd done this to her had stepped flawlessly around those papers. Unless he'd simply collected any he had tagged with his feet, but that seemed equally unlikely, given how thoroughly the distance was covered by them.

It'd been dark, Skinner noted, glancing up at the porch's front edge and then over his shoulder toward the street. No street light within view, no lights on the driveway, a single bulb by the door itself but that hadn't been on. So Malloy had been right about one thing, it had been pitch black. But how had her assailant gotten around all those papers, then? And why would she think it had been raining when it wasn't?

This case isn't right, Skinner decided, straightening from his crouch. The pieces don't add up. Which made him think of the X-Files. Mulder would be all over this. For a minute Skinner was tempted to call him in. But no, that wouldn't help any to let the lanky agent start spinning his wild theories and citing obscure folklore. Still, Skinner decided to treat this attack as if it were an X-File. Throw out the rules of reality, he told himself. Anything is possible, no matter how crazy. So what did he know?

First, someone had attacked Malloy here in her driveway.

Second, it had been pitch dark, yet the attacker had not only hit her repeatedly but had stepped around obstacles to do so.

Third, this was personal. That wasn't a fact, but Skinner knew it nonetheless. It was too violent to be anything else. There had been real anger, real hatred, behind those blows. And the attacker had sought Malloy out specifically. Whoever it was had wanted her to suffer.

His knee-jerk response to that was "obviously I'm not the only one whose budget she threatened." That was uncharitable, of course. But perhaps there was some truth to it. He didn't think for a second that the attacker was FBI, if for no other reason than he'd have an agent's badge for being this sloppy. But had Malloy always been with the Bureau? There had been that coffee cup, he remembered. What had it said? Rice & Sloan. That would be his next stop. They should be open by the time he got there.

GEORGE WASHINGTON UNIVERSITY HOSPITAL
WASHINGTON, D.C.
FRIDAY, 10:41 a.m.

"I talked to your old bosses," he told Malloy when he stopped by to see her an hour or two later. He'd been pleased to find her awake and more cogent today. "Thought this might have to do with something you'd worked on there. But they couldn't think of anything that might fit the bill."

"I'm an accountant," she reminded him, "not a prosecutor. I don't get people coming after me." Which was ironic, given that she looked like she'd gone ten rounds with a city bus, the bruising now purpling clearly beneath and around the bandages.

"Whoever did this was after you in particular," Skinner argued. "I know it. And you do too." He saw the way her eyes flickered away from him for just a second. "What?" he demanded, leaning forward in the chair he'd dragged next to her bed. "What aren't you telling me?"

"It's nothing," she answered after a second, her voice smaller and more malleable than before, the brittle steel missing for a change. "It doesn't mean anything. I was delirious."

"Maybe you were," he agreed, "but that doesn't mean you didn't pick up on something. Tell me."

She sighed. "I thought I heard... a voice. Right before I blacked out."

"A voice?" Skinner was all ears. "Man? Woman? Young? Old? Accent? Range? What did it say?"

"Man, I think." She frowned and squeezed her eyes shut for a second. "Soft. Husky. No real accent. He said 'in the kingdom of the blind there are no kings.'" She laughed, wincing as the movement caught at her bruised chest and wrapped ribs. "Sorry. I thought I imagined it. Maybe I did."

"Maybe," Skinner agreed, but he was already turning the phrase over in his head. "In the kingdom of the blind there are no kings." He knew there was a phrase, maybe from the Bible? Something about the kingdom of the blind and the one-eyed man. This could be a twisted version of that. He was absolutely certain she hadn't imagined it. Her attacker had whispered this to her, which meant it was important. But what did it mean?

The brief conversation had worn Malloy out, so Skinner left the room to let her rest. A quick search on his phone had turned up the original quote "In the kingdom of the blind, the one-eyed man is king." It was Erasmus, not the Bible. Even so, he'd said "there are no kings." That sounded bitter. Angry. Were they looking for a blind man? Or was that only a metaphor?

A blind man wouldn't have cared that it was dark, Skinner realized. And her injuries, from something thin and heavy like a pipe or a cane— or a walking stick. Could a blind man have navigated his way through those files? Not easily. Not with any speed. X-Files, Skinner reminded himself. Maybe this wasn't just any old blind man.

He felt like the pieces were there, only just out of reach. And he had the sinking feeling he wouldn't be able to grasp them on his own. With a sigh, he called up a number on his phone.

"This is Skinner," he said as soon as it picked up. "I need an answer, and I don't have time for twenty questions. How would a blind man find his way through a pile of papers without touching them, at high speed?"

The reply was immediate. "Echolocation."

"That thing that bats do?"

"There have been theories," Mulder started, but sped up when Skinner cleared his throat. "Some think we could learn to do what bats do. Echolocate, find our way by sonar. See our surroundings by letting reflected sounds paint a mental picture."

"Anybody doing research on that?"

He heard the sound of Mulder typing at his computer. "There was a guy," the agent said after a minute. "Doctor Gerald Rasmussen. Published a paper on it several years back. Lots of promise." More typing. "It doesn't look like it ever went anywhere, though."

"Where did this Rasmussen work?" Skinner asked.

The sound of more keys being struck. "Patton GenTech," Mulder replied.

"Thank you, Agent Mulder." Skinner tried not to let the words stick in his throat. "You've been a big help." He hung up before the agent could launch any more theories at him, or ask why he'd needed to know.

Rasmussen. Patton GenTech. Published years ago and nothing since.

Skinner had a pretty good hunch that, if he asked at Rice & Sloan, he'd learn that Patton GenTech had been a client of theirs, and that during budget review one year the firm had recommended Rasmussen's funding be cut. "At best questionable results," he was sure.

Just as he was sure Tracy Malloy had been the accountant in charge.

It looked like the good doctor's research had borne fruit finally. And now he'd decided to prove it and get revenge, all at the same time.

But Malloy had survived the attack.

Which meant, Skinner knew, that her assailant was sure to try again.

He frowned and glanced at the clock. It was almost noon. He had until nightfall, at least, and probably a few hours past that. More than enough time to go home, grab a shower, change, eat something, and then get ready.

And he could stop at a flower shop along the way. If he stepped inside bearing roses, Sharon wouldn't kick him out right away. He hoped.

GEORGE WASHINGTON UNIVERSITY HOSPITAL
WASHINGTON, D.C.
SATURDAY, 12:13 a.m.

It was late, just past midnight, when Skinner started awake. He'd been dozing off in the chair outside Malloy's room, where he'd stationed himself right after dinner. Now he looked around to see what had awakened him, squinting in the dark.

Dark. Why was it dark? This was a hospital, even late at night on a recovery wing like this there were always lights. But he didn't see any at all. Total blackout.

That wasn't good.

No one was around, which was also odd, and wrong. But if the power had failed the staff would be busy trying to get that sorted, and seeing to those in immediate danger, the patients on life support and so on. This wing was for those already in recovery, which meant all the heart monitors and what not were no longer functioning but that was less crucial than getting somebody's insulin pump going again. There had probably been a bustle of nurses gathering supplies and running for the other floors, which might have also contributed to his waking up. Someone would be back to check on the floor soon, he was sure. Right now, though, he was alone out here.

The next thing he noticed was the sound. It was a soft, rapid patter—a lot like rain, he realized. *Score one for you, Malloy.* It wasn't rain, though, not exactly. It sent a shiver down his spine, and left an uncomfortable near-buzzing in his ears and behind his eyes.

And it was getting closer.

After a few seconds he could discern a figure approaching out of the shadows, emerging from them as if shedding an inky curtain, edges and details slowly resolving against the black. A tall figure, tapping a long, thick white cane on the ground in front of him, the cane the only bright spot in the darkness. That was the sound, Skinner realized, fighting down a second shiver. And, if he was right, the man used that sound, and its echoes, to paint a mental picture of his surroundings. Just like a bat. The mental image only added to the eeriness of the situation.

"Doctor Rasmussen, I presume?" Skinner called out, rising to his feet and reaching into his jacket pocket at the same time. Taking action helped push back the child-like fear of the dark that had been gnawing at him since he'd opened his eyes to blackness.

"Stand aside, whoever you are," the good doctor replied, his voice soft and low like a whisper and chilling as a winter wind. "I only want her."

"Can't do that," Skinner said, shaking off the last of the gloom. "Walk away, doctor. Walk away now, while you still can."

The doctor smiled as he tapped his way closer, moving unerringly around various chairs and carts in his path despite the inky black that made them barely more than vague outlines lingering in the shadows. "I don't think so," he replied. His total ease in the darkness would have been enough to unsettle anyone.

Skinner shrugged, now intent enough upon his plan to ignore any fear.

"Your funeral." And he switched on the device in his hand.

Instantly Rasmussen froze, head tilting this way and that in obvious confusion. His cane hovered where it was, in mid-tap, its end less than an inch from the floor. "What have you done?" he demanded, his voice rising to a shriek.

"Ultrasound recording," Skinner answered, approaching the doctor but staying wary. His other hand retrieved a ziptie from his other pocket. "From a hawkmoth. They cancel a bat's echolocation. Figured they'd do the same for you." It was useful to have friends. Especially ones at the Smithsonian. And astounding just what they had on file in the digital archives over at the National Zoo. He'd stopped there on the way back.

Rasmussen thrashed about, swinging that cane of his in a vicious arc, but now he was just as blind as Skinner. Moreso, apparently—as Skinner got closer and his sight adjusted he could see that the doctor's eyes were dull and filmed over, as if a fog had seeped into them, masking the colors beneath. No wonder the man had been so focused on a cure for blindness—he had been hoping to use it himself. And he had. Too bad he'd decided his first action with it should be one of revenge.

Even though he still couldn't see much, Skinner was able to duck the blind swing easily, and he stepped into the arc of the cane, catching it with one hand and wrenching it from Rasmussen's grip. With his other hand he grabbed the doctor's shoulder and spun him around, a foot to the back of the man's knee, forcing his legs to buckle and driving him to the ground. From there it was an easy thing to zip-tie his hands behind his back. Problem solved.

He was already dreading how insufferable Mulder was going to be once he found out.

GEORGE WASHINGTON UNIVERSITY HOSPITAL
WASHINGTON, D.C.
TUESDAY, 5:22 p.m.

A few days later, Skinner dropped by to see Malloy again. "You're looking better," he commented as he entered her room. There was a lightweight cast on her arm, and a foam cast along the side of her face, but a lot of the bruising was starting to fade.

"Better," she agreed, "but still a long ways to go. At least they're letting me go home." She was already dressed in regular clothes, jeans and a long-sleeved T-shirt, rather than hospital garb. "Thank you," she said, forcing herself to look him in the eye. "For catching Rasmussen. For stopping him."

Skinner nodded. "Glad I could be of service."

A small smile crept onto Malloy's face, and her eyes had a hint of their old fire when she replied, "And is this the part where you tell me what that service will cost me? Like sparing your precious X-Files?"

But Skinner shook his head. "No, this is the part where I give you my defense." He dropped a file onto the bed beside her.

She flipped it open, then looked up at him, frowning. "This is my incident report. So this is some kind of weird blackmail?"

"Not at all." Skinner crossed his arms over his chest. "You cut off this man's funding years ago, and probably never even knew his name. He continued his research, which was so cutting-edge it sounds like fairy tales and make-believe, and then came after you for revenge. This is exactly the kind of case the X-Files handles—the ones that can't be explained any other way, the ones that have long-term repercussions even when there's no clear immediate effect. This is why that unit needs to stay."

Malloy considered that, flipping pages idly as she thought. Finally, she nodded. "I see your point," she admitted. "I deal in hard numbers, clear gains, quantifiable results. But yes, maybe there should always been one unit that handles things a little... differently. Things like this." She nodded again. "All right, AD Skinner. The X-Files can stay."

He did his best not to grin as he nodded back. "Thank you. Good luck with your recovery."

As he let himself out and headed down the hall, he thought about it. At first he'd been defending the X-Files partially out of sheer stubbornness, like the dog that doesn't want the bone anymore but will fight if you try taking it from him. But he'd known for a while that the X-Files did have value. And now he even knew how to explain it, at least a little, so others could see that value, too.

Now if only Sharon could see the value in letting him out of the doghouse and off the couch. But Skinner suspected that was something even Mulder couldn't help him with.

Though chocolate might. Lots and lots of chocolate.

THE END

DUSK

By Paul Crilley

CASTLE BLUFF, NEW HAMPSHIRE
16th MAY, 2015, 2:16 a.m.

K im Duncan had made many dodgy decisions in her seventeen years on this planet, but this, she reckoned, ranked right up there with the worst of them.

But what could she do? When she'd caught Briony and her hell-spawn friend sneaking out of the house in the middle of the night she *had* to tag along. How else was she going to humiliate her sister? She needed hard facts for that. And hard facts meant threatening to tell the parental units unless she could go with.

She was kind of regretting it now. Kim shivered and pulled her dad's quilted jacket tighter around her body. Heavy mist coiled slowly between the tree trunks. She couldn't see more than five feet in front of her and it was getting colder with every passing minute.

"Marco!" she called out.

Audrey, Briony's friend and the aforementioned hell-spawn, lunged out of the mist at her. "Shut up!" she snapped. "God, you are *so* annoying. You're going to screw everything up."

Kim shone her cell phone flash directly into Audrey's eyes, holding it there till she squinted and looked away with a muttered insult.

Briony, Audrey, and Briony's killjoy sister, Kimmy. It was like some bad teen sitcom.

"Let's go home," said Kim. "It's going to snow soon."

"I told you not to come," said Briony.

"Yeah, and if mom found out I let you come out here on your own? I'd be grounded for a month."

"What difference would that make?" asked Audrey. "It's not as if you have any friends. You'd be able to just sit in your room with your stupid books."

"Seriously?" said Kim. "That's your best insult? That I sit in my room and *read*?"

Audrey turned away with a flick of her perfectly straightened hair and moved deeper into the woods. She only got two steps before she lost her footing and fell to her knees.

"Yeah," said Kim, "high heels, forests and hiking. Hashtag *not-too-clever*."

"We're not hiking," said Briony. "We're searching."

And there it was. The lame-ass reason they were floundering around the woods on a freezing night three days from Christmas.

Searching.

For Callum James, the mysterious, five hundred year old vampire from the multi-*quadrillion* selling *Dusk* novels.

"How long will it take to convince you he's a character in a stupid book and not *actually* a real person who hangs around in mist-shrouded forests?"

"Shows what you know," sneered Audrey. "Sarah and Jasmine and Shauna *all* saw him. He was amazingly hot? But modest with it too," she added.

Briony nodded. "Like, he looks like a Greek God but he's not really aware of it?"

Kim gritted her teeth. She hated the way her sister spoke like almost everything was a question.

"And Sarah said she and Callum shared a moment? And that she just *knew* she was special to him."

"So they spoke to him, did they?" asked Kim.

"No. It was the way he *looked* at her?" said Briony. "You wouldn't understand."

"She's lying, anyway," said Audrey. "No way would Callum James pick her. She's such a loser."

"Let me guess," said Kim. "You're more his type?"

Audrey flicked her hair. "Of course I am."

"Hate to break it to you," said Kim. "I've read the first book. His type is the quiet loner without any friends." Kim flashed a grin at her sister. "So if anyone here is his type, it's me."

"Oh my God, you're *such* a sad case," said Briony. "As if he'd go for *you.*"

"Yeah. *I'm* the sad case. Says the one wandering around the woods in the middle of the night hoping a fictional vampire will notice her."

Audrey whirled around and grabbed Kim's jacket. Kim blinked in surprise as the girl's face twisted with fury. "He is *not. Fictional,*" she snarled, her face only inches from Kim's.

"Okay, okay. Fine. God, calm down."

Audrey glared at Kim for another five seconds, then released her jacket, smiled sweetly, and smoothed the material down. She turned away and started marching deeper into the forest.

"You *do* know that even if there *is* someone out here it will probably turn out to be a catfish creep?" she called. But Audrey ignored her.

They carried on walking. The mist grew thicker, a white haze that draped across the forest, blocking out the trees until they were almost on top of them. A branch got tangled in Kim's hair. She swore and pulled up short.

"Guys!" she called. "Hold up."

She winced, moving her head around as she tried to unwind her hair. She had to eventually yank it free, leaving behind a clump in the process.

"Perfect."

She snapped the branch in irritation, dropped it to the ground.

That was when she realized she was alone.

Kim looked around. The mist had closed in even more, a gauze bandage across tired eyes.

"Briony?"

No answer.

"Audrey?"

She moved a few paces, then stopped. She had no clue where she was going. Couldn't see more than three feet in front of her. She'd read once that if you get lost you were supposed to just stay where you were and wait for someone to find you. But... she looked around, shivering as the mist brushed wetly against her cheeks. She couldn't hang around here all night. She'd freeze to death.

She decided to keep moving.

She kept her eyes downcast, watching where she put her feet. Last thing she needed was to fall and twist an ankle.

Every few minutes she paused to listen, wondering where the other two went.

And then she saw the white glow from up ahead.

FBI HEADQUARTERS
WASHINGTON, D.C.
MONDAY, 8:54 a.m.

"I'm nobody special. I'm not one of the cool kids. I'm not one of the emos. And I'm not one of the goths. I'm just somebody trying to get through high school so I can leave this crappy town and study journalism in Chicago.

"Which was why I found it so weird when Callum James kept bumping into me. Almost like he was doing it on purpose. Which was crazy. Because hot guys don't hit on girls like me. That's not how it works. They prefer the cheerleaders. The airheads. Somebody who won't challenge their already tiny mindset.

"To be honest, Callum freaked me out a bit. He was a loner. A bit of a weirdo, really, with skin so white it was like the smiles on Hollywood stars. And his eyes...

"...His eyes were deep, dark pools, hiding everything. Giving away nothing."

Scully slammed the book shut in disgust. "Sorry. Not really my thing."

Mulder nodded gravely. "More of a Dan Brown fan?"

Scully tossed the book on the desk. It hit a pile of papers and fell to the floor with a heavy thud.

"Hey. Easy on my book." Mulder swung his legs off the desk, picked the book up and carefully brushed it down.

Scully frowned. "*Your* book?"

"Yeah," said Mulder, checking the spine for damage. "A first edition."

Scully watched him, waiting for the punch-line. It didn't come. "Seriously?"

"What? A guy can't read books about teenage girls and vampires without it being weird?" He paused, obviously running this last sentence back through his mind. "That came out wrong. Thing is Scully, I was a fan of the writer way before the *Dusk* books. Eugene McEllroy. He was a contemporary of Hunter S. Thompson. The two of them blazed the trail of gonzo journalism back in the seventies. You should hear some of the stories about them. They took every drug known to man. Mescaline, LSD, uppers, downers, you name it. Apparently, McEllroy's favorite was MDMA. Said it was the only time he didn't want to kill everyone in the world."

"That's so sweet. And he went from gonzo journalism to writing books for teenagers how exactly?"

Mulder shrugged. "No idea. But when *Dusk* started outselling all his other work a thousand times over, he must have decided he was on to a good thing. You should read them, Scully. You might be surprised."

"Mulder, what year is it?"

"Why?" He sat up straight and leaned forward eagerly, a slight grin on his face. "Have you experienced lost time? Did you come to in your car on a lonely road with no recollection of how you got there?"

"What year?"

"2017."

"*Mulder!*"

"Fine. 2015."

"Which means we've known each other how long?"

"Twenty-one years?"

"And in all that time have you ever seen me reading a book like that? Just from the first page you can see they're marketed to lonely teenagers and frustrated housewives. The main character is ordinary in every way. Much like how most teenagers feel about themselves. A blank template that they can imprint on while they read the books. If such an ordinary character can draw the attention of a centuries old vampire, then there's still hope for them."

Mulder was nodding. "That's why I thought you'd be into it."

Scully raised an eyebrow. Mulder held up his hands in defense. "Kidding."

"Besides," said Scully. "I get enough weird stuff in my day job without reading about a three hundred year old man who spends his time hanging around the local high school."

"Yeah, McEllroy explained that. His vampires also feed on high, intense emotions. Not just blood. And what better place to pick up that kind of energy than a high school?"

Scully sighed. "If you say so. And we're talking about this… why?"

Mulder handed her a file. Scully flipped it open and scanned the top page—a missing persons report.

"There have been reports of teens going missing in a little town called Castle Bluff," said Mulder. "Three so far."

Scully flicked through the file. Basic police reports. Three teens. All disappeared during the night. And all gone missing within three weeks of each other.

"Do they have a connection?"

"They're all obsessed with the *Dusk* books," said Mulder.

Scully waited. Nothing else was forthcoming. "Mulder, half the teens in the *country* are obsessed with the *Dusk* novels. That's not a connection."

"What if I told you people have sighted Callum James in the vicinity of the disappearances?"

Scully blinked. "The vampire from the books?"

Mulder nodded. "And what if I told you that Eugene McEllroy lives in the same town?"

"I'd tell you to find out if he has a new book coming out, because this sounds like a cheap publicity stunt that's gone wrong."

"That's what I thought at first. Then I saw this cell phone footage."

Mulder swung his monitor around to face Scully and hit a button on his keyboard.

Scully leaned forward. It was footage of a snow-covered forest floor. Leaves and twigs, a pair of feet. She could hear frightened, panicked breathing. A moment later the image swung upward as the cell phone was raised to shoulder height.

In the distance, glimpsed between tree trunks, was a figure. But the figure appeared to be glowing. Scully squinted. No, not glowing. The figure… sparkled. Silver and white motes of light flashing around it like dust caught in the sun. A trick of the light? Moon reflecting off the mist?

Scully wasn't sure. She leaned closer. The figure was staring down at two girls kneeling on the forest floor. The image shifted as whoever held the phone used the optical zoom. The image lurched closer, losing definition in the process. But Scully could still see the rapt looks on the faces of the girls—the look of devotion in their eyes.

Whoever held the cell phone shifted slightly. A twig snapped underfoot. The glowing figure whirled around. Scully heard an indrawn breath of fear, then the image shifted crazily as the person turned and ran. The image blurred and tilted. Panicky sobs came from Mulder's speakers.

Then nothing.

"The two girls who looked like they were kneeling before an altar are Briony Duncan and Audrey Caplan. Both haven't been seen since they disappeared two nights ago. Local police have drawn a blank. Same as with the previous case."

"Why have the FBI only been notified now?"

"There was a possibility the first case wasn't an abduction, but a runaway. The local PD reassessed the case in the light of the most recent incident and called it in."

"Two nights ago, though? The crime scene will be contaminated."

"I know. Agent Peters is already there with the Evidence Response Team. He's the one who put the call through to me."

"What did he say?"

"He said, and I quote, 'Hey spooky. How'd you like a multiple abduction case carried out by a fictional vampire who has the hots for high school kids?' " Mulder grinned. "I mean, when he puts it like that, how could I resist?"

CASTLE BLUFF, NEW HAMPSHIRE
3:23 p.m.

Mulder drove through a wintry tunnel of black trees, the leafless branches twisting up toward the leaden sky. He shivered and cranked up the heating. Snow tonight. A white Christmas. Been a while since they'd had one of those.

He checked the GPS. They should arrive at the town in a few minutes. He glanced across at Scully. She was fast asleep, a tiny line of drool hanging from the side of her mouth. Mulder stared at it for a while. She was adamant she didn't drool in her sleep, even when he pointed out the damp patch on her pillow. He'd tried explaining that it wasn't gross, manly drool. That it was dainty, *classy* drool. But that hadn't done much to make her any less irritated.

He glanced in the rear view mirror then pulled over. He fished his cell phone out and was about to take a picture of her drool when she snorted and opened her eyes. Mulder quickly hid the phone.

"We there yet?" she asked, stifling a yawn.

Mulder pointed out the window. He'd stopped—more from luck than anything else—just shy of the town marker. It was a huge billboard with a bird's eye view of 1950s suburbia. For some reason a cartoon vampire was flying through the sky above the houses.

She squinted at the sign. "What's with the vampire?"

Mulder shrugged and started the car. "Maybe it's a new addition. To drum up some tourism."

"Classy."

Written across the bottom of the sign were the words, *"Castle Bluff. Pop. 3546. Stay the night. You won't ever want to leave."*

"Is it just me, or is that slightly ominous?" said Mulder.

"It's not just you."

"Good to know."

They drove into town about five minutes later. Mulder squinted through the fogged window. Not much to see. A general store, a few bars, a couple of old, family-run restaurants. The place looked like it was stuck in a time warp. But he supposed that was understandable. A town with a population of just a few thousand was going to be pretty insular. They were probably still on dial-up internet here.

"You want to stop in and meet the sheriff or should we look for a place to crash?" he said.

"Sheriff, I think. We can see if there's been any progress and he can recommend a local hotel."

Mulder eased to a stop at a red light. Four kids were pulling a wooden sled along the slush-covered sidewalk. Norman Rockwell, eat your heart out.

"I think a B&B might be our best bet, Scully. I don't think hotels have been invented here yet."

The Sheriff's Department was located halfway along the main street, on one side of what Mulder assumed was the town square. (A square that consisted of a ten by ten patch of snow-covered grass with a dry fountain in the center.)

There were only two parking bays outside the station and both were occupied by police cruisers that looked like they were from the seventies, the kind you saw on reruns of *Kojak*.

Mulder parked on the street. The freezing air stung his face as he climbed out and made his way onto the porch along the front of the building.

"You sure this is the Sheriff's Department?" asked Scully as she joined him, nodding at a rocking chair with a folded blanket draped across it.

Mulder pointed at the door. Painted on the glass were the words, *"Castle Bluff Sheriff's Department. You have a nice day now."*

They both stared at it these words for a while. Mulder wondered if they were meant to be ironic. Somehow he didn't think so.

At least the inside looked a bit more like a proper police station, albeit a small one.

In a provincial town.

On a Sunday afternoon.

In the fifties.

A small waiting area greeted them, padded benches lining the walls and a table covered in old magazines planted in the middle of the room. A tiny cubicle to their left was occupied by a woman who looked like she was about eighty years old.

She was knitting.

They approached the cubicle. The walls inside were covered with faded pictures torn from ancient magazines. Mulder squinted at them. Dallas. Dynasty, that kind of thing.

"Afternoon ma'am," said Mulder.

The old woman carried on with her knitting, the tip of her tongue poking out the side of her mouth. Mulder glanced at Scully. She shrugged.

Mulder tapped on the glass. "Ma'am?"

The old woman finally looked up and scowled at him. He flashed his badge.

"Special Agent Fox Mulder. This is my partner, Dana Scully. We're here to see the sheriff."

She squinted at their badges, her lips moving with the effort. Mulder could actually see her forming the words "FBI" as she read the badge. She finally sighed and heaved herself out of her chair. She pulled open the door to the cubicle and leaned out.

"*Lester!*" she shouted. "*Visitors!*"

She slumped back into her chair and resumed her knitting. A few seconds later, a tall, thin figure appeared in the reception area. Mulder blinked. The new arrival was wearing a sheriff's uniform, but he looked like he was only about twenty years old. That couldn't be right, surely.

Lester strode forward and shook hands with them.

"Lester Goodman. Acting Sheriff."

"Acting?" asked Mulder.

"Yeah. My dad's the real Sheriff, but he's… out of action for a while. Follow me."

They followed Lester along a corridor lined with police circulars and Missing Person posters issued from out of state. Lester paused before a door, then gently pushed it open, gesturing for them to look inside. Scully looked first, then turned to Mulder, her face inscrutable. She moved aside to let him look.

The room was dark, but he could see it was kitted out with hospital gear. Machines hummed and buzzed. Blue and green lights flashed comfortingly.

A large figure rested in a wheelchair, IV lines arcing across the desk to saline pouches mounted on stands behind him. The figure's head was resting on the desk. Mulder couldn't be sure the guy was still alive. He didn't look it.

Lester reached past his shoulder and closed the door. "My dad. He's been Sheriff in this town for forty years. He's… a little reluctant to pass on the torch. He'll come around, but in the meantime I'm Sheriff by proxy. You see that movie? With Bruce Willis and the bad wig? Where they put their minds in robots and let the robots do their day to day? That's me. I'm the robot."

Mulder couldn't detect any resentment in his tone. Just resignation.

"And the town is okay with that?" asked Mulder.

Lester shrugged. "No complaints. 'Course, they're all watching to see how I handle these missing kids."

Mulder almost snorted with laughter at that. Lester couldn't be more than a year or two older than the victims.

"The thing is, there's not usually much for me to do. Most recent hassles we had were some earth tremors a couple months back. Old Elsie's chimney collapsed. Folks were still talking about it a month later."

"Has there been any progress?" asked Scully.

Lester blew out his cheeks. "Well, old Bill Wicks—he owns the hardware store—has offered to rebuild it for her—"

"I meant about the missing girls," said Scully gently.

Lester's face flushed red. Mulder felt sorry for the kid. "Sorry. Right. Uh... no. No progress. Your friends have been out searching the forest. Where Kimmy said it all happened."

"Kimmy?" asked Scully.

"Sorry. Kim Duncan. The witness."

"Of course. We'll need to speak with her."

Lester nodded.

"The previous missing girl," said Mulder. "There's been no progress there either?"

"None. The woods cover a forty-mile area. We've sent dogs through, and every weekend the family organize searches." He shakes his head. "But there's been nothing. I'm sure they'll all turn up. Just kids out having a good time."

He didn't sound like he believed it.

"And you're sure none of them were having problems at home?" said Scully.

Lester shook his head. "According to the families, everything was good. Lucy—that's the first missing girl—was a straight-A student. Spent all her time reading. Mostly those stupid *Dusk* books." He made a sour face and shook his head.

"I take it you're not of the opinion that the perp is a three hundred year old vampire?" asked Scully.

"Come on. That's just stupid girls getting their panties in a knot."

"So how do you explain the footage?" asked Mulder.

Lester shrugged. "A prank. You know McEllroy's fans - Duskites, they call themselves - believe that he based his books on a real vampire? The one that was supposed to have terrorized the town in the fifties—"

Mulder held a hand up. "Back up. What are you talking about?"

"Oh, yeah. Sorry. I suppose it wasn't in the report. Back in the 1950s we had a spate of attacks. Similar to what's happening now. Missing girls. *And* a couple of boys. Eight in total. Not sure how the rumor got started, but people said it was a vampire. Word is McEllroy got his idea from those attacks, and these Duskites think Callum James is the real deal.

The one responsible for the attacks in the fifties. Me, I think it's a couple of jocks on the football team having a laugh."

"I fail to see the humor in the situation," said Scully. "Three girls are missing and if this is just some… high school prank then those responsible will have to be punished."

"Did the missing kids ever turn up?"

Lester shook his head. "And no bodies either. Nothing. If you want more details, ask Tom across the square. He runs the B&B. You checked in yet?"

"Not yet."

"Well, he's a character. Claims he witnessed one of the original abductions back in the fifties."

"Where exactly does McEllroy live?" asked Scully.

Lester looked at them in surprise. "Why?"

"I'm a fan," said Mulder. "Thought I'd get my book signed while I'm here."

"He has a house on the outskirts of town. Follow the main road through and take the dirt track on your right. House is at the end. Don't know if he'll sign your book though. He's a grumpy bastard. Only comes into town to buy whisky and cigarettes."

The B&B was a double-story house on the opposite side of the town square. Mulder pulled his overnight bag out of the trunk and joined Scully inside.

A cramped welcoming area greeted them. Wood paneling. Leather armchairs, a deer's head mounted on the wall. Scully was waiting by the reception desk. She glanced over her shoulder and held something out for him, a brochure of some kind.

Mulder glanced it over while Scully rang the bell. It was a history of the original vampire attacks, ending with an ad for a guided tour of the locations where the kids went missing. The brochure looked like it had been put together in MS Paint about twenty years ago. It even used Comic Sans.

Mulder skimmed through it. The attacks took place over a six-month period. The brochure listed the names and even had black and white pictures of the victims.

The beaded curtain behind the desk was pushed aside and a couple in their seventies stepped through.

"Hiya there," said the woman. "I'm Aileen."

"And I'm Tom." The man held his hand out to shake. "Are you two the FBI fellahs who're gonna find our girls?"

"We'll certainly try," said Mulder. "Do you have a room? A double?"

"You folks a couple, then?" asked Aileen.

"Um… yes," said Scully.

"That's nice," said Aileen. "It's good that you work together. Especially when you're away from home. Right, Tom?"

"You know it's the same vampire, right?" said Tom, leaning forward.

"From the fifties?" said Mulder.

"Yes. He's come back."

"Any idea why he would do that?"

"To finish what he started."

Aileen's smile had turned brittle. She quickly handed the key to Scully. "Here ya go. Supper's between 6 and 8. Will you be eating with us?"

"I think we'll need something."

"We have steaks," said Tom, turning his attention to Scully.

"Sounds good," she said.

"How'd you want them? As Count Dracula intended or crisped in the light of the sun?"

"As the good Count intended," said Scully.

"Same for me," said Mulder.

Tom stared at them both suspiciously, then reached under the desk and came up with a mist spritzer. Aileen's eyes widened and she tried to stop him, but he was already squeezing the trigger on the plastic bottle.

A stream of water hit Mulder in the face. He blinked in surprise as Tom turned the bottle to Scully and sprayed her too.

The four of them stood for a moment, confusion and embarrassment hanging in the air. Tom finally smiled and put the bottle away.

"Holy water," he explained. "Just checking."

Mulder wiped the water away.

"I'm so, so sorry," said Aileen.

The afternoon light was fading as they headed toward Kim Duncan's house. The grey sky was low and heavy. About to dump another few inches of snow on them, Scully thought.

Kim's mother opened the door. Her eyes were glazed and empty. She looked like she hadn't slept since her daughter went missing.

"Special agents Dana Scully and Fox Mulder. We've come to see Kim."

Mrs. Duncan nodded and led them through the house to the kitchen. Scully could see through the windows to the backyard. Kim was seated on an old wooden swing, swathed in a massive, quilted jacket that had to be her father's. Her hands were cupped around a mug of something hot. The steam drifted up into the air and was swallowed by the cold wind.

Mrs. Duncan stared out the window. Scully could only imagine what she must be feeling. Did she blame Kim? She was the older sister. She should have been looking out for Briony. Not that anything was ever that simple, but those treacherous thoughts must be sliding around her head. Questioning. Wondering. Did Kim do enough? Why didn't Kim stop Briony leaving the house? Why, why, why?

"Mrs. Duncan?" prompted Scully.

Mrs. Duncan started, looking at them as if seeing them for the first time. "Can we talk to Kim?"

"You can try," said Mrs. Duncan. She glanced back out the window. "We've all tried," she added softly. "She's... different. She was always a bit distant. But now..." she shook her head. "She barely speaks. Just stares into the woods."

Scully and Mulder headed out the kitchen door and approached Kim. She was pushing the swing slightly, bending her knees and pushing back, then letting it swing gently before pushing off again.

"Kim?"

No answer.

"Kim," repeated Scully. "We'd like to ask you a few questions."

"What for?" she snapped. "You've got the cell phone footage."

"We're more interested in what happened after you stopped recording," said Mulder.

She turned her head to stare at Mulder. "What are you talking about? Nothing happened."

Mulder nodded. He glanced up at the grey sky, then down at the snow. He kicked it with his foot, digging a hole in the snow. "It's just... in the report, I wonder if you forgot something. If something was left out."

She turned away again and hunched down deeper in the jacket. "Nothing was left out. I ran. I got the hell out of there as fast as I could. I ditched my little sister and I saved my own skin. Now leave me alone."

"Kim—"

"I said leave me alone!" she screamed, tears in her eyes. "Why are you even here! Go and find her! Find my sister and bring her back!"

Kim leaped out of the swing and sprinted back into the house, slamming the door behind them. Scully caught Mrs. Duncan's eye through the window. The woman just shrugged helplessly.

The snow finally started to fall as they followed the road out of town. The heavy, pregnant flakes fell silent and thick, flaring white as they cut through their headlights.

They missed McEllroy's drive the first time, had to double back when they'd driven over the town limits. They moved slowly, finally spotting the driveway obscured by bushes that had been coaxed and cut to hide it from view.

"Doesn't seem to like visitors, does he?" said Scully.

Mulder nodded. "A journalist turned up unannounced at his door once. Back in the seventies. McEllroy tied him to a chair and kept him prisoner for five days."

Scully glanced at Mulder to see if he was joking. Always hard to tell with him.

"Why wasn't he arrested?"

"The journalist wrote a story on it. Won the Pulitzer."

They edged the car along the rutted track until they arrived at a surprisingly modern house nestled among the tall firs. The whole front of the house was glass. Scully could see straight into the lounge. Old, comfortable chairs. Bookshelves lining the walls. A roaring fire. No television, she noted. Rare, these days.

They got out and Mulder knocked on the front door. "Be prepared," he said. "He's got a reputation for being difficult."

"You mean normal people *don't* hold journalists prisoner for five days? I'm shocked, Mulder."

The door swung open. Scully immediately took a step back and drew her gun. "FBI. Drop the weapon!"

McEllroy stood before them wearing nothing but a pair of boxer shorts, a double-barrel shotgun held in his hands. A homemade cigarette hung from the corner of his mouth.

He squinted through the smoke at them.

"Who?"

"FBI," said Mulder. "Sir, please put down the weapon."

"FBI?"

Mulder reached into his overcoat and pulled out his ID. McEllroy frowned at it, then leaned the shotgun against the wall.

"Thought you were fans," he muttered.

Scully warily holstered her gun. "That's how you treat your fans?"

"Only the loyal ones. The ones that track me down."

He turned and walked back into the house. Scully glanced at Mulder. He shrugged and followed after.

McEllroy led them into the kitchen where it looked like they had interrupted him making a milkshake. He carried on where he left off, spooning ice cream into the jug. Then he emptied half a bottle of whisky on top. He gave it a few blitzes and poured it into a glass.

"Want some?"

"We're on duty," said Mulder.

"Suit yourself."

He downed half the glass, smacked his lips and sighed. "Good stuff."

"Mr. McEllroy, we'd like to ask you a few questions," said Scully.

"What about?"

"The missing girls."

He looked perplexed. "What missing girls?"

"Sir," said Scully, trying her best to keep the exasperation from her voice. "Are you honestly saying you don't know what's been happening in your own town?"

"*My* town? This isn't my town. I *hate* this place."

"So… why are you here?"

"Only place I can write. I grew up here. Doesn't mean I like the place, though. Can't stand it."

"Three girls have gone missing, Mr. McEllroy," said Mulder. "And people are claiming the perpetrator is Callum James. The talk around town is that you based your books on a vampire that terrorized this town in the 1950s. That Callum James, is in fact, real."

McEllroy shook his head in disgust. "This town is filled with idiots. I knew some people thought Callum was real but I didn't know any girls had gone missing. You know where I got the idea for *Dusk* from? I wanted to see how stupid, how *mindless* a book I could write and still get people to buy it. It was meant to be satire. A commentary on modern society and the mindless fashion in which we consume entertainment. How teenagers today are so stupid they'll buy into anything. The vampire as a metaphor for the mindless trash we're all addicted to. How we can't survive without our gossip rags and 24-7 entertainment." He barked out a laugh. "Only problem is, teenagers today don't know satire. Or irony. They lapped it up. Bought into it as if I was writing a serious novel just for them." He shook his head in disgust. "If they're running around thinking Callum is real, I guess I succeeded. Just not in the way I'd hoped."

"You sound like you wanted your book to fail," said Scully.

"Don't be an idiot. I wanted it to succeed. But for the right reasons. For people to realize it for what it was. A hate letter to everything that's wrong with today's world. I despise the *Dusk* books. Loathe them with every fiber of my being. They're everything that's wrong with modern society. Mindless crap passed off as something meaningful. Pop psychology disguised as deep thinking. Teen relationships distilled into the most destructive form I could think of—stalker and the stalked— hunter and the hunted. When I realized no one actually understood what I was trying to say I even threw in some necrophilia fetishism, making it clear Callum was dead—had been for centuries. When that didn't work I turned him into a controlling, abusive creep who wouldn't let the main character have a life of her own." He shrugged. "They thought it was romantic. If I could go back in time I would burn the manuscript of the first book before it left the door. I'd kill myself before I even had the idea."

McEllroy was practically frothing at the mouth, his face flushed. He forced himself to calm down, taking another hefty gulp of his milkshake.

"So... what are you working on now?" asked Scully, trying to deflect the conversation slightly.

McEllroy looked at her as if she was insane. "The new *Dusk* book, of course."

Mulder took out the photographs they'd taken from the police station. "Mr. McEllroy did any of these girls come to see you in the past month?"

McEllroy studied them while finishing his drink. "That one," he said, pointing at the photograph of Tracy Sullivan, the first victim. "She was obsessed. *She* thought Callum was real. That I knew him and should introduce them. Apparently they were soul mates."

"When was this?"

McEllroy shrugged. "Few weeks ago. I was pretty wasted at the time. I just slammed the door in her face. Only reason I remember is the red hair."

"Are you aware of anyone around here who likes to dress up as Callum James?" asked Mulder.

He shook his head. "No one that I know of."

"And there's no movie being filmed? Any book trailers, that kind of thing?"

"Christ, no. It's bad enough now. You think I want a movie out there as well?"

Scully closed her notebook and smiled politely. "Thanks for your time, Mr. McEllroy," she said. She handed over her card. "Give us a call if you think of anything that might help."

Back in the car, Scully stared out the window, watching as McEllroy flopped down in his couch. "Do you believe him?" she asked.

"That we're living in a culture obsessed with pop culture, instant celebrity, and simplistic answers to complex relationship issues? Sure."

"You know what I mean. Mulder, I think McEllroy should be our prime suspect here. When word of this gets out the publicity for him will be huge. His sales will go through the roof."

"His sales are already through the roof. And he said himself he doesn't *want* any more publicity."

"Doesn't mean it's true. I think he's our man. He admitted that at least one of the girls came to see him. Plus, he's not exactly… stable."

"Who can define stable, Scully? The guy's a creative genius. And he took a crap load of drugs back in the day. I think he's doing pretty well, all things considered."

"Mulder, you're not being objective. You're letting the fact that you're a fan interfere with you thinking."

He grinned. "I'm not. I hear you. I do. He's definitely a suspect, but that wasn't him on the cell phone footage. The figure who abducted those girls looked to be over six feet tall. McEllroy barely stood taller than you."

Scully sighed, then stifled a yawn. "We're not going to get anything more done tonight. I say we get something to eat and turn in. We can head out to the woods tomorrow. Check out the crime scene."

Mulder nodded.

Mulder was awoken the next morning by a frantic banging on his door. He sat up, befuddled with sleep. Reached out for his gun, then blinked and poked Scully in the back. "Someone at the door," he mumbled.

Scully grunted and pulled the blankets higher around her shoulders. Mulder blinked at the clock. 06:20.

"Agents Mulder and Scully?" called a voice from the hallway. Mulder thought he recognized it. Acting Sheriff Goodman. "You need to get out here," called Lester. "The missing girls have turned up."

When the Sheriff said the girls had turned up, Scully had felt a flicker of hope.

She should have known better. Hope was not something you culti-vated in this job. Realism, yes. Pessimism, sure—if you weren't careful. But hope? No.

The girls had been dumped in the town square during the night. By the time the bodies had been discovered, they were covered with snow, and any footprints that might prove useful long since gone.

She stared at the first body that had been lifted onto the medical table. (The other two bodies were waiting outside in the police cruisers. No morgue in Castle Bluff.) It was Briony Duncan.

Scully hadn't had time to perform proper autopsies yet, but she didn't need to. At least, not to determine the cause of death.

"Exsanguination," she said to Mulder. "Total."

Mulder raised his eyebrows. "*Total?*"

"As near as." Scully pointed to a bruised area on her inside thigh. Two puncture wounds were clearly visible. "The blood was drawn from the femoral artery."

"Any signs of struggle?"

Scully shook her head. "Which leads me to believe the victims were drugged."

"Or under some kind of glamor?"

Scully sighed. "No, Mulder. Drugged. Agent Peters took some tissue samples to Washington for me. It shouldn't take long to hear back. I told them to test for rohypnol, ketamine or zolpidem."

"Date rape drugs?"

Scully nodded. "That could also explain the lack of vasoconstriction. If the victims were drugged there would be no fear. No adrenalin pumping through their bodies to contract the blood vessels."

"But how does that explain the draining of the blood?"

"There are any number of methods if the victims were drugged. Drawing the blood with syringes, for example. That would also explain the puncture wounds. The killer could have injected some kind of anti-coagulant to keep the blood flowing."

"So you're still saying this was done by human hands?"

"Yes. There's nothing here to indicate any supernatural or unexplained forces at work. Mulder, I believe we have a serial killer on our hands. Someone who read about these missing girls from the fifties and is now copying those murders himself. He might even possibly suffer from haematodipsia."

"A sexual thirst for blood?" Mulder shook his head. "I don't buy it, Scully."

"Why? What better place to satiate such a thirst but a town that thinks it has its own personal vampire? It's the perfect cover. In fact, an even better cover for someone who suffers from such a condition would be to build a career writing about vampires."

"This *is* a vampire, Scully. I'm not saying it's Callum James, but it's definitely some kind of blood-sucking predator."

"Fine. You go look into that aspect and I'll perform the autopsies."

Mulder turned away.

"Mulder."

He paused.

"Just don't stick a stake through anybody. At least not until I get the lab results back."

Mulder headed over to the B&B to find Tom sitting behind the reception desk reading an Anne Rice novel.

"Terrible thing," said the old man. "With the girls, I mean."

"It is. Listen, I want to ask you something. The attacks back in the fifties. How did they stop?"

"Ah, now if you book my tour you'd find that out right at the end."

"Don't really have time for that, Tom."

"No. I suppose not. Well, the vampire was hunted down by a foreign fellow. Named Stefan Kurzweg. He'd been living in the town for a year or so when the attacks started."

"Was there any proof he'd killed the vampire? A body? A pile of ash?"

Tom smiled in satisfaction. "No. Just his say so. Which is why I think it's the same vampire."

"What happened to Kurzweg?"

"He stayed in town. Died in 1986."

Mulder nodded thoughtfully. "Thanks, Tom."

Mulder hesitated outside the B&B, wondering if he should tell Scully. But what was there to tell? Nothing that would change her mind.

Instead, he took out his phone and put in a call back to Washington. He gave his ID and security codes and asked to be put through to the Directorate of Intelligence, finally managing to track down Emily Doyle, someone who he and Scully had worked with before.

"Hey Doyle. It's me. Need a rush job."

"Why, I'm fine, Mulder, thanks for asking," she said sarcastically. "How are you, Mulder?"

"Sorry, Doyle. In a rush. I need you to get me anything you can on Stefan Kurzweg. Died in eighty-six in a place called Castle Bluff."

"That's it?"

"Afraid so. Did I say it's urgent?"

"I think you did, yeah."

"Because it is."

He heard Doyle sigh. "I'll get on it."

He hung up and looked around. The streets were deserted, the discovery of the three girls sending everyone inside their homes. Scully was right about one thing. McEllroy *was* somehow connected to this. It had to be more than a coincidence that the vampire was hunting here, where the writer of the *Dusk* books lived.

Mulder decided to question him again. Hopefully this time the man would be sober enough to talk.

As Mulder pulled up to a stop outside McEllroy's house his phone rang. Doyle.

"What d'you have?"

"Hello, Doyle. How are you Doyle?"

"Hello Doyle. How are you Doyle? Now what do you have?"

"Your really need to work on your social skills, Mulder. Okay, it seems your Mr. Kurzweg led a very interesting life."

"How so?"

"First off, he worked in the Nazi weapons program. You know anything about Operation Paperclip?"

Operation Paperclip was the program hatched up by the Office of Strategic Services in the aftermath of the Second World War. German scientists and technicians were brought over to the States to work on various government projects, mainly so that Russia didn't get their hands on them.

"I know of it."

"He was part of that."

"Doing what?"

"Classified. Couldn't access his files. That was literally all I could get."

Interesting. "Thanks Doyle."

"No problem. Although you could have just got this from Scully."

"Scully?"

"Yeah, she asked me to look into McEllroy's past?"

"What's that got to do with Kurzweg?"

"Ah. You guys off on your own missions, huh? Here's the thing.

McEllroy is Kurzweg's son. He changed his name as soon as he was of
legal age."

Mulder hung up and stared at McEllroy's house. He was Kurzweg's
son? He checked his gun and climbed out of the car. He knocked on the
door but there was no answer.

"Mr. McEllroy? FBI."

Still nothing. Mulder tried to door. Locked. He looked around, then
used the butt of his gun to smash a pane of glass. He reached in and
unlocked the door, stepping into the house.

The place was empty. He could feel it. He checked through all the
rooms just to make sure, but his instincts were correct. Deserted.

Mulder headed back to the door, then stopped suddenly. He hadn't
seen an office anywhere. Where did McEllroy write his books?

He went through the house again, this time focusing on the floor. He
found the trapdoor in the kitchen, pulled it up to reveal a set of stairs
leading into the basement.

Mulder climbed down, finding a locked door at the bottom. He
kicked it in, gun held in the ready position. The door smashed back
against the wall.

"Mr. McEllroy? Are you in here?"

No answer. Mulder reached into the room and found the light switch.
He flicked it on, revealing a cluttered office. An old desk, wooden filing
cabinets. The walls were plastered with yellowing newsprint and pieces
of paper covered with an untidy scrawl.

Mulder scanned the untidy handwriting. Half of them were ideas for
Dusk stories, and the other half were raging screeds against society. Mulder
approached the desk, riffled through the drawers until he found an old,
leather-bound notebook. He opened it up. Not McEllroy's handwriting.
This was much neater, a cursive script written with a fountain pen.

Mulder realized it was a diary. The diary of Stefan Kurzweg.

He started reading.

Scully dropped her scrubs into the bin and took the spatter goggles
off. Cause of death was the same in all three cases. Exsanguination.
Puncture marks in the thigh. No signs of struggle.

Her phone buzzed. "Agent Scully," she said, answering it.

"Scully? It's Peters. Your results are in."

"And?"

"Negative on all your hunches."

Scully's shoulders sagged. "Seriously?"

"Afraid so. But they did find something else you might be interested in. High levels of MDMA."

Scully straightened up, her heart racing. "Ecstasy?"

"Enough to make an elephant fall in love with all the other elephants and want to open up night clubs with them."

"Thanks."

Scully hung up. She tapped her phone against her chin. What had Mulder said about McEllroy? That his drug of choice was MDMA?

She hurried to Sheriff Goodman's office. He wasn't there but she logged into the department intranet and tracked down Kim Duncan's cell phone footage.

She skipped ahead to the point where the glowing figure came into view. It was hard to make out any features, but the figure really didn't look like an old man with crazy white hair. And Mulder was right. It *was* too tall. There was no way McEllroy could dress up to look like that.

Which didn't mean he wasn't involved. Just that he had an accomplice.

But who? Sheriff Goodman had seen the footage. He knew everyone in town. If it was someone from around here, he would have said.

Scully was staring absently at the shaky footage. It had reached the point where Kim was discovered, the glowing figure whirling around. The view shifted, swinging wildly as Kim turned and ran.

Scully frowned. She paused the footage, then stepped back one frame at a time. She'd seen something... something familiar.

Her finger froze over the keyboard and a satisfied smile spread across her face.

Leaning up against one of the trees on the outer edge of the clearing was a double barrel shotgun. It would have been invisible but for the white glow from the alleged vampire reflecting from the metal. A hand was there as well, resting on the gun. The rest of the figure was cast in shadow, but the hand looked old.

"Got you."

An hour later Mulder looked up, blinking in the dim light. He knew the story behind the vampire now.

It seemed that during the war Stefan Kurzweg was a member of the Institute for Occult Warfare, an elite unit of psychics, occultists and mediums led by Heinrich Himmler. Himmler thought using occult warfare was the only way Germany would triumph.

But this started even before the war. Himmler had heard legends about a vampire that once terrorized the village of Wewelsburg. He signed a hundred year lease on Wewelsburg Castle, hoping to track down this vampire and turn it to the cause.

Mulder already knew about the castle. Himmler wanted to turn it into a training facility devoted to occult and pagan rituals that would make Germany the rulers of the world. He called it the Grail Castle and spent most of his time searching for occult artifacts like the Spear of Destiny.

But it seemed the castle was also a secret laboratory. Himmler and the IOW did indeed capture the vampire. But they couldn't convince it to join the cause. So they did what the Nazis did best. They formed a team to experiment on it, tried to turn it into a weapon they could control.

Kurzweg was the leader of that team.

They managed to take away some of the vampire's weaknesses. The shimmering around the creature was like a shield. Sunscreen. It could come out during the day if it so wanted. They took away its weaknesses to religious symbols. Only problem was, the thing went mad. Utterly insane. It became fixated on Kurzweg. Wouldn't do anything it was told. Himmler tried to test it as a weapon, released it into a nearby village. It wiped everyone out.

They recaptured it, locked it away in a crypt.

Then the war ended. Kurzweg was recruited to the US, but the vampire got loose and tracked him down. This was back in the fifties, when it went on its killing spree through Castle Bluff. Kurzweg managed to lure it into one of the abandoned mines around the town and used dynamite to bring the whole thing down on its head. According to the diary, Kurzweg thought he'd finally killed it.

Mulder stared thoughtfully at the wall. The recent earth tremors Sheriff Goodman mentioned. Maybe they shook something loose, allowing the vampire to get free again.

And now it was carrying on where it left off.

So the vampire *wasn't* Callum James, the vampire from McEllroy's novels. McEllroy had taken the idea from his father's diary.

He took out his phone and called Scully.

"Mulder? Where are you?"

"At McEllroy's place. Listen, I need to tell you—"

"Not now," said Scully. "McEllroy's the one doing it. He's—"

"You shouldn't be down here," said a voice behind Mulder.

Mulder spun around just in time to see the butt of McEllroy's shotgun coming straight for his head. A flash of pain. A burst of light. He dropped to the floor. Found himself staring at his cell phone.

He could hear Scully's voice. "Mulder?"

He reached out and weakly grabbed his phone. Then he felt someone dragging him. He moved his arm and shoved the phone into his pocket. His thoughts were scattered, but he knew one thing. He had to keep his phone close by.

"Mulder! Mulder are you okay?"

No answer. A moment later the line went dead. Scully stared at her phone in frustration. That was McEllroy's voice she'd heard.

Mulder was in danger.

She called Director Skinner. "Sir. Mulder's in trouble. I need an immediate track on his cell phone."

"I'll authorize it now."

"Get them to feed it to my GPS on my phone."

She hung up just as Sheriff Goodman burst into the office.

"More girls have gone missing!"

"How many?"

"Nine."

"*Nine*..." How the hell did McEllroy kidnap nine girls?

"They left notes this time."

Scully pulled up short. "What?"

"They think that since the other three girls were found, they'd been rejected by Callum. They think there's still a chance they'll be chosen as his mate. They've gone to *look* for him."

Mulder woke up with a hangover so bad it felt like his skull had split in two.

Oh wait. McEllroy. His skull probably *had* split in two. He tried to raise his hands but realized they were tied behind his back.

Mulder forced his eyes open, wincing at the pain. A dim orange glow picked out his surroundings. Dirt walls. Timber supports. Narrow passage.

He was in a mine. Most likely the one the vampire had been trapped in since the fifties.

He looked to his left. Huge piles of earth and rocks blocked the passage. But there was a hole in the ground, a wide fissure.

"He has to feed, you see."

Mulder looked right and saw McEllroy approaching with his shotgun.

"McEllroy. Let me go. There's still time to stop this."

"Stop this? You can't stop this. No one can. It's the way of the world."

He squatted down in front of Mulder.

"I created him you know. Callum. He came to life from my books. That's why I have to keep feeding him."

"No. McEllroy, you based your books on your father's notes. *He* made the vampire what it is."

"Liar!" McEllroy backhanded Mulder. "He came because of me. They're all the same, don't you see? The vampire? My fans. They're always hungry. Always need feeding."

A white glow appeared in the fissure in the tunnel floor. McEllroy nodded toward it. "He's coming."

McEllroy straightened up and took out a needle. "MDMA. He likes his victims willing, you see. Doesn't like the taste of adrenalin."

The snow had left the forest difficult to navigate. Scully's feet kept sinking into deep drifts. She was breathing heavily by the time they were only five minutes from the road.

She checked her phone again. The GPS signal said Mulder's phone was only about a kilometer or so away.

"This way," said Scully, pointing.

"Can I see?" asked Sheriff Goodman.

Scully handed her phone over and he studied the screen. "That's the old mines. They've been closed since the turn of the century."

"You know where they are?"

Lester nodded. Scully took her phone back and slid it into her pocket. "Lead the way."

"Wait!" Mulder desperately needed to buy time. "You don't need the drugs. I'll go. Willingly."

McEllroy frowned. "What?"

"You think I don't understand? You think I don't get it? The vampire. He's *us*. He's our culture. Never-ending hunger for the latest thing. The latest book. The latest gossip. Twenty-four hour channels that need constant feeding. Manufactured news. Fame hunting. Reality shows about talentless morons whose only claim to fame is that they filmed themselves having sex. Endless reboots of movies that are only a couple of years old. Cancelled television shows brought back to life as comics and novels. Social media this. Facebook that I *understand*, McEllroy. You and me, we crave a simpler time. Do you know they actually asked me to join Twitter? I'm talking about my department. The X-files. All the other FBI departments have signed up and they wanted me to as well."

McEllroy's gun dropped slightly. "Goddamn it. I *hate* Twitter. My publishers asked me to sign up. I told them I would burn my latest manuscript if they even mentioned it again."

"See. I get that. What's with the constant need to share everything? Selfies and pictures of what you're eating. Who cares, right?"

"*They* do. *He* cares. That's why we have to keep feeding it," whispered McEllroy. "If we don't feed it, it will devour us. It will get worse."

"No. It's not like that. If we don't feed it, it will wither up and die. We can fight this together."

McEllroy shook his head sadly. "No. It can never die. *I* have to do this. Don't you see? So others won't have to. The human race has become corrupted. No one cares anymore. There will always be someone willing to feed the beast, willing to sacrifice their pride, their lives, others, just for a few minutes of fame." McEllroy straightened up. "'Even the enemy

of God and man had friends and associates in his desolation; I am alone'."
He shook his head again. "*I have to do this. To stop it getting worse.*"

Scully paused. She'd seen something up ahead. The flash of bright
colors. She drew her sidearm as she and Lester drew closer. She could
hear voices now. Voices raised in argument.

"He won't want you, you cow. He'll want someone pure."

"That rules you out. Everyone knows what you blew Donny behind
the science block."

"FBI," called Scully. "Arms where I can see them."

She moved around a tree to find a group of five girls - they looked
about seventeen - standing in a huddle. They were dressed like they were
about to go clubbing. Scully frowned and holstered her gun.

"What are you doing out here?"

"What's it to you?" asked one of the girls.

Scully raised an eyebrow. "I'm a Federal law enforcer. I'm on the hunt
for a murderer. So it's *everything* to me. I won't ask again, young lady."

"We're looking for Callum," snapped another of the girls.

Lester leaned in to Scully. "These are some of the girls who have been
reported missing."

"Why are you searching for the vampire?" asked Scully.

"Because he rejected those other girls. The ones who turned up dead.
That means he's still on the lookout for a *real* girlfriend. Someone who
understands him."

"And he'll pick me," said another.

"In your dreams. It will be me."

"It will be none of you," snapped Scully. "Because you're all going to
go home."

The girls looked Scully up and down. "I don't think so, bitch," said
one of them.

"*NOW!*" shouted Scully.

The girls jumped. Even Sheriff Goodman jerked upright.

"You can't speak to us like that. It's an infringement on our human rights."

Scully sighed and turned to Lester. "Sheriff. See these girls are
returned home. And if they give you and problems, charge them with

obstructing a federal officer in the course of her duties."

Scully took her phone out again and set off, ignoring the complaints and protests behind her.

The glow from the fissure was growing brighter. McEllroy pulled Mulder to his feet.

"I'm really sorry, man," McEllroy said. "You seem really cool. Under different circumstances I'd have loved to get high with you. But I have to feed it. It's my responsibility."

"It doesn't have to be like this."

"It does. It's my punishment. It's penance for writing those books."

He shoved Mulder with the shotgun, angling him toward the crevice. The white glow was growing stronger, spilling out and illuminating the dirt walls. McEllroy pushed him until he was standing on the edge. Mulder couldn't help it. He peered down into the hole.

He saw a deep shaft. Broken timber supports jutted out of the walls.

And he saw the vampire climbing nimbly toward him, almost at the top of the crevice.

"FBI," shouted a voice behind them. "Raise your hands where I can see them!"

Mulder felt the shotgun leave his back. He turned and saw McEllroy swinging the weapon around, aiming for Scully. At the same time he realized she couldn't fire. He was standing too close to McEllroy for her to make a safe shot.

He lunged forward and grabbed the shotgun with his tied hands, shoving it upward just as McEllroy pulled the trigger.

The explosion was deafening in the narrow tunnel. The pellets hit the support beams above them, shredding the ancient wood. Earth and rocks poured from the ceiling. Dust clouds billowed through the passage.

"Mulder *move!*"

Mulder staggered forward, heading toward the hazy light. He heard McEllroy shout in anger, turned and could just make out the old man swinging his gun at him.

Then through the choking clouds of dust Mulder saw two glowing hands rise up through the crevice and grab McEllroy's ankles.

Mulder and McEllroy locked eyes.

Then he was yanked backward down the hole.

Mulder hesitated, debating whether to go back.

"Mulder! The roof's going to cave in."

Mulder glanced up just as a huge chunk off the wall slid free, rocks and stones following in its wake as they covered the crevice hole.

Mulder turned and ran just as the entire ceiling came down.

Mulder and Scully sprinted from the mineshaft, coughing and spluttering, waving the clouds of dust away. They collapsed onto the snow as the mine entrance caved in, a huge grey and brown cloud billowing up into the sky.

When Mulder had cleared his lungs he sat up and stared at the pile of dirt that had once been the mine entrance.

"Did you see it?" he said.

"See what?"

"The vampire. It grabbed his legs."

"Mulder, all I saw was McEllroy falling down a mine shaft. There *was* no vampire."

Mulder sighed. He held out his hands to Scully and she cut the rope with her pocketknife.

"His fans aren't going to be happy," said Scully.

"No," agreed Mulder.

They got to their feet.

"Still," he said. "There's always fan fiction. Maybe I'll give it a try. I could put you in it. Dana Scully versus Callum James."

"You do that and I'll leave you."

"Come on, Scully. It will be cool. Just you against a three hundred year old vampire, having to fight your own attraction for the creature as you hunt him down. It's solid gold."

They started walking back through the forest. Mulder glanced back over his shoulder, watching the cloud slowly dissipate.

"Solid gold, I tell you."

THE END

LOVING THE ALIEN

By Stefan Petrucha

FBI HEADQUARTERS
WASHINGTON, D.C.
6th OCTOBER, 1997, 3:15 p.m.

S tuck in any routine we crave the new, forgetting how easily it can betray us, or how deeply we might miss habit's comfort when gone. Even fear and paranoia can become banal if that's all there is. That morning in the office felt so routine, it was hard to pay attention. For instance, I had to ask, as I had a dozen times:

"Mulder, how can you *possibly* think this isn't a complete waste of time?"

And, of course, he answered with a joke: "A little green man told me, Scully. Or do you find that assertion Scooby-dubious?"

His sheepish smile earned my expected eye roll, but it wasn't bad for a bad joke. Maybe he'd held onto it for days, waiting for the right moment to spring it on me. Either way, those were his last words before Agent Mulder, as the cliché goes, disappeared into thin air.

Not that I didn't *want* to investigate the case with him, but I'd already objected. "Wait a day, or I could cancel…"

"No. You have an appointment with Dr. Zuckerman."

"The check-up's a formality."

"So's this."

He held up two local newspaper articles and a post-it. It was scant even for an X-file, not even worth a slide show. The small-town alien sightings were exactly the sort of tabloid nonsense that crops up in bored towns craving anything new.

As for the post-it, Mulder dismissed it, too. "It's like a hand-written version of Nigerian email offering 5 million dollars, only I'm getting an exclusive look at a live EBE. At least six people a year claim to capture Bigfoot, the Chupacabra, or living aliens. But there's only one Dana Scully."

We've been protective of each other from the beginning. Since my cancer, Mulder's awkward motherliness, touching at first, had become irritating. Being alive, I wanted to be allowed to live. But that's what I mean about habit and the betrayal of the new.

I sighed an old sigh. He smiled and winked as always. "Come on. It's not like the shadow government would send anything this goofy. I'll be back in two days, and you can tell me again how Klerksdorp spheres are really natural formations and not proof of ancient astronauts."

Ever since Michael Kritschgau convinced Mulder that our very human military is behind the mass abduction of American citizens, his self-deprecating humor has acquired an almost masochistic quality. The thought of a world without aliens seemed to dull him.

"If it's obviously fake, why go?"

"Because it's from Bishopville, South Carolina, home of the Lizard Man of Scape Ore Swamp!"

Speaking of Scooby-dubious, he first brought up the 1988 sightings of a reptilian humanoid years ago just to prove he wasn't completely gullible. One witness admitted lying, the footprint casts were shown to be fake and the deep "claw" scratches on the cars were probably caused by a power tool. Even Mr. *I Want to Believe* thought it was embarrassing.

Which meant he was leaving something out, so I waited for the truth.

It seemed we were always waiting for the truth.

"Okay, you caught me. The handwriting looks familiar."

"Familiar? How?"

"Can't place it, but it's bugging me. It's probably, probably nothing, but....?"

"You've got a better shot at the five million," I told him. But I was telling myself, *Let him go alone. It may improve his mood.*

So, without further objection, I did exactly that. I let him go. At least physically.

That night, as I lay half-asleep, I thought I saw him standing in a corner by my dresser, all in shadow. But it was nothing, or a dream, a Mulder-shaped dream.

Next day, when he didn't answer my calls, I contacted Bishopville's sheriff, John Quinlan, who seemed to have a lot of time on his hands.

He'd not only met Mulder, he provided a simple explanation:

"He lost his charger and couldn't get a replacement. The way he dresses, he stands out like a pine tree in a parking lot, so I'm sure I'll see him. I'll have him call."

The call never came.

That night I saw another shadow. This one looked like my father, dead three years now. Seeing him was comforting rather than frightening. I even wanted a closer look. But with a twist of my head, Dad vanished, a trick of the light. Disappointed, but expecting as much, I stared at the white ceiling, remembering how he used to call me Starbuck.

Starbuck was chief mate from *Moby Dick*. He was a practical man devoted to keeping the ship and its crew working, while mad Captain Ahab set course for the unknown. In other words, Starbuck was the one who made sense. Dad never met Mulder. I don't know whether he'd have liked him, but I have a pretty good idea what he would have called him.

Next morning, after receiving Dr. Zimmerman's expected clean bill of health, I was about to leave his waiting room when I noticed everyone staring at the television. CNN was airing a report on the Bishopville sightings. They even had an 'exclusive' blurry alien video taken by an anonymous viewer. It showed a dim figure among dimmer trees, making dazzling leaps from branch to branch. Of course, the anchor failed to mention the lack of any reference that would enable you to judge its size. In the past, the Barred Owl, an albino species with highly reflective eyes, was taken for Mothman. This skittering thing on cable TV's most respected news source looked like a squirrel.

But Mulder still hadn't called. Sheriff Quinlan, now frazzled by an influx of press and sightseers, hadn't seen him. A credit card check revealed Mulder had rented a room in a motel charmingly named *Inn or Out?* When my calls there went unanswered, I packed an extra cell phone charger and scheduled a flight.

REGIONAL AIRPORT
FLORENCE, SOUTH CAROLINA
WEDNESDAY, 4:57 p.m.

Hours later, I stand in Florence Regional airport, 35 miles northeast of Bishopville, agitated by a too-familiar concern for my partner's life. I long for distraction, but nothing works; not the quaint airport, the people, or the car radio. I hope for interesting scenery, but pass mile on mile of flat farmland along Interstate 20. The trip is nearly over before I even glimpse a swamp. A lazy sun sets low behind it, teasing me with odd silhouettes that refuse to resolve into recognizable objects.

And, of course, I wonder, if Mulder is one of them.

I don't think his disappearance has anything to do with a military conspiracy. I'm imagining something more mundane. A fringe believer or two-bit con man, upset when Mulder realizes his *alien* is a pet monkey with mange, murders him in a drunken rage.

But Mulder is too well-trained to be taken off guard easily. More likely he'd gone into the swamp alone and slipped. Or was bitten by a snake. There are six venomous varieties common to South Carolina, including three types of rattlesnake.

Alligators are also not an unreasonable concern.

By the time I near Bishopville I find my own motherliness as irritating as Mulder's.

He's probably fine.

The cheery reptilian face on the sign for the Lizard Man Souvenir Shop is strangely reassuring. Nothing so gaudy could be real. The two motels I pass are full. The view of the town center from the base of an old water tower tells me why. Network satellite trucks, reporters and curiosity-seekers overburden the main street. Must be a slow news week. My destination, the one-story brick police department is, of course, at the center of the crowd.

In a town just four blocks wide, I'm forced to park four blocks away and walk. Dressed for Washington, the heat and humidity feel like a quilt wrapped around my body. At the office, a dark business suit all but fades into the wall. Here, portable lights veer in my direction. Excited journalists thrust microphones and shout stupid questions. They're all, I imagine, eager to make a name for themselves, if only so they never have to cover a story like this again.

"Are you a MIB?"

"Do I look like a man?"

"No."

"Am I wearing black?"

"No, but…"

By then I'm pressing my badge against a glass door at two doe-eyed deputies. Inside, beyond an aged Formica counter, I see two more deputies and three non-uniformed staff. Several phones ring with loud, old-style jangles, but everyone's eyes remain on the crowd outside.

A compact women with coiffed blonde hair claps her hands and points to the phones. After introducing herself as Deputy Sherry Tate, she ushers me to a windowless backroom. In it, the sheriff, ball point pen in hand, slumps in a plastic chair at a table piled with paperwork and photos.

"Still tied up, John?" Deputy Tate asks.

He's younger than she is, broad-shouldered and fit, with short, sandy hair. The shadows cast by a lamp's bare bulb give the cramped space a vaguely noir feel, so I almost expect him to sound like Bogart, but he doesn't. Not looking up, his lips curl.

"Yeah, but I'm dying for a different kind of tie-up with you, Miss Velvet."

I cough. He sputters. "Oh. I... You... Agent Scully?"

"Did my clothes give it away?"

He motions me in. "Thank-you, uh, Deputy Tate. That'll be all."

Miss Velvet curtsies and leaves.

"That must've sounded bad."

With Mulder at risk, I don't make an issue. "I'm sure you're used to talking informally in a small office."

He tosses his pen on the table. "Small, stretched and stressed. There's enough press to make the sewers back up if they all take a piss. And in about an hour, I'm giving my first national press conference, during which I'll be expected to explain how I'm gonna handle over *eighty* sightings. Frankly, I have no idea."

"Are you getting support from other jurisdictions?

"For the people who brought you the Lizard Man? They're laughing their asses off. Besides, without a crime, what are they supposed to do? Allot overtime to search for a big-headed squirrel? If I said the FBI was here, they might, but you asked me not to."

Because with the conspiracy operating in the Bureau, I'd rather word didn't get out until I know what's going on.

"I appreciate the cooperation. No sign of Agent Mulder, I assume?"

"Nope. He's not the sort to go traipsing off into a swamp on his own, is he?"

"I don't know if *traipse* is the right word, but… yes. Aside from the charger, did he say anything at all?"

"Just that he was here to *see a man about an alien*. I took it as a way of telling me to mind my own business, at least before that CNN video. Now…. Agent, between you, me and the wall, does the FBI think this shit is real?"

"The FBI definitely does not. Agent Mulder… not lately."

He raises an eyebrow. "And you?"

"Well…" I clear my throat. "A visiting extraterrestrial isn't a theory I'd embrace without compelling evidence, and as of now, there isn't any…. is there?

He waves a dismissive hand. "Looks to me like tall tales, wobbly video and blurry pictures taken by drunk high schoolers who'd rather get on TV than graduate. But I'm no expert."

"May I?"

His eyes light up. "Do you one better. Cut that pile in half before my conference and first thing tomorrow, and I'll free up two deputies to help find your partner."

It's already dark. Not being the type to *traipse off* into the swamp, I agree.

Already familiar with the two incidents that brought Mulder here, I'm thinking this more recent slew should be as easy to dismiss. Even in mundane circumstances, eyewitnesses are notoriously unreliable. William James once said *belief creates fact*. More accurately, expectation can alter perception. Take a white light for a spaceship and that *becomes* the memory.

Not that reconstructing the truth is impossible, but you have to earn it. It helps to realize that the paranormal has habits. Before 1977's *Close Encounters of the Third Kind*, alien descriptions varied wildly. After, short, baby-headed, big-eyed Grays became the norm. As expected, these reports fit Spielberg's archetype almost to a tee. There is, however, one fairly consistent difference.

"Half these people say they're seeing something six to eight feet tall. I'm surprised no one's claimed the Lizard Man is back."

The sheriff rises and looks over my shoulder, the way Mulder sometimes does. "Around here, that's the quickest way to get called a liar. I figure most are seeing something. I've heard of mangy bears with wounded paws forced to walk on their hind legs. That'd look six feet, and they can climb."

"That doesn't explain the wild leaps in sixteen of the reports."

I imagine Mulder's reaction: *Maybe the gravity on its home-world is weaker. Like the astronauts jumping on the moon*

The dozen photos and three videos take a few more minutes. With Quinlan watching, I rattle off what earmarks the fakes: "Perspective off. Shadows out of place. Squirrel. Color inconsistent. Someone in a mask. Squirrel. Tree stump. Papier-mâché on wires. And this... this is someone with tin foil around their head, eating a sandwich."

As I recite the old reasons, spot the same old problems, again, I hear Mulder:

But, Scully, how do you explain...?

Only this time, I can't imagine how he'd end the sentence. I do know that even when his questions confirmed my opinion, they forced me to look again. Alone, I have to make sure I don't miss anything important *because* it strikes me as stupid.

Wouldn't want to miss the truth for aesthetic reasons.

As the sheriff points to the final fuzzy image, his arm rubs against mine. "That one had me going."

"It can be anything."

"But if it can be anything, how can you be sure it's not something?"

I squint. "I can't, but it's useless as evidence. People see patterns everywhere. It's in our nature to perceive vague stimuli as significant—a process called *pareidolia*. Arguably, we evolved to see things that aren't there as a survival mechanism."

The room is small. We're examining the same photo, but when Quinlan turns his head toward me, I realize how close he is.

"How can hallucinating help you survive?"

I move back a half step. "Not exactly hallucinating, more like the brain guessing. Say you see what *might* be a tiger in the brush. Sometimes it's a tiger, sometimes not, but if your brain always insists it *is* a tiger, you're more inclined to run. Over time, you have a better chance of surviving and passing on that trait." Personal space varies between cultures, but the distance between us is still uncomfortable. I shift a few more inches away. "So... not only are we geared to see things that aren't there, we're geared to assume they want to eat us."

In my mind, Mulder says, *Funny, Scully, whenever I seen an indistinct figure in the dark, I walk toward it.*

All the more reason to worry, but the thought makes me take that second look. I do see the sheriff's point. A shape haunts the blur. From the neck down, it's human, or, as Mulder might say, *humanoid*, but the head is wrong, so wrong, it's easy to dismiss as noise.

But does that mean I should?

The sheriff's nonchalant nod brings his head closer. "Interesting how much of this paranormal stuff is really about who we are, y'know? Today, I was reading how the whole alien abduction story is like a bondage fantasy. You're tied down, poked, prodded, usually in a sexual way. Maybe people who feel like they have to be in control all the time, like us, tend to fantasize about *not* being in control."

Having been effectively raped and impregnated by my abductors, the notion of bondage as an erotic role-playing game is as alien to me as, well... aliens. I debate whether I should tell him the more compelling theory, that the abductions are part of a military experiment, and a horrid crime against humanity.

Instead, I say, "I've heard that."

"Be tough to find a motel tonight..."

"I'm sure I'll be fine."

Thankfully, I'm done. The stack of material I've dismissed is huge. What's left, surprisingly, is more than nothing. I place the last photo on the smaller pile, scoop it up and turn to leave. "Time for your conference isn't it, Sheriff? I'll see you in the morning if I haven't found Agent Mulder by then."

With a smile, Quinlan gets out of my way.

I don't know how long Deputy Tate's been at the door, but her gruff manner makes me think she was listening in. Hurriedly, she escorts to me a backdoor and out into a trash-filled alley.

"So you can avoid the press." The steel fire door slams.

Other than the smell, I appreciate the gesture. The sky above the front of the building is scarred with fake daylight. I hear the bored reporters chatting idly, but then a wave of quiet rolls through them. Sherriff Quinlan's first press conference is starting.

"An expert review has concluded absolutely that the vast majority of these reports..."

Concluded absolutely makes me wince. Despite popular belief, science operates primarily on inductive reasoning, which deals in probability, not absolutes. Science can't *conclude absolutely* that the sun will rise tomorrow. It can only say sunrise is extremely likely, and that there's no known reason to believe it won't happen. It's misunderstandings like this that can give science a bad name.

How one reaches these imperfect conclusions is another question. A good scientist looks at the evidence and *then* forms a theory. The uninformed might think my partner does the opposite, forming theories based on emotion, on what he *wants* to believe. True, emotion provides the energy, but Mulder's suppositions are born from *intuition*, an innate ability to understand a situation immediately—or at least to believe he does.

I don't dismiss intuition. In 1865, Friedrich Kekulé day-dreamed about a snake biting its own tale, and so discovered the ring-shape of the Benzene molecule. Yet, exhilarating as an instinctive leap might be, landing somewhere unexpected can leave you lost. At least my more methodical approach allows me to go back to square one.

To that end, my next stop is the *Inn or Out?* Rather than risk being asked if I'm Will Smith or Tommy Lee Jones, I decide to head the back way. The small cemetery across from the sheriff's office is soothing. The large abandoned building beyond it, less so. But before my mind can conjure any tigers in the gloom, the motel parking lot comes into view.

I avoid mentioning the FBI, saying Mulder is a missing friend. The owner, Peggy White, lit cigarette dangling, a curl of smoke splitting her unfriendly face, is less than helpful. A day with the media has taught her how easily information can be converted to cash.

A little girl, Maggie, five or six, mutely clutches her side. She moves only to avoid the lit cigarette when her mother swings her arm. There's a dullness in her eyes, a fear-reaction from all the strangers in town. When I smile at her, she smiles back.

Though I didn't intend to be manipulative, Peggy softens, admitting she remembers Mulder. "Didn't like his look. Checked in, left after a few hours, now he owes me. That's all."

Maggie's pretty face and lanky body remind me of Samantha, the sister Mulder lost as a child. If he saw the same resemblance, maybe he spoke to her. Not only does she not remember him; Peggy, no longer trusting my intentions, sends her off to watch TV.

It's only when I pay Mulder's bill that she lets me into the dingy room.

It smells of both mold and bleach. At first glance, there's nothing here other than his half-open suitcase. A closer look will take time, but Peggy won't have it. When I ask for an hour, she laughs. "That's as funny as a three legged dog in a horse race." She pats the wobbling door. "You're looking at the last available room for fifty miles. A ton of sleepy reporters with expense accounts will be falling over each other to pay six times my usual rate. And if I tell them the previous occupant has *mysteriously* vanished..."

"I never said it was mysterious."

"Guess I'm a better storyteller then you are, then."

I argue that the room is a potential crime scene. I threaten to call the sheriff. In response, she spits a bit of filter onto the carpet. I consider taking Mulder's things and spending the night in my rental car, but he may have left some clue behind. We settle on three times her "usual rate." I hope Skinner accepts the charge when I file my expense report.

I'd asked for an hour to search, but spend two. The only thing I find gives me too much of the wrong kind of information. Curled in a rusted wastebasket by the desk is one of Mulder's porno magazines. Heavier stock pokes from the center.

But he probably already has a subscription.

Fortunately, the outlets work, so I plug in my laptop, curl up on the over-bleached sheets, and stare at the blurry photo from the sheriff's office. I see a face, then a bunny rabbit, then a fairly clear image of our 26th president, Teddy Roosevelt.

I am asleep in minutes.

I don't know how long I'm out before a sound makes me open my eyes a slit. My room, *Mulder's* room, is dark, but I don't recall turning off the lights. I've no idea what made the sound, a slamming car door, a bottle tossed in a garbage can, or the pop of settling support beams. I'm under the blankets, head on a pillow, smelling bleach and dank air, but I don't even remember getting undressed.

And again, someone is there with me, again, all in shadow.

He's over by the pressboard desk, beside the wastebasket and tilted standing lamp. He's not Mulder or my father, though he looks, in turns, like both. He's taller, thicker. There are curves above his shoulders. I assume it's the drapes, but they suggest large wings. I'm not afraid. If anything, I barely feel like I'm in the room, as if my body is something I'm imagining.

Almost idly, a question comes to mind: *Who are you?*

Likewise in my mind, an answer appears: *Uriel.*

I know the name. Uriel's an archangel, the one God sent to block Eden's gates after the fall, to prevent humanity from ever reentering paradise. He's a cherub. Not the cute pudgy type on Valentine's Day cards—the fierce sort that battles fallen angels with a huge flaming sword.

But I'm still not afraid.

What do you want?

The room remains undisturbed by sound, while in my mind he speaks louder and deeper than my own inner voice: *Leap. Or he'll die.*

Then it's over.

I'm awake. Really awake. The lights are on, as I left them. I'm on top of the bedspread, next to the blurry photo and my laptop. My side aches from having slept in the odd position.

I assume I've experienced *hypnagogia*. Awake, the brain responds to external stimuli—reality, asleep, to internal stimuli—dream. Chemicals paralyze the body so we don't act out those dreams. In threshold states, however, the stimuli mix, producing vivid hallucinations. Dark figures in bedrooms are common. So, for some reason, are flying dogs.

It wasn't real, but at the same time, Kekulé dreamt a real molecule's shape. At any given time, we're aware of only a small percent of our brain's processes. Not believing that an archangel manifested in a crappy motel room doesn't mean refusing to accept the possibility *I* was trying to tell myself something.

I reexamine the spot Uriel stood. The desk drawers remain empty. I pull each out, look underneath and along the sides. Nothing. The floor has only dust bunnies. The porno mag remains alone in the trash.

Or does it?

I take it out. The shells of a few sunflower seeds tumble from its pages. I look again at the heavier rectangle in the center. It's not a subscription card; it's the back of a memo pad. Mulder must have used it as a bookmark.

Aware that my partner's obsession has left him with a solitary life, I try not to question his private habits too closely. At the same time, I have to ask, do you really need to keep your place when reading a review of *A Decade of Dirty Delinquents*?

The cardboard seems blank, but intuition brought me this far and I'm not willing to give up yet. Using an old trick I first saw on TV, I rub a pencil against the surface. It works. Two words, scrawled in Mulder's familiar hand, appear: SWAMP SHACK.

There are numbers, too, coordinates.

Remembering the GPS in the glove compartment of my rental car, I head out to retrieve it. In the quaint graveyard, I nearly trip over some empty beer cans and a broken Ouija board. The board reminds me of a George Carlin joke: "Tell people there's an invisible man in the sky who created the universe, and the vast majority believe you. Tell them the paint is wet, and they have to touch it to be sure."

He was wrong. They want to touch the invisible, too.

The glow from the press is gone. The main street is empty save for a lone SUV from the sheriff's office, slowly cruising the other end of the short town. Beyond it, a mustard-colored streak spreads along the bottom of the sky. The sun is rising, fulfilling expectation.

I reach my car without incident. The GPS puts the location six miles into Scape Ore Swamp. No roads visible, I can't get there from here, not without help. I tell myself there's no time to waste, but it's a theory of convenience. Mulder may be fine, or already dead. I grab my phone to wake Quinlan, but as I dial, the SUV pulls up.

Miss Velvet is at the wheel. A pimple-faced male deputy rides shotgun.

"Any luck?" she asks, friendly enough. I show her the coordinates. "Could be worse. Could be ten miles in instead of six. Things are quieter, most everyone's finally asleep. You want, we'll take you out there now." She looks at my shoes. "Got extra snake-waders in the trunk. I'll radio the troopers to keep an evac helicopter on standby, just in case."

Hoping Mulder wore more than his shoes, I climb in. Mark Hickmon, a fair-haired twenty-something, introduces himself and pours me some coffee from a Thermos.

"You said *finally* asleep. What did I miss?"

Hickmon's red eyes open a little wider, "It was quiet until around one. Then, out of nowhere, we get like ten calls, sightings. Sheriff mapped 'em as they came in. We think the thing came in from the southwest, around

Al's Topiary Garden, jumped through the fields, climbed up the roof of an abandoned warehouse right where the streetlights start, then turned tail and hopped back the way it came."

Using his hand to illustrate the leaps, he almost spills coffee on Tate, earning a light slap.

"Did anyone photograph it?"

Hickmon shakes his head. "It was all over in about ten minutes. One of those TV action crews chased after it, but got nothing. Lots of witnesses, but the sheriff said you don't think much of them. Me, I don't see how so many people can be lying."

"I never said they were lying, only that they didn't necessarily understand what they were seeing. If it's not a misidentified animal, it could be a hoax."

"Jumping around like that?"

I shrug. "Someone who wanted to drum up business for the town could've hired an acrobat, or… a parkour expert."

"Parkour?"

"A discipline developed in France. Using only your surroundings, you propel yourself around and over any obstacles. It's based on military training."

I flash on Mulder smiling. *It's not like the shadow government would send anything this goofy.*

What if they would?

SCAPE ORE SWAMP
LEE COUNTY, SOUTH CAROLINA
THURSDAY, 5:16 a.m.

The view shifts from flat fields to thick trees. We turn onto what I wouldn't even call a dirt road, more a path that barely fits the SUV.

"ATV trail," Tate explains. "How far we get depends on how the drainage's been. I only hope we don't trash the vehicle."

We bounce hard. Branches scrape and thud the sides so loudly, I have to raise my voice.

"I appreciate you taking the risk."

She shrugs. "It's my job."

Given what I took for jealousy last night, her professionalism is refreshing. Maybe we all just needed some sleep. An instant later we're surrounded by incredibly tall, thin pines. The swamp is thick with them, the way a field of grass might look to a mouse.

"Why's it called Scape Ore Swamp?"

They look at each other. "It's short for Escaped Whore Swamp. During the Revolutionary War, a British camp in town was ambushed. Three of their 'pleasure' women ran and hid here."

After about two miles, a front wheel spins in the spongy ground, then two. Forced to stop, Tate passes out the high, rubber snake-waders and some orange vests.

"Don't want to be taken for a deer... or an alien."

The vest is tight, the boots too big. I can only hope both will serve their purpose. Once they're on, we begin what Tate says will be "a long march." Given the damp, muddy ground that gives way to stretches of shallow, murky water, the better word is *slog*.

I let those with experience lead, try to walk where they walk, do as they do. But when I'm the third to climb over a particularly fat, rotting tree trunk, it collapses. Tate and Hickmon catch me, but not before mossy water tips over a loose boot top, drenching my foot and ankle. I about removing it to dump the water, but a slithering feeling across my calf changes my mind.

Long hours later, the GPS coordinates are a half-mile off. Knowing we'll arrive soon, Hickmon heads to the privacy of a thick-bottomed cypress to relieve his bladder. Despite the constant insect drone, he is... loud.

Tate and I look around awkwardly, then at each other.

She grimaces. "About last night. I've known John Quinlan since grade school. We been together three years."

"It's none of my business, but, don't you think it effects you professionally? He is your superior."

She gives me a look. "Maybe in some corporation, but it's no secret in that office who gets promoted or why. John ever did anything funny on my account, he'd get it bad. Mostly from me."

"But..." Remembering I'm a visitor, I cut myself off.

"Now, flirting with *you* was out of bounds. He *will* be apologizing next he sees you."

Tate's easy confidence makes it easy to imagine her the dominant partner.

"You got someone?"

"No."

Her brow acquires the smallest of wrinkles. "I'd have guessed different from the look on your face when you talk about Agent Mulder."

"It's not like that. He's my partner."

"It can be like that without being like that, if you know what I mean."

What she may consider southern friendliness is beginning to feel intrusive.

"I admit our relationship is complicated, but…"

Before I can think how to explain, Hickmon, finished at last, calls out: "I see something."

Sloshing from behind the cypress, he points toward a vague rectangle between the trees, maybe a hundred yards away.

Tate squints. "What the hell…? I've seen deer stands out here, but no more than a ladder and a platform."

The *swamp shack* sits in a small clearing surrounded by a deep mesh of branches that has to be cut away by Hickmon's machete. I'd pictured a rotting wooden hut held up on aged dock pilings, but it seems made of the sort of PVC composite used in decks. The windowless shack has one door, but a series of air vents line the low-angled roof. The chug of a gas generator disrupts the insect noises.

Silver screw tops wink in the sunlight, telling me: "It's new."

Tate kneels beside me. "Want to tell us what we're getting into?"

This isn't a risk I can ask them to take without an explanation, so I sigh an old sigh.

"Agent Mulder was here to meet someone claiming to have captured a live alien."

There's an expected beat of incredulity, then: "And he *believed* him?"

Hickmon looks around. "Why not? Topiary garden's due east. If there's a path, that thing last night *could've* come from here."

I touch his shoulder. "I assume it was a hoax, but that doesn't make this less dangerous. If someone's holding him inside, they won't be happy to see us."

"Still…"

His fear isn't as contagious as Mulder's desire to believe, but, given all I've seen, I have to acknowledge I may be wrong.

Tate shrugs. "Your partner, your call."

Fortunately, alien or not, the play is the same. "No windows works both ways. We can't see in, but unless they have cameras, they can't see us. I'm thinking we turn off the generator and see if anyone comes out."

Staying low, Deputy Tate and I take up positions on either side of the door. A nervous Hickmon makes his way to the generator. It sputters, then stops, the sudden quiet revealing the previously inaudible whirr of fans in the vents. As they slow and stop, I wonder what's so wrong with the air inside that the swamp smell is preferable. The shack is the right size for a meth lab.

Mulder, what did you wander into this time?

We wait, guns out, but down. After a slow thirty seconds, a mosquito lands on Hickmon's cheek. I put a finger to my lips to warn him, but he slaps it hard, leaving a bright red smudge. The slap is sharp, loud.

And all hell breaks loose.

They say that in a crisis the adrenaline rush makes time seem slow, but it doesn't happen now. The moments that follow are as blurry as any bad photo. A thunderous blast tears a head-sized hole in the door. What's left of it flies open. A wiry figure, at least six feet tall, rushes out, shotgun in hand.

Before I can tell if it's alien, man, beast, or Mulder, Hickmon fires. Though I assume he's never shot at a human being before, he hits it in the chest. His next two shots come in such rapid succession, the body doesn't have time to fall before the third bullet makes contact. When it does, it lands on its back. The black oatmeal of the marsh oozes around it. The sinking face belongs to an older man, maybe seventy, balding, pink skin red from sunburn. It disappears with a moist *plop*.

Now is not the time to stare. There may be more in the shack.

As if obeying Uriel's command to *jump,* I all but leap in. A gross smell hits me, so thick, even the best ventilation couldn't keep it in check. The single room is dominated by a large empty cage, the source of the odor. Otherwise, the place is empty. Mulder isn't here and my only chance to find him may already be dead.

I rush back out. Tate, having pulled the man's head above water, presses a fistful of gauze from her First Aid kit into the wounds. Ignoring the wetness filling both my boots, I straddle him at the waist. Hickmon's aim was true. The fading heart pumps a stream of blood from the largest of three entry wounds. The man's eyes waver like small boats about to tear loose from their mooring. He's barely conscious, if at all.

I have seconds.

"Look at me!" I scream. Our gazes meet. We both know I'm the last thing he'll ever see. "Where's Agent Mulder? What have you done with him?"

A gleam of pure hatred flashes from the man's eyes—and he dies.

Tate already has a walkie-talkie in hand. "No need for Evac?"

Heart pounding, I fall back. "No, but I want a forensic team out here, stat."

A loud panting turns us toward Hickmon. He's on his knees, eyes wide, chest rising and falling so fast he's in danger of hyperventilating.

"You did the right thing," I tell him, though part of me wishes he hadn't. "Keep your head down. Sherry, do you have a bag, anything he can breathe into?"

As she tends Hickmon, I check the corpse. It isn't easy, but I squeeze my hand into each wet pocket. Empty. No ID, nothing. It's a small town. He might be local.

"Either of you recognize him?"

No such luck.

Before going back into the shack, I restart the generator. The whirring fans don't relieve much of the awful smell, part chemical, part fecal. The soiled cage is six by four. Two of its thick bars are impossibly bent and marred by what could be scratches or bites. The lock has been snapped, the cage door ajar. Whatever was inside wanted out, and was powerful enough to get its way.

I hear Hickmon. "W-was that thing locked up in here?"

He, still pale, is at the door. Tate's beside him.

"Or someone wants it to look that way. Let's stay out until forensics gets here. I don't want any contamination."

Tate's nose wrinkles. "Already looks pretty contaminated to me."

"Once they test the biological residue we'll know if it's human or…"

"Alien?" Hickson offers.

"Animal. I was going to say, *animal*."

It is hours before forensics arrives, hours more before I learn that the elderly man's photo and fingerprints, faxed from the site by satellite phones, aren't in the national criminal databases. I'm told it'll be morning before they can even start on the lab-work.

Meanwhile, Mulder, like the truth, is out there.

Soggy, antsy, lacking better ideas, I decide to retrace the "alien's" path from last night.

"How far is that topiary park?"

Hickmon, though distracted by all the activity, seems no calmer. "Two miles?"

"Whyn't you show her, Mark? You can still get there by sunset. I'll have a car meet you," Tate says. After any shooting, it's protocol to offer the involved officer an opportunity to step away from the scene. Being stuck in a swamp hasn't afford any easy opportunities.

And so we begin another slog. While the ground gets drier, the path becomes less clear. Moving inch by inch, it's clear we won't beat the sunset. I doubt any alien, real or not, came this way. Hickmon says little. It's not unusual under the circumstances, but not knowing him, I can't say how well he's taking it. I tell Hickmon he had no choice, that he likely saved our lives.

When he finally does speak, it's a shout: "Cottonmouth!"

Four feet of dull yellow and earthy brown dart in front of me, disappearing behind a stubby branch. My eyes are riveted on the wood, watching for any sign of movement.

"Don't worry, he's gone. He's more afraid of you than you are of him."

Really? Then 'he' must be having a heart attack.

Before I let myself breathe again, I notice that the frayed wood on the branch-end branch is almost white. It's freshly fallen. I look up and find a spot on a tree. In fact, more than a few tree branches have been snapped recently. Together, they form a rough line headed east.

Hickmon guesses what I'm thinking. "Parkour?"

I nod.

Whatever the explanation, following the line speeds our trip. We're out of the swamp by nightfall. Better yet, as my aching feet squish in the wet waders and stars wink into the sky, Al's Topiary Garden appears on the horizon.

Heartened, I pick up speed, only to stop short at the hint of a cool breeze. In this heat, it's stranger to find than an alien, and I don't want to let it go. It hits my fingertips, not my face, as if rising from below. By the time I turn toward it, it's gone.

The Lizard Man supposedly frequented an abandoned subway. I doubt there's a subway around here. A salt cavern might not be out of the question.

"Are there any underground caves here?"

"In Linville, about two hundred miles."

The breeze gone, there's nothing to follow. The dark growing, there's nothing to see. In any event, I have no reason to pursue it.

By the time we reach the garden, there's barely enough light to make out the topiaries. What I can see impresses me. I expected animal-shapes, but these are abstract; entwined trees curving up in a double helix, pyramids, spirals, and wilder shapes that look like freeform doodles.

Halfway across the three short acres, I make out headlights at the far end. Our ride from the sheriff's office, I assume. Hickmon's a few steps ahead when I notice that the chorus of crickets, our company for miles now, has stopped. Along a row of bushes looped in serpentine waves, I think I see someone. It could be the owner, or part of the garden. I take a few steps closer. When the thing moves, I remember my words to Sheriff Quinlan—*you see what might be a tiger*.

It rises like madness—garish, terrifying, but not at all like a dream. Uriel came along with a heaviness in my mind that reassured me he was an illusion. No such comfort here. I'm completely, horrifyingly aware, my inner-animal fearing for its life, my intellect repulsed that a world I'd thought mostly predictable would *dare* present me with anything so ridiculous.

In a theoretical conversation, reason can debate with the instinct to assume. In the moment you have to choose.

Of course it's a monster.

Of course it's not.

I want to believe it's an animal, but the skull-size and huge, pupil-black eyes make that impossible. A costume? Yes. It must be a costume. Whatever it is, it's lean, lithe, and about six feet tall, with grey, leathery skin. No sooner does it crouch than it leaps, rising so quickly it looks like a blurry, oversize squirrel. I've certainly never seen anything human move so quickly.

A being from another world with heavier gravity, like the astronauts on the moon.

But the astronauts seemed to move in slow-motion. This thing's free-standing jump, from ground to high branch, is more explosive than a cobra strike. A second leap nearly cracks the branch. It wraps itself around the double-helix trees. They waver, surrounding me with a rain of small leaves. Another jump takes it back to the ground, four short yards away, facing me.

One more leap and it'll be on me. I seize.

My brain howls: *Idiot! It is a tiger. You should've run!*

"Get down!"

I'm already ducking when the air near my ear sizzles and burns. I hear a pistol's firecracker pop. The thing somersaults backwards and dives into a bush as if it were water. I hear it flee, or rather, hear brush snapping in its wake.

Hickmon helps me up. We chase after crunching leaves and cracking twigs. They soon dissolve, leaving us at the garden's end, staring at a wall of shadow. Our brains ache to find a pattern in it, but the blackness only throbs.

Neither of us mention parkour.

Sheriff Quinlan rushes toward us. He's shouting, but I don't hear what he's saying. I train my eyes on the topiaries. I see no blood or no torn clothing, but I'm so exhausted I can't trust that I'm not missing something. If I don't get some rest, my uselessness will only increase.

Quinlan, tired and pale himself, escorts us back to the car. A few moments after I climb in, he hands me a note, a hand-written apology for his flirtatious remarks. His description is so objective and complete, if I wanted to press harassment charges, I could use the letter as evidence. I want to question his timing. Instead I thank him and ask to be dropped off at the motel.

The little town center is day-bright again, bullied by klieg lights, packed with people.

"They can't all be press."

Quinlan grows grim. "They're mostly locals. First two sightings, no one blinked. After eighty, people got a little tense. Something goes strolling through town, they get a little more tense. Now, rumors flying that the government's involved, they hear about our first shooting in decades and everyone's more skittish than a cat in a roomful of rocking chairs."

"Rumors of government involvement?"

"Sherry said not to mention it until you got some sleep, but…"

He nods at a newspaper on the seat floor. The front page half-covered by a blurry photo in the digitized black and green of night vision. The bobbed hair and business suit indicate it's not any alien. It's me, walking to the motel last night. I was a fool. After I answered the questions from the press so smugly, some enterprising journalist decided to follow me.

Ahead, people mill and swarm, a mob changing shape in insect waves. If they don't already know about the topiary garden, they will soon. Without some explanation that puts the world back roughly where they left it, things could get ugly.

The main street impossible to navigate, we drive around the long way to the *Inn or Out*. In the cheap, moldy room, I take what is arguably a shower before collapsing into bed.

Something happens, call it sleep. At least for my body, but my mind will not let go. It careens, counting the possibilities, ruthlessly discarding data and dream. It may be obsession that drives me, inflamed loyalty, even love, but I can't name it. It's a habit beyond habit. My partner, my friend, the man who found the cure for my cancer, is out there somewhere and I have to find him.

I think I open my eyes. I see scant, yellow streetlight behind the blinds. As I watch, breathing slowly, the air acquires an odd quality, as if taking on a presence. To get away from the light, I think I roll over. Uriel waits in his spot by the desk, patient, as if he's been there all eternity. I don't have to ask, I don't have to think a word before he speaks:

Jump or he'll die.

Again, the voice feels like it's in my mind, very different from the harsh scraping that fills my ears. Uriel is intimate, as close as the air. The scraping is loud, but distant, as if coming from some other room. My best guess is that Uriel is a dream, but the sound is real.

I pivot to pinpoint the source. This time, Uriel doesn't vanish so easily. He's sticky tonight. The scraping is clearer. It's coming from above me, on the motel roof. Human, animal, wind, it moves along the room's width. Is it the thing from the garden? Did it follow me?

Jump or he'll die.

I'm not clear if Uriel's speaking, or I'm remembering his words. Is there a difference with dreams? I hear screaming. Is it mine?

Uriel, am I screaming?

He vanishes without answering, taking enough shadow with him to change the room. The screaming remains. It's not just screaming—it's words, but I can't make them out. I stumble from bed. When I stand, my head lolls, as if my lower body's awake, but the rest of me hasn't caught up. Before my hand can turn the knob, my forehead bangs the door.

"Ow!"

At least I'm more awake now. Outside, the air smells less of mold and bleach, but it's still too thick to be refreshing. Peggy White stands in the parking lot, wearing a white housecoat, angel sleeves marred by old cigarette burns. She's the one screaming. Groggy reporters surround her, but keep their distance, as if she's a tiger.

"It took my baby!" she roars. "That thing took Maggie!"

Apparently I'm skeptical even half-asleep. I consider the possibility she's faking.

The nearest reporter's hair is a mess, yet he managed to get on a tie. His cameraman adjusts the lens for a tighter shot. "The alien kidnapped your daughter?"

"I don't know what the hell it was!"

"Can you describe…?"

Peggy snaps. She lashes out. Polished nails rake across the reporter's face. "It's your fault, all of you! I'll kill you!"

I move to intervene, but there's no further violence. She collapses and sobs convulsively. One of them kneels beside her. Another gives her a water bottle. The camera keeps shooting.

I no longer think she's lying.

Unnoticed, maybe because I'm still in my bathrobe, I scan the roof. A pattern in the damaged shingles, real or not, leads toward the trees. There, a patch of white peeks from the shorn bark of a newly cracked branch.

I no longer doubt the thing was here.

Carrying a child might slow it down. It may even need to rest. The most reasonable course of action would be to run after it, calling the sheriff as I go. But I don't.

Instead, for the first time in my life, there's something I just *know*.

Barefoot, I run to my rental car. As I drive, I almost feel the story of

Maggie's kidnapping nipping at my heels, spreading from the motel to the street, where hundreds wait to catch the panic. Speeding through the center of town, I honk to warn the crowd. I swerve, skim a klieg light, but barely slow down.

Past the outskirts, I'm doing eighty. The road ahead is empty, until the headlights hit a black sedan sitting catty-corner, blocking my path. Someone in a dark suit stands by its open door, trying to wave me down. At this speed, he's mostly a blur. He could just as easily be a well-dressed hitchhiker or a dapper Lizard Man.

Since meeting Mulder four years ago, I can't count how many times I've been on a lonely road only to have the driver of a mysterious black sedan try to wave me down. Usually, I stop. This time, I don't. He leaps out of the way. Tires squeal and dirt churns as I leave the road long enough to maneuver around the sedan. Whoever it is will follow, but after a sharp right, nothing's visible in my rearview mirror for the rest of the trip to Al's Topiary.

AL'S TOPIARY GARDEN
ELIZABETHVILLE, SOUTH CAROLINA
FRIDAY, 4:12 a.m.

I grab a flashlight from the glove compartment and head out. The beam dances along the abstract vegetation. As I make my way, a waxing moon pokes from behind the clouds. The pebble-covered paths hurt my feet, but I can't slow down. When I reach the flat field beyond the garden, my soles are grateful. I search both my memory and the terrain, trying to find the spot I stood on a few hours ago, when my fingers caught a cool breeze.

I think I find it. It's terribly soft, nearly not there at all, but as I follow the feeling, step after step, it gets stronger. When I pause beside a lone cypress, a wave of rising air curls along the tips of my toes. The flashlight beam reveals the edge of a ragged hole. The moonlight hints at its far side, five feet away.

Jump.

The voice is so clear and strong it makes me feel as if I've been yanked back to the motel bed. I even feel the mattress lump under my left shoulder and smell the heavy bleach in the pillow case. For an instant, I'm not sure if I'm really there or here. But then I feel the soft earth beneath my feet and the updraft from the hole chills the sweat on my cheeks.

I'm here all right.

And again, Uriel says, *Jump.*

So I do.

Eyes closed, I jump.

The fall is a flash, an instant that goes by too quickly to ever recall. Hitting the hard ground, curling and rolling into a cold, shallow puddle seems to take much, much longer. Nothing is broken, aside from the flashlight, so I stand. Moonlight reflects from the puddle up into salt crystal deposits along the walls. I can make out what's in front of me, but not much more.

I am about to conclude that I've gone insane, that there's no point to what I've done, when the plinking of water drops falling from my soaked bathrobe's hem melds with the sound of a sniffling child.

"Maggie?" I whisper.

I'm not sure why I whisper, but her response is even quieter: "Help."

I take a few steps, maybe three, and then, at long last, see clearly, see *it* clearly. It's perched on a flat rock, bobbing, breathing heavily, its long grey arms and legs wrapped tightly around the girl. It's not *just* that I see it. I recognize it for what it is.

It's Mulder.

The prosthesis enlarging his head has been torn along the forehead. One huge black eye, having fallen out, lies beside him like a giant's lost contact lens. He gasps, he's hurting, deep in the grip of some delusion.

"Scully?" he says, gulping down air. "I found her. I found Samantha." Gently, sweetly, he kisses the forehead of the shivering, terrified child. "See? She's still so young. Nothing's been lost. Nothing."

"Mulder, try not to talk. Can I see Samantha... please?"

Head bobbing like a broken doll, he smiles. "Skeptic. You have to see if she's all right, don't you? She is. She's fine. But, sure." He let's go. "Go on Samantha. You can trust Scully. She's a friend."

Before Maggie can leave his lap, a voice shouts down from the world above.

"Hello? Agent? Are you all right?"

Mulder grabs Maggie, covering her mouth. "Shh..." he says, petting her.

I look up into Assistant Director Skinner's agitated face. Seeing only me, unharmed, he says, "I caught a late flight, drove all night to bring you the file on the man who was shot and you nearly run me over." But then he catches himself. "Agent, are you alone down there?"

TRINITY HOSPITAL
WASHINGTON, D.C.
MONDAY, OCTOBER 13, 1:08 p.m.

Three days later, Mulder remains in the private wing of a Washington hospital, the extra expense covered by no less than the CIA. While Mulder understands the basics of what happened, I've yet to share all I've learned. I don't want to create any anxiety that might exacerbate his lingering disorientation. I will, of course, eventually tell him everything.

According to the file Skinner brought, early in Mulder's career, while still assigned to the FBI's Behavioral Science Unit, he was respected enough for the Central Intelligence Agency to request his opinion. They were considering a revival of MKUltra, the infamous mind control program halted in 1973. A Dr. Jacob Elman was convinced that a combination of hypnosis and drugs could make a given subject to perform actions they might otherwise consider abhorrent, say, a covert assassination—on command. Not only that, Elman believed he could convince them they were someone else entirely.

Beyond the fiction of *The Manchurian Candidate*, there is reason to suspect this is actually possible. We now know that under hypnosis, individuals lose track of both their normal judgment and their sense of identity. At the same time, their ability to focus on imaginary situations increases significantly. But a young, idealistic Mulder, presenting arguments both pragmatic and ethical, effectively scuttled the project and ruined Elman's career. Destitute, Elman dropped out of sight.

From there, I surmise he somehow continued his research, and, achieving success, embarked on a plan for revenge. I can't imagine it was difficult to learn of the reputation 'Spooky' Mulder had acquired. Providing suitable bait in the form of a few staged alien encounters (perhaps wearing the elaborate costume himself), he lured Mulder into a trap. Then, in that awful cage, Elman convinced Mulder he was the very thing he'd spent his life trying to find—an alien.

I don't know if Elman's ultimate goal was to vindicate his career while only humiliating Mulder, or if, in the end, he planned to kill him, perhaps by ordering him to attack the police. I do know that whatever information was found in Elman's South Carolina home was confiscated by the CIA, and is now available only on a need-to-know basis. AD Skinner tried to follow up, but apparently the FBI does not need to know.

Maintaining such an extreme altered state must have required regular drugs as well as psychological reinforcement. With Elman dead, the effects dissipated. Mistaking Maggie White for his lost sister was an indication Mulder's true identity was returning.

This leaves an elephant in the room; the faux alien's astonishing acrobatic feats. I have no definite answers, but offer three possibilities. Some, none, or all may be true.

First, high levels of epinephrine were found in Mulder's blood, indicating that artificial adrenaline was part of Elman's concoction. Second, anecdotal evidence suggests the existence of what's called hysterical strength. The common example is a panicked mother lifting a heavy car off her trapped child. Such feats usually occur in life and death situations, but there are exceptions. Lastly, there is belief itself, a powerful motivator. If a stage show hypnotist can turn a wall-flower into an expressive dancer, Mulder's own conviction that he was capable of wild leaps would, at the very least, make accomplishing them more likely.

In any event, a price was paid. In addition to a series of sprains, a torn ligament and two bruised bones, the medical examination showed that Agent Mulder had experienced three mild heart attacks. Fortunately, the myocardial infarctions left no major damage—though I check again every time I visit.

As much as we crave the new, in the end, our very sense of self is based on routine. As Mulder recovers, it's the familiar things about him, about us, even those traits I find irritating, that give me the most comfort. While he seems more himself, he has developed a tendency to repeat himself, which I hope will vanish in time. Today, for instance, he greets me by saying the same thing he said yesterday, and the day before:

"Y'know, Scully, being the hunted instead of the hunter gave me a whole new perspective."

Rather than point it out, I ask, "How so?"

The last two times, he described the profound loneliness of trying to make his way in a completely unrecognizable world.

This time, though, he surprises me. Instead of confessing profound angst, he twists his head and squints at me. "Wait a minute…"

His eyes go saucer-wide. "Whoa! Has your hair always been that red?"

"Uh… yes?"

"It's amazing," he says. "Absolutely amazing."

I'm about to thank him, but then he looks around, as delighted by the drops of moisture against the ice-pitcher and the sunlight against the windows as he is by my hair color.

"Everything looks so *new*. Must be a holdover from Elman's drugs, but I guess that's a plus, huh?"

Before I answer, I think about my leap of faith. While I suspected there was a cave, I'd no reason to think Mulder would be there. So, was it my subconscious, or did that knowledge come from somewhere else? Maybe my personal sin, if such things exist, is being unable to say *I don't know* when I can. But that's Mulder's sin as well, isn't it?

It's a monster!

No it's not!

As for Uriel, I decide not to decide.

After all, I am Starbuck, keeping the ship running while Mulder's mad Ahab tells it where to go. I am Starbuck. The ship must survive or all is lost.

As I try to see whatever it is Mulder's seeing in this horribly boring hospital room, I tell him, "Yes. I'd definitely count that as a plus."

THE END

NON GRATUM ANUS RODENTUM

By Brian Keene

WASHINGTON, D.C.
23rd JUNE, 1994, 9:46 a.m.

A s the hallway lights dimmed and the janitorial crew began their nightly rounds, Assistant Director Walter Skinner considered going for a run. Boxing and jogging had always been hobbies for him, but recently, jogging had become something much more—an escape. In the last few months, the public sidewalks and monuments he jogged around had provided a solace and comfort he couldn't find at home or at work. Given the disarray in both his personal and professional lives, those few moments of peace were something he desperately needed.

He glanced down at his desk. To the left was a framed photograph taken sixteen years ago on the day of his and Sharon's wedding. To the right sat an ashtray overflowing with stained Morley cigarette butts. Both the picture and the ashtray made his stomach hurt. He had a physical coming up, something the Bureau required annually, and although he was in solid shape for a man his age, Skinner already knew what the doctor would find—an ulcer. The usual reasons would be cited. Bacterial infection. Stress. Poor diet. Smoking (which he didn't do). Drinking (which he did). A host of other sources. But Skinner knew what the real culprits were. He was looking at them right now.

Since coming home from Vietnam and getting clean, Skinner had lived each day like it mattered. The war and his time in the Bureau had taught him that anything could happen at any time. It didn't matter how prepared you thought were, or how confident you felt. Things could— and did—change on a dime. He'd heard a rock song once, in which part of the lyrics had been that changes weren't permanent, but change was.

There was truth in that. Skinner tried to treat every minute with purpose. He tried to enjoy every good moment, be it something as simple as a hug from his wife or as complicated as helping to bring down a child pornography ring. He cherished those moments, and banked on them during the bad times.

Lately, however, it seemed like there was nothing but bad. His marriage was crumbling. Looking back, it hadn't been good in a long time, but it felt now as if the damage had already been done, with no hope of reprieve or repair. Separate bank accounts. Separate friends. Separate lives. When he and Sharon were home at the same time, which wasn't often these days, they were like strangers. He remembered their early years together, when they'd talk for hours about everything. Now, their conversations were polite but forced and clipped, focusing on trivial inanities. He couldn't remember the last time they'd touched, and saying "I love you" had become as perfunctory and rote as saying "Bless you" after someone sneezed.

Like others, he could have lost himself in his work, except that this was an even bigger source of stress. As an Assistant Director, making choices was part of Skinner's job description. Now, he was stuck in the middle between a resentful employee and a duplicitous superior who usurped the chain of command and whose goals and reasons were cloaked in a frustrating shroud of secrecy and potential maliciousness—the same superior who had filled up the ashtray on Skinner's desk.

Logically, Skinner knew that Agent Mulder didn't blame him for the closure of the so-called X-Files, and his subsequent reassignment to general duties (which currently involved a wiretap detail). Those orders had come down from the top of the FBI's executive branch, prompted no doubt by directives from Skinner's unofficial smoking overseer. But as Mulder's immediate superior, Skinner nevertheless bore the brunt of the agent's condescension, insolence, and simmering resentment with the Bureau itself. He understood the younger man's anger and disillusionment. He felt them, too. It was heartbreaking. Mulder had been one of the finest, most promising agents in the Bureau's sixty-year history. He'd already made a name for himself before even graduating from the academy. Now, those talents were being wasted because of the smoking man's murky agenda. When Skinner had pressed his superiors on the reasons why, he'd been met with the same stonewalling and frustrating silence that Mulder himself railed against.

And yet, no matter how sympathetic he was to Mulder's grievances, to protect the agent—as well as Mulder's partner, Scully—Skinner had to disassociate himself from those emotions and straddle the line that Mulder kept crossing, becoming a barrier of sorts. Because if he didn't, Skinner had a very strong suspicion that being reassigned to general duties wouldn't be the worst thing to befall Fox Mulder. And so, Skinner spent each day choosing not to choose, caught between two very different masters and trying to provide a balance between their disparate interests. He wondered how much longer he could hold that position, defending a line that was about to collapse in upon itself?

Yes, he decided, a jog would do him good. A late-night run under the stars might give him some perspective, or at the very least, a few moments of reprieve. Good. Bad. The stars were indifferent. The universe didn't care about a person's trials, triumphs, or tribulations. The universe just was.

Maybe he'd be able to sleep afterward, although he doubted it. Before their marriage had begun to fall apart, Sharon had been after him to see a doctor at a sleep disorder clinic. He'd awake shrieking, clutching the sheets, bathed in sweat. He told Sharon he had dreams about Vietnam, and that wasn't a lie. But the truth was far more than simply dreaming about the war. Skinner suffered from recurring nightmares of an old woman he'd encountered only once in Vietnam. He'd never told Sharon about that meeting. Indeed, he'd never spoken of it to anyone.

One night while on patrol, Skinner's unit had been ambushed. Every single man had fallen, including himself. Moments after being shot, he had looked down upon his body, lying motionless in the jungle beneath him. He'd watched, peaceful and unafraid, while the Viet Cong stripped off his uniform and seized his weapons and gear. Eventually, after looting the bodies, the enemy had moved on. At sunrise, another Marine unit had arrived. Skinner had watched them zip his corpse inside a body bag. He'd awoken two weeks later in a hospital in Saigon, and was told that the Marines had found a pulse on him shortly before processing his remains.

That much Sharon—and only Sharon—knew. What he hadn't told her, or anyone else, was that an old woman had remained with him that entire time. She had appeared when he first looked down at his body, and had stayed with him until he'd woken in the hospital, ultimately lifting him up and carrying him away from a bright light before departing.

Skinner didn't believe that he'd had what Mulder would have called a near-death experience. He had always chalked the old woman and the rest of the matter up to a hallucination, one he had suffered while gravely injured and no doubt exacerbated by the amount of drugs he took just to cope with the things he'd done while in the country. He was certain of it. Nevertheless, he still dreamed about her, years later, and woke screaming.

He sighed. No wonder his marriage was coming undone.

He removed his glasses and rubbed the bridge of his nose. A headache was starting to form there. Someone knocked on the office door. Skinner put his glasses back on and straightened up.

"Come in."

The door opened, and a member of the janitorial staff peeked inside—a Guatemalan kid, barely twenty-one, by the looks of him. He smiled at Skinner, who returned the gesture with a curt nod.

"You here late," the youth said, grinning. "You work hard."

"Somebody has to."

"You want I come back?"

"No." Skinner shook his head. "That's okay. I was leaving for the night anyway."

He made sure that his computer was powered down and locked, collected his briefcase, coat, and weapon, and walked to the door. Behind him, the young man hummed tunelessly and emptied the trash can. Glancing back at him, Skinner was reminded of himself at that age. Except that instead of passing a security clearance and getting a job as a custodian inside FBI headquarters, he'd voluntarily enlisted in the Marine Corps and—three weeks into his tour—blew the head off a ten-year old North Vietnamese boy strapped with grenades.

Voluntarily enlisting. Shooting a suicide bomber. Those were choices he had made, and good or bad, they were his choices to live with. Now, he was trying to live with not making any choices at all.

Skinner wondered which was worse.

"Do me a favor? Make sure you dump that ashtray. It stinks."

The janitor nodded. "Sure thing. It's full. You smoke a lot."

Skinner decided not to bother explaining that he didn't smoke.

He made his way to the basement of the building, intent on retrieving his running clothes and sneakers from his locker in the employee gym. On his way there, he passed by Mulder's office. When Skinner had been starting out, the cramped, dingy room had been where they kept the copier. More recently, it had housed the X-Files.

Now, it merely held a sense of despairing air of futility.

Mulder was the only person Skinner knew who slept less than he did. Chances were good that the younger man would still be there, working late. Deciding to check on the agent's progress with the wiretapping detail, he knocked on the door, steeling himself for some sarcastic quip. When Mulder didn't answer, Skinner opened the door and looked inside. The room was vacant, but the light was still on. Frowning, he crossed over to the desk and rifled through the transcripts and reports. He couldn't help but smile wistfully at the doodles Mulder had scrawled on a nearby notepad—several flying saucers, a naked woman, spiral shapes, and something that he guessed was Bigfoot—but his frown returned when he caught a glimpse of something buried beneath the mound of paperwork.

He pushed the transcripts and notepad aside and picked up a series of newspaper clippings that had been paper-clipped together. The top article was dated from two weeks before, and at first glance, had nothing to do with Mulder's current assignment. The headline read 'TWO DEAD IN SEWER SLAYING'. Skinner scanned the lead, which reported that two metropolitan sanitation workers had been mauled to death in the sewers beneath the nation's capital by an unknown animal.

"Damn it, Mulder."

Clearly, the agent was still collecting potential X-Files, something he'd strictly been forbidden against doing.

Clenching his jaw, Skinner flipped through the rest of the clippings, all of which detailed further reports of an unknown wild animal on the loose in the sewers, along with the deaths of several homeless. Skinner shook his head and turned to the last clipping, dated from that morning. As he did, it felt as if someone had punched him in the stomach. His ulcer burned, and he gasped, staring at a photograph that had been taken next to a manhole cover, apparently near the scene of another homeless person's death. A large group of people was congregated in the picture—emergency responders, law enforcement, and a few street people. It was the latter that caught Skinner's eye, particularly a homeless man standing apart from the others, to the far left of the photograph.

"Ramirez?"

Could it be? He stared intently. The photo was in black and white, and the man was out of focus. He looked much older than Ramirez would have been, but that could be accounted for by his rough condition. He was dressed in dirty clothes and his long, thin hair and beard were matted and unkempt. His hands and the exposed skin on his face were covered in what was either filth or sores. Skinner couldn't be sure which. But when he studied the man's eyes, and then noticed the scarring on the man's left cheek, visible despite the thick beard, there was one thing he was certain of.

"Ramirez…"

Skinner decided not to go jogging after all.

He folded up the last newspaper clipping and stuffed it into his pocket. After returning the others to Mulder's desk, he left the room and closed the door behind him.

Before leaving the building, he checked his weapon and briefcase, and took possession of his personal sidearm. Agents were encouraged to carry while off-duty, and Skinner obliged, but he much preferred his 1911 to the shitty department issue handguns.

The guard eyed him as he swiped his badge through the scanner.

"No civilian clothes tonight, sir?"

"Not tonight. I'm going to meet an old friend."

DUC PHO, VIETNAM
AUGUST 1970

Even at night, the jungle was hot—a wet heat that seemed to cling to everything. The rain just made it worse.

Nineteen-year old Walter Skinner hunkered down in a banana grove three kilometers west of Duc Pho, listening to the raindrops pelt the thick vegetation. Droplets fell from his poncho. He swatted in annoyance at a mosquito. In Vietnam, even the insects were tenacious, and not scared away by a storm the way their American counterparts would be.

He slapped his neck with both hands, crushing two bugs, and then wiped the smeared remains on his legs.

When he looked again, there was still blood on his hands.

An hour earlier, their patrol had discovered an underground Viet Cong tunnel complex, embedded in the heart of the banana grove. Their orders were to guard the entrance until the Army could dispatch a tunnel rat to search and destroy the facility. The Marines were scattered across the area, and although Skinner couldn't see them, he knew they were there. He himself was positioned to the right of the tunnel entrance. Kyle Lybeck, a native of Seattle and fresh out of boot camp, crouched to his left. Skinner had been tasked with showing the new recruit the ropes, which so far had pretty much consisted of getting him high.

"We gonna smoke one later?" Lybeck whispered in the darkness.

"It's the only way to deal with this shit," Skinner answered. "But not now. You light up now, and Charlie can take your head off from out there in the brush just by tracking your match. Don't give them a target. And besides, I'm still coming down from the acid I took yesterday."

Lybeck's eyes widened. "You mean…? Out here? Man, that's insane."

"It's not so bad," Skinner replied. "It's mostly just the after-effects now. Just a few vapor trails."

"God, Skinner…"

"I'm fine. I could do without standing out here in this rain, though."

"How long do you think we'll wait here?"

"As long as it takes. You know the drill. Hurry up and wait."

Somewhere in the distance, a radio squawked. Bird and insects created their own cacophony. The rain continued to fall, turning from drops to mist. Skinner shivered, despite the heat.

Eventually, the lieutenant called out, signaling his approach in the dark and identifying himself so they wouldn't mistakenly shoot. With him was a new arrival—a soldier from the Army.

"Skinner, Lybeck," the lieutenant said, "this is Sergeant Ramirez from 1st Battalion. He's here to deal with the complex. I want you both to assist him. Show him what you've found."

"Yes, sir," both men replied, without saluting.

They studied each other as the officer disappeared back into the darkness.

"You're both too tall to fit inside," Ramirez said, "so don't worry about assisting me. Just show me the entrance. I'll take care of the rest."

"What are you going to do?" Lybeck asked.

Ramirez shrugged. "What I always do. Head down inside, explore the place, watch for booby traps, recover any intel, and then blow the fucking thing sky high."

"Sounds dangerous," Skinner observed. "You sure you want to go it alone?"

"I prefer it that way. Truth is, things gets fucked up down in those tunnels. I've got a lot better chance of staying alive if I can focus, and I can't focus if I'm babysitting two jarheads."

"Fuck you," Skinner replied.

"No offense. You can call me a grunt if it'll make you feel better. All I meant is that you guys don't know what's probably waiting down there. I do."

Lybeck glanced at the entrance to the tunnels. "What *is* down there?"

"Booby traps, for sure. Bats, sometimes, and snakes and rats. I went in this one tunnel in the HoBo woods north of Saigon. The VC flooded it with poison gas."

"Hope you were wearing a gas mask," Skinner said.

"I was that time, luckily. Usually, I don't. It's hard to see down there. Even harder with a fucking gas mask. But something told me to wear it that time, so I did. Anyway, listen. You guys stay here, topside. You hear any shooting, that's just me saying hello to Charlie."

"And you're sure you don't want any help?" Skinner asked.

Ramirez grinned. "Not unless you hear me start screaming. Then… sure, you can lend a hand. Or say a prayer, maybe."

"I'm not much for praying. I lost whatever faith I had left during my first month here."

Ramirez's smile grew broader as he stripped off his extra gear and sat it in a neat pile. "You're a serious motherfucker, aren't you, jarhead? What's your name?"

"Skinner."

"No, I mean your real name."

"Walter."

"Well, take it from me, Walt. You need to loosen up. You're wound too tight. And if I'm not mistaken, you look like you're on something. That's no way to experience the Nam."

Skinner snorted. "What would you suggest?"

"Just try to enjoy the ride. This place is Disneyland and we're all on vacation."

Then, without another word, Ramirez ducked low and entered the tunnel, disappearing into the darkness.

Skinner and Lybeck waited in silence. The minutes seemed to crawl by. The mist turned back into rain, and the mosquitoes returned in force. Then, slowly, the jungle began to fill with sound again. One of their fellow Marines coughed somewhere in the shadows. A radio crackled sporadically. The birds and insects resumed their chattering.

And a muffled gunshot echoed from beneath their feet.

Startled, Skinner and Lybeck both turned to the tunnel entrance as two more shots boomed below. These were followed by an agonized, monstrous squeal and then three more gunshots in quick succession. All around them, their fellow squad members called out, wondering what was happening.

"What the hell was that?" Lybeck's voice went up an octave. "Sounded like an animal."

Instead of responding, Skinner crouched down and stepped inside the tunnel. It sloped steadily downward into the darkness, barely wide enough for him to traverse without turning to his side. Cold air wafted up from below, along with acrid gun smoke. Squinting, he peered into the blackness and listened for more gunshots, but the tunnel was silent.

"I can't see anything." Skinner turned back to Lybeck. "Do you have a flashlight?"

"Yeah. I almost left it behind when you told me not to hump so much stuff, but then I didn't, in case I wanted to read comic books out h—"

"Give it to me," Skinner interrupted. "Then go get the lieutenant and the others."

"Shouldn't I go with you?"

"Just do what I said."

Lybeck's expression betrayed his relief at staying topside. He rummaged through his pack, found the flashlight, and handed it to Skinner. Then he ran to get the others.

Skinner clicked on the flashlight and trained the beam downward. The darkness seemed to surround it, as if annoyed by the intrusion.

Taking a deep breath, he bent over and crept forward, alert and listening for any movement. He knew better than to call out for the tunnel rat. The burrow was quiet. He swept the beam back and forth, watching for traps. The further he went, the tighter the tunnel walls seemed to become. Even though he walked hunched over, his head still scraped against the roof.

Eventually, the passageway leveled out, but he had to drop down to his hands and knees to fit through it. He crawled along, struggling to hold both his rifle and the flashlight, while also watching for booby traps or enemy combatants. He sputtered as strands of spider webs brushed against his face and clung to his skin.

Then he saw the first corpse.

The dead Viet Cong lay sprawled on his back in the middle of the tunnel. His clothing was torn, and his chest, arms and face were covered with deep scratches and odd bite marks that seemed almost like singular puncture wounds. After a moment's hesitation, Skinner placed his palm against the dead man's face, making sure it was real and not some drug-induced hallucination. The skin was cold, slick, and felt like cheese.

He noticed a discarded pistol next to the corpse's left hand. He sat his rifle aside and claimed the weapon, hoping it would make his crawl easier. Then he moved forward again. The passageway was still quiet. When he glanced behind him, he could no longer see the entrance.

Soon, Skinner came to a section where the excavators had dug two holes to each side of the tunnel. He peered into both. One was empty. The other contained a second corpse. This one bore the same bite and claw marks as the previous body, but it was missing its head. A broken bamboo spear lay by its side. He found the head twenty yards further down the passageway. The eyes were still open.

The tunnel narrowed again, squeezing against his shoulders, but Skinner pressed on. He noticed claw marks in the soil, and an odd, wide track that looked like it had been made by something dragged through the dirt—perhaps a tail or a very large snake. He had to crawl over three more corpses, including one whose abdomen had been ripped open and emptied of its innards. Skinners hands and knees sank into the still-warm cavity as he wriggled over the body. All of the dead had similar wounds. There were no bullet holes, and the puncture marks were definitely some type of bite, rather than being made by a knife or bayonet. Skinner wondered what had happened to these men. It couldn't have been Ramirez. He'd only been armed with a handgun and a knife. None of these corpses had been shot, so how then to explain the gunfire he and Lybeck had heard? What had killed these men? And where was Ramirez?

Then he heard a moan.

He fought the urge to call out, unsure if the voice belonged to the missing soldier or another Viet Cong. The passageway widened, allowing him to stand up again. Soon, the tunnel opened up into a large underground chamber. Skinner stretched his aching muscles and stepped inside. Another agonized moan echoed softly through the room, followed by harsh breathing. Skinner raised the pistol and trained the light over the walls. He saw crudely-fashioned bunk beds, storage lockers, a table and chairs made from tree stumps, and other debris, all of it damaged or askew, as if a struggle had taken place. The room still stank of gun smoke, and beneath it, there was a wetter, muskier smell.

"Who's there?"

Startled, Skinner shined the light toward the voice. Ramirez sat propped up against a dirt wall, chest rising and falling as he struggled for breath. His uniform was in tatters, and his body bore the same wounds that covered the dead.

"Ramirez!" Skinner rushed over to him and knelt by his side. "Hang on, man. Help is on the way."

"Can't hear you so well, Walt," Ramirez wheezed. "Shot that fucker but my ears are still ringing. Damn muzzle flash nearly blinded me."

"Help is on the way," Skinner repeated, raising his voice. "Are there any other VC?"

Ramirez shook his head. "All dead."

"What the hell happened down here?"

The injured soldier motioned weakly to the corner. Skinner turned the flashlight in the direction he'd pointed, illuminating yet another corpse. But this dead body was no Viet Cong. It wore the torn and barely recognizable remnants of a North Vietnamese uniform, but that was where all similarities ended. For one thing, it was much larger than a human. Skinner estimated its height to be about seven feet and its weight just over two hundred pounds. He idly wondered how something that size had even fit in the tunnels. It had two arms and legs, but was covered in coarse brown hair. Its head was distinctly rat-like, with a pointed snout, beady black eyes, ears, and sharp teeth. A long, hairless tail lay limp in the dirt behind it.

"It has to be the acid," Skinner whispered, shaking his head.

"No," Ramirez gasped. "It's real, all right."

Skinner quickly rummaged through the chests and lockers. He found some clean clothes and ripped them into rags. Then he began binding Ramirez's wounds. The man bled from over a dozen bites and scratches. The deepest was on his chest, where the rat-man's incisors had left a large, ragged puncture. The soldier's left cheek hung down, the flap of skin moving every time Ramirez tried to talk.

"Stay with me," Skinner told him. "And stay awake."

"It was denned up in here," Ramirez said. "Must have killed the others not too long ago. I interrupted its snack. Took every round I had to kill it."

Skinner glanced back at the body again, and was disturbed to see it changing. The rat-like features had begun to fade, and its size seemed to be shrinking.

"I'm more messed up than I thought I was," he muttered.

"Speak up, Walt. Can't hear you."

"I'm going to have to move you. Can you crawl?"

Ramirez shrugged. "I don't think so. Fucked my leg up pretty bad."

"Okay. Wait here."

Skinner hurried back through the tunnel until he'd reached the section with the guard holes on each side. Then he cupped his hands over his mouth and shouted.

"I need a medic down here!"

His pulse quickened when he heard Lybeck and some of the others shout an affirmative. Then he crawled back to Ramirez. As he reentered the room, he noticed that the rat-thing was now just a dead Viet Cong. It still wore the shredded uniform, but the tail and all the other fantastical features were gone. Instead, there was just a bullet-riddled corpse. Skinner nodded in affirmation, convinced now that it had indeed been the drugs in his system.

"Walt?"

"Yeah, buddy." He returned to the soldier's side. "I'm right here."

"Stay with me a while?"

"Absolutely."

Skinner sat down beside him, with his back to the wall. Ramirez rested his head on Skinner's shoulder, while Skinner held his hand and promised him everything would be okay. It wasn't the first time he'd held the hand of an injured man. He remembered one Marine, whose body had essentially been turned inside out by a claymore. Skinner had held his hand and told him it would be okay, knowing all the while that the man was dying. At the time, he'd considered it a prayer of sorts, hoping that, if his mangled comrade couldn't hear him, then maybe God would, and that He would see to it that the man was okay, after all.

He knew better now. And yet, he comforted Ramirez as best he could, and the two of them were still praying when the rest of the squad arrived.

WASHINGTON, D.C.
TUESDAY, 11:51 p.m.

Skinner arrived on foot at the crime scene, his personal sidearm concealed beneath his coat, and the newspaper clipping still stuffed in his pocket. The air blew cold, tossing trash and leaves down the sidewalk. Yellow police tape fluttered in the breeze like party streamers. Other than four homeless people, the street was almost deserted—no cars or pedestrians, although both could be heard blocks away. Urban ghosts—unseen but audible. Three of the homeless were huddled together in a swaddling of filthy blankets and sleeping bags. The fourth sat apart from the others, taking furtive, cautious sips from a brown-bagged bottle of liquor.

Skinner unfolded the clipping and approached the first group—two men and a woman. They eyed him warily, muttering among themselves and refusing to make eye contact. Skinner was struck by how young the three of them were. Still in their twenties, he was certain, although it was obvious that living on the streets was beginning to age them.

"You smell like five-oh," one of the men muttered. "Don't hassle us. We're not hurting anybody."

"I'm not here to hassle you. I'm just looking for someone."

"Are you looking for Tony?" The girl sat up, suddenly interested. "Or Frankie, maybe? Seems like everybody is looking for them."

"Never mind her," the first man said. "She hasn't made sense since that Herod thing."

Skinner struggled to hide his frustration, and forced a smile. "Herod? You mean the serial-killer? I work for the people who caught him."

"You got Herod off the street? Well shit, dude. Have a drink with us. You guys slide the fuck over and make some room for him."

The young man began nudging his companions, both of whom groaned at the request.

"They take us at night, you know," the girl said. "Big lights come down and then, whoosh, we're gone. They're doing experiments and stuff. That's why I can't have no babies!"

Where's Agent Mulder when I need him? Skinner thought.

Skinner held out the newspaper photo and pointed at Ramirez. "I'm looking for this man. Have you seen him?"

The three of them squinted at the photo.

"What did he do?" the younger man asked.

"He didn't do anything. He's an old friend, and I'm trying to find him."

"Ain't seen him, dude. Hard to tell for sure from that picture. That paper is kind of crinkled."

Skinner pulled out his wallet and produced a ten dollar bill. "How about this kind of paper? Can you tell from this?"

The homeless man smiled. "I'll take your money, but I still haven't seen the guy."

Skinner studied them for a moment. Then, sighing, he handed the younger man the money.

"Thanks, dude. You sure you don't want to party with us?"

"Yeah," the girl chimed in. "Maybe the lights will come back tonight."

"No thanks." He nodded at the fourth homeless man. "What about him? Do you think he might be able to help me?"

The younger man shrugged. "I don't know. Maybe. He keeps to himself. Doesn't talk to anybody."

Muttering a quick thanks, Skinner approached the loner and repeated the inquiry. The homeless man studied the picture carefully, and then made a small whimpering sound. He looked up at Skinner with hollow, sunken eyes and then pointed at the manhole cover.

"He's down there?"

The man nodded.

"You're sure of it?"

Another nod.

"Shit."

Skinner handed the man his last ten dollar bill and then approached the sewer. Four stanchions surrounded the manhole. The breeze picked up again, causing the police tape to flutter again. Skinner debated his next course of action. He was an Assistant Director at the Federal Bureau of Investigation, and yet here he was, contemplating disturbing a crime scene and venturing into the sewers beneath the nation's capital in the middle of the night. It occurred to him that no one even knew where he was. He wondered if Sharon would even notice that he wasn't home yet. If something happened to him, how long before she'd worry? If she worried at all...

He turned his head from side to side, cracking his back and neck. Then, he pushed his glasses up on his face and ducked beneath the caution tape. He had difficulty getting his fingers beneath the manhole cover, but he managed to pry up one end, and then lifted, grunting with the strain. The heavy lid clanged loudly as he dragged it aside. Skinner glanced around, but the street was still deserted. The only people paying attention were his four new companions.

"Good luck," the young guy called as Skinner climbed into the hole. "Hope you find your friend."

The loner said nothing, but his frightened, mournful eyes were the last thing Skinner saw before descending below.

After climbing down the ladder, Skinner realized too late that he should have brought a flashlight. The streetlights above filtered down through the hole, providing a small amount of illumination. It wasn't enough to clearly see his surroundings, but his vision adjusted to the point where he wouldn't have to stumble around blind. He was able to stand at his full height.

It was warmer in the corrugated steel passage than it had been topside, but the atmosphere was humid and smelled like rotten eggs. The air seemed to cling to his face like wet cheesecloth. It reminded Skinner of Vietnam, and the night he'd met Ramirez. Here he was, years later, plunging into a tunnel again in search of the man.

He unholstered his 1911. The weight of the weapon felt good in his hand—reassuring. Skinner glanced back and forth, wondering which way to go. The pipe stretched in both directions, and he saw nothing but shadows on either end. After a moment, he started forward. His shoes splashed in water. It was only ankle deep, but warm and tepid. The rotten egg stench grew stronger. Skinner wrinkled his nose, wondering what he was stepping in. He pushed the thought away and slogged ahead.

The pipe ran in a straight, horizontal line. The only sound was the steady, monotonous drip of water. The darkness was broken every few yards by shafts of light from sewer gratings and other openings. On a whim, he fumbled in his pocket and pulled out his mobile phone. When he flipped it open, he was surprised to discover that he still had service, albeit only one bar.

He wondered how he would explain himself if he was caught down here. What if he encountered a sanitation worker, or a police officer? He'd be hard pressed to explain why he had violated a crime scene, let alone offer a reason why an Assistant Director from the FBI was stumbling around in the sewers beneath Washington D.C. in the middle of the night.

Then he heard a scream.

The tunnel seemed to vibrate from the noise. The shriek echoed all around him, the sound continuing on even after its issuer had stopped. He couldn't be sure, but he thought it had come from directly ahead of him. Skinner pressed forward, quickening his pace. His shoes splashed loudly in the water. After a moment, the pipe began to curve. He rounded the bend, and nearly screamed himself.

There, illuminated by a shaft of streetlight filtering down from above, crouched an acid flashback from Vietnam. It was a man-rat, except much bigger than the one he had hallucinated all those years ago. Tattered rags clung to its hairy, sleekly-muscled frame, and something shiny and silver dangled around its neck. Its pointed snout and coarse whiskers were slick with blood. So were the long, filthy talons at its fingertips. Another set of black claws protruded from the toes of its boots. The beast's pointed ears twitched. The stench wafting off the man-rat was terrible, even worse than the smell of the sewer.

The creature was hunched over the still-twitching body of a homeless man. The victim had been disemboweled, and steam rose from the open wound. Horrified, Skinner realized that the man was still alive, even as the were-rat reached into the open cavity with its two clawed hands and pulled out more warm organs to feast upon.

The monster gazed up at him and squealed. The sound was much like the feral shriek he and Lybeck had heard in Vietnam. But while that one had echoed of pain, this one promised anger.

"Don't move," Skinner said. His voice was barely a whisper. Suddenly, his mouth seemed to have gone dry. "Keep your hands up and step away from him."

The creature blinked its beady black eyes and tensed. There was a malevolent intelligence in that stare.

Skinner's attention was drawn once again to the silver object hanging around the beast's neck. He realized it was a pair of dogtags.

"Ramirez? Is that you?"

At this, the rat-thing seemed confused. It glanced down at its unfinished meal, and then back up at Skinner. Then, with another squeal, it leapt to its feet.

Skinner fired two shots, aiming for center mass. The creature tumbled backward against the pipe. Then, it pivoted, lashing out with its massive tail. The appendage struck Skinner in the chest, knocking him to the ground. His handgun skittered away in the darkness.

Gasping, Skinner sat up. His pants and coat were soaked with foul sewer water, and his glasses were fogged over. He hurriedly wiped the slime from them as best as he could, and then scrambled around for his weapon. He found it lying slightly above the water level. When he turned back, the creature was gone, but he could hear the echoes of its talons against metal as it fled.

He bent over and checked the victim's pulse, not expecting to find one. Sure enough, the man was dead. Rising to his feet, Skinner hurried off in pursuit. He noticed a splash of blood against the side of the tunnel, and knew that he'd wounded the—whatever it was. It couldn't be real. There wasn't enough light down here, and the situation was enough like what had happened in Vietnam that his mind was playing tricks on him. If Agent Scully had been here, she'd have verified the same thing.

Soon, the sound of his quarry's scrabbling ceased. Skinner slowed his pace, wondering if the killer had stopped, and was waiting to ambush him, or if it had given him the slip and escaped. When he rounded another turn, he saw that neither had been the case.

Ramirez sat in the water, legs outstretched, shoulders slumped, resting his chin upon his chest. He was dressed in the same rags the creature had worn, but they were looser now, barely clinging to his frame. The dogtags were still around his neck. At the sound of Skinner's approach, he raised his head wearily. His mouth and hands were smeared with blood. More blood streamed from the bullet wounds in his chest.

"Ramirez? Is that really you?"

The injured man frowned. "Who's there?"

"It's Skinner. The Marine. We met in Vietnam."

"W-walt?" Despite his pain, Ramirez grinned. "Holy shit! It really is you, isn't it?"

Skinner approached him cautiously, weapon at the ready. Ramirez shook his head.

"You don't need that, Walt. Not anymore. I'm dying. A lot of the shit from movies isn't true. You don't need silver bullets. Regular bullets work just fine."

"Ramirez... I..."

"It's okay. It's okay. I want this. This is good."

Skinner holstered his weapon and knelt down beside him. He pulled out his phone and saw that he still had a weak signal.

"Hang on," he said. "I'll call for help. Just stay with me."

"No," Ramirez wheezed. "Don't call anyone. Just stay with me."

"Bullshit. We need to get you help or you're going to die."

"I want to die, Walt. But I don't want to die alone. Just stay with me, okay? Please? Stay with me, like before."

Nodding, Skinner slipped the phone back into his pocket. Then, without hesitation, he reached out, took Ramirez's bloody hand, and held it.

"What...what happened to you?"

Ramirez coughed blood. "It was back in that tunnel. You should have let me die that night, but I don't blame you, Walt. You were just trying to help. But when I got attacked...the bite...it infected me, I guess. It didn't happen right away. They medevac'd me out of the jungle, and I did two weeks in a hospital in Saigon before they shipped me back to the world. Before the end of the month, I was back in the States. And that's when it happened."

"When what happened?"

"The change. It comes once a month, kinda like a woman's period, I guess. Doesn't seem to be connected to the moon or anything like that. Sometimes it happens early. Other times it comes late. But once a month…"

He broke off as another round of coughing racked his body. Blood flew from his mouth and nose. When the spasm ended, he gasped for breath.

"Once a month, I turn into this. I don't want to… but I can't help it. And it's hungry… it gets so hungry, Walt…"

"Just rest," Skinner choked, the words catching in his throat.

"Soon… I will. But I need to tell… need … I've done some… bad things, Walt. Some really bad shit. Worse than… worse than anything we did over there. I've been… trapped all this time. Caught between two masters… you know? Me… and the other. And when it takes control… when it takes control, I can't help myself… I feel so goddamned guilty… I don't want to be trapped… anymore… but I couldn't… I couldn't make the choice… myself."

He trailed off, and his breath hitched in his chest. Skinner squeezed his hand, certain that he was dead, but then Ramirez wheezed.

"Do you… understand, Walt?"

Closing his eyes, Skinner nodded. "I do."

Ramirez squeezed his hand and smiled.

"That's… twice you've… saved me now… jarhead."

Then he stopped breathing again, this time for good.

Skinner pulled him close, and wept in the darkness.

"I want to know what happened down there."

The speaker angrily jabbed a smoldering Morley cigarette butt into the ashtray on Skinner's desk. Then he shook another cigarette out of his pack and lit it.

"I told you. He was responsible for attacking and murdering several people."

"I want details, Mr. Skinner."

Skinner nodded at a manila folder on the desk. "If you want details, they're all right there in the police report."

"You know damn well what I mean. You don't seem to appreciate your position. Perhaps I need to remind you."

"If you have a problem with my performance, maybe you should take it up with the Director. Or talk to Security Chief Blevins. I understand he's on good terms with you."

The smoking man's eyes narrowed. "What's that supposed to mean?"

"It means maybe you should go hang out in his office. I'm busy."

"I see." He exhaled a large cloud of smoke. "Perhaps I'll have to look into your workload."

Skinner shrugged trying to appear nonchalant. Then he pulled the ashtray toward him.

"One other thing. I'd appreciate it if you didn't smoke in here."

"There are worse things than can happen to a person than second hand smoke, Mr. Skinner."

He reached across the desk and snuffed the half-smoked cigarette out in the ashtray. Then, without another word, he left, slamming the office door behind him.

Sighing, Skinner opened a desk drawer and put the ashtray inside. Then he slid the drawer shut and stared out the window. His fists curled at his sides. He didn't realize he was crying again until he felt the wetness roll down his cheeks. He thought back to what Ramirez had said the night before—his dying words. Of how he'd been caught between two masters, and unable to make a choice for himself.

Then, with the smoke still lingering in the air, Skinner stood up and decided to go check on Mulder.

THE END

BACK IN EL PASO MY LIFE WILL BE WORTHLESS

By Keith R.A. DeCandido

THE J. EDGAR HOOVER BUILDING
WASHINGTON, D.C.
3rd APRIL, 1994, 9:17 a.m.

S pecial Agent Jack Colt arrived at the Assistant Director's office feeling very much like a schoolkid who was sent to the principal's office. Usually the Assistant Special Agent in Charge doled out his assignments, but it was the ASAC who told him to report to AD Skinner.

The AD's assistant smiled at him. "One moment, please." She pushed a button on her phone and said, "Agent Colt is here."

Skinner's tinny voice sounded over her phone's speaker. "Send him in."

Colt nodded to the assistant and opened the wooden door to Skinner's expansive office. The AD was standing at his desk, back to the window, while a familiar man in a plaid shirt, jeans, and cowboy boots sat in one of the guest chairs. The latter rose to his feet, running one hand over his balding head.

"Thanks for coming, Agent Colt," Skinner said. He always sounded like he was speaking through a clenched jaw. "I believe you know Detective Johnson."

"Of course." He reached out to shake the man's hand, and Martin Johnson of the El Paso Police Department returned it firmly. "What brings you up from El Paso, Martin?" His face fell. "Oh, Christ, don't tell me Nobilis is putting together another appeal?"

Johnson sat back down. "No, but I reckon he'll be puttin' one together soon. I'm afraid we've found two more bodies. Brunette women, both strangled, sliced across the stomach—"

"So it's a copycat."

"—and with the skin cream on the women's nether regions."

Colt winced. "Somebody must've let that out to the public."

"No sir, they did not," Johnson said tightly. "As God is my witness, the only folks who know that particular detail in El Paso are Doc Gardner, me, and Detective Martinez. That's why I flew up here instead'a calling. Loose lips sinkin' ships and all that."

Colt shook his head. "And Nobilis is still in prison?"

"Hell, he's in solitary. He ain't had no visitors, and he ain't sent no mail out, and we ain't let him see any'a the mail he gets."

"Who's he get mail from?"

Johnson shrugged. "The usual—groupies, lawyers, fetishists. He don't see none of it, so it ain't that. I'm thinkin' we got the wrong guy. Again."

"That's not possible," Colt snapped.

Skinner snapped right back. "That's enough, Agent Colt. Obviously, this new set of murders needs to be investigated."

"Look," Johnson said, "most'a the murders we gotta deal with back home are morons killin' other morons. Kids fightin' over sneakers, drug dealers fightin' over street corners, men fightin' over women. This freako stuff is outta our league, which is why we called y'all in the first place two years ago."

Colt noticed the file on Skinner's desk. "May I?"

Skinner nodded.

Picking it up, Colt said, "You called us in, Martin, because more murders kept happening after you put people in jail. You arrested Arlo Montrose, then two more murders. You arrested Buck Halverson, then four more murders. You arrested Jebediah Zipkis, and then five more murders and I'm on a plane to El Paso."

"An' *you* arrested Frank Nobilis, and now we got two more."

"I arrested Nobilis because he's who the evidence pointed to. Evidence doesn't lie."

Skinner's phone buzzed, followed by his assistant's voice over the speaker. "Agents Scully and Mulder are here."

Colt's head snapped up toward the AD.

Skinner pushed a button on the phone. "Send them in."

The door opened to a tall, skinny dark-haired man in a gray suit very much like the one Colt was wearing, and a petite redhead in a green pantsuit.

Pointing at the two new arrivals, Colt asked, "What're the two nutjobs doing here?"

Smirking, Fox Mulder said, "Actually we prefer the term 'sanity challenged'. And technically, *I'm* the nutjob. Scully here's the skeptic."

"Agents Scully and Mulder have a lot of experience with cases that are out of the ordinary," Skinner said.

Rolling his eyes, Colt said, "Oh, please. This isn't one of Mulder's whackadoodle alien things—it's a serial killer. And yes," he said quickly as Mulder was opening his mouth, "I know you worked in Behavioral Sciences and Violent Crimes."

"Actually," Mulder said, "I was just going to ask if we could sit down."

Johnson had risen to his feet, prompting Skinner to say, "Detective Johnson, this is Special Agent Fox Mulder and his partner, Special Agent Dana Scully. They'll be assisting Special Agent Colt."

Mulder shook the man's hand, as did Scully. "Pleasure to be meetin' you both," Johnson said. "I gotta hit the road—I'm flyin' back tonight. I'll pick y'all up at the airport tomorrow."

"Thank you, Detective," Scully said with a small smile.

Colt turned his gaze upon Skinner. "I work alone, sir."

"No, Agent Colt, you work for the Federal Bureau of Investigation. Whether or not you are permitted to flout FBI procedure regarding partnership is entirely up to the people who supervise you. While your ASAC is willing to indulge you on the majority of your cases, I am not willing to do so on this case. All three of you are on a plane to El Paso tomorrow morning to investigate these latest murders, see if they match the ones that Frank Nobilis is in prison for. My assistant will send you your tickets through interoffice."

Colt blew out a long breath. "Happy happy, joy joy. Fine, we'll fly to El Paso."

VISTA ATLANTIC FLIGHT 1013
IN TRANSIT BETWEEN WASHINGTON, D.C. AND DALLAS, TEXAS
4th APRIL

"You know, I get why you two were assigned to me now."

Colt was staring at Mulder and Scully, sitting across the aisle from him. The Bureau had sprung for first-class seats, which Colt had made a mental note to thank Skinner for, and Colt had been fortunate enough not to have a seatmate. The X-files goons were in the two seats across from him. Mulder had a Walkman in his lap, headphones in his ears, eyes closed. He was in the window seat, leaving Scully to read over files in the aisle seat.

Scully removed her reading glasses, set the file down on the tray table, and stared at him, green eyes flashing. "And why is that, Agent Colt?"

"Same reason why the Bureau keeps your little goon squad running. Keeps the clearance rate up."

"Excuse me?" Scully asked with a frown.

"C'mon, for what other reason would you guys be allowed to continue? You get all the crazy cases that can't actually be closed, but since you're a special unit, you don't get counted with the regular stats. So the public thinks that we have a better clearance rate than we actually have and they feel safer."

"You really believe that?"

"You *don't*? C'mon, Agent Scully, I spent last night looking over your recent case history." Colt started enumerated on his fingers the files he'd read last night while staying late at the office. If he *was* going to be stuck with these garbanzos, he wanted an idea of their casework. "In the last few months alone, we've got Mount Avalon: four deaths, two people missing and presumed dead, no arrests. Worcester, Massachusetts: a woman raped and assaulted, two orderlies murdered, Agent Mulder assaulted, no arrests. Milford Haven, Massachusetts: six people killed, a woman missing and presumed dead, no arrests. The USS *Ardent*: almost the entire crew missing and presumed dead, no arrests. Gibsonton, Florida: three people murdered, the suspect still missing, no arrests. Murray, Virginia: three members of a family, including a three-year-old, murdered, and you guessed it, no arrests."

"We've also closed a few cases. The chicken plant in Dudley, Arkansas, the murders in Fairfield, Idaho and the INS station in North Carolina, the death fetishist in Minneapolis..."

Colt held up a hand. "Yeah, sure, you've run into a couple—and I gotta give you credit for that loony Pfaster in Minneapolis, that was a good bust—but let's face it, the only reason the Bureau puts up with your crap clearance rate is that it makes the rest of us look good."

Scully shook her head. "That's one theory."

"Look, whatever, but I prefer to work alone, all right? You two can come along and cover the Bureau's ass in case it winds up going into the toilet, but stay out of my way when we get down there. I've had enough of partners." Then he recalled something else he'd read the previous night. "And I think you're in a good position to understand why."

"How's that?"

"The last regular partner I had got shot in the head. And he was already pretty crazy before that, and the bullet rattling around in his cranium just made him worse. Name of Duane Barry."

Scully went rigid. Most people wouldn't notice any difference, but he could see her entire body freeze up, even though there was almost no discernible change to her facial expression.

"He was always wound too tight even before he caught a bullet. Always talking about himself in the third person, it was like being partnered with Bob Dole." He gave her an apologetic look. "I'm sorry you had to go through that with him."

"I'm fine." Scully said those two words with the same lack of conviction that relatives of murder victims did when people idiotically asked them how they were doing.

"Either way, after two years of being partnered with *that* jackass, you can see why I'm not exactly eager to embrace the notion of teamwork."

Scully had been staring at an indeterminate point on the plane's floor, but now she looked up and stared intently right at Colt once again. Despite everything, Colt actually flinched, and then decided that Agent Scully must've been damn good at interrogations...

She said, "You mentioned our clearance rate. Maybe it's not what it could be, but at the very least, we've been able to put a stop to more than one tragedy before it could happen, or failing that, before it could get worse. And the successes we have had are due to Agent Mulder and I working *together*."

Colt shrugged. "If you say so. But I got a lot more closed cases under my name than you do, or that I did when I was partnered with your erstwhile kidnapper."

EL PASO COUNTY MEDICAL EXAMINER'S OFFICE
EL PASO, TEXAS
4th APRIL

"Damn."

Colt regarded the two bodies on slabs with a depressing sense of *déjà vu*.

"Something wrong, Agent Colt?" Mulder asked.

"Hm?" Colt looked up, having momentarily forgotten that he had two tagalongs. The three of them had been led by an assistant to this exam room, containing the two latest victims of what local news had been calling "the El Paso Ripper" for the past several years. "No, just—well, up until now, I was kind of half-entertaining the notion that EPPD screwed up, that this was just an unrelated double murder. But looking at these two now..."

A voice came from the doorway. "Nice to see you're still a judgmental bastard, Jack."

Looking over, Colt smiled at the entrance of the stooped-over form of Louise Gardner, the chief medical examiner for El Paso County. "Always, Louise, you know that."

"You brought company this time?"

Indicating the other agents with his left hand, Colt said, "Dr. Louise Gardner, these are Agents Dana Scully and Fox Mulder. They'll be helping me out."

"Seriously? Your parents named you Fox? You got brothers named ABC, NBC, and CBS, too?"

Without missing a beat, Mulder said, "My oldest brother is named Dupont, but he's kind of the black sheep of the family."

Scully interjected before the banter could continue: "I'm also a medical doctor. I'd like to assist on the autopsy."

Gardner grinned, showing off her dentures. "Agent Scully, you just made my assistant's day. He's been dreading this, and he'll be more than happy to defer to you."

Colt nodded. "I need to reinterview the witnesses."

"I'll come with you," Mulder said.

With a wince, Colt started, "Look, Agent Mulder why don't you—?"

"Do what Skinner asked and back you up? Sure." Mulder shot a sardonic grin at Colt.

"Fine." Colt let out a very long, very annoyed sigh.

"I'm gonna get started on Mrs. Underwood here," Gardner said, pointing at the body of Eleanor Underwood, the first victim. "Agent Scully, whyn't you scrub in and tackle Miss Alvarez?"

Scully nodded, and went over to the closet to get a set of scrubs.

Colt sighed, grateful that he'd managed to ditch one of them. With luck, he'd be able to dump Mulder, too.

The first person Colt and Mulder talked to was the husband of the first victim, Todd Underwood.

"Can you tell us where you were on the night of the 2nd, Mr. Underwood?"

"I *told* the cops all this already. Why you askin' me this stuff?"

"We're not the cops, Mr. Underwood," Colt said patiently, "we're the FBI, and we believe there may be a connection between Eleanor's death and other deaths in the city over the past few years."

Underwood blinked. "Say what? You talkin' about the El Paso Ripper? Man, they got that sonofabitch in jail. Anyhow, I was at work."

Mulder then asked, "Did Eleanor meet anyone new recently? Or did someone come back into her life that she hadn't seen in a while?"

"Nah. I mean, she worked at one'a them call centers, and they got people comin' and goin' all'a time, so there was always new people there, but that's it."

Frowning, Mulder checked the file. "This says she's unemployed."

"Yeah, she got fired last week."

Colt sighed. That wasn't in the file, and he made a mental note to yell at Martin Johnson later.

Their next stop was Dona Alvarez's roommate, Katarina Rossov. They both worked as nurses in the Bliss Private Hospital just outside of town.

"I'm glad you're here, actually," Rossov said with a slight Russian accent. "That detective asked me to telephone him if I recalled something, but I am afraid that I misplaced the business card he handed me. There was a man at the hospital who was very rude to Dona. He was visiting another client—this was about a week before she was attacked. It was either the 30th or the 31st. I know it was before the 1st, because it was before the doctors decided to play April Fool's jokes on the nurses." Rossov's tone indicated how little she thought of that particular tradition.

"Why didn't you mention this to the police?" Colt asked.

Rossov looked sheepish. "I had forgotten about it as soon as it happened, honestly—we get rude people in the hospital all the time—but I remembered this man after thinking because he was *so* rude."

"Can you provide a description of him?"

"I am afraid not, but our hospital uses videotape surveillance. They keep all the tapes once they have been fully recorded on, for security purposes."

Colt asked a few more questions, confirming as it said in the report that Alvarez didn't have a boyfriend, then he and Mulder took their leave.

"Well," Colt said, "I don't want to get too optimistic, but we're already in better shape than when we started, between this cranky hospital visitor and the job that Underwood got fired from. I don't want to count out the husband—though it's too bad that Alvarez wasn't seeing anyone."

Mulder frowned. "What difference does that make? Serial killers like the El Paso Ripper almost never know their victims intimately. Sometimes they suffer delusions that they do, but they're most often strangers. For that matter, all the people that the EPPD *and* you imprisoned have been strangers to the victims."

"Yeah, and they've all been the wrong guy. Maybe it's time to take a different approach."

"Intimate contact doesn't make sense," Mulder said, "unless you think there's a huge field of commonality between an unemployed telemarketer and a nurse at a private hospital." He smiled. "Besides, people don't usually need a *reason* to want to kill a telemarketer. And anyhow, your theory still holds—we already talked to Alvarez's significant other."

Colt frowned. "What?"

Indicating the small house with a shake of his head, Mulder said, "Didn't you take a good look at the place? Only one bedroom, and the living room sofa doesn't fold out. They slept in the same room, likely the same bed. They probably kept it quiet since they work together, and private hospitals in Texas tend to be funded by old-money Southern types who wouldn't look kindly on a homosexual relationship."

For several seconds, Colt just looked at Mulder. He wanted to argue the point, but looking back over his memory of the house, all the clues were there, not to mention how grief-stricken Johnson said that Alvarez was over her roommate dying.

"Sonofabitch."

Mulder smirked. "Not bad for a sanity-challenged special agent."

Colt sighed. He hoped Mulder wasn't going to be this self-righteous for the *entire* case. "Fine, I think at this point we need to split up. I'll go check out the place where Underwood worked, you go to Bliss Hospital and go through the tapes." If he *was* going to get saddled with partners, he was damn well going to let one of *them* do the drudgework.

THE DEW DROP INN, ROOM 120
EL PASO, TEXAS
4th APRIL

Very reluctantly, Colt had to admit that having two other pairs of feet to do legwork had its uses. He sat in his hotel room's comfy chair while the X-goons sat in the two chairs by the table near the window.

Scully was filling them in on the autopsies of the two latest victims first. "There were no real surprises in either case. Which is unfortunate, since something new might provide us with a lead. However, both Eleanor Underwood and Dona Alvarez were killed by a serrated blade cutting open their carotid artery. Both stomachs were slashed post-mortem, and both women had a skin cream applied to their genitalia. The cream is still out for testing, but both Dr. Gardner and I are fairly certain it's the same cream that was used in the other El Paso Ripper killings."

Colt snarled. "Can we *please* not call them that?"

Giving a small smile, Scully said, "Sorry, that's the phrase Dr. Gardner used. She's an excellent pathologist. In any event, just as with the others, there's no useful trace evidence. However, two things did give me pause."

That got Colt's attention. As Scully had indicated, something discrepant from the previous murders would have been useful, but hearing that it was the same thing again just made him want to bang his head against the wall.

Scully continued. "We did find some trace evidence, but it tested as inert matter."

"So?"

"I checked the files, and that same inert matter was found on several other victims. I had Dr. Gardner pull the particles from the other cases so the lab can run more tests." She sighed. "I may need to ship them to Quantico, though, the lab here is not exactly up to standards."

"Yeah, welcome to West Texas," Colt muttered. "After the last time I was here, the mayor, the governor, and I had a long talk about the inadequacy of the labs here. Nice to see they listened."

Mulder shook his head. "I'm shocked, *shocked*, to learn that politicians misled you."

Colt shot Mulder a look. "*Casablanca*? Didn't think that was your kind of film." Colt had no idea if the rumors about Mulder's tape collection were true, although Agent DelVecchio had insisted that those tapes were his if something ever happened to Mulder.

Since Mulder didn't rise to the bait, Colt turned his attention back to Scully. "You said there were two things?"

Nodding, Scully said, "There was dust in the mouth. Lab says it was disintegrated bone fragments."

Colt leaned back, disappointed. "Yeah, that was in all the bodies. Figured it was part of the fetish thing."

Mulder, though, after sitting slumped in his chair, sat ramrod straight all of a sudden. "Bone fragments? You sure?"

"The lab's not so bad that it can't identify bone," Scully said with another of her small smiles. "Yes, I'm sure."

"It could be corpse dust."

"What kind of dust?" Colt did not like where this was going.

"Several Native American tribes have legends of skin-walkers— shapechangers who can take on the forms of different animals. Agent Scully and I encountered one last year in Browning, Montana."

Colt shot Scully a look, but she had her poker face on. Of course, she wasn't denying it...

Then he recalled one of the files on a case they had in Browning, where a local Native American was killed by a ranch owner, who was then killed, probably by the first victim's son, who was shot by Scully in self-defense. Mulder's report had mentioned skin-walkers and werewolves, while Scully's only made a passing mention of "clinical lycanthropy."

Mulder was still babbling. "In Navajo folklore, the *yee naaldlooshii* blows corpse dust into a victim's face. It's made from ground-up bones, ideally the bones of a small child."

Speaking in what Colt instantly identified as a long-suffering tone, Scully said, "Mulder, even if this is like what we saw in Browning, in every legend, skin-walkers take on the form of animals."

"True, but it's not much of a leap to go from changing into an animal to changing into a person. Scientifically speaking, it's probably easier, because there's less shifting of mass."

A bitter laugh burst from Colt's mouth. "I can't believe you used the phrase 'scientifically speaking' in *that* sentence."

"But it does fit the evidence," Mulder said insistently. "A killer who can change shape would explain why we have the same murders committed with the same methods, including the portions not revealed to the public, while having four wildly different suspects. It also might explain the inert matter. It could be the altered skin cells that the skin-walker uses."

Tightly, Colt said, "Agent Mulder, I know for a fact that you graduated at the top of your class at Quantico—which leads me to think that it was a particularly dumb class that year—so I know that you simply *had* to be there for the part where they told you that an investigator doesn't come up with a theory and find evidence to fit it. We find evidence and *then* concoct a theory." Mulder started to talk again, but Colt cut him off. "I don't want to hear it. What did you find out at the hospital?"

For a few seconds, Mulder just looked at Colt with that vacant stare of his. Then he grabbed a folder filled with several 8 ½ x 11" sheets of paper. "Private hospitals get all the best toys. Their security videos record onto super-8 tapes and they have a four-color printer. This is the guy Nurse Rossov was talking about. He started yelling at Nurse Alvarez at a little after three p.m. on the 31st."

He handed Colt the folder. Opening it, he saw several slightly curled pieces of paper that felt a bit cool to the touch. Each sheet had screen captures from the surveillance tape of a tall man with short, dark hair and thick plastic-framed glasses arguing with Rossov. Each printout had a date and time stamp on the lower left-hand corner: "3/31/95 15:07," and so on.

Colt let out a huge grin. "We got him." He grabbed a file folder of his own. "Underwood was fired after she got into a fight with another tele-marketer, a guy named Orville Hobloch. And when I say 'fight,' I mean a physical altercation. I got the photocopy of the Hobloch's driver's license. The staff kept them on file."

He pulled out the photocopy in question and handed it to Scully.

The picture on the Texas state driver's license belonging to one Orville Hobloch was an almost perfect match for the picture of the person on Mulder's fancy color printout.

EL PASO POLICE DEPARTMENT HEADQUARTERS, CITY HALL
EL PASO, TEXAS
5th APRIL

"Look, I'm telling you, I didn't kill those women! I wasn't even in El Paso!"

Colt shook his head. They always pulled this.

EPPD had brought Orville Hobloch in without a fuss, as he was still unemployed and was sitting at home watching television, according to Detective Johnson. Now he was sitting in one of the small interrogation rooms in the portion of City Hall that was used by the local cops.

"Mr. Hobloch, we have video surveillance of you getting into a verbal altercation with one of the victims, and eyewitness accounts of you getting into a physical altercation with another."

He shook his head. "I knew it. I knew you bastards would try to tie Ellie's death to me. Look, yeah, we got into a fight. She was an uptight bitch and she got in my face. But I didn't kill her. And I don't even know who the other one *was*."

"Nurse Dona Alvarez." Colt placed the color printouts Mulder had gotten in front of him on the metal table. "This is you yelling at her on the 31st. She was dead two days later."

"Look, I didn't—" Hobloch looked at the printouts and his eyes went wide under his plastic-frame glasses. "Holy crapola. That guy looks just like me."

"It *is* you."

"No, it isn't!" Hobloch started fidgeting in the chair. "You said that was the 31st? I wasn't even in El Paso; I was in Corpus Christi. After I got fired, I went to visit my Dad out there. He doesn't have a guest room, and I can't sleep on his couch without it chewing up my back, so I stayed in a Days Inn. I was there from the 30th to the 3rd, including when that pop singer got shot."

"What?" Colt knew that a Latina singer named Selena had been shot by the president of her own fan club in Corpus Christi on the 31st. He'd only paid mild attention to it because DelVecchio's daughter was heartbroken and he couldn't shut up about how little Maya was pounding her chest over it.

For the next two hours, Colt continued his interrogation of Hobloch.

The man was temperamental, and he lost it and yelled more than once. It wasn't hard to see how he got into an altercation with Underwood. But it *was* getting hard to see how such a hothead could be the meticulous serial killer he'd been chasing.

At one point, a knock came at the door, and Scully stuck her head in. "Excuse me, Agent Colt? Your wife's on the phone. She says it's urgent."

Since Scully knew damn well that Colt wasn't married, she was letting him know that she needed to see him outside without Hobloch knowing anything was amiss.

"Excuse me," he said, following Scully out the door.

As soon as she shut the door behind him, Scully said, "It's not him. He didn't kill Alvarez, and I don't know who Agent Mulder saw on the tape, but that wasn't him, either." She led him down the hall to a room with a VCR and a television. Mulder and Johnson were already there.

"Detective Johnson, Agent Scully, and I have been busy while you've been distracting Hobloch. Take a look at this," Mulder said, and he pushed PLAY on the VCR's remote.

"I got this from my granddaughter," Johnson said. "She's a huge Selena fan—got a shrine in her bedroom, even."

The tape started showing a local news story from Corpus Christi about Selena's murder. They were interviewing people who were staying in the same hotel where Selena was shot. The first was a hysterical woman, the second a black man who was pissed at all the people in the way of his hotel experience, and then a very familiar man with plastic framed glasses.

"Look, I think it's a tragedy, but more because she was such a young woman. I mean, I don't listen to the music myself, I think it's garbage what kids listen to these days, but she wasn't even 25 years old yet. That's really just horrible."

As he spoke, the caption at the bottom of the screen read ORVILLE HOBLOCH.

Colt shook his head. "That isn't possible."

Johnson said, "I talked to the hotel. They kept *real* close track of who was stayin' and for how long on account'a what happened. Hobloch was there the dates he said he was, which means there ain't no way he killed either Alvarez or Underwood."

"All right, fine," Colt said. "He's out as a suspect. Go ahead and kick him."

"We still have a suspect," Mulder said. "Somebody who looks *a lot* like Hobloch was at that hospital yelling at Alvarez."

Pointing a finger at Mulder, Colt said, "Don't give me that shapeshifter crap, Mulder. We'll check the evidence again, interview more witnesses, and find out who did this and how they found out about the skin cream."

Rising to his feet, Johnson said, "'Scuse me?"

Scully cut off Johnson before he could continue in that hostile tone. "Agent Colt, the press coverage of these latest two murders has had *no* mention of the skin cream. It's probably still a secret."

"Well, obviously Frank Nobilis didn't commit *these* two murders," Colt said, "but the evidence that he killed the others is pretty compelling. Certainly the jury thought so."

"Actually," Mulder said, "I've been looking over the files on Nobilis, and there are a lot of holes in the case. There's no physical evidence tying Nobilis to the scenes, the eyewitness accounts—"

Colt nearly exploded, and actually felt an urge to hit Mulder. "Where the *hell* do you get off? You're here to *assist* me on *this* case, Mulder! You've got *no* business going back over old files."

To Colt's annoyance, it was again Scully who spoke. "They might be the same case. The whole reason you came down here is because it looked like it might be the same killer. We have to look at the case against Nobilis for the same reason why *you* looked at the cases against Montrose, Halverson, and Zipkis before going after Nobilis two years ago."

Colt glowered at Scully. He couldn't come up with a good response to that, so he stormed out of the video room rather than try to utter a bad one.

THE DEW DROP INN, ROOM 120
EL PASO, TEXAS
7th APRIL

For the next two days, Colt decided to hammer on Hobloch. He was on the videotape, he was the only thing Alvarez and Underwood had in common, he *had* to be the one.

Unfortunately, he had an airtight alibi, especially since the footage of his being interviewed in the wake of Selena being shot was picked up by several stations. To add insult to injury, he rented a car to make the nine-hour drive to Corpus Christi and back, and his credit card was used at several gas stations and service stops along I-10 and I-35. The mileage on the rental car when he returned it matched the fifteen hundred miles it would have taken to drive there and back, plus a little extra.

Mulder and Scully weren't doing much better. Reluctantly, Colt met with them in his hotel room again at seven p.m. The nutjobs were kind enough to bring some takeout from a local Tex-Mex place.

After swallowing a bite of enchilada, Scully said, "We reinterviewed the witnesses you talked to about Nobilis. Sue Dietrich said she wasn't sure it was him anymore. Don Egan said you quoted him out of context."

Colt rolled his eyes as he picked up his chicken taco. "Yeah, there was a reason why we didn't put *him* on the stand. What about that old guy, Jim Tolley?"

"He refused to speak to us, saying you coerced him into testifying."

"What? I did no such thing! Dammit! Two more murders, and now everyone's backing off." Colt slammed a fist on the desk.

After sipping his soda, Mulder said, "It wouldn't be the first time that people rushed to make an eyewitness account in the heat of the moment. Especially regarding a serial killer that has been around as long as the El Paso Ripper has."

"So we've got nothing?" Colt asked.

With a tilt of his head, Mulder replied, "Well, we've got a good case for Nobilis's appeal."

"That isn't even a little funny, Mulder."

"It wasn't meant to be."

Colt smirked. "Yeah, well it's hard to tell with that deadpan of yours." The smirk fell and he thought for a moment while gnawing on his taco. Much as he hated to admit it, the nutjobs were on the right track. "All right, let's take what you're doing one step further. I want to look back over *everything*, going all the way back to the first murder back in '88."

The phone rang. Colt climbed out of his chair and went over to the table between the two double beds and picked up the receiver. "Colt."

"This is Detective Johnson. You need to get down to Concordia Cemetery right away, Agent Colt. We got us another body."

CONCORDIA CEMETERY
EL PASO, TEXAS
7th APRIL

"Keep the damn press out of here, will you please?"

An EPPD uniform grabbed the photographer who had apparently climbed the metal fence on Yandell Drive to get into the cemetery to see the latest victim of "the El Paso Ripper." The paparazzo was tossed out the cemetery gate, where plenty of other members of the fourth estate were congregated about.

The latest victim was named Julianne Koogler. Just like the others, it was a brunette woman with a slash across her belly, strangulation marks on her neck (but no evidence of a weapon that was used, just the ligature marks), skin cream applied to her genitalia, and dust in her mouth. Plus there was that inert material near the wounds.

Koogler had been placed on the ground of the cemetery, which was, unusually, more dirt than grass. It was the first cemetery Colt had visited that looked more like a ranch than a park.

Scully was off on the side talking on her cellular while Mulder examined the body alongside Colt. Pointing at the mouth, Mulder said, "More corpse dust."

"Enough with that, please," Colt said angrily.

Scully ended her call, lowering the small plastic antenna on her phone before pocketing it. "That was Quantico. They examined the inert material that was on all the crime scenes, and they don't have any answers. They did detect some DNA markers, but nothing they could identify."

"So it's from something alive?" Mulder asked.

"Maybe—but they can't figure out *what* it is. There's not enough there."

Colt frowned. "That doesn't make any sense."

"If anything about this case made sense," Scully said, "Ms. Koogler would probably still be alive."

"Yeah." Colt sighed. "All right, let's bag her up and get her away from the vipers. There's no blood here, so she was probably dumped."

Johnson had been chatting with uniforms and other detectives, and came over to where the three federal agents were standing. "We got us some good news there. Our bad guy made his first mistake. Whole mess'a people saw him dump the body."

"When?" Mulder asked.

"'Round 6:30 or so. Uniforms're takin' statements now."

Colt nodded. "Okay, get the body to Gardner. Agent Scully, if you'd be so kind as to assist her?"

Scully said, "Of course."

Colt noticed Mulder gazing out at the crowds of press and civilians all gathered at the entrance, held from squeezing through by a phalanx of cops. On the sidewalk by the metal fence on Stevens Street, several plain-clothes and uniformed officers were talking to civilians and taking notes. "Maybe we'll get lucky," Mulder said. "The witnesses to the previous victims caught glances and quick looks from far away. This is the first time we've got really solid eyewitness accounts. If he screwed that up, maybe he screwed up something else."

"Let's hope," Colt said.

As the three FBI agents walked past that part of the fence, one of the witnesses, a taller, older man wearing a cowboy hat, caught sight of them. "That's *him!*" he cried while pointing a finger right at Colt.

A short teenaged Latina woman suddenly let loose with a barrage of Spanish. Colt was rusty, but he recalled enough of the language to know that she was doing the same thing as the man in the cowboy hat: pointing at Colt and saying that he did it.

"What the hell?"

All the witnesses now were screaming and crying and pointing fingers right at Colt.

"That's him!"

"He's the killer!"

"Arrest that bastard, *now!*"

"*Ay dios, el asesino!*"

'Johnson glared at the trio, then said to Mulder, "Get him the hell outta here!"

Colt was just staring at the people who all looked at him with fear and loathing. "I don't—"

He felt Mulder's surprisingly strong grip on his arm. "Let's go."

But Colt just stood there, staring incomprehensibly. "How can they think that I—"

"Jack," Mulder said forcefully, and the nutjob's use of his first name finally snapped him out of it. "We have to go."

"Yeah, of course." He let Mulder lead him through the crowd, which was quickly mutating into an angry mob, calling for the head of Jack Colt.

EL PASO POLICE DEPARTMENT HEADQUARTERS, CITY HALL
EL PASO, TEXAS
8th APRIL

"Quite a view."

Colt turned away from the magnificent sight of the sun rising over the Franklin Mountains to see Scully standing behind him at the east-facing window of the police HQ section of El Paso's City Hall. She was still wearing blue scrubs from her all-night autopsy of Koogler, though she wasn't wearing the cap, gloves, or goggles.

While Colt shared Scully's understated appreciation of the view, he had bigger fish to fry. "What the hell's going on, Agent Scully?"

"I'm afraid there isn't a lot of good news," she said slowly. "The trace evidence is exactly the same as the other victims, but we're no closer to knowing what the inert material is or where they're getting ground-up bones from to put in the mouth. The only other biological trace we found belongs to the victim." She had been staring off to the side for a bit, but now she looked up to face Colt directly. "In addition, eight eyewitnesses describe the person who dumped the body in the cemetery as you. With two exceptions, that being a pair of sisters, none of the eight know each other, and didn't meet until they were brought here last night."

"They're crazy!" Colt took a deep breath to keep himself from getting hysterical. He'd been up all night. "Look, Dana, I didn't do this."

"I know you didn't, but these witnesses are sure that the perpetrator at least looked a lot like you." Scully blew out a breath. "I need you to account for your whereabouts yesterday."

Colt rolled his eyes. "You *know* my whereabouts."

"No, Jack," Scully said intently, "I *don't*. You've spent the last several days avoiding Mulder and me, keeping us away from you. Yesterday, we didn't see you at all until seven o'clock last night in the hotel, and only heard from you when I called you to check in first thing in the morning. That's an entire day—during which a murder happened and you were sighted dumping the body—where Agent Mulder and I can't back you up. And to make matters worse, you're familiar with the MO of the murders and you're a trained federal agent, so you have the means."

"All right, all right." He thought back over the day. "I was making phone calls from the hotel room, trying to find a hole in Hobloch's alibi."

"From the hotel phone?" Scully asked hopefully.

Colt shook his head. "No, I used my cellular. It's easier to keep all the calls there, easier on the expense reporting." He sighed. "And the reception was for crap, so I walked around outside until I could find three bars. I honestly have no idea where I went, I don't really know my way around this town."

"This isn't good, Jack."

"Yeah." He sighed. "I need a Coke." He wandered back down the hallway toward a vending machine. Reaching into his pants pocket, he was shocked to find nothing in the back left pocket. "Oh, for God's sake. I don't have my wallet."

"What happened to it?" Scully asked.

Colt thought back over the previous night. "I took it out to pay you guys for the Mexican food, and I must've left it on the desk when we got called to the cemetery." Relieved for so quotidian an explanation, he then turned to Scully. "I don't suppose I can borrow fifty cents for a Coke?"

"Unfortunately, scrubs don't have pockets." Scully actually smiled a little. The whole situation was absurd, and he was very grateful that she was the one talking to him. If it was Mulder, he'd be hip-deep in nonsense about shapeshifters.

Speaking of whom, Mulder turned the corner and said, "Scully, Colt, there you are. EPPD just got an anonymous tip that the killer is in a house on La Luz Avenue."

"Let's go," Colt said, eager to find *something* that would give them a proper break in this case—and one that didn't put his head on the chopping block.

"I'll meet you there," Scully said, heading to the women's room, no doubt to change out of her scrubs.

Colt and Mulder went downstairs to the motor pool to find Johnson and his partner Detective Martinez putting on Kevlar vests. Martinez silently handed one to Mulder, but Johnson was staring at Colt. "You ain't goin', Jack."

"Oh, come off it, Martin, I'm the lead investigator."

"You're a *suspect*, Jack. I can't—"

Holding up a hand, Colt said, "Stop it right there, *Detective*. Until I'm given instructions by someone a helluva lot higher up in the food chain than *you*, this is still *my* case. So either arrest me on the flimsy-ass evidence you have, or give me a damn Kevlar."

There was a brief, ugly pause, and then Johnson nodded at Martinez, who slowly reached into the trunk of the car and pulled out another vest.

By the time Colt had velcro'd himself into his, Scully had arrived and got a vest of her own.

As they sat in the back of the EPPD Chevy Cavalier, Mulder whispered to Colt, "You do realize that a shapeshifter would explain both how Hobloch could be in two places at once and how someone who looks just like you could kill Koogler, right?"

"Shut up, Mulder," Colt muttered.

They arrived at a one-story house on La Luz, the only one on the block that had the driveway gate shut and padlocked. The padlock itself had plenty of rust, too.

An EPPD SWAT team went in first, clearing the house, which didn't take too long, as the house looked abandoned.

Colt, Mulder, and Scully went in once the SWAT leader gave the all-clear. The place was all hardwood floors, with laminate that was starting to wear off, and the floor was covered in blood spatter at varying levels of dryness. No furniture at all, not even internal doors on any of the hinges.

But lots and lots of blood stains.

"Ladies and gentlemen," Colt said with a smile, "I think we may have us a crime scene."

"We've got more than that," Mulder said.

Turning Colt saw the agent going for a wallet that was sitting on a windowsill. "God, he left his *wallet*? Whoever called in the tip must've spooked him."

But Mulder was looking through the wallet with a haunted expression.

Colt stared at him. "What is it, Mulder?"

The wallet looked a lot like Colt's own, a simple brown leather fold-over, with clear plastic cardholders inside.

Mulder held the outermost cardholder, which revealed a very familiar

Maryland driver's license.

Colt felt his stomach rumble, and he suddenly found himself short of breath. "That—that can't be my wallet."

"Unless there's another Jackson P. Colt living in Gaithersburg, who has a Platinum American Express card and a membership to Blockbuster Video..." Mulder looked up, stricken. "I'm sorry, Agent Colt."

"So'm I," Johnson said, grabbing Colt by the arms. "Jackson Colt, you are under arrest for the murder of Julianne Koogler. You have the right to remain silent..."

EL PASO COUNTY JAIL
EL PASO, TEXAS
9th APRIL

"I'm sorry, Jack."

Colt found Mulder's words to be the coldest of comforts as he sat in the jail cell. He'd never been inside one of these when it was locked before. Visually, it wasn't all *that* much different from what it was like when the door was open, but psychologically, the difference was vast. Colt had never been claustrophobic, but it wasn't difficult to get such pangs now knowing that he was fully restricted to this tiny space.

There were six cells on this floor, but his was the only one occupied. A uniformed officer sat at a desk on the far end of the room, a TV monitor on the desk that showed that officer images of each of the cells.

He'd been arraigned within a few hours of being arrested. The prosecutor provided affidavits from Johnson and Martinez, the bastards, who said that Colt was surly and unstable and unpleasant and insulting, and then he said that Colt was a flight risk because of his FBI ties. And then he mentioned Barry and how his ex-partner's recent death while in FBI custody might have unhinged him.

"I called Skinner—well, actually, Scully called him. But he said the bureau can't do anything officially except cooperate with local authorities."

The judge was all too eager to remand him without bail until trial. After all, another judge had just granted Frank Nobilis an appeal hearing based on the reasonable doubt created by the murders of Dona Alvarez, Eleanor Underwood, and Julianne Koogler while Nobilis was incarcerated.

"For what it's worth, I think this just lends support to the shapeshifter theory. I believe the inert matter is the skin cells of the shapeshifter. Scully said it was DNA that they couldn't identify, and it would make sense that we wouldn't know what to look for in this kind of DNA profile."

Colt was barely paying attention to Mulder. None of it made any sense. How could Hobloch be in two places at once? How could someone who looked enough like Colt that eight different people swore it was him exist without his knowing about it? How could so much evidence point to so many different people who *weren't* the El Paso Ripper?

"Great," he muttered, "now *I'm* calling him the El Paso Ripper."

"What was that?" Mulder asked.

"Nothing." He shook his head. His life was falling apart, and all he could do was castigate himself for using a stupid nickname.

Mulder looked nonplussed for a second, then continued. "Well, anyhow, Agent Scully and I plan to—"

"Go home," interrupted the voice of Martin Johnson. The man himself was coming through the door. Scully came in behind him, looking annoyed.

"Excuse me?" Mulder got nonplussed again.

"The FBI has been uninvited from participating in this investigation, Agent Mulder," Johnson said formally. "This is a crime that ain't crossed state lines, so y'all are only here by our invitation. That invitation's been revoked."

"Detective, there's still a case to be solved here," Mulder started, but Johnson held a hand up.

"I don't wanna hear it, Agent Mulder. I'm sorry I flew to Washington, and I'm sorry this all happened. I want you an' Agent Scully outta my jurisdiction by tomorrow mornin'." He turned to look at Colt. Johnson's eyes were haggard and sad, Colt noticed, though he was hardly about to sympathize with the detective given his own position. "As for you, Jack—you'll be stayin' here in regular lockup. You'll get this floor to yourself. I ain't about to put no federal agent in a max security prison, your life wouldn't be worth a wooden peso. So you'll stay here until trial."

Mulder stared at Johnson. "You're making a mistake, Detective. The killer's still out there, he can look like anybody, and he'll kill again."

Colt rolled his eyes and lay down on the wafer-thin mattress on the rickety bunk. Count on good old Spooky Mulder to keep hammering the nonsense.

But was it nonsense? As he watched Mulder and Scully reluctantly leave the floor, each giving him an encouraging look before departing, Colt wondered if Mulder's notion was so crazy. After all, *somebody* was on that hospital video footage, and *somebody* dropped Koogler's body in the cemetery.

Johnson gave him a sympathetic look of his own, but while Colt was willing to accept such from Scully and Mulder, he had no interest in doing so with the one who put cuffs on him. "Get the hell out of here, Martin."

"I'm sorry 'bout this, Jack—but you said it yourself, the evidence don't lie."

With that, Colt was left alone with his thoughts.

No, not quite alone. There was the guard at the desk. About thirty seconds after Johnson left, the guard got up and walked over to the cell.

"I'm really sorry about all this, Agent Colt. If it makes you feel any better, they don't have any evidence supporting the notion that you killed any of the others. Just Miss Koogler. She was a sweet lady, I didn't particularly want to kill her like I did the others, but I needed to set you up."

Colt looked at the guard, whose nameplate read NIVEN. "What are you—"

"See, you were getting too close. Well, *you* weren't, Mulder and Scully were. Those two are good. Mulder actually colors outside the lines every once in a while, and Scully's brilliant. Between the two of them, they probably would've tracked me down. Hell, Mulder's the only one who recognized the corpse dust. I figured *somebody* from around these parts would get the reference, but no such luck. Anyhow, I couldn't afford to let you feds get too close, so I found a brunette to fit the profile, killed her in the usual way, and then framed you for her murder."

Now Colt was staring openly at Niven. "This can't be."

"Oh, it is. It was fun there for a while, watching Detective Johnson and then you run around like hamsters on a wheel. But now they're sending in the big guns. I can't have that, so I'm done. I'm leaving El Paso—probably won't even kill anymore. Honestly, the thrill of that was going away anyhow. I'll just go somewhere else, find another hobby to occupy myself."

Finally, Colt realized what was happening. "All right, Officer Niven, very funny, but I'm not in the mood for jokes."

"Oh, this is no joke, Agent Colt." He sighed. "Fine, I'll prove it to you."

To Colt's horror, Niven's features began to shift and move and undulate.

Colt's stomach rumbled, and bile rose in his throat as Niven's eyes changed position, his nose shrunk, his mouth widened, his skin tone altered.

"It can't be," he whispered. Mulder's nonsense was just that: the deranged ramblings of a brilliant mind that had been twisted by trauma, just like every third serial killer out there. Mulder's sister had gone missing when he was a kid, and he concocted some fantasy about aliens because that was easier for him to believe than his sister running away from home.

But that whole shapechanger garbage was just that: garbage. Things like that and aliens and werewolves and things that went bump in the night weren't *real*. Colt *knew* that.

Yet a different person stood before him now, wearing Officer Niven's uniform.

"You'll forgive me," this new person said with Niven's voice, "if I don't do that again. It *hurts*. S'why I usually only change shape once a year or so. But I wanted you to know the truth. I figured you deserved that much, since I went and ruined your life and all."

Colt continued his incredulous stare. "This isn't possible."

Niven shrugged his new shoulders. "Fine, don't believe it. Makes no difference to me one way or the other. Like I said, I'm leaving El Paso. Good luck with the trial."

Then Niven—or whoever he was now—just turned and left.

Colt was now alone on the floor.

Mulder was right.

The El Paso Ripper was still out there.

And he would never catch him.

Jack Colt screamed.

REPORT FILED BY SPECIAL AGENT DANA SCULLY
ON THE "EL PASO RIPPER" CASE
11th APRIL

S.A. Jackson Colt was found dead in his cell this morning, an apparent suicide. Officer Darren Niven of the El Paso Police Department, who was assigned to be guarding S.A. Colt's cell, has gone missing.

S.A. Colt's suicide has led to the murder of Julianne Koogler being closed, but the murders of Dona Alvarez and Eleanor Underwood are still open, since S.A. Colt was here in Washington when those murders took place. Detective Martin Johnson of the EPPD has stated that he intends to search for an accomplice of S.A. Colt's who might still be operating in El Paso. In a press conference, Detective Johnson stated unequivocally that Frank Nobilis remains the guilty party for all previous "El Paso Ripper" murders, with S.A. Colt and his theoretical accomplice responsible for the three copycats.

S.A. Mulder's hypothesis that the perpetrator might be a shapechanger is unsupported by any evidence, although there has yet to be a proper explanation for the duplicate of Orville Hobloch who appeared on the Bliss Private Hospital videotape surveillance.

It is also my belief that S.A. Colt is not guilty of the crime for which he was arrested. I do not believe that S.A. Colt is capable of this act. However, his suicide, the evidence against him, and the lack of evidence supporting any other perpetrator leaves any alternative avenue of investigation closed.

This is, sadly, another X-file that remains an open case for the bureau.

THE END

PARANORMAL QUEST

By Ray Garton

REDDING, CALIFORNIA
2nd DECEMBER, 1997, 9:37 a.m.

"They're all pretty much the same wherever you go," Fox Mulder whispered as he and Dana Scully were led into the refrigerated room. "What's that?" Scully said.

"Morgues."

The man leading them was Dr. Oliver Copper, Chief Medical Examiner with the Shasta County Coroner's office, a tall, pear-shaped man in his fifties with a fringe of silvering black hair around his bald spot and stubble on his jowls.

"I've found that the occupants don't mind the uniformity," Dr. Copper said over his shoulder as he led them around a corner. "In fact, they never bring it up."

Mulder gave her his smirking we've-got-a-live-one look and said, "How does the staff feel?"

Dr. Copper stopped, turned to them, tipped his head forward and looked over the top of his half-glasses. "We think it sucks. I can say that out loud now because I'm retiring at the end of next week."

"You seem a little young to be retiring, Dr. Copper," Scully said.

He gave her a warm smile. "That's very sweet of you, but the truth is, if you can find a young spot anywhere on my body, I'll have it grafted to my face. Now. You were here to see Milsap, is that right?" He turned to the two levels of square doors in the wall and opened the center one on the bottom. "This would be the talk of the internet if we hadn't been told to sit on it."

Mulder said, "Who told you that?"

"Your people. The FBI. They told me to lock it down tight and they'd send someone. And here you are."

"You called them, correct?" Scully said.

"Yes. I wanted to know if they'd ever seen anything like this before." He bent down and pulled out the drawer.

Brandi Milsap, 22 years old, was stretched out on the slab. Her head was framed by her long blonde hair and there was a hole between her breasts. It looked to Scully like an exit wound from a high-caliber weapon. Below that, the stapled autopsy incision began.

"Have *you* ever seen anything like this before, Dr. Copper?" Mulder said.

"Not without an entrance wound. You'd expect to find one in this woman's back, but it's not there."

Mulder hunkered down beside the body for a closer look. "You're saying this originated ... *inside* the chest cavity?"

"I have the entire autopsy on video, you can look over everything for yourself. It's clear to me, as crazy as it sounds, that her heart exploded. But not in any way that would be consistent with a ... a natural cause of death."

Scully said, "You're saying her heart exploded with enough force to blow a hole through her chest?"

"I'm afraid so."

"That seems pretty unlikely," Scully said. "Do you have any theories as to how it might have happened?"

"Not a one," Dr. Copper said. "I was hoping you'd have something to offer. Have *you* ever seen anything like this?"

"I haven't," Mulder said as he stood. "But Agent Scully is the M.D."

She shook her head. "No, I haven't. I'm still not sure what I'm seeing now."

"Were there witnesses?" Mulder said.

The doctor nodded. "Yes, a room full of people. Brandi Milsap is the oldest of four children, two sisters and a brother. She lived with her extended family just outside of town in Bella Vista. A big old house."

"The family was present when this happened?" Scully said.

"Some of them, along with several people from a TV show about ghosts and haunted houses." Mulder nodded as the doctor continued. "They've been investigating the house because the Milsaps claim some ... well, weird things have been happening." Dr. Copper rolled his eyes.

"You seem skeptical."

"I was. Until this. The Milsap family is ... well, they've been in the area for a few generations and people are ... wary of them."

"I understand your hesitation, Dr. Copper, but you can speak freely. I take it this family has a bad reputation?"

"Yes. And it's earned. They have no interest in anything legitimate or above board. They're grifters. To the bone. People who've lived around here a while know to steer clear of them, but there are plenty who aren't aware of their reputation. When they started saying their house was haunted, most people knew better than to believe them. Myself included. I figured they were bucking for some book or movie deal." He looked down at Brandi Milsap's body. "Now I'm not so sure. This is ... bizarre. To say the least. I have no explanation for it."

Mulder turned to his partner. "Dr. Scully? Any thoughts?"

"On violently exploding hearts? Not at the moment, no." She turned to Dr. Copper. "I would like to see the autopsy video."

He nodded. "Come right this way."

BELLA VISTA, CALIFORNIA
12:24 p.m.

Mulder drove down Dry Creek Road in Bella Vista with the air conditioner blasting. It was a hot and humid August day. They had been talking about the autopsy video since leaving the morgue.

"I assumed there would be some answer in the video," Scully said. "Something Dr. Copper had missed or misinterpreted. But he did everything right. It was just as he described it."

"Do you know of anything that could cause something like that?"

"Aside from a bullet, no. How much do you know about this TV show?"

"*Paranormal Quest*. It's a syndicated show that follows a team of paranormal researchers as they investigate alleged hauntings, possessions, and other phenomena. The third season starts this fall. It's a hit."

"Are these serious researchers, or are they TV researchers?"

Mulder smirked. "Are you suggesting, Scully, that some of the things we see on television may be less than authentic?"

"Let me guess. You were a fan of the show long before this case came along."

"Not a fan, no. If I were, I would refer to the show as 'the PQ.' That's what fans call it. I've seen it, and other shows and so-called documentaries like it. They're all showbiz. This one is a group of young people who travel around the country with their equipment to investigate paranormal activity. They rope ordinary people into the show, residents and locals, and proceed to scare the hell out of them."

"Equipment?"

"You gotta have equipment, Scully. Electromagnetic field monitors, motion detectors."

"I'm not aware of any evidence that suggests supernatural phenomenon can be detected by EMF monitors, are you?"

Mulder shook his head. "There is none. It's all smoke and mirrors. Most people don't know what an EMF monitor is or what it does, so they're impressed because they're blissfully unaware that those monitors are set off by a wide variety of things and have no way of determining the source of the fluctuations. What makes this show different from most is that we're shown what appears to be, and what we're told *is*, actual paranormal activity, and the locals are interviewed afterward. They aren't actors, but they seem genuinely frightened and upset. And all that fear is captured by the cameras, of course, for the enjoyment of the viewing audience."

"But you think they're frauds?"

"I don't know if I'd go so far as to call them frauds. They are, after all, doing a TV show. I think most people know better than to think anything they see on a TV show about ghosts is real. Reality is not what TV does. That's why I don't think shows like this will ever catch on. This one's a hit, though. And very entertaining. But it's showbiz."

"Do you think it's possible that they've … well, stumbled onto something real this time?"

"I'm guessing nobody in the cast of *Paranormal Quest* has ever been anywhere near an actual paranormal event, and I'm not sure they'd recognize one if they saw it. Which is why I'm so interested in their reaction to Brandi Milsap's bizarre death. And in how much of it they got on video."

"There's video of the incident?" It was the first time Scully had heard anything about it.

"If they're doing an episode about the Milsap house, they've got that place wired for sound and video. It seems unlikely that they missed this."

"I don't understand. There was nothing in the file about a video."

"No, there wasn't. So far, the show's host and co-executive producer,

Brody Walsh, denies that any video exists."

"Why don't you believe him?"

"Same reason again. They're doing a TV show."

MILSAP RESIDENCE
12:32 p.m.

The Milsap house loomed at the end of a narrow, half-mile-long dirt road that cut off of Dry Creek. It passed through a dense patch of woods and was flanked by mounds of blackberry vines. Several cars and pickup trucks were parked in a graveled oval clearing in front, along with one white van.

The house was just as Dr. Copper had described it: big and old. Mulder got out of the car and glanced back at the trail of dust it had kicked up, then squinted in the sunlight at the house. At one time, it probably had been as well cared for as the land on which it stood. If so, those days were far in the past.

Only small segments of the house were visible through the thick tangle of trees, shrubs, and vines surrounding it. An enormous birch tree stood in the front yard, its branches drooping low. There was a plum tree, a pomegranate tree, a couple of huge oaks, and towering above the house in back was a muscular cedar. They all crowded in close, as if protecting the house, which was swallowed up in all the branches and dark shade. One side of the yard disappeared into a wall of blackberry vines and the front of the house was mostly hidden behind drapes of ivy. From what Mulder could see, it appeared to be an odd blend of Tidewater and French Colonial styles, and it was not in the best of shape.

The pale curtain in a second-story window half obscured by branches was pulled aside slightly for a moment, then dropped back into place.

A low stone wall crawling with ivy surrounded the yard. There was no gate, but the entrance opened to a narrow path that cut through two rectangles of untended grass and weeds. It ended at steps that ascended into the black cave of the covered porch.

Mulder looked at Scully across the roof of the car. "Looks pretty ripe for a haunting, doesn't it?"

"It looks ripe for something," she said as she closed her door.

Mulder did the same. They walked away from the car and up the path. The steps creaked beneath them, and they crossed the broad, cluttered porch to the front door. Mulder knocked, then they removed their badges from their pockets and prepared to show them.

Voices inside stopped abruptly and heavy footsteps approached before the door was pulled open. A large man stood just inside the doorway—tall, with broad shoulders and a barrel chest. An explosion of wild white hair rose from above his long forehead and fanned around his narrow face, which was lined with wrinkles like razor-slashes. Bushy gray eyebrows huddled low and close over his deep-set eyes. He wore a white T-shirt with what looked like two spaghetti sauce stains on the front, and denim overalls.

"Help you?" he said in a suspicious voice made of crushed stones.

Mulder recognized him from photographs: Barney Milsap, the patriarch of the clan.

They raised their badges and Mulder said, "FBI. I'm Agent Fox Mulder, this is Agent Dana Scully. I'm sorry to come at a time like this. I know you've experienced a terrible loss. But we'd like to ask you a few questions about the death of Brandi Milsap. I believe she was your granddaughter, Mr. Milsap?"

For a moment, Mulder thought the old man was going to slam the door in their faces. Then the wrinkled face slowly relaxed into an expression of disdainful resignation. He took a couple of heavy steps backward and gestured for them to come inside.

As Mulder had suspected, there were cameras and lights everywhere. It looked as much like a set in a studio as a private home. It was crowded inside, but he had no trouble telling the Milsaps from the PQ crew. All of the Milsaps looked at him and Scully with quiet suspicion or hostility or both.

Introductions were made and Mulder took quick mental notes of names and faces. But he focused his attention on one face and made his way through the group to Brody Walsh. He was a fratboy type, but at 33, that was all performance and image. He was a shrewd producer, businessman, and showman with two other cheaply-produced but highly successful syndicated TV shows to his credit. His blond hair was cut short and his skin was nicely tanned.

"Is there someplace quiet where we can talk?" Mulder said.

They went to the laundry room.

"This is a hell of a thing, huh?" Walsh said grimly, frowning.

"It is, yes. How much of it did you capture on video?"

"Oh, I already told the police we didn't get any of — "

"I know, but, see ... I'm not the police."

"The equipment was put away by then and nothing was turned on when it happened."

"Then you haven't been entirely honest with your audience."

"Audience?"

Mulder smiled. "It's in the introduction to every episode. 'In the course of investigating a house, the *Paranormal Quest* team monitors every room, from every angle, non-stop, for the duration of the investigation.' I guess ... that's not true."

"You watch the show?" Walsh said with a smile, but that dropped away quickly. "No, wait, I'm not saying that's not true, it's just that, well, we have to give families a little privacy, you know what I'm saying?"

"It's either true or it's not."

His eyes widened slightly. "Am I in some kind of trouble?"

"That depends. If there's no video, then I'm sure your fans will be disappointed to learn you haven't been entirely honest with them in your introduction. They'll probably get over it. But if you're withholding evidence which you plan to incorporate into your TV show, you'll be going away for a while, Brody."

Walsh leaned back stiffly against the dryer.

"On the other hand, if, say, between the time that you spoke with the police yesterday and our arrival today, you discovered that some of your equipment *had* been running and happened to catch — "

"That's *exactly* what happened," Walsh said, smiling as his posture relaxed. "Yes, it was earlier today that we found it. That's exactly what happened."

Mulder returned the smile.

"This is a modified security van," Walsh said as he opened the doors in the rear of the white van parked in front of the house. He continued as he went inside, "It's the kind private investigators use, you know? Same equipment and everything."

Scully pressed her lips tightly together when Mulder turned to her with eyebrows raised high above his eyes, wide with mock enthusiasm, as if the same equipment that private investigators used was an exciting detail. She turned away to keep from laughing.

The equipment left little room for comfort. Walsh squeezed into a seat facing a monitor and Mulder and Scully hunkered down behind him.

"What you're going to see happened yesterday evening," Walsh said, turning on the equipment. "We'd finished for the night and we were starting to break up and head back to the hotel."

"No one in your crew stays at the house overnight?" Mulder said.

"Always. Sometimes we take turns, but usually it's Annie who stays overnight. One of my production assistants, Annie Jervik. She doesn't care much for motels and she knows the equipment."

"She's been staying with the Milsaps?"

"Yes. We need somebody there to keep an eye on the equipment, make sure it's functioning. The cameras are motion activated, *very* sensitive, and all the microphones are sound activated. Drop a dime on the carpet and they'll catch it."

The monitor's screen glowed with a frozen gray image.

Walsh said, "We were all in the dining room saying our goodnights, when I heard ... I didn't know what it was at first, a laugh, a yelp of surprise. It was Brandi at the other end of the room, clutching her chest. There are three cameras in the room, but this is the best angle by far."

He hit a button and the figures in the dining room, shot at a downward angle from above, began to move and talk around the remains of an impromptu buffet on the dining table. A few of them held paper plates with some food left on them. There were about a dozen people in the long, rectangular room, but Scully's eyes went to Brandi Milsap standing at the far end of the table.

She was tall, slender, shapely, and her spun-gold hair fell past her shoulders. She wore a snug, low-cut, red tank top and denim Daisy Dukes that made her look like she was auditioning for a part in something on Cinemax.

She held a paper plate with a plastic fork and a few pieces of watermelon rind on it as she talked to a young man Scully assumed to be with the TV crew. He was tall, handsome, with black hair and nice blue eyes, but he gave the impression that he did not know it. His gray pullover shirt and black jeans were too big for him and he looked uncomfortable, not only in the Milsap house, but in his own skin.

"Who is that with her?" Scully asked.

"One of my camera guys, Tony Barbieri. I think she had a crush on him."

Brandi stood close, facing Tony, but she leaned even closer to say something, and as she did, she tugged on the collar of his shirt. He laughed at whatever she said.

"We'll need to hear the sound, too," Scully said.

"From each microphone," Mulder added, never taking his eyes from the screen. "And we'll need to see video from each camera."

"Yeah, sure, we can do that," Walsh said. "But for now... " He turned up the volume.

They heard a murmur of conversation, occasionally interrupted by laughter.

Brandi touched Tony's chin with her fingertip as she said something, and they both laughed. She stopped abruptly and her smile quickly changed to a look of confusion and distress. She said something inaudible to Tony, put her left hand to the bare flesh in the deep scoop neck of her tank top, and her long fingers curled into a fist. She cried out as the paper plate fell from her other hand and she staggered forward, clutching the back of the chair at the end of the dining table.

The microphone picked up a thick popping sound as the center of her chest blew outward behind her hand, spattering the table with red, and she dropped to the floor and out of sight.

It was so sudden and over so quickly that Scully could not yet be sure of what she'd seen.

The young man who'd been talking to Brandi bent down behind the table and chair, but only for a moment. He stood upright again, shouting, "Oh, god!"

Everyone rushed to that end of the table and there were a few screams.

Walsh stopped the video and looked over his shoulder at Scully. "I've watched it again and again, and I still don't know what I saw. I was *there*, and I don't know what I saw."

"Any speculation?" Mulder said.

He slowly shook his head, then shrugged, then shook his head again. "I don't know. I'm a talker, but this knocks the words right outta me."

"You must have some thoughts or observations," Scully said.

"Let's get out of this van before we bake."

Outside, they walked a few steps through the heat to the shade of an oak tree on the edge of the clearing.

"How long have you been here?" Scully asked.

"Two days."

Mulder said, "What's it been like so far? The house, I mean. Do you think this incident is related to your reason for coming here in the first place?"

"You mean the haunting? I don't know if it's related, but we *have* seen a lot of activity here in the last couple of days. More than usual. Objects moving around, even heavy furniture. Doors opening and closing on their own. No apparitions yet, but after what we've seen, I wouldn't be surprised."

"What were you going to do with the video?" Mulder asked with a smirk.

Walsh shrugged. "I don't know. I just didn't want anyone else to know about it until we could find out what we had."

"We need to see and hear all of it," Mulder said. "I'd like to take everything you have to the local FBI office and watch it there. Can you put it all together for us?"

"Sure, I'll box it up if you'll tell me exactly what you want to see."

Mulder smiled. "Everything since you got here."

Walsh's smile melted from his face as his eyes grew wide. "Uh, well, I'm kind of doing a show here, you know?"

"During which someone was killed," Scully said.

"But not *murdered*."

"We don't know that," Mulder said.

"I don't understand," Walsh said. "Why is the FBI involved? Shouldn't this be handled by local law enforcement?"

"Would you like us to hand it off to the Sheriff's Department?" Mulder said. "We'd have to tell them that you withheld evidence, though, and I don't think they'll — "

"Okay, okay," Walsh said, hands raised and waggling in a gesture of surrender. "I'll box up the tapes for you. There's a lot of them, though. It'll take some time."

Mulder said, "We'll wait inside."

Walsh turned and went back to the van.

As they walked slowly back to the house, they spoke quietly.

"Beautifully handled, Mulder."

"What did you think of the video?"

Scully shook her head. "I'm baffled. I've never seen anything like it. There's nothing in my medical training or experience that could explain it."

"You asked about the guy standing with her. Did you notice anything in particular?"

"Only that she was flirting with him with no subtlety whatsoever."

"I noticed that, too. Let's go inside and start asking questions. You want to take the object of the deceased's flirtation, or shall I?"

"He looked uncomfortable with her. I got the feeling that uncomfortable is his natural state. He might be more at ease with a man than a woman."

Mulder nodded. "Good thinking." As they entered the yard, he said, "I wonder if Walsh knows they're a family of grifters."

"Like you said, reality is not what TV does. I doubt Mr. Walsh cares."

Scully first talked to Denise Milsap, Brandi's mother. She was a gaunt woman with straight dishwater-blond hair that fell limply past her shoulders. Almost frail in appearance, Denise had come downstairs from her bedroom to talk with Scully. The gray crescents beneath her dismal brown eyes stood out against her pale skin.

"I'm terribly sorry for your loss, Mrs. Milsap," Scully said once they were both seated on the couch. "I know this is a difficult time to answer questions, but I think it's important we learn what caused your daughter's death. Did she have any heart problems? Any medical problems at all?"

"She was as healthy as a horse." Denise turned her head slowly back and forth, starting at the center of the room. "No heart problems, nothing wrong. It just ... happened."

"You weren't present at the time, were you?"

"No. I'd already gone upstairs."

"Do you have any idea what might have caused it? Any suspicions at all?"

Denise looked briefly at Scully with heavy-lidded eyes, then turned toward the foyer, as if to make sure they were alone. "Well ... I, uh ..." She lowered her head and frowned at her lap.

"Yes?"

She spoke barely above a whisper. "Some pretty scary stuff has been happening in this house."

"Are you referring to the things that drew the TV crew here?"

"No, I … I mean — " Another quick glance around. " — since they got here."

"What kind of scary stuff?"

Denise chewed her lower lip as she considered her answer. "Ghost stuff."

"Wasn't that happening *before* they arrived?"

Sounds of movement made both of them look toward the foyer. A tall, heavyset man entered the living room and said, "Shouldn't you be in bed, honey?"

Scully heard Denise's quiet gasp even though she cut it off before her husband heard it.

"Randy," she said, standing.

"I thought you took one a them pills," he said, putting an arm around her shoulders.

Scully stood, too, and said, "I'm Agent Dana — "

"Yeah, I know. My wife can't talk right now. She needs to lie down."

Scully noted the resemblance to Randy's father, although Barney Milsap had held up better at twice the age. She said, "I'm going to need to talk to everyone at some — "

"Yeah, well, we can't talk now." He led Denise out of the living room and toward the stairs.

Barney Milsap came around the corner and spoke to them quietly, then Randy and Denise went upstairs. Barney turned and looked sternly at Scully in the living room.

"Mr. Milsap," she said. "I need to ask you some questions."

While Scully talked to members of the Milsap family, Mulder found Tony Barbieri at the kitchen sink with a woman washing dishes.

The woman was short, had brown hair cut in a bob, and wore a baggy blue shirt and olive green peasant skirt.

"Tony Barbieri?"

Tony turned around and looked at Mulder with large eyes. He couldn't decide if Tony looked nervous, afraid, or simply uncomfortable, as Scully had said.

Showing his badge, he said, "I'm Agent Mulder, FBI. Could I have a word with you?"

"Sure." He rinsed his hands and approached Mulder as he dried them on a dishtowel.

"Is there someplace we can go to talk?"

"Um ... the back porch." He tossed the towel onto the counter and led the way to the back door.

They stepped out onto the covered, screened-in porch, which was just as cluttered as the one in front. As Mulder turned to keep the screen door from slamming shut, he saw the woman who'd been washing dishes with Tony following them out.

"What's your name?" he said, smiling.

She blinked at him rapidly, opened her mouth, and stared for a moment. She had a round, pale face, worried green eyes behind black-framed glasses, and she did not smile.

"Annie," she said.

"The production assistant."

Her eyes widened and her head pulled back slightly. "Yes. Why?"

"We were talking to Brody Walsh earlier and you came up in the conversation."

"I ... I did?"

"We'll need to ask you some questions. But for now, if you don't mind, I'd like to have a word with Tony alone."

"Oh. Sure. Okay." She turned, went back inside, and gently closed the screen door. But she left the back door open.

Mulder turned to Tony. "Are you two friends?"

Tony nodded. "We live in the same building. In fact, she got me this job."

"You were standing next to Brandi Milsap when she died."

Tony frowned, swallowed hard, then nodded once. "Yeah. We were talking."

"What were you talking about?"

"Nothing important. Music, TV shows we like, that kind of thing."

"When did you know something was wrong?"

His cheeks rose in a slight wince as he ran a hand back through his thick black hair. "I didn't at first. That's what bothers me. She was telling me about this new song she'd just heard on the radio and she was ... well, she wasn't *singing* it, but she was making this sound the singer makes in the song, and then ... the sound changed. It was like she was panting. I thought she was still doing the singer, you know? But then her expression changed and grabbed her chest and I knew something was wrong, that she was in some kind of pain."

"Did she say anything?"

"Yeah. As soon as she grabbed her chest, she said, really soft, she just kind of breathed it, she said, 'It's hot.' Then she ... cried out."

"Anything else?"

He shook his head and his face darkened. His eyes glistened and he seemed near tears. "Then it happened. And it ... I was ... I just couldn't ... "

"Was this the first time you'd talked with Brandi?"

He took a deep breath, sniffed once. "No, we've talked a few other times since we got here."

"Was there a relationship developing?"

"A relationship?"

Mulder shrugged. "Were you interested in each other? Romantically?"

Tony's cheeks became rosy and he turned away from Mulder to look through the screen at the spacious back yard. "Romantically? Well, we just met a couple of days ago."

"It only takes a second to fall for somebody. And she was very attractive."

"No, really. We were just talking. She was friendly; we got along. That's all."

"My partner and I just watched the video of the incident and we both noticed that Brandi seemed quite taken with you."

He turned to Mulder slowly and looked at him first with confusion, then disbelief. "What makes you say that?"

"You were there. Standing right next to her. Didn't you notice that she was flirting with you?"

"Flirting? Really?"

"How old are you, Tony?"

"I'll be 26 in October."

"Do you date much? Have a girlfriend?"

He looked down at a rusty old kerosene heater against the wall. "No. I don't date and I don't have, um ... no. I'm just ... I guess I've never been any good at that."

Scully had been right about Tony. Discomfort was his natural state.

Mulder said, "Well, I don't think Brandi knew that because she couldn't keep her hands or her eyes off of you."

Sadness passed over Tony's face as he continued to stare down at the heater.

"Do you have any idea what might have happened to her, Tony? You were standing the closest. Did any of what happened make sense to you?"

He shook his head back and forth forcefully. "No, it didn't. And it was the most horrible thing I've ever seen in my life. I don't think I'll ever be able to forget it. No matter how hard I try."

Mulder heard a sound behind him and turned to see a figure standing a few feet down the hall just inside the screen door. Against the light coming from the kitchen, it was no more than a silhouette. He reached out and opened the screen as the figure turned and hurried away. But he caught a glimpse of Annie's skirt as she disappeared around the corner at the other end of the hall.

Barney Milsap was 86 years old but he was quite sharp and regarded Scully with unveiled suspicion as they spoke in the living room. He sat on the edge of a throne-like recliner and leaned forward with elbows on the armrests. His ice-blue eyes were slightly narrowed as they looked unwaveringly into Scully's. She seated herself at the end of the couch.

"Look, if you're the *federales*," he said, "then there probably ain't much about me you don't already know, so it won't come as any surprise to know I don't like cops. I'm just telling you up front so you'll know. If I'm unfriendly, it ain't personal."

It's probably a family tradition, Scully thought.

"I'm not here for you, Mr. Milsap. I'm simply investigating the cause of your granddaughter's death."

"Heart blew up."

"Yes. Do you have any idea what might have caused that to happen?"

He slowly turned his head from side to side.

"Do you think it could be connected to the reason the TV crew is here?"

He leaned back in the chair and chewed his upper lip for a moment, fidgeted, opened his mouth to speak, then closed it and fidgeted a bit more. Finally, he moved forward again and said, "I wouldn't know."

Milsap had something on his mind and he'd come close to saying it out loud. Scully lowered her eyes for a moment, deciding how to proceed. When she looked at him again, the old man had not moved a muscle. "Look, Mr. Milsap, if you don't like cops, then I'm assuming you'd rather we not stick around."

"That's right," he said with a single, slow nod.

"Well, if you give us the impression you're withholding information about this case — and that is the impression you're giving me — we'll only stick around longer. And look closer. It would be in your best interest to tell us everything, even if it's something you don't think is important."

He leaned back again, stared down at his hands for a moment, then locked his fingers together and cracked his knuckles. Looking at her again, he said, "Some ... strange things have happened here in the last couple of days. Since they arrived."

"My understanding was that strange things were happening before they arrived, and that's why they came."

"Yeah. But ... *different* strange things have been happening since they got here."

"What kind of different strange things?"

"Stuff moving around. By itself."

"That wasn't happening before they arrived?"

"Yeah, but ... well ... " He took a deep breath, then surprised her by pushing on the armrests of the chair with his big hands and getting to his feet. "You're right. It's probably just the same stuff, huh? Sorry. Wish I could help, but I got nothin' to tell ya."

Scully stood as he walked out of the living room. "We'll talk again later today, Mr. Milsap," she said firmly.

He stopped walking, but he did not turn around.

Scully said, "I strongly suggest you reconsider and tell me what's on your mind."

He stood with his back to her for a long moment, then walked through the foyer and past the stairway. As he rounded the corner to go down the hall, he passed a dark-haired young woman coming in the opposite direction. She headed for the front door and Scully heard it open, but not close.

Scully headed out of the living room to find Mulder. She took only a few steps before the young woman returned, accompanied by Walsh. She was animated and seemed angry as she spoke to him, too quietly for Scully to understand what she was saying. Walsh stopped and faced her, shushed her, and put his hands on her shoulders in an apparent attempt to calm her. Then, as Scully entered the foyer, he turned and led her up the stairs, talking to her quietly but urgently.

Scully went upstairs a moment later and followed the sound of their voices to a closed door. She could not make out their words, but the exchange was intense. Then it was silent beyond the door.

The door opened and Walsh stepped out, pausing for a moment when he saw Scully standing in the hall.

"Is something wrong?" she said.

He pulled the door closed. "Annie's sick. My production assistant. I don't know if it's something she ate or a bug she's caught."

Scully did not believe him.

Walsh said, "I've got those tapes boxed up for you, by the way."

"Thank you."

"If you can wait for me to make sure Annie's okay, I'll meet you at the van and hand them over."

Scully nodded, then went back downstairs. She met Mulder in the foyer.

"Did you see a short, dark-haired woman pass through here?" he said.

"Annie?"

"That's the one. Where'd she go?"

"She's in a bedroom upstairs. Walsh says she's sick, but I saw her talking to him and she didn't look sick at all. Excited, maybe upset, but not sick."

Mulder nodded. "She was eavesdropping on my conversation with Tony Barbieri on the back porch."

"Any idea why?"

"No, but I intend to find out."

Footsteps hurried down the stairs and Walsh joined them a moment later.

"Shall we go get the tapes?" he said with a smile.

"How is Annie?" Scully said.

"She's not feeling well. She's going to lie down for a little while."

Mulder said, "What's wrong with her?"

"I think it's something she ate. We've been eating too much fast food lately. Come on, let's go."

He went to the front door and left the house.

Mulder and Scully exchanged a skeptical look as they followed Walsh out of the house.

REDDING, CALIFORNIA
3:14 p.m.

On the drive to the FBI office in Redding, Mulder said, "Anything strange happen while we were apart?"

"Define strange."

"Paranormal. Ghostly."

"No. But the Milsaps were strange enough. Brandi's mother and grandfather both told me that weird things have been happening in the house *since* the TV crew arrived. Weirder than the things that were allegedly happening before, they claim."

"Did they get specific about these weird occurrences?"

"Objects moving around by themselves, the same things Walsh described."

"Did they suggest that the PQ crew were *causing* these things to happen?"

"No, not explicitly. They seemed ... intimidated."

"Barney Milsap? Intimidated?"

"He had something to say, but he seemed afraid to say it. And then he abruptly ended the interview."

"Given the kind of people the Milsaps are, do you think it's possible there was no paranormal activity occurring in their house?"

"After what Dr. Copper told us, that seems likely. They were just looking for attention."

"And the attention they got was Walsh and his TV show. It only makes sense that they're worried about strange things happening in their house if those things weren't happening before Walsh and his crew arrived."

"What about you, Mulder? Did you have any paranormal experiences?"

"No. But maybe that's because we aren't the people meant to experience them."

FEDERAL BUREAU OF INVESTIGATION
REDDING, CALIFORNIA
3:29 p.m.

Agent Yolanda Kim led Mulder and Scully, each carrying a large cardboard box of videotapes, down a sparse corridor and through a door on the right. As she flipped on the lights, she said, "We're not very high on the funding ladder here in Redding, which is why this will probably remind you of your old high school's audio-visual room."

She was not exaggerating. There were two TVs, two VCRs, and some sound and editing equipment, all of which were arranged on a long counter that ran across the rear wall. Two tables and several chairs took up space in the center of the room, with another TV on one of the tables and more chairs at the rear counter.

They placed the boxes on one of the tables.

"The equipment isn't complicated," Agent Kim said. "If you have any questions or problems, I'll be down the hall. And if you want coffee or snacks, the break room is next door."

Walsh had labeled all the tapes that included footage of Brandi Milsap's death, but there were only a few. The rest contained video shot in every room of the Milsap house since the crew had set up their equipment two days ago. Mulder and Scully split up the tapes and used both TVs and VCRs at the same time.

After watching for about fifteen minutes, Scully was the first to speak up. "Mulder, look at this." She rewound the tape as Mulder left his chair and joined her, then turned up the volume. "Watch this."

It was a view of the Milsap kitchen. It was dark outside the window and the digital clock on the microwave read 1:17. Annie stood alone wearing a T-shirt and baggy pajama bottoms and dipping a tea bag into a steaming mug on the counter. She took the cup, turned and started to leave the kitchen as a heavyset woman in her fifties wearing a robe shuffled into the room, her slippers hissing across the tile floor. It was Sarah, Barney Milsap's oldest child.

"Can't sleep?" Annie said quietly.

"Insomnia," the woman said. "I can never sleep. I need a snack."

Annie nodded and left the room as Sarah reached up and opened both doors of a cupboard at once. The contents — bags of potato chips, boxes of cookies, crackers, and cereal, a tin of candy, jars of nuts — flew out and rained down on Sarah in an explosion of clatter. She cried out in shock as she flailed her arms and stumbled backward, finally falling on her ass.

The doors of the cupboard slammed shut with a bang, then flew open again. They flapped like broken shutters in a windstorm, moving so fast that they sounded almost like machine-gun fire.

One of Sarah's slippers came off as she crawled backward, screaming, away from the scattered bags, boxes, and jars. The lid had come off the tin and wrapped hard candies littered the floor.

The cupboard doors slammed shut and did not open again.

Annie ran into the room and went to Sarah's side. A moment later, other members of the Milsap family joined them.

"Thoughts, Mulder?"

"Let's see it again."

FEDERAL BUREAU OF INVESTIGATION
REDDING, CALIFORNIA
4:31 p.m.

Throughout the tapes, there were scattered incidents similar to the one in the kitchen.

A chair sliding across a room... a bed shaking with visible help from no one... dresser drawers opening and closing... dishes thrown from the kitchen counter to the floor, where they shattered into pieces.

"Are you seeing a pattern, Scully?"

"Are you?"

"I asked first."

"I'm ... not sure. These incidents take place both day and night, no two have been exactly alike, and they look pretty convincing. The only consistent thing I've seen is the presence of Annie."

He nodded enthusiastically. "Yes, exactly."

"You don't believe Walsh's story?"

"What he told us may be true, but I don't think he's telling us everything."

"Are you suggesting that Annie is responsible for the activity in the house?"

"If it wasn't happening *before* the TV crew arrived, then somebody in that crew must be making it happen."

"I'd like to know how. Everything we've seen has looked pretty convincing. If Annie's doing it, she's fooled me."

"I want to see the tape of the death again, the one trained on the other end of the dining room. And the one we haven't gotten to yet — the kitchen at the same time."

They slipped the tapes into the VCRs and synched them up.

The first tape was shot by a camera mounted in a corner of the dining room that was behind Brandi and Tony and provided a view of the kitchen doorway near the opposite corner. The other tape showed a view of the doorway from the other side, in the kitchen.

In the first tape, while everyone stood around the table chatting and laughing in the minutes before Brandi Milsap's death, Annie stood alone in the doorway that led into the kitchen, talking to no one. Her shoulder leaned against the doorjamb, arms folded across her chest, completely motionless as she stared.

"She stands like that for a long time without moving," Mulder said.

"And she never takes her eyes off of Tony and Brandi."

Annie's face remained expressionless for some time, then it slowly changed. The inner tips of her eyebrows rose above her eyes tense, giving her a sad expression for a moment. Then her face tightened and she dropped her head abruptly, reached up and covered her mouth with her right hand. She spun around and disappeared into the kitchen.

They turned to the other TV. The kitchen was empty.

Mulder rewound the tape until he could see Annie standing in the doorway from behind. When he replayed it, Annie remained in the door only for a few seconds. Then she simply disappeared.

"He's altered the tape," Scully said.

"A hail Mary pass. He didn't have time to do even a halfway convincing job, so he slapped this together quickly and hoped we wouldn't notice. Whatever Annie was doing in the kitchen when Brandi's heart went off like a firecracker, Brody Walsh does not want us to see it."

"You think she has some kind of... ability?"

"Yeah. The ability to turn a pretty ridiculous little TV show into a big hit."

MILSAP RESIDENCE
5:12 p.m.

Tony Barbieri answered the door when Mulder and Scully returned to the Milsap house. When he saw them, he stepped back and pulled the door all the way open so they could enter.

"We need to speak to Brody," Mulder said as they went inside.

"He's around here somewhere," Tony said, closing the door.

Mulder turned to him. "Tony, tell me about your friend Annie."

"Annie? What about her?"

Mulder noticed that Tony had the same kind of deer-in-the-head-lights look that Annie had given him earlier on the back porch. They seemed to have general discomfort in common.

He said, "You told me you live in the same building and she got you this job. How long have you known her?"

"Not long, really. I moved into the building, uh ... seven months ago. That's when I met her."

"What's the relationship been like?" Mulder said.

"Well, like I said, we're just friends."

"I know, but I mean, what kind of... well... Scully?"

"She pays a lot of attention to you, doesn't she?" Scully said.

Tony arched a brow. "What?"

"She gives you little gifts, does a lot of favors for you, maybe cooks meals for you. Isn't that right?"

He looked as if he felt the need to apologize for something, but he didn't know what it was. "Uh... yeah, but... I don't understand these questions."

"Tony, do you have any other female friends? Any women you know who, since you met Annie, have gotten ill, maybe? Or injured?"

The tension left his face slowly. "Uh, well, not a friend, but... yeah. A few weeks after I moved in. Nina. She lived across the hall. She had a... a stroke."

"An elderly woman?" Scully said.

"No. She was in her twenties. A dancer. Well... a stripper."

"Had she been sick?" Mulder said.

"No. In fact, I'd just seen her that night. Her car wouldn't start, so she called me and asked for a ride home from work."

"You'd become friends?"

Tony frowned as his eyes moved back and forth between them. He spoke slowly, preoccupied with the workings of his own thoughts. "Just neighbors. She said she was desperate and had my number, so she called me."

"If you weren't close," Scully said, "why did she have your number?"

"Right after I moved in, she introduced herself, said she liked to know her neighbors. She lived alone and sometimes, she said, guys would try to follow her home from work. She didn't want to have to wait for the cops if something happened, so she gave me her number and asked for mine."

"Seems a little forward for a new neighbor," Scully said.

"Yeah, that's what Annie thought. Anyway, I brought Nina home from work and went into her apartment because she insisted on giving me some money for gas. And that night... she died." He turned to Mulder. "Why is this important?"

"Is that the only one you can think of?" Mulder said. "Any other female friends have... problems?"

Tony's eyes slowly turned toward the doorway of the dining room where he had watched Brandi die.

To Scully, Mulder said, "I think he's doing the math."

"Can you tell us where Annie is right now, Tony?" Scully said.

"Brody said she was upstairs sleeping because she didn't feel well."

"We've been gone for more than three hours," Scully said. "She's still up there?"

He shrugged. "Far as I know."

"Thanks, Tony," Mulder said, then he and Scully went upstairs.

She led the way to the bedroom and knocked on the door. "Annie? It's Agents Scully and Mulder. We need to speak to you."

There were no sounds in the bedroom. Scully opened the door.

Strands of sunlight bled through the tree branches outside the window. The room was a mess and smelled heavily of perfume. A dressing table had been cleared, and perfume bottles and makeup and the contents of an open jewelry box were scattered over the floor around it. A web of cracks ran through the dressing table's large mirror. A straight back chair lay on its side. Some of the drawers of a dresser were open and one side of the dresser had been pulled away from the wall by more than a foot. A framed poster lay on the floor in front of the closet door on which it had been hanging.

Annie lay fully clothed in the center of the neatly made queen bed with her back to them. Her glasses were on the pillow behind her head.

"Annie," Scully said, hurrying to the bed. She placed the glasses on a night stand, put a hand on the young woman's arm and shook her gently.

Annie did not stir or make a sound.

Repeating her name loudly, Scully rolled her onto her back. When Annie remained unresponsive, Scully brushed a fingertip over the lashes of one closed eye. The eyelid did not twitch. "She's been drugged. There's a syringe on the night stand."

"See if you can wake —"

A toilet flushed on the other side of the closet door. It wasn't a closet.

Mulder drew his weapon and leveled it at the bathroom door.

It opened and Brody Walsh stepped out. He lifted both hands, smiled sheepishly, and said, "It's only me."

Mulder lowered his gun, but he didn't put it away.

"I told you she was sick," Walsh said, nodding toward Annie on the bed.

"She's been drugged, Mr. Walsh," Scully said. "Would you happen to know anything about that?"

He looked at Scully, bent over Annie, checking her eyes, gently shaking her, and said, "Uh... what are you doing?"

"Trying to revive her."

Walsh lunged for the bed, saying, "Don't do that!"

"Freeze!" Mulder shouted, raising his gun again.

Walsh lurched to a halt and lifted his hands. He looked terrified. "You don't understand—it's a big mistake to wake her up. I mean, it could be dangerous."

Holding the gun on Walsh, Mulder slowly made his way around the foot of the bed. "Has she been getting unpredictable, Brody? Hard to control?"

Walsh's eyes darted back and forth between Mulder moving around the bed and Scully trying to revive Annie. Finally, he said, "Whuh-what are you talking about?"

"Annie is the reason that every house you investigate is haunted, isn't that right? She's the reason every episode includes footage of paranormal activity, isn't she? She allows you to fake the whole thing so perfectly that even the people whose homes you investigate don't know they're being fooled. How did you find her, Brody?"

Still eyeing Annie on the bed and looking ready to run out of the room, Walsh spoke haltingly. "She used to babysit for us. My ex-wife and me. Aiden and Emma loved her. Our kids. They used to tell me that she entertained them by doing magic tricks. Making things move around and float in the air. I didn't think much of it. They were just little kids. But then I found out their mother had installed a couple of nanny cams in the house, so I watched some of the video, and... sure enough. That's what Annie was doing."

"And you've been using her ever since, right?"

"*Using* her? She's well-paid. The thing is, she's not, uh… very stable."

"And I bet she's been even less stable since she met Tony Barbieri, right?"

Walsh dropped his hands and his shoulders sagged as he nodded. "Yes. Tony. He's all she's been able to talk about since he moved into her building. I had to give him a job just to keep her happy."

Mulder stood at the foot of the bed and lowered his weapon. "Did she intend to kill Brandi Milsap?"

"No. That's the thing, see, she's been losing control of it ever since Tony came along. Sometimes she even does it in her *sleep*. It scares the hell out of me. These days, I'm afraid to be *around* her. What happened with Brandi… no, it wasn't intentional, and she's been very upset about it. She tried to stop herself."

Mulder said, "That's why she went into the kitchen, to stop herself. That's the part of the video you cut out. You didn't want us to know because you were afraid she'd be taken away from you and your show would be left high and dry."

Creases cut into Walsh's tan forehead as he nodded heavily. "That's why I've been carrying around a tranquilizer. Just in case. And it's a good thing because today I needed it. She just… well, she *lost* it. She did this," he said, waving his hands at the mess in the room. "She didn't do it consciously. She wasn't even *trying*."

"What did you give her?" Scully said.

"It was, uh… midazolam, I think."

"You *think*?"

"I-I'm not sure I'm pronouncing it correctly, but that's what I gave her, yes."

"If you can't pronounce it," Scully said, "it's a good idea not to *inject* it. She's not coming around. Mulder, can you get my medical bag out of the car? I have ammonia inhalants in there."

He holstered his weapon and said to Walsh, "Come with me."

"Gladly," Walsh said, hurrying after Mulder.

Rushing down the stairs, Mulder heard voices coming from the dining room. He went out the front door, down the porch steps, and through the yard.

"What do you know about Annie?" Mulder said as they hurried across the gravel.

"Lonely, socially awkward, a little neurotic."

"And how much do you know about her ability?" Mulder said.

"When we started, she'd move some furniture, make doors open and close, that sort of thing. But she could only do a little at a time because it drained her. She told me back then that she didn't use it very often. She'd play little tricks on people she didn't like, or entertain children. Like mine."

Mulder went to the passenger side of the car and opened the rear door.

"But while she worked for me, she got better at it. And stronger. She started breaking things without meaning to. Glass stuff at first, but then a chair, a door."

Leaning into the back seat, Mulder took Scully's medical bag from the floorboard, then stood and closed the door.

Walsh said, "In one house — the show never aired — she accidentally killed the family's cat. That's when I started getting worried. Now I'm... scared."

As they headed back toward the house, Mulder heard a rattling sound and stopped walking to listen. It was coming from the house.

"What's that noise?" Walsh said.

It grew steadily louder. Mulder looked at the upstairs window. A patch of the blue sky was reflected in the pane, which was trembling.

"I think it's the house," Mulder said before he burst into a run through the gate, across the yard, and onto the porch.

Someone inside screamed before he reached the front door. And then something inside exploded.

Scully brought a glass of water from the bathroom to the bed and was going to sprinkle some on Annie's face, but the shaking started before she got that far. She thought, for a moment, that it was an earthquake. The windowpanes shuddered and a mobile of barnyard animals hanging from the ceiling in a corner jittered and swayed.

She gasped when all of the bottles of perfume and jars of creams and scattered jewelry that had been knocked from the dressing table rose swiftly in a single, unified motion. They hovered in the air almost six feet from the hardwood floor for no more than a heartbeat before rocketing directly toward her.

She dropped the glass of water and lifted her arms protectively across her face and chest as she dropped to the floor. Two of the bottles hit her before she dropped flat to the floor — one on the elbow, the other on the left side of her neck — but the rest shot over her and hit the wall with sharp pops. Some of them went through the open doorway and hit the opposite wall outside the room.

The door swung as if kicked and slammed with a bang.

"Annie!" she shouted as she got up and knelt on the bed.

Annie lay on her back, mouth open, eyes darting around behind closed lids. Her lips and cheeks twitched, but she remained unconscious.

The house was shaking harder now, enough to do structural damage if it continued for long.

A woman screamed downstairs and a jarring explosion followed a moment later.

Scully clutched Annie's upper arms and shook her against the mattress, shouting her name over and over.

The panes of both windows shattered and blew inward, as if a powerful bomb had been detonated just outside the house. Instead of falling to the floor, the shards swirled in the air, chattering like glass teeth, spinning fiercely around Scully in a sparkling vortex that gradually closed in around her.

"Annie! Wake up! You have to wake up, Annie!"

When she felt the first stinging, biting cuts, Scully shouted Mulder's name twice.

Mulder pushed the door open and walked into a smoky cacophony. His training kicked in and he quickly began to process the details of his environment.

Dark smoke rolled out of the kitchen doorway and he assumed something in the kitchen had blown up, perhaps the stove. A moment later, the flaming shape of a man ran out of that smoke, screaming and flailing his burning arms like a child pretending to be a bird. Randy Milsap.

There were more screams from the kitchen as someone ran after Randy, holding up a tablecloth and shouting, "On the floor, Randy, drop to the floor!"

Walsh stopped in the doorway behind Mulder and shouted, "Dear god, she's snapped!"

The shaking house began to sway. Pictures dropped off the walls and knick-knacks clattered over shelves and fell to the floor. As he sprinted up the stairs, Mulder heard Scully's voice.

"Annie! Wake up! You have to wake up, Annie!" As he reached the top of the stairs, she screamed, "Mulder! Mulder!"

When he tried to enter the bedroom, the door was met with resistance from inside. Mulder pressed his shoulder against it and shoved. It felt like he was pushing against a powerful wind.

The resistance gave way abruptly, and he fell into the bedroom in time to see, through a spinning, tinkling blur, a drawer shoot like a missile from the dresser. It hit Scully, who was on her knees straddling Annie and shaking her, across her shoulder blades and knocked her flat on her face on top of the unconscious woman.

Mulder dropped to the floor and crawled to the bed with the medical bag in hand, shouting Scully's name. Staying low, he released the bag, climbed halfway onto the bed, wrapped his arm around Scully's waist, and pulled her off of Annie, then onto the floor.

"How bad?" he said.

There were three small, freshly-opened cuts on her face crying tiny crimson tears. They matched the small cuts in her blazer. Pain twisted her features as she lay on her back beneath Mulder. "Don't know yet."

The tornado of broken glass began to break up and shards embedded themselves in the walls with small pops.

"We've gotta get out of here," he said. "There's a fire downstairs."

Scully's tense eyes widened at something above and behind Mulder.

He sat up and lifted an arm to protect his face from flying bits of glass. He found Annie on all fours on the bed, jaw still slack, the corners of her mouth glistening with moisture, peering over the edge of the bed at them with closed eyes that fluttered under the lids.

The remaining vortex of broke glass above the bed collapsed and the pieces rained loudly onto the hardwood floor.

"Annie, you've got to wake up!" he shouted as he got to his feet.

She did not respond or move in any way.

Mulder felt a sudden spike in the room's temperature. He looked around for flames but saw none, then down at Scully. Her palms were pressed to her cheeks as she looked up at him with fearful eyes.

Touching his face, Mulder knew that it was not the room's temperature that had changed but his own. His head was growing hot.

He thought Brandi Milsap whispering, "It's hot," before her heart blew through her chest.

Scully rolled onto her side with a pained expression, saying, "We've got to get out of here!" She started to get to her feet, but dropped flat when a gunshot exploded in the room.

Much of Annie's head vanished in a fleeting splash of red and her arms and legs collapsed beneath her. She lay face down with what remained of her head sagging limply over the edge of the mattress, dribbling on the floor.

Mulder turned to see Barney Milsap filling the doorway. He lowered the shotgun from his shoulder, jutted his chin, and turned to meet Mulder's eyes.

"I shoulda done it sooner," he said.

Firefighters managed to save most of the house, but the kitchen and dining room were gutted. Two ambulances and six Sheriff's deputies in three cars arrived quickly. One of the ambulances rushed Randy Milsap to the hospital while two EMTs from the other ambulances treated minor wounds.

Barney Milsap did not resist or make a sound when he was read his rights by one of the deputies.

"Looks like you really did it this time, Barney," the deputy said as he put the cuffs on Milsap's wrists.

Scully sat on the porch steps while one of the EMTs cleaned her small cuts. Mulder stood nearby with Brody Walsh, whose tan seemed to have drained from his face. He looked somehow smaller, deflated.

"They told me to stay in town," he said in a thin voice. "I'm supposed to go to the Sheriff's Department from here. They're going to question me. All of us, I guess. Everyone in the crew."

"I suggest you answer all of their questions honestly and accurately," Mulder said.

"I... I've never been... questioned before."

"You'll get lots of practice from this. And don't worry, they probably won't believe you, anyway."

Walsh gave him a long look. "But you knew. You figured it out. Why? I mean... how?"

Mulder smiled. "Just doing my job."

Walsh stepped over to Scully and muttered, "I'm sorry. Very sorry." Then he turned and wandered off in the general direction of the white van.

Tony Barbieri stood alone beside the van looking lost and stunned. When he saw Mulder looking in his direction, he lifted his hand and gave a half-hearted wave.

Mulder drove out of Shasta County that night going south on Interstate 5 to Sacramento. There, he and Scully would board a plane and fly back to Washington, D.C.

In addition to the cuts, Scully had a large bruise across her upper back. She had seen a doctor before leaving Redding and was given a painkiller, the effects of which were still giving her voice a certain thickness.

"I can't help feeling bad for Annie," she said. "She thought she'd found someone like her, someone who would understand her. I wonder if she'd ever been in love before."

"She and Tony seemed to have a lot in common," Mulder said.

"He was too dense to see it. Too... shy and afraid."

"Which is exactly what they had in common. I suspect both of them have been told in ways both explicit and indirect that they're never good enough, never measure up to anyone else."

"We all have those experiences in life, Mulder."

"Yes, but we're all not the same person. Some hardly notice those experiences and simply move on unscathed. Others are strengthened by them, see them as a challenge, something to prove wrong. But some people, the Annies and Tonys, are not equipped with the same defense mechanisms. Whatever allows some people to ignore the barbs and move on, whatever that is, the Annies and Tonys don't have it. It's as if it were snuffed out in vitro. Or maybe it simply was never there. Whatever they're missing, they're not able to get through those experiences unscathed. Because of that missing... something, they aren't able to defend themselves emotionally. And some of those blows are self-inflicted because they don't know of any other way to think of themselves than as... something less than."

"In this case, Annie had something *more* than."

Mulder nodded and smiled. "She was missing something most of us have, but she had something *none* of us have. It was so... *alien*, even to her, that she didn't understand it or know how to use it."

"Let's hope it's not an evolutionary change that's in the works. If it is, I think it's coming much too soon. Can you imagine somebody like Brody Walsh with that kind of ability? At least this will put an end to his show."

Mulder chuckled. "That would surprise me."

"You don't think this will ruin any credibility that show has?"

"First of all, it's a TV show, which means, as I'm sure Walsh himself would tell you, that it has no credibility at all. Because it's just a TV show. Credibility isn't an issue. Publicity is, and this will give him plenty of that. Secondly, the real story won't be reported. No one will know that Annie was behind it because the local cops won't believe or accept that story. Especially not from the producer and host of a paranormal TV show. They'll come up with something, and that will be the story. As long as Walsh isn't convicted of anything, and it's doubtful that he will be, he can go back to his show. And probably to a gigantic spike in the ratings."

"Without Annie?"

Mulder smiled. "Don't worry, Scully. He'll think of something. It's showbiz, and the show must go on."

THE END

KING OF THE WATERY DEEP

By Tim Deal

OFF THE COAST OF JEDDAH, SAUDI ARABIA
11th MAY, 2000, 11:00 a.m.

A thick cloud of dust and sand settled over the Red Sea and shrouded the forty foot Marietta in parched gloom. Jane Pepper pulled her sleeves down and flipped up her sweatshirt hood. Grant Hicks walked by, his wetsuit unzipped to the waist.

"No dive?" she said.

"Captain's lost," he said over his shoulder. "Can't see a damn thing."

The crew was posted around the Marietta keeping a lookout for the jagged coral that could rip a hole in the hull.

"Grant, relax, let's go into the cabin and have some wine."

He waved a hand in the air.

A shout punctuated the air—from the bow, one of the crew members spied something. A dark shape loomed just a few meters ahead.

"What the hell is that?" she said.

"Land!" yelled Tito, one of the Filipino hands.

A sharp outcropping of rock pierced through the sandy veil. It was charcoal gray, mottled with barnacles and broken crab shells.

Jane flipped on her camera and recorded the approach to the cluster of rocks. The expanse of land widened, revealing a small island or peninsula. There was not but small sagging trees, scattered, dry shrubs and dead vegetation.

Jane headed to the cabin and walked into the galley. Her friend Maggie Pelham sat at the table, one hand clutching a novel, the other gently rubbing her husband, Gavin's, head. Gavin, meanwhile, lay on the galley bench with a plastic bag hovering near his face.

"You're missing all the excitement," said Jane.

"I don't know, things are pretty exciting here," said Maggie.

"Hang in there, Gavin. We've had to anchor near an island until the sandstorm blows over."

Gavin lifted his head up. "Island?"

Jane grabbed a bottle of white wine from the refrigerator and popped the cork. She filled a glass for Maggie, then filled hers. "Happy early birthday my friend." They clinked glasses.

Gavin sat up, and Maggie looked him. "Feeling better?"

"No," he said. "I need to get off this boat, I—" he paused and dry-heaved into the plastic bag. He stood, grabbed the table for balance, then left for the deck.

"The air will do him good," said Maggie. "This wine however..."

"It's consulate stock, and it'll have to do," she said.

The galley door burst open. It was Tito.

"Miss Maggie," he said. "Your husband swam to the island."

"Should I be worried?" said Maggie.

On the deck, most of the crew was perched on the bow calling out to Gavin. Jane could see no sign of him. She looked around for Grant.

"Where's Grant?"

She yanked the sleeve of one of the crewman, an Indonesian named Bayu, she thought.

"Where's Grant? The American?"

"The American? He there, he follow." He pointed at the island.

A scream, sharp and desperate, pierced the air. The crew froze and went silent.

Jane looked at Maggie, saw the smile slip off her face, her eyes widen, hands move involuntarily to her mouth.

"That was Gavin," said Maggie.

Bayu started hoisting the anchor, Tito and the rest ran towards the cabin.

"What are you doing?" said Jane. She grabbed Bayu's forearms, tried to stop him from cranking up the anchor. "What the fuck are you doing?"

He continued, his eyes wild with fear.

"That's my husband," said Maggie. "He needs help. For god's sake stop!" She turned back towards the island, screamed out for Gavin, tears beginning to form in the corner of her eyes. Jane hammered at Bayu's hands with her fists, bellowed into his face.

Bayu turned and was about to say something when he was yanked violently over the bow of the boat. Jane heard the splash, heard the man saying something she could not understand, then nothing.

A sound from shore. She looked up. It was Grant, running towards the boat. He reached the shore, climbed one of the rocks and dove in.

Jane went back to the bow. Grant swam towards her. She found the rescue line with an orange floatation ring and tossed it overboard. Grant got his arm looped around it. The boat suddenly lurched backwards, taking Jane off her feet. She hit the deck hard and smashed her mouth on the stainless steel cleat on the bow. She tasted blood, felt the shards of one of her cuspids on her tongue and spat it out. The boat sped backwards, the engine throttling thick and loud.

Jane got up to her hands and knees and crawled to look over the gunwale. Grant still clung to the ring, pulled by the boat. She looked up at the captain. His face was bathed in the glow of his instruments. The boat veered sharply to the right and stopped in a jarring crunch of fiberglass. It sent Jane soaring backwards onto the deck. The Marietta's stern was now raised about a foot higher than its bow. The captain shifted into forward, but the boat remained, despite the angry growls of the engine.

Grant had released the ring and swam towards the dive ladder on the aft-end of the boat. She could see a large coral formation on the starboard and aft side of the boat. They had run aground. The engine continued to grind, belching diesel smoke into the foggy air. Grant was able to pull himself onto the dive platform. Jane reached down to help him over the gunwale, grabbed his right hand in hers, and pulled. He caught the railing in his left hand and hooked a leg over.

Thank God.

The boat lurched forward and Grant stumbled back into the water. The engine sputtered, popped, and died in thick plume of black smoke. When it cleared, she saw Grant floating face down in the water.

"No, no, Grant, no!"

She climbed over the gunwale onto the dive platform. She could almost reach him. She started to slip in when the water around Grant began to churn and bubble. The water turned crimson and Grant was pulled violently beneath the surface.

With her free hand she wiped salt water from her burning eyes. She blinked until the tears cleared and she was sure what she was seeing was real.

It climbed out of the sea and onto the deck, a man-thing, tall and slender, covered in iridescent aquamarine scales, its wide mouth opened and closed revealing sharp rows of teeth. It made it over the gunwale and paused. It turned its head towards Jane, curved its rubbery mouth into something resembling a grin, then ripped the cabin door from its hinges. It entered.

Screams poured from the cabin.

AIR FRANCE FLIGHT 71
FRIDAY, 2130 HOURS LOCAL TIME

Special Agent Dana Scully rubbed her eyes and stared down the aisle until it came back into focus. Dinner service had started, and she contemplated waking Mulder, who had dozed off beside her after three gin and tonics.

"Front-loading," he'd said. "In preparation for the dryness."

Three hours since their connection left Charles De Gaul. Three more until they landed at King Abdulaziz Airport, Jeddah, Saudi Arabia.

Dryness. It transcended climate, temperature, and spoke to the restrictive cultural expectations placed on residents and visitors to the Kingdom. Imposed Sharia law. Headscarves and abaya. The ban on alcohol and pork. Public prayer five times a day. Jeddah was supposedly a bit more cosmopolitan than landlocked Riyadh, but the distinction was lost on her. Women couldn't drive in Jeddah; couldn't travel by car without a male escort—husband, brother, or father. She bristled at the marginalization, but was concerned more about the practical, operational obstacles such restrictions would create. She thought about the case file in her attaché case under the seat in front of her. She considered variables, weighed options, programmed herself for worst-case scenarios. She suppressed an urge to retrieve the file and look at it again, found herself drifting towards possible conclusions, then stopped herself. Let it sit for now.

The dinner cart stopped a row ahead and Mulder stirred, sat up, and unlatched his seat back tray.

"Impressive," said Scully.

"Pavlovian conditioning," said Mulder. "My brain is hardwired to recognize the sound of an approaching food cart even while in deep REM sleep."

It was chicken or lamb. Mulder chose the chicken accompanied by a glass of Pinot Grigio. Scully wasn't hungry and asked for a sparking water.

Skinner had been reluctant to approve this investigation. He didn't think it was an X-File, and was further worried about the possibility of diplomatic gaffes associated with such an investigation in a culturally sensitive part of the world. There was little to suggest a paranormal link to the Pepper and Hicks disappearance. Saudi authorities firmly believed that Sudanese pirates were to blame—or possibly Somalis that drifted north around the Horn of Africa up from the Gulf of Aden.

Still, there was the video. Scully hadn't seen it yet, but it was enough for the Riyadh office to give Skinner a call.

Mulder held a fruit cup in front of her face. "Eat something," he said. "After today, you'll be eating through a burkha."

Two hours later and the captain announced the initial descent. The cabin awoke with a flurry of motion. Dark-haired women, who had previously been wearing tight jeans, miniskirts, and low-cut tank tops and blouses, one-by-one emerged from the aircraft lavatories in long, black, shapeless abayas. All had their hair hidden beneath black headscarves, or hijab, and some concealed their faces as well. Scully realized that these women, whom she found previously indistinguishable from their western counterparts, were Saudis. The abaya was not so much a cultural signature as she thought. Instead, it was a state uniform, a means of controlling personal expression. And its wear is not a point of pride, but of obligation.

She took a deep breath, let it out and unfastened her seatbelt. She bent and retrieved the folded black garment from her attaché and placed it in her lap. She looked over at Mulder—his smile a combination of sardonic humor and sympathy.

Scully stood and went to the lavatory to change.

KING ABDULAZIZ AIRPORT
JEDDAH, SAUDI ARABIA
SATURDAY, 0215 HOURS LOCAL TIME

Fox Mulder turned his head side to side, slowly, and stretched the clenched muscles in his neck. Two hours in the immigration line had worn him thin. For a while, he thought that he and Scully would never get through, that they'd become mired in Purgatory, locked in an existential broken record.

They retrieved their luggage and passed it through the electronic scanners at customs, then made it out to the terminal. Scully looked irritated and uncomfortable in her abaya. The terminal was a scene in black and white—scores of women, head-to-toe, in shapeless dark drapes. Men, on the other hand, wore crisp white robes, and red and white checkered keffiyah held to their heads by thick cords.

The State Department had sent a driver to meet them—a young Filipino named Jack. He held a sign that read "Mr. Fox." If Scully was offended, she didn't show it. Jack lead them out to a gray van. The heat and humidity descended on him like a heavy shroud. He felt the sweat begin to dampen his navy blue suit. Once inside the van, Mulder noted the armored reinforcements and bulletproof glass.

"Expecting trouble?" he said.

"I'm sorry, Mr. Fox?"

"The armor plating?"

"We worry about terrorists. We have briefings."

They pulled out of the airport into the city, full of lights, the coastline, and traffic circles with statues of colorful cars, skinny camels, and giant ships.

Jack drove them to a nondescript gate north of the city to a place he called "North Obhur." No hotel signs, no indication that anything existed there. They paused for a few minutes then the gate opened. They pulled in and found themselves in a small compound with an office and tennis courts.

They checked in to separate villas. It was a beach resort, right on the Red Sea. Like many other western resorts, it was marked discretely so as not to attract, and subsequently offend, the Saudi Arabian Ministry of Virtue and Vice.

Mulder dropped off his gear in his bungalow and met Scully in the outdoor restaurant by the water. She was no longer in her abaya, and had switched to a pair of shorts and a tank top.

"Feel more normal now?" he said.

Scully opened her mouth to respond but was interrupted by the blast of three different Mosque loudspeakers as the early morning, or *Fajr*, call to prayer echoed across the neighborhood.

BORDER GUARD STATION
OBHUR BAY, JEDDAH
SATURDAY, 1115 HOURS LOCAL TIME

There was no relief in the shadow of the palms and her abaya sucked in the heat, trapped her sweat, and made her itch. The bay, a sliver of water slicing eastward into North Jeddah, was full of activity. Dive boats and luxury yachts made their way west to the open sea while young men on jet skis cut across their wake, launching themselves into the air. Two boats docked at the station while the Saudi Border Guards checked manifests. One, a dive boat laden with a mix of smiling, sandy-haired expats; the other a smaller craft with two Arabic men in shorts and tank-tops, and four women covered head-to-toe in black, their bright orange lifejackets a stark contrast to their abaya, hijab, and niqab.

"Will they swim in that?" this to Raymond Bates, a State Department Diplomatic Security special agent who had met them there.

"Oh yes," he said. "They'll remain covered in the presence of men, most of them at least."

"What's the point of being in the water if you can't feel it directly against your skin?"

He smiled, kicked a stone loose from the ground. "Welcome to the Magic Kingdom."

Mulder, meanwhile, turned from the chain link fence that separated them from the station. He had forgone a suit and was better dressed for the 112-degree heat in khakis and a loose fitting white shirt, no tie. Despite the lack of sleep, he looked comfortable. Scully shot him daggers.

"The Saudi guys," said Mulder. "You confirmed eleven, right?"

Bates continued to toe the rock. "You have to figure in the *insha'allah* factor," he said. He went on to explain the indeterminateness of Saudi culture. Nothing concrete; everything left to God.

"If Allah wills it," he said.

They didn't have to wait for long. A gleaming silver Land Rover pulled up and parked across two parking spaces. Two men got out. One, a tall willowy man in a bright white robe and checkered kefiyah, spoke into a cell phone. His feminine features were framed by a meticulously trimmed beard. It was as if it had been carefully painted on his face. His partner was shorter, though obviously fit. He wore a tan suit and powdered blue shirt that was open at the collar. In contrast, he was clean-shaven, his black hair thick and unruly, his smile wide and white and persistent.

They exchanged greetings with Bates, the Suit effusive, loud—his handshake vigorous and lingering. White Robe was more reserved, his face scarcely shifting from its bored, impassive expression.

Bates made the introductions, "these are Inspectors Mahmoud Mohammed Bakhsh, and Saleh bin Taha of the Saudi *Mabahith*, the General Directorate of Investigation." He motioned to White Robe and Suit respectively, both of whom honed in on Mulder first, then turned to Scully. Mahmoud offered a curt nod, Saleh, however beamed at her.

"It is a rare pleasure," he said, extending his hand. She took it and shook it firmly, then disengaged before he had a chance to latch. He hovered within her personal space for a moment. His cologne was strong, cloying; would have been pleasant at a smaller dose.

"Agent Bates tells me you studied at the University of Maryland," he said. "I studied under Doctor Henry Grange for a year. Foreign exchange program from King Abdulaziz University. Cultural Anthropology."

"Grange retired during my junior year," said Scully. "He was well respected, if I remember correctly."

"I would welcome the opportunity to speak more about Doctor Grange," he said.

Scully felt Mahmoud's glare, his disdain for this interaction, palpable. Mulder came to the rescue.

"Gentleman, should we look at the boat?"

Mahmoud nodded. Saleh smiled and turned towards the gate, his eyes lingering on Scully until she was lost in his periphery.

A quick flash of Mahmoud's badge, and the gate guard allowed them in into the base, which was comprised of a small administrative building, a boat shack, and six gray vessels of varying size tied to the docks. The Marietta was dry-docked on metal stands, a canopy had been erected above.

Scully noted the condition of the boat exterior. The hull's outer layer of fiberglass was scratched and torn in several places. The railing that lined the gunwales had been ripped loose in spots, and was missing in others.

"Our forensic team has already processed the boat," said Mahmoud. "I'm not sure you'll find anything more of interest."

"I've seen the translated report," said Mulder. "It indicated the discovery of blood, purportedly from the crew. However, there was no mention of spent shell casings. Was that detail missed, or did the attackers use daggers and cutlasses?"

Scully shot him a glance. "Mulder," she said.

"Funny, Agent Mulder," said Saleh. "Red Sea pirates have become much more sophisticated since the nineteenth century. I think you'll find that the *Mabahith* possess a forensic team on par with the FBI's. Those crime scene specialists that weren't trained at the New Scotland Yard, received their training from your own agency."

Mahmoud looked at his watch, sighed. Saleh gestured towards the stepladder next to the boat. Scully pulled a pair of latex gloves and plastic shoe coverings from her briefcase, put them on, and then glanced down at the hem of her abaya trailing on the ground. She pulled it up and tucked it into her shorts. Mahmoud made a sound she couldn't interpret. She climbed the ladder, stopped at the top, and observed the deck.

The deck and outer bulkheads were stained with the charcoal gray smudges of fingerprint powder residue, and the ruddy brown patches of dried blood. She felt her stomach tighten. So much blood—more than the file photographs depicted. Great violent spatters, large dry pools, streaked up and down the deck.

Scully took it all in, tried to envision the moment of panic, the blood-bath that ensued. The railings told her that whoever entered the boat used them to gain purchase. That meant they had to climb *up* into the boat, which supported the idea of pirates in small-motorized craft—likely inflatables.

This raised a question that had been nagging her since reading the case file. If their goal was to kill everyone on board, why didn't they just shoot up the boat, hit it with a rocket-propelled grenade, and sink it? Instead, they boarded the boat, and seemingly butchered everyone. She let that sit for a moment and climbed over the gunwale. The still hot air trapped the stench of old meat, rotten fish, and the tide. She gagged, put her hand to her mouth then stopped and swallowed it down.

Scully crouched and looked at the blood-streaked deck. There were two things she noticed immediately. Within the streaks and pools of dried blood she found vague remnants of footprints, the pattern and activity of bare feet—the pirates' or victims' she could not be sure.

"Were you able to get print patterns from the deck?" she called over her shoulder.

Silence. A wave of dizziness passed through her—the heat and fetid air.

"There are footprints here," she said. "Did you—" she stood and looked around. The men were near the water, Mahmoud and Saleh smoking, Mulder and Bates smiling, laughing at something that was said.

"Great." She turned back to the Marietta.

The second thing she noticed were patches of faint iridescence scattered across the deck. She pulled out a small Maglight and shined it at an oblique angle. The iridescence had minute shadows and depth. She pulled out tweezers and evidence bag. Working carefully, she was able to collect a few of the iridescent pieces.

Scully could think of only two reasons why they would board the boat. The first, if it held cargo of interest to the pirates. This seemed unlikely. It was a pleasure boat, routinely used for recreational diving. The other would be to capture someone alive.

Alive. The thought tugged at her, built a rising sense of urgency deep inside. She stood and called out, "Mulder!"

"Yes Scully."

She started. He was standing at the top of the ladder.

"Pepper may be alive."

"Alive?" said Mulder, then covered his mouth and nose. "After all of this?"

"It's a long shot, but it's possible and we'll need to move fast."

"Finish up here," he said. "I've got a copy of the Marietta's manifest. We're meeting Bates back at the consulate to take a look at that tape."

"The report mentioned an island. If Pepper's alive—"

"Saleh said they scoured the island. They've got a few boats out there now, just in case," said Mulder.

Scully looked past Mulder and found Mahmoud's eyes locked on hers.

U.S. CONSULATE
JEDDAH, SAUDI ARABIA
SATURDAY, 1300 HOURS LOCAL TIME

Mulder and Scully sat in Bates' office, a laptop set up in front of them, a camcorder attached to the laptop.

"The GDI is every bit as thorough as Saleh indicated, only they weren't the first ones on the scene," said Bates.

"The report indicated that the Border Guard received a call from a passing trawler that the Marietta had run aground on a reef," said Mulder.

"Correct. They responded, then boarded the vessel in search of survivors. They found no one onboard, but came across a damaged camcorder lying on the deck. They seized it, then brought it back the station. The officer in charge couldn't get the camera to operate, so he attempted to pull the mini DV tape in order to watch it on one of their own cameras—only there was no tape."

"No tape?"

"This is a high-end camcorder. It records video to a proprietary storage media. The disc is not easy to locate, especially if you're not familiar with the camera. The Border Guard called the consulate after checking the Marietta manifest. Then they called the GDI. We got there first. When I arrived, they showed me the camcorder, and I promised to provide the GDI with a copy of anything I may find on the disc."

"And you found something?" said Scully.

"I'll let you be the judge of that."

He pressed play. The video opened on the bow of a boat—presumably the Marietta—and showed the approach to the cluster of rocks and the island.

"Is that fog?" said Mulder.

"Sandstorm," said Bates.

The video spun and caught a young, fit, dark haired man reaching up to cover the lens.

"Captain says we'll need to anchor here until the sandstorm dissipates," the man said. The video bounced around then went dark. However the audio continued to record, and captured Pepper's voice and the ambient sounds of he people around her. Mulder and Scully listened in silence as the chaos escalated into terrifying screams. For Mulder, it was almost unbearable to hear. After a moment, the screams subsided. The screen brightened, the camera bounced on the deck, the lens cracked.

"I think that the camera fell from Pepper's pocket at this point, keep watching."

Through the damaged lens, Mulder caught movement from the lower left of the screen, a figure, just a glimpse, then the screen went black. Bates reversed the video then paused it. Mulder leaned closer.

"Someone jumping off the boat, but—" he said.

"Is that a wetsuit?" said Scully.

"I've watched this at least seven times. I've shown it to the Bureau guys that came in from Riyadh. I'm not sure what we are seeing," said Bates. "We're sending the disc back to the States for forensic examination, but that will take time."

"I've never seen a wetsuit like that," said Mulder. "Every bit of his skin is covered. Look at the way it captures the light."

The figure on the screen, frozen in mid leap, was human in shape, but was covered in shimmering green and blue from its feet up to its head, which featured a small mohawk-like crest.

"The camera was damaged in the fall," said Scully. "Is it possible that the image became distorted, the color altered by the impact?"

"Possible," said Bates. "But that will be for the experts to figure out."

"Are there any witness accounts of such things before the Marietta attack?" said Mulder. "Any incidents, rumors, legends?"

"That, you'll have to ask your GDI counterparts," said Bates.

Scully stood and retrieved the bag she filled from the deck.

"Agent Bates, do you have anyone on your staff that has access to a lab and can identify this? It appears to be fish scales, and if we can identify the type of scales, we may be a little closer to determining who the attackers were. If my suspicions are correct, the pirates were Somali fishermen."

"This would be a little far from their territory, but I have a contact at the Office of the Deputy Ministry of Fisheries Affairs who may be able to help out. I'll have a courier run this over."

The consulate van picked up Mulder and Scully and they exited the gates. They sat outside the consulate, snarled in heavy traffic.

"The Arabian Peninsula has a rich history of paranormal activity. We've had our own experiences with djinn, and we know that djinn can take on a variety forms," said Mulder.

"There's very little to suggest that this is an X-File, Mulder. All we have is a blurry snippet of video. A State Department diplomat is missing, and may be still alive. I think we have to admit that we're out of our element here. Jane Pepper's life may be on the line, and I don't have confidence in the Saudis' conclusion."

Mulder felt that familiar frustration rise up. Despite years of investigations of unexplained events, Scully always defaulted to skepticism.

"So what do you suggest?"

"We know the attack took place near an undocumented island in the Red Sea. We know that the boat was boarded. If Pepper was taken, it stands to reason that she was taken because of who she was. This would mean that someone had tipped the pirates off."

Mulder pulled a business-sized envelope from his back pocket.

"According to Saleh, only the boat captain and the Border Guards had access to the manifest," said Mulder as he opened the envelope. "Besides the crew, the only other passengers were Gavin and Maggie Pelham, British expats with an address at Al Basateen."

"When we listened to the tape audio, Gavin Pelham was not on the boat at the time of the attack. He had swam to the island and the boat disembarked before he returned."

Mulder paused for a moment to let it sink in. Then he leaned forward to the driver. "Do you know where Al Basateen is?"

AL BASATEEN RESIDENTIAL COMPOUND
JEDDAH, SAUDI ARABIA
SATURDAY, 1515 HOURS LOCAL TIME

The security gate was manned by Saudi soldiers armed with AK-47s and an MG3 machine gun mounted on a HUMVEE. However, once the van passed through security, the compound looked like any western condominium complex. They located the Pelham villa, a large town-house in beige stucco, with a ceramic tiled roof. The door opened after two rings of the bell. A middle aged Filipina woman stood in the doorway with a worried look on her face.

"Mr. And Mrs. Pelham no return from boat trip," she managed after Mulder and Scully introduced themselves.

"May we come in?" said Scully.

Tina had been the housekeeper for the Pelhams for six years, three of those in the Kingdom, three in Jakarta. Gavin was a tobacco rep for a big US tobacco firm, while Maggie taught English at the International School.

"Do you know Jane Pepper?" asked Mulder.

"I know Miss Pepper. Very nice lady, she lives two villas over."

"Did the Pelhams ever talk about Miss Pepper in a an angry way?"

"No, never. They like Miss Pepper very much. They have many parties together."

"Parties? What sort of parties?"

"Parties with neighbors. Mr. Pelham would always bring his happy juice."

Tina brought them into the kitchen and opened the pantry. Within were steel pots, tubing, and a pressure cooker placed neatly on the same shelf. "Mr. Pelham gave many people happy juice. They pay him money."

She led Mulder and Scully out of the kitchen, up the stairs, and to a closed door. She unlocked the door and opened it. Scully counted thirty or so cardboard boxes in neat stacks inside.

"Happy juice," said Tina.

Scully walked in, opened a box, and pulled out a 1.5 liter plastic bottle. "Water?" she said.

"You try," said Tina.

Scully twisted off the cap and sniffed. She looked at Mulder.

"Alcohol," she said.

Mulder walked over, took the bottle, and swigged.

"Sidiki," he said. Saudi moonshine."

SHERATON RED SEA HOTEL
NORTH OBHUR, JEDDAH
SATURDAY, 1720 HOURS LOCAL TIME

Scully's cell rang as the consulate van pulled into the hotel, the gate sliding closed behind them.

"Scully? I see... okay. Thank you." She thumbed the disconnect button and looked at Mulder.

"Preliminary examination of the scales are inconclusive. They don't match up with any of the common fish species in the Red Sea. They're running further tests."

Mulder raised his eyebrows.

"It doesn't mean anything, Mulder."

"If you say so."

Scully went back to her bungalow eager to rid herself of the abaya. Once at the sliding glass door, she noticed the light on, though she was certain she had turned it off. She reached for her Sig Sauer P228, but had to pull her abaya up past her waist to retrieve it. She stopped and listened. She could hear nothing from within, the sound of the surf on the rocks and the quiet chatter of diners at the restaurant behind her.

She quietly slid the door open, then pulled the cobalt blue curtain to the side. No sound or movement from within. Nothing, at least in the living room. She slipped in and moved towards the bedroom. Again she paused and listened. The bed was covered with brightly colored boxes, dozens of them. A vase of roses sat on her nightstand, a card leaned against the vase. After confirming that the bedroom and bathroom were empty, she removed her abaya, then holstered the sig. She picked up the card and opened it.

"Welcome to Jeddah,
Saleh"

The gifts, the flowers were not only profoundly unprofessional, they were excessive. She could not discern what behaviors she could have displayed in the last few hours that would have prompted this lavish gesture.

Scully headed to the door to tell Mulder, but the phone rang.

"Hello?" she said.

"Agent Scully, this is Saleh. I trust you received my welcome gifts?"

"About that, I'm not too familiar with the customs of your country, but—"

"I'm sorry Agent Scully, but I actually called to give you some important news. Jane Pepper has been found alive. She is under protection and being treated at the International Medical Center. In her condition, I think it best if you could handle her debriefing. There may be others alive."

"Of course. I'll call the consulate about transportation."

"No need," said Saleh. "I have sent a car. It should be there soon."

Scully hung up, then called Mulder. It went to voicemail. She explained the situation. Scully sighed, shook the wrinkles out of her abaya, slipped it over her clothes, then went to meet the car.

Mulder got out of the shower, dried off, and noticed a message on his cell phone. He listened to Scully's message and made a mental note to check in on her if he hadn't heard back within the hour. He was relieved to hear that Jane Pepper had been found alive. Not only did it mean the prospect of more answers, but it also meant that the Saudis were keeping their word about the ongoing search.

He dressed in shorts and a t-shirt, then sat in front of laptop at the small desk in his bedroom. He read a research article on Enki, the Sumerian God of the Sea.

The main temple to Enki is named E-en-gur-a, meaning "house of the subterranean waters," a ziggurat temple on an island near the Red Sea coastline where the Yemeni Quda'a tribe settled. He was the keeper of the divine powers called Me, the gifts of civilization. He is often shown with the horned crown of divinity dressed in the skin of a carp. In Babylonian mythology, Enki is known as Ea, and is depicted as half-man, half-fish. Ea was also referred to as the Skar Apsi, or, "King of the Watery Deep."

Mulder typed in a search for "Yemeni Quda'a tribe," which resulted in a number of web articles on "Jeddah." He then tried "Skar Apsi." The first search result was the copy of a journal article entitled "From the Depths: The Ocean Cults of Arabia." Mulder's pulse quickened. Before he had an opportunity to read the article, his gaze drifted down to author's name:

Dr. Henry Grange, PhD, University of Maryland School of Anthropology.

He picked up his phone.

NORTH OBHUR, JEDDAH
SATURDAY, 1835 HOURS LOCAL TIME

Scully sat in the back of the Lincoln Town Car and began to suspect that it was not an official vehicle. The pristine leather interior, integrated

DVD player, and well-manicured driver suggested otherwise. She tried to enquire, but the driver did not seem to understand English.

She watched the gated resorts and marinas roll by through deeply tinted windows, as the car traveled south towards Jeddah proper. She recognized the onramp to Medinah Road ahead, but the driver continued on another quarter mile before turning right and coming to a stop in front of a gate. A moment later and the gate began to slide open, and the Town Car entered a long driveway.

"Is this the medical center?" she said, but the driver replied in Arabic.

The car continued until the driveway opened up to the ocean on the right. There she saw a massive yacht, and Saleh standing next to the gangplank. The car stopped, and Scully got out.

"Forgive the detour Agent Scully, but given that this is your first trip to Jeddah, I thought you may appreciate the scenic route to the medical center. We can travel south along the coast and put in at the city docks."

Scully felt the anger rise up at the suggestion. Pepper had been through hell, and there was a chance the information she provided could prove useful in locating Hicks, the Pelhams, and the crew.

"I'm sorry, but I don't have time for the 'scenic route.' It's critical that you get me to Jane Pepper immediately."

Then she saw it—something in his expression, something a little too amused. She sensed the presence of the driver, close, looming, tense. Her hand drifted towards her Sig, but she realized the abaya was in the way.

"Do not worry, Agent Scully, I will take you directly to Ms. Pepper without further delay."

SHERATON RED SEA HOTEL
NORTH OBHUR, JEDDAH
SATURDAY, 1915 HOURS LOCAL TIME

Mulder had left two messages with Scully, and one with Agent Bates. His concerns may have been unfounded. He wasn't sure how robust the cell signals were in Jeddah, and he wasn't positive there was cause for alarm to begin with. He ran the facts down: someone or something came from the water and boarded the Marietta; no survivors remained on the boat, and no bodies were found; Pepper had been found alive by the Saudis (but how and where?); Gavin Pelham was not on the boat during the attack; Gavin was bootlegging siddiki from his home; then there were the identified scales, the video, and Professor Henry Grange, who quite possibly linked the whole thing to—

A knock on the door. Mulder pulled his Sig from its holster on the nightstand, and peered through the curtains. For a moment he didn't recognize the tall man with the close-cut beard, then he realized it was Mahmoud, this time dressed in a pair of jeans and a black t-shirt. Mulder slid the door open, placing the handgun behind his thigh.

"Inspector Mahmoud," he said. "What brings you here?"

Mulder stepped aside, and Mahmoud stooped to enter, his demeanor sunken, tired.

"I wanted to personally inform you that the bodies of Ms. Jane Pepper, Grant Hicks, Maggie Pelham, and most of the crew of the Marietta were recovered about an hour ago by the Border Guard. Although their identities will not be officially confirmed until DNA or Dental records are consulted."

Mulder felt his chest tighten. "That can't be right, I—Agent Scully received a call from Inspector Saleh. He said that Pepper had been found alive, that she was going to debrief her."

Mahmoud met his gaze. "Saleh you say? Impossible. He was with me when we received word. You must be mistaken. No matter now. We have been pulled off the case. The case has been picked up by the General Intelligence Presidency. It's been declared a matter of national security. I came here as a courtesy."

Mahmoud began walking towards the door. Mulder blocked his way.

"Listen, Saleh, or someone claiming to be him, called Scully, sent a car to pick her up. I haven't been able to reach her."

Mahmoud sidestepped Mulder. "I am sure she simply misunderstood the message. Saleh has taken a, well, a personal interest in Agent Scully. Perhaps she was too ashamed to admit that she simply went out on a social engagement with him."

Saleh reached for the door and Mulder grabbed his arm.

"A social engagement?" he said, his face inches from Mahmoud's. "You don't know my partner. I believe she's in danger. I need you to call Saleh."

Mahmoud stared at Mulder, his features cold and impenetrable. "I'm risking my career by being here."

"Call Saleh," said Mulder.

6 NAUTICAL MILES OVER THE RED SEA
SATURDAY, 2030 HOURS

Mulder and Mahmoud sat in the troop compartment of a UH-60 Blackhawk Helicopter as it soared over the dark swells and whitecaps of the sea below. Both wore headphones and mics.

"Saleh's driver said he brought Agent Scully to Saleh's private yacht just before 1900," said Saleh.

"Private yacht?"

"The royal family is pretty expansive in the Kingdom. Saleh is one of many minor princes."

"How can we be sure that he took her to the island?"

"The driver said that Mahmoud was acting strangely, and that he made references to 'bringing Agent Scully to the scene of the crime.'"

"How well do you know Mahmoud?"

"Well enough to know that his piety is far eclipsed by his vanity."

Mulder felt the Blackhawk begin to descend. The helicopter's floodlights exposed the rock-strewn shore of a sparsely vegetated island. They flew inland for another few minutes and then landed on a flat stretch of land.

"Shouldn't we check the coast for the yacht?" said Mulder.

"The pilot received a report of a sandstorm moving over the island. We're grounded. We'll move by foot to where the bodies were located. It's not far from here."

Mahmoud led Mulder across an open expanse of terrain towards higher ground. The wind picked up and showered them with warm, sand-filled blasts of air. They climbed up several large boulders until they reached a plateau. Through the darkness and the sandy haze, Mulder made out a large spire jutting from the middle of the plateau.

"What is that?" he said, his voice fighting the increasing howl of the wind."

"This would be the scene of the crime," said Mahmoud. "E-en-gur-a, the Temple of Enki. It is an archeological site of one of the many pre-Islamic pagan deities."

"The water god? Saleh studied under Doctor Grange, an expert in Enki's cults," said Mulder.

"We will search inside the temple. Saleh may have very well brought Scully here," said Mahmoud. "The subterranean passages lead to an underwater sacrificial chamber. It's there that the Border Guard found the victims."

Once upon the spire, its clear geometrical lines were more obvious. It was an obelisk thirty to forty feet high. At its base, a stone archway, black within. Mahmoud illuminated the archway with a flashlight, revealing a myriad of worn symbols. "Mostly cuneiform," he said. "Some symbols, have yet to be deciphered."

He moved within the arch, and Mulder followed. It narrowed into a short hall that then began to steeply descend.

The condition of the bodies suggested the possibility of international terrorist involvement."

"What was the condition of the bodies?"

"They were beheaded. All of them."

It wasn't long before Mulder smelled seawater, and the heard the splash of water on stone. The corridor widened, then opened up into a large chamber. Here, a path lead out into a pool of seawater and stopped at another obelisk, this one a smaller replica of the one aboveground. The chamber was otherwise empty.

"The bodies were found arranged around the obelisk."

"No Scully, or Saleh. They must be above."

"Perhaps they haven't arrived yet."

"Mahmoud, she's in danger, we just can't wait here in hopes that she'll show up."

"Perhaps you should worry less about your partner."

"What—?"

Mahmoud illuminated the gun he pointed at Mulder, then blinded him with the beam of light.

"Remove your weapon and drop it on the ground."

Mulder reached into his jacket and pulled out his Sig. For a moment he considered taking a shot at Mahmoud, but he couldn't see anything with the light in his eyes.

"Back slowly towards the obelisk. I think you'll find what happens next to be... fascinating."

"What have you done with Scully?" he said. "Look, you have me now, you don't need her. Let her go."

"Scully, I'm sure, is in good hands," said Mahmoud.

Mulder felt the cold stone of the obelisk press into his back. Mahmoud was upon him quickly, handcuffing his hands behind the stone monument. The light was now gone from his eyes, leaving drifting motes and spirals. His eyes adjusted. Mahmoud was busy lighting torches around the perimeter of the chamber.

"Enki is a god that requires balance," said Mahmoud. "Like many of the older gods, he is sustained by sacrifice. In the Abrahamic traditions, those sacrifices are largely personal and symbolic. During Ramadan, Muslims forego food and negative behaviors from sunrise to sunset; For Catholics, they sacrifice something for Lent; and the Jews have Tish B'Av. Enki and his kind are not so figurative."

Mahmoud finished with the torches and moved to the path that crossed the water in front of Mulder. He began to remove his clothing.

"Enki represents the relationship of the land and the sea; the balance that is struck when two powerful elements clash—the explosion of surf on the rocks, the estuary that carves through landscapes, and the hurricanes and typhoons that level human settlements. Enki also represents the harmonic nature of that balance—the bounty of the depths, the life-giving supply of rain, trade and transportation."

Mahmoud now stood nude in front of Mulder, his thin body flickering orange in the torchlight. Mulder pulled at his cuffs, tried to squeeze his hands out of them to no avail.

"These are ancient ideas," said Mulder. "Antiquated, dead. Nothing will come from my sacrifice but your arrest."

"These ideas are very much alive, as you'll have the privilege of witnessing first hand," said Mahmoud.

He dropped to his knees and began to utter a series of harsh, guttural sounds—a language Mulder could not understand. When he raised his head, his eyes had turned black, his face more aquiline, and his skin a shimmering green and blue.

Mulder's pulse quickened, his breathing shallowed. The water in the pool around him began to churn. He felt panic rise as Mahmoud's fingers grew webbed membranes and sharp talons. Mahmoud's skin transformed into glimmering scales. His unintelligible gibbering, now further garbled by a viscous gel that formed strands over a gaping carp-like mouth, increased in urgency and crescendo.

Mulder pulled at the handcuffs until he felt blood trickle onto his hands. The water around him came alive as bubbles roiled the surface. This too excited Mahmoud, his black eyes wide with delight over the arrival of his minions. He shambled towards Mulder on unsteady, webbed feet, his enormous mouth, now ringed with jagged teeth, sucking at the air.

His presence spoke of vast unexplored depths and long dormant Gods. As Mulder anticipated the tearing claws and ripping teeth, his thoughts became murky, invaded by a submerged plume of malevolence, both ancient and alien.

Mahmoud was close enough to Mulder that he could smell the creature's rotten breath. He turned his head away, awaited the inevitable, and watched as several figures broke the surface of the pool, their skin glistening, heads misshapen, and their breath coming in deep labored exchanges.

He howled.

AN UNIDENTIFIED ISLAND IN THE RED SEA
SATURDAY, 2143 HOURS

From above, a pale orange light and the dance of shadows. The surrealism of the moment struck her. Breathing underwater. Clouds of bubbles rising over her head. Beneath the Red Sea.

Scully followed the others towards the light. Besides Saleh, there were four men—operators from the Ministry of the Interior's Special Response Team. She kicked until she was alongside them, then they surfaced together.

As her head rose above the water she was met with a collage of images: a cavernous chamber, golden light, two men and a stone pillar—but something didn't look right. She pulled off her mask and for a moment it looked as though one of the men was covered in scales, his great webbed talons grasping at the throat of Mulder, chained to an obelisk.

Saleh yelled something in Arabic and one of the MOI men fired a burst from his HK MP5 submachine gun. The man with scales dropped at Mulder's feet. The operators quickly climbed out of the water and approached the body.

Scully removed her fins and walked to Mulder.

"For a moment I thought—" she said.

"That I was being attacked by a fish man? Come on, Scully, we've danced this dance before" Mulder nodded towards the body on the ground. "See for yourself."

Scully looked down at the body. "Mulder?"

Mulder followed her gaze.

Mahmoud laid dead and naked, blood seeping from several bullet wounds in his side.

"But..." said Mulder.

Saleh stepped up. "There are others just like Mahmoud, cultists, worshippers of old Sumerian gods. The attack on the Marietta was not the first of its kind. They've kept to the ocean, so far, but our fear is that they'll eventually begin operating further inland. My studies with Doctor Grange have been invaluable in hunting them down. So far it has been targets of opportunity, and those have been in line with the ancient calendar. Your sacrifice was to be aligned with the Ara Tisritum, the Sumerian 'Month of Beginning' which signals the start of the new year."

"Mahmoud said something about Enki's need for 'balance,'" said Mulder. "As if my sacrifice was the second half of the ritual. Was Pepper the first?"

"Mulder, Pepper is alive. It was Maggie Pelham that they were after," said Scully. "Mahmoud had been leaning on her husband Gavin over his siddiki business. Gavin told Mahmoud about the boat trip, gave up his wife to save his skin."

"The worshippers of Enki have very specific criteria of their offerings," said Saleh. "They must not be of Sumerian birth or descent, and they must have been born on the mid-month day of Arah Tisritum."

"In the Gregorian calendar," said Scully. "That day is October 13th."

"Maggie Pelham and I shared the same Birthday?" said Mulder.

"Let's get you up to the boat and see to those wrists."

AIR FRANCE FLIGHT 718
SUNDAY, 2330 HOURS LOCAL TIME

Scully sat in the first class cabin and sipped at a glass of champagne. She set her glass down and let her eyes close. A moment later, she sensed

Mulder's presence, looked up and saw him standing in the aisle.

"I'm sorry that there were no more seats in first class, Mulder. I can come back to coach if you want. It is *your* Birthday."

"Enjoy it," he said, "While you can."

"I'm trying to," she said, and closed her eyes. "Let's not tell Skinner about the Prince's upgrade."

"I can't wrap my ahead around one thing. Mahmoud would have access to MOI databases with dates of birth of all expats in the Kingdom. That explains Maggie. What about me? How did he know?"

"I don't know Mulder, maybe Bates said something. Maybe he got it from the passport officials at the airport."

"But that would mean it was all chance, my coming here."

"All chance Mulder."

"I've been reviewing the case file. What if I were to tell you that the FBI office in Riyadh only requested us at the behest of a Saudi Prince?"

Scully opened her eyes. "Is that true?"

Mulder shrugged and smiled.

THE END

SEWERS

By Gini Koch

BAILEY'S CROSSROADS, VIRGINIA
8th DECEMBER, 1990, 10:09 a.m.

The sewer was dark and dank and smelled far worse than Arthur Dales imagined it would. But there was a monster down here he had to stop.

Thankfully there were concrete walkways on either side of the wide trench that was filled with water, waste, and God alone knew what else. He walked quickly but quietly, his flashlight in one hand, his Colt .45 in the other. A sound caught his attention—something rough rubbing against the concrete. Something scaly. He moved towards the sound.

The creature leaped out from around a corner. Hard to see clearly, but the elongated, fang-filled snout and the giant, spiky tail didn't seem like a costume—especially as the tail slammed into Dales and threw him against the other side of the tunnel.

"Where's the boy?" Dales managed to shout as he kept his feet under him, his gun in his hand, and didn't take a dive into the sewage, though his flashlight did. "Give me the boy!"

The creature roared, then turned and ran, in the water that filled the sewer drain. It ran faster than its size would indicate possible. Dales ran after it. He was so close now. He aimed and fired.

The bullet deflected off the creature's body. Unless this was a giant man in a bulletproof alligator suit, the creature had hide that repelled bullets.

The creature was strong, and Dales' weapon wasn't going to make a dent. It didn't matter—the life of the boy mattered. He ran on into the dark.

VISTA BUENA, CALIFORNIA
DECEMBER 1990

Jason was late and his mom was going to be pissed. And more pissed that he was with the ABC Girls. "I should probably go."

"Come on, Jay," Amanda said. "Since when are you chicken?"

"I'm not. It's just.. ,we're supposed to be home now."

Brittany rolled her eyes. "And since when do you care about that?"

"Jason's worried that his mom's going to freak out," Caitlin said. "But you know she's buzzed at best, Jay. She's probably passed out."

There was a lot of truth to that. And they'd biked all the way to the fairgrounds to see the carnival. That his mom didn't want him going to. Then again, his mom never wanted him going anywhere. She only wanted him to go to school so she'd know where he was most of the time.

"It's kind of crummy looking," he pointed out.

"It's old," Brittany said with a shrug. "So what? I want to ride the Zipper."

"I want to see the freaks," Amanda chimed in.

"Cotton candy," Caitlin said. "And funnel cake. And Cokes."

"We don't have money," Jason pointed out.

The ABC Girls gave him the exact same look. It was easy because they were triplets, but it was always unnerving to see them all stare at him with their heads cocked to the right, little smirks on their faces, and their left eyebrows raised.

"Since when has that ever stopped us?" Amanda asked finally.

"Never," Jason admitted. Their middle school counselor had called them all budding delinquents. But whatever. The ABC Girls were his friends, and Jason didn't have a lot of friends. Besides, the Girls were great pickpockets. Jason wasn't, but his job was to be the distraction. And to spot the right marks.

As he looked around, a man approached them from inside the carnival's chain link fence. "You kids want to come in?" The man was tall and looked like a body builder, and his voice was deep and raspy.

"Are you the strongman?" Brittany asked.

"Nope. I'm not the lion tamer or the ringmaster, either." He winked, and his eyes looked odd—yellow and more like a cat's than a human's.

But the next moment they looked normal again.

"Are you one of the freaks?" Amanda asked.

"You shouldn't say that!" Jason said.

The man shrugged. "You four look like kids who skipped school to come to our carnival but don't have any money to get in."

They looked at each other. "We might have no school today," Caitlin said.

"We might have money, too," Brittany added.

The man laughed. "Right. Look, we're slow—so I know that school is actually going on today. I have a soft spot for truants. So come around to the back—I'll let you in the employee's entrance." With that, he turned and headed off.

"Do his pants look weird to you guys?" Jason asked the Girls. They looked like there was something big shoved down the back of one of the man's pant legs. Something big that was moving differently than the man's legs were.

"Don't care," Amanda said. "He wants to let us in, we're going in."

They rode their bikes to the back and sure enough, the man was there, waiting for them. The day was overcast, since winter in a beach city meant a lot of fog and rain. More clouds blocked the sun and Jason shivered. The fairgrounds were on a mesa overlooking the beach. He watched the waves crash angrily. "Maybe we shouldn't go in."

Caitlin grabbed his hand and pulled him off his bike. "Don't be such a sissy, Jay." Amanda grabbed his other arm and, following Brittany, they pulled Jason through the employee's entrance.

The man grinned at them. His teeth looked really big. "Glad you four decided to take advantage of getting in for free." He turned around. "Come on," he said over his shoulder. "I'll show you those freaks you want to see so badly."

"Can we get cotton candy first?" Caitlin asked as they trotted to catch up to him. "So we eat long enough before we ride the rides so we don't get sick."

The man shrugged. "Sure. My treat."

"Why are you being so nice to us?" Jason asked. He tried not to sound as suspicious as he felt. He failed, if the man's smirk was any indication. There was something wrong about how the man looked—as if he was wearing a costume that didn't fit him just right.

The man shrugged. "I like kids."

"What's your name?" Brittany asked.

"You can call me Gator. It's my nickname."

"Why do you have that nickname?" Amanda asked.

Gator grinned, showing long teeth that looked like fangs. "Because, like you guessed, I'm one of the freaks. I'm the Alligator Man."

"Cool!" Caitlin squealed as they approached the cotton candy vendor.

"You don't have scales," Brittany said accusingly.

"That you can see." Gator chuckled. "Besides, I have other attributes." He smiled at the vendor. "Four cotton candies for my kiddos, please."

The vendor twirled the pink sugar onto the cones. Gator paid. The money smelled bad but the cotton candy man didn't seem to notice or mind. He smiled when he handed Jason his treat. "You have a nice dad."

Jason stared at him. His father had left his family years ago. And besides, didn't the cotton candy man know Gator? "Ah…"

Gator laughed. "Come on, kids. Time to see the show."

He led them to the Freak Show tent. Like where they'd come in, it was near the back and also by some toilets. The tent looked old and creepy. Gator pulled back a flap—it was pitch black inside. The Girls raced in.

Jason held back. "I'm not so sure I want to."

Gator reached out, put his hand on Jason's shoulder, and propelled him inside. "You want to. Trust me."

As the flap closed behind them, Jason was sure that he heard someone scream. It sounded like one of the Girls. He looked up at Gator. Then Jason screamed, too.

FEDERAL BUREAU OF INVESTIGATION
WASHINGTON, D.C.
DECEMBER 1990

"Here's one for you, Spookster." Johnston tossed a file onto Mulder's desk.

"Fox."

"What?"

Mulder sighed as he picked up the file. "I'd rather you called me Fox.

Well, honestly, I'd rather you called me Mulder, but if you're going to insist on something else, call me Fox." He'd asked Johnston to call him Mulder every day for six weeks. He was trying now for his first name. He hated it, but it was still preferable to the nickname he'd earned at the Academy.

Johnston stubbornly insisted on calling him by variations of his nickname, but always in a buddy way—Mulder never picked up any real malice or ridicule. That he'd been partnered with Johnston was one of life's mysteries. Probably because Patterson from ISU didn't care for him. Probably a lot of his superiors didn't care for him. Like Johnston, though, this wasn't worth a lot of Mulder's focus.

"Why?" This was the first time Johnston had ever asked.

"It's better than Spooky or its derivatives." Mulder took a drag on his cigarette as he looked at folder. An abduction case. Only...not quite. Four kids, all aged twelve—three girls, triplets, and a boy, all friends. All from the bad part of wherever Vista Buena, California was. Ah, Johnston had added a note—an hour north of Los Angeles, thirty minutes south of Santa Barbara. So Johnston was good for something. No ransom involved. The missing kids were all delinquents and truants, at least per their school records, so logic would dictate that they were more likely to be runaways or hanging out at some friend's house than kidnap victims.

However, there were eye witnesses to the abduction. There weren't a lot of them, but the few who'd given statements all corroborated each other. What they corroborated, though, was unbelievable. "What the hell is this?"

"I see you found our 'gold'. Yes, witnesses say they were dragged down into the sewer. By a giant alligator with glowing yellow eyes."

"You're kidding."

"You wish I was. Local police are assessing—if the kids aren't found by tonight, then ASAC Carter wants you to take the lead on this one. Kids disappeared at a carnival, and he thinks it could be a publicity stunt. But we'll need to close it out, give it the Agency's stamp of unsolvable or reveal the hoax."

"This is in California. Don't we have agents out there?"

Johnston shrugged. "ASAC Carter tapped you for this one—newest guy always gets the shit jobs and lunatics. But I'll be riding shotgun, so no worries, Spookarino. It'll be a fun vacation. We leave tomorrow at six a.m. if the local LEOs don't have them back by then. I'll pick you up at your place. Give the wife my apologies in advance." Johnston walked off.

Mulder read the rest of the file. Police had investigated the sewer and found no evidence of any of the kids or a giant alligator. Then again, he'd already experienced enough police incompetence, corruption, and cover-ups to understand why ASAC Carter wanted the Bureau to investigate.

He ground out his cigarette. There was something familiar about this. He'd seen something similar, and not that long ago.

Mulder headed for the records room, the old one, where the X-Files were stored. Since meeting Arthur Dales last month, he'd been looking at these files more and more. As Dales had said, they were interesting. They might also have some clue about his sister's abduction. Though he was certain she hadn't been taken by some urban myth.

Finding the file didn't take long—he'd read this one about ten days ago. File X-528791, regarding Allan G. Sewers.

He took the file back up to his desk. This was a case Dales himself had covered. And it sounded eerily similar to the situation in Vista Buena.

Mulder put both files into his briefcase, grabbed his trench coat, and headed out.

"Need help, Spookins?" Johnston asked as he walked by.

"Nope. Going to see an old friend who may have some insights. He's not much for company, so it's better if I go alone. Figure I'll see you tomorrow, bright and early."

With that, Mulder headed for the parking lot.

ARTHUR DALES' APARTMENT BUILDING
WASHINGTON, D.C.

Dales' building was older, just like Dales. Maybe that was why he stayed there. Mulder went upstairs, down the hall, and rapped on the door. "Mister Dales? It's Fox Mulder."

The door opened, though the chain lock was still on. "Ah. It *is* you. You're back sooner than I'd expected."

"A strange case just came across my desk and I think you may be able to give me some insights."

Dales closed the door, unlocked it, and let Mulder in. "You're unclear on the concept of retired, aren't you?"

Mulder shrugged. "I'm clear on the concept of getting an expert's opinion."

"Ah, flattery. That I can never get enough of. So," Dales asked as he sat on his sofa and Mulder took the easy chair he'd occupied the last time he'd been here, "what can I do you for?"

Mulder handed him the old X-File. "I need to know how much of this case was bullshit and how much was real."

Dales' eyes widened as he glanced at the file number. "Why?"

"Because we have a case that sounds just like it in Southern California right now. I fly out tomorrow morning with my partner, assuming the missing kids don't turn up before then. And I want to know if this is a hoax. Because it sounds like a hoax."

"It's no hoax. But, dammit, I thought I'd gotten him." Dales sighed. "Though, to be honest, I've heard rumors…I guess I just wanted to believe I'd taken the bastard out."

"Who? Sewers or the alligator?"

"One and the same, son. One and the same. So, you'll need to go armed for bear. Take guns with high velocity and large rounds. And lots of rounds. He won't go down easily."

"Wait, seriously? You want me to believe that alligators in the sewers are real?"

"You believe in aliens. What's the difference?"

"The fact that alligators need a certain temperature range to survive and thrive, and New York, D.C., most of the places where we get alligator in the sewer stories, aren't the right climate."

"Southern California would be. Besides, he's not an alligator. Well, not only an alligator."

"Right."

Dales sighed. "All that I told you before, all that you've already seen—all the unexplainable by rational means. Somehow, those things you accept. And yet you want to argue this one with me?"

"Alligator in the sewer rumors have been around longer than you've been alive, sir."

Dales nodded. "Rumors usually have some grain of truth in them, son. Sometimes much more than a grain."

"So, tell me about it, why you think this is real."

"Because I followed up on the rumors even before I was in the Bureau."

"You're kidding."

"Nope. I was always fascinated by the rumors, in part for the reasons you gave earlier—alligators can't really survive a New York winter, not without the protections a zoo or an animal park would give them. But the rumors never let up. Some of them were just bullshit, of course. But more than you'd think weren't. And I found a pattern to them. Then I joined the Bureau and I had to focus on finding so-called communists."

"And you told me how well that went."

Dales chuckled dryly. "I thought the business with your father had ended my career, but I was too good to waste, and Mister Hoover chose to keep me around. And then I discovered that a missing persons case intersected with my lifelong alligator in the sewers hunt…"

BAILEY'S CROSSROADS, VIRGINIA
NOVEMBER 1963

The small carnival was set up, but not opened—it was too early in the morning.

"Artie, are you sure this is the place?" Hunter asked as they got out of their sedan.

"I'm sure." Dales wasn't just sure—he was positive. "I've tracked this thing for too long, Jack."

"Yeah, yeah, since before you were in the Bureau, I know, I know. We need to find those missing kids, though."

"They'll be here. They'll be wherever it is."

The carnies were here already, setting up. A quick flash of their badges got them access. Dales headed straight for the Freak Show tent. A man raced up to them. He was about Dales' height, stout, hairy, and half-dressed, which was how Dales knew he was hairy. "I'm the owner. What's this about? We have our permits."

"It's not about your right to be here. What kind of background checks do you do on your employees, Mister…?"

"And for God's sake, button your shirt up," Hunter added.

"Zartec," he said as he so buttoned. "Emilio Zartec. We're a carnival. We don't do background checks. If someone has a talent, and is willing to work, I put them to work. This isn't a lifelong career choice for most."

"Where do your freaks come from?" Dales asked as they reached the tent.

"All over. Are you going to make me prove that the freaks are real?" Zartec didn't sound worried about this, more annoyed than anything else.

"Possibly." Dales went into the tent. It was dark, and the setup inside made it darker. The interior was a maze, with the walls made up of canvas stretched between wooden stakes, interspersed with "cages" that held the freaks. "Get me to your Malligator."

"Half man, half gator," Zartec said rather proudly. "He's been with us for years."

"I'll bet he has," Dales muttered under his breath.

Zartec cleared his throat. "That one is, ah, a costume, you know. I mean, Gator, as we call him, has an issue with his teeth, but the rest is, ah, showbiz magic. He's my man in charge of the Freak Tent—sets it up, makes sure we give the people what they want."

Zartec led them through the maze towards the back of the tent. "So, where is he?" Dales asked—the Malligator cage was empty.

"Possibly getting breakfast," Zartec said. "He's an employee, not a slave, and the tent, as you can see, is already set up and just awaiting its cast and audience." Zartec looked at his watch. "And I have a carnival to prepare for opening."

"We'll have a look around," Hunter said. "You don't need to stay with us."

Zartec didn't look happy, but Hunter was a big man, like his late partner, Hayes Michel had been, only he had more muscle than Michel had ever had. Zartec took Hunter's hint and left them. Dales pulled out his flashlight and took a closer look.

Like the rest of the freak cages, this one was Plexiglas on three sides with wooden bars in front—presumably so the freaks could grab at the gawkers and make their experience more thrilling. A wooden box at the back was both a trunk and a seat, and there was a great deal of sawdust on the floor. What was absent was the Malligator and anyone, or anything, else.

Dales opened the wooden trunk. There were some shelf stable food-stuffs and a thermos filled with water. No false bottom, no missing kids.

"I'm going to take a look at the rest of this area," Hunter said. Dales grunted and Hunter wandered off.

Dales kicked the sawdust around and was rewarded by finding a manhole cover with "Sewer" on it. "Interesting location."

"Artie!"

Dales ran towards the sound of Hunter's voice. He was a few yards away at another freak cage, with the wooden bench trunk opened. Dales looked in to see a young girl, covered in what looked like mud but smelled like something else. "Is she alive?"

Hunter nodded. "Just barely. We need to call for an ambulance."

"We need to check the rest of these trunks." Dales ran off, through the maze, checking each cage, while Hunter shouted for Zartec. Sure enough, Dales found two more girls, both covered in sewage, both barely alive.

Local police were on their way—he could hear the sirens in the distance. Hunter was locking down the carnival personnel with Zartec's frantic help. But the Malligator was still nowhere around.

Precious time was wasted waiting for the local LEOs to arrive, but Dales had an obligation to the girls' families to not allow their daughters to be left without his guard—and it wasn't as if he and Hunter could reliably trust the carnival people to guard and not destroy evidence.

"What now?" Hunter asked as the local police cordoned off the scene and the emergency personnel tended to the kidnapped girls.

"There's still one kid missing, the boy. And I think I know where he and our suspect are." Dales strode back to the Malligator's cage, Hunter following. Dales pulled up the sewer manhole cover. "This moved pretty easily, Jack. He's down there, and he's got the boy with him. And," Dales said, stepping onto the metal ladder, "I'm going after them both."

ARTHUR DALES' APARTMENT BUILDING
WASHINGTON, D.C.
DECEMBER 1990

"So, what happened after you went after them?" Mulder asked. Dales was a good storyteller and he wanted the ending.

"I tracked them for hours to the spillway that went to the ocean. Emptied my gun into the Malligator's eye. He went down, but he had a good hold on the boy and took the child with him." Dales shook his head. "I went back for reinforcements and to call the Coast Guard, but as soon as I got up onto land, Hunter told me we'd been called off."

"Why? Was the Malligator actually an alien?"

"I doubt it. No, we were called off because President Kennedy had been assassinated, and Hoover wanted a full showing of all Special Agents to work the case."

"But you still had a child missing!"

"And he was a kid from a poor neighborhood. Meaning no one in authority cared. I tried to follow up, but by the time we were done with the Kennedy investigation I was at retirement age and decided I was getting too old for the game. And I hadn't seen any activity in the sewer rumors for a couple of years. So, I had hope that I'd gotten him and stopped him, even though I'd lost the boy."

"So, this could still be a hoax or a bunch of kids hiding from their parents."

"No. It's not. You need to take this seriously. Have you read the file?"

Mulder nodded. "But it was incomplete."

"Because we were pulled off the case. The girls were mutilated."

Mulder repressed a shudder. "What happened to them?"

"Externally? Nothing. But internally? He removed their ovaries somehow, without cutting them open."

"Why?"

"I have no idea. However, there was raw sewage inside them, where their internal organs had been. Two of the girls died by the time they got to the hospital. The third girl survived, but she hanged herself before she turned eighteen." Dales' eyes flashed. "Every time, the times that it's real, he does this—takes three girls and takes their ovaries. The girls almost always die. And the boy he takes, we have no idea what happens to him—none of the missing boys have ever been found."

"And the Bureau just ignored this? Despite your evidence?"

"Just like they ignore most of the X-Files. Doesn't mean they're right to ignore it, and you're not right to dismiss it, either. He's a murderer, and he's been doing this for far too long. He has to be stopped. You *have* to stop him."

"I'll take it under advisement." Mulder stood to go. "Thanks for your help."

"Where in California is this going on?" Dales asked as he walked Mulder to the door.

"Someplace called Vista Buena."

"Ah. Good luck. And please keep me posted."

"Will do." Mulder shook Dales' hand, then left. He respected Dales, but the story was still hard to swallow. Lurid and horrific, but still, difficult to believe. "I want to believe…I think."

He got into his car and considered what to do from here. He could go over this with Johnston, but they'd have far too much time together on the plane tomorrow, so reviewing what he'd learned could absolutely wait.

He checked his watch. Samanda would be home by now. Might as well use a perk of marriage and discuss this with her.

ARLINGTON, VIRGINIA

"Hey honey, I'm home." Mulder opened the apartment door and sniffed. "Pupusas tonight?" They were his favorite, the El Salvadoran version of tamales. So the evening promised to be much better than the day had been and the next day would be.

Samanda came out of the kitchen. Her long, black hair was pulled back into a thick braid, which was his favorite look for her. She was in Georgetown sweats, but clearly hadn't run yet. "Yes, but dinner won't be ready for another hour. You're early. Everything alright?"

"Yeah. Weird new case that might not actually be weird. If it's not actually weird, it's a standard missing kids case, meaning that there's a small chance I won't be flying out at the buttcrack of dawn tomorrow."

She laughed. "You want to sleep in the bedroom tonight?"

"Nah. I kind of like the couch. It's more comfortable than the bed."

"Says you. So, you able to share all the weird that's taking you away from your wife?"

"Sure." He handed her the file, then glanced at the end table where the mail lived. "Hey, is that what I think it is?" He picked up a letter from the University of Southern California addressed to Dr. Samanda Rodriguez-Mulder.

"It is." Samanda looked nervous. "The offer came sooner than I expected."

Mulder scanned the letter. "You're going to be a law professor at USC. You're going to take it, right?"

"If I can." She grimaced. "They jumped on me a lot faster than I thought anyone would."

"You're an expert on immigration, congressional, and entertainment law. I can understand why they wanted to tie you up before your alma mater could."

"You know why I can't take Georgetown, even if they offer me more money than USC." She took his hand. "It wouldn't have been possible if not for you, Fox."

He squeezed her hand. Samanda was the only one he liked calling him Fox. Possibly because she reminded him of Samantha. Her hair, her smile, her name—they were like his little sister's. Which was why he'd been willing to marry her to keep her safely in the country as opposed letting her be deported back to El Salvador. Someone like Samanda could do so much more here than she could as a warlord's daughter trapped in a war-torn country. "Well, I think you taking a job across the country is a good reason for us to divorce, even though we still love each other."

"Hopefully the Department of Immigration will buy that story and agree."

"You interned with the top immigration firm in the country. I feel confident that they'll help us get divorced or annulled without the government causing a problem."

"Probably," She said absently, as she read the file. "Mister Dales was part of this? Have you spoken with him?"

"Right before I came home. He thinks it's real."

"I think he's right." She closed the file and handed it back to him. "Besides, you owe it to him, and those children, to treat it as if it's real until such time as you discover it isn't."

"Yes, Counselor."

"Have you gone over this with Clayton?"

He grimaced. "No. I asked him to call me Fox today."

"Really? Did he?"

"No." He sighed. "I don't get him."

"And yet you're the one who majored in psychology. If you want my opinion, he wants to be your friend, and he thinks nicknames mean friendship."

"They don't."

"Not to you, no. But to most people? They do."

"Only nicknames you like."

Samanda grinned. "Not always. You want to run before or after dinner?"

"Probably before." He liked to have a cigarette after dinner, not a run.

She sighed. "You need to quit smoking. Change and let's go, Mister Wheezy."

"Hey, I'm in shape."

"Not the shape you could be in. I'll race you. Whoever does the slowest mile has to clean the dishes and kitchen."

Mulder laughed. "You're on."

Later, as he did the dishes and cleaned the kitchen, Mulder thought about what Samanda had said about Johnston. Maybe he should give the guy a chance. Maybe if he did, Johnston would stop calling him stupid names and use the one Mulder liked.

LOS ANGELES INTERNATIONAL AIRPORT
CALIFORNIA

The flight into Los Angeles had been uneventful. Mulder had filled Johnston in on his conversation with Dales and let Johnston read the X-File. Johnston shared Mulder's skepticism about an alligator man or alligators in the sewers in general, but also agreed with Samanda that they needed to treat this case seriously, particularly since the kids hadn't been found yet.

"Those kids are gone," Johnston pointed out. "Their bikes were found outside the carnival. No matter who actually took them, I think we need to assume they've been kidnapped."

"Any ransom requests yet?"

Johnston shook his head. "Which gives your Mister Dales' suspicions a little more credence."

Once on the ground and luggage in hand, they headed for the rental car area. Johnston insisted on doing the driving—not because Mulder wanted him to, but Johnston said he'd been in Los Angeles several times and the idea of being the driver seemed vitally important to him. As with so many things about Johnston, it just wasn't worth arguing about. The idea of being friends with Johnston had worn off by the time the plane had taxied down the runway in D.C.

As they reached the rental desk, a man in a light blue raincoat and fedora turned around and Mulder jumped. "Mister Dales, what are you doing here?"

"Making sure Sewers goes down for good." Dales nodded to Johnston. "Thanks for pulling those strings."

"What?" Mulder stared at Johnston. "What's he talking about?"

Johnston shrugged. "Artie called me last night, explained his concerns about the case, I took those concerns to ASAC Carter, and he approved us bringing on a consultant." He cleared his throat. "Artie was on our flight. Sitting a few rows behind us."

"Which you didn't notice," Dales pointed out. "Shocking lack of attention to detail, son. You need to focus. It's a good thing for you Clay and I are here."

"How the hell did you know to call Johnston?" Mulder asked.

Dales' eyes twinkled. "I'm retired, son, but I'm a retired Special Agent. I still have my ways." He clapped Johnston on the shoulder. "Clay, let's get rolling, time's wasting."

Johnston beamed. "It's an honor to work with you, sir."

"I may be sick," Mulder muttered.

Dales chuckled. "Likewise, Clay. Mister Mulder, try to keep up."

Mulder gave Dales shotgun, but quickly regretted it, because Dales and Johnston had spent the first half of the hour-plus drive discussing how agency procedures had changed throughout the years. And Dales made him roll down his window when he had a smoke.

"Death sticks, son. That's what those are. You need to take up something less deadly for your oral fixation." Then it was back to Agency Procedure Throughout the Ages.

Finally Mulder couldn't take it anymore. "Does anyone besides me remember that we're here to investigate the disappearance of four kids which could be linked to a gigantic alligator? Anyone?"

Dales turned around and winked at him. "I do. But you're the holdout. You're still expecting those children to be found by the time we reach our location."

Mulder had to admit that this was true. He pulled out the files and re-read them, while Johnston verified with Dales the weaponry that would be waiting for them once they reached their destination.

VISTA BUENA, CALIFORNIA

The Girls were crying. Jason had never heard them cry before, ever. But they were crying now. He was crying, too.

Gator had taken them into the Freak Show tent and, as soon as the flap closed behind them, his whole body had bubbled and boiled and *shifted*, as his clothes ripped off and he turned into something that looked a lot more like an alligator than a man. A gigantic alligator, standing upright like a cartoon did, but this wasn't funny at all. Its hands were almost human, but with sharp claws at the end of the fingers. However, the long, wide mouth filled with razor-sharp teeth and a writhing tongue weren't human at all. The eyes were the worst—kind of human and kind of not, glowing yellow, filled with evil and satisfaction both.

And yet, he could still see Gator somehow in the alligator's face, though Gator no longer looked like he was wearing a costume. The Alligator Man was what Gator really was.

He was a fast alligator, too.All four of them had tried to run but the Alligator Man had caught them, easily, slamming them around with his huge, powerful tail, the tail Jason realized had been the odd shape in Gator's pants.

Once they were all knocked down, Gator had gathered up the Girls in one arm like they were dolls, and took hold of Jason with the other. They'd screamed, but no one had come to help them. Jason wasn't sure if anyone could hear them, or if everyone could and no one cared. Then Gator dragged them down a hole into the sewers.

Jason knew they were in the sewers because of the smell. It was worse than the smell of a million farts, an ocean of piss, and a ton of dog vomit.

Gator dragged and carried them through sewer tunnels. Jason tried to pay attention to where they were going, but he was too afraid to notice much and it was too dark to really see anyway. Then they'd reached a spillway or something like it, something narrower than the regular tunnels. Gator just fit into it. The spillway widened at the end into what seemed like a small, round room. And in here was Gator's nest.

Not that this was someplace homey. It was filthy and disgusting— sewage-soaked rags making a bed, a rickety metal chair next to a rotting wooden box holding some weird-looking little statues, and some kind of stuff on the walls that Jason was pretty sure his science teacher would say were phosphorescent, giving off a sickly green glow that somehow was worse than darkness.

Gator had tossed the Girls onto the bed. Jason he shoved into the chair. Gator's body and horrible tail blocked them in, so there was no hope of escape. Then he started to chant in a language Jason had never heard, while he moved the little statues around on the box.

Gator's voice was raspy, but soothing in a way, and the movements he was doing with the statues was kind of hypnotic. Despite his terror, Jason felt his head nodding. He tried to look at the Girls, but his eyelids were too heavy and they closed without him wanting them to.

Jason woke up. There was no sound of chanting anymore. He looked around. The Girls were still lying on the filthy rags and Gator was still there and still more alligator than man. It hadn't been a dream.

"Please don't kill us."

Gator looked over at him, his yellow eyes reptilian, not human. "You have nothing to fear from me, son."

"You're not my father."

Gator grinned and opened his fang-filled snout. "So sure about that, are you?"

"I knew my dad. Before he left us."

"There's all kinds of fathers." Gator turned back to the Girls. They seemed asleep, but not in a normal way. Their breathing was shallow and they weren't moving at all. "I'd spare you, because I know they're your friends, but you need to watch this."

"Why?" Jason fought down panic. "What are you going to do?" Gator spread Amanda's legs. "Oh, God, don't do that! They're just kids!"

Gator laughed. "These girls were born old. But in order to live, we need something they have. And you need to see how it's done."

Gator's incredibly long tongue flicked out and into Amanda. Jason jumped on him, to make him stop, but Gator just held Jason up and away, with one of his powerful arms. And, as he watched, Jason added to the vomit smell, as Gator pulled something out of Amanda and swallowed it.

Blood was pouring out of her, but Gator didn't pay any mind. He just did the same to Brittany and Caitlin.

"You're killing them!"

Gator swallowed and turned to him. "Yes. So we can live."

"I'm not like you. I don't know what you are, but I'm not whatever it is."

Gator nodded. "Not yet. But you will be." He put Jason back down on the chair, fiddled with the statues some more, and began chanting again.

Despite his horror and terror, Jason fell asleep again. And when he awoke, Gator and the Girls were gone.

VISTA BUENA COUNTY FAIRGROUNDS

"Why?" Mulder asked, when there was a lull in the discussion of the number of rounds of ammunition ordered, which coincided with their pulling off the freeway.

"Why what, Spookster?"

"If we take as our active theory that there's an alligator-man who's responsible for these attacks, why does he do it? There's no sign of sexual assault. I mean, yes, he's taking the girls' ovaries, but the MEs never mentioned any evidence of normal sexual activity."

"He's not having sex with the girls," Dales said. "He's taking their ovaries for a reason, however."

"The victims are all young, never older than fourteen, usually around twelve. Why those ages? And what happens to the boy? I mean, why does he take a boy, every time, along with three girls? And why three? And why do we never find the boy? Boys, really. What happens to them? Does he eat all of them as opposed to only taking their reproductive organs?"

"Good questions," Dales said. "Now you sound like an investigator."

"Do you have any good answers?" Mulder asked hopefully.

"Not a one. Well, not one you'll like."

"Sounds like Voodoo to me," Johnston said offhandedly, as he flashed his badge at the police officers blocking the entrance to the fairgrounds. "They believe in shape shifting, right?"

The local LEOs had cordoned off the fairgrounds, which wasn't as difficult as it sounded, since the grounds were on a mesa overlooking the ocean and there was only one road that led in or out.

"Ah," Dales said. "That's the one."

"Voodoo? Seriously?" Mulder considered the possibility. "I haven't spent a lot of time on Voodoo or any other African and Caribbean belief systems," he admitted. "But from what I can remember, they believe they can change shapes. And reanimate the dead."

"Wouldn't have to be a real Voodoo practitioner," Johnston said as he parked the car. "Could be someone who has some of the spells down and altered them for his own use."

"Sounds like he'd be a very real practitioner if he could do that," Mulder said dryly. "But what's the motivation?" he asked as they got out of the car.

"Why create a zombie?" Johnston countered. "Because you can?"

"Because you want a slave," Dales said. "That's the reason for zombies." He shook his head. "That's not Sewers' reason, or else we'd have found at least one of the boys he's taken somewhere along the line."

They were taken to the head detective, a man named Lambert, who looked grim. "We've found bodies," he said, after badges were flashed and introductions were made. "Down on the beach."

"How many?" Dales asked.

"Three. It's the missing girls." Lambert shook his head. "The boy's still missing. Think he might have done this."

"He didn't," Dales said strongly. "He's a victim, too, and we need to search for him before it's too late."

"I want to see the bodies," Mulder said. "And talk to any witnesses. We also need to take a look at where the children were abducted."

"Bodies are on the beach, like I said. Some witnesses are here, most are home, but we have their statements that you can read. Initial abduction site is the Freak Show tent on the fairgrounds."

"We need to get some more guns and see where the sewers go around here," Dales muttered impatiently. "We already know who killed those girls."

Mulder pulled Johnston aside. "Look, you brought Mister Dales onto this case, so why don't we split up? You two go check out the abduction site, get all those guns and ammo you two are so happy about, and, you know, go down into the sewers. I'll examine the bodies and check the statements for anything that could give us a lead."

"Hey, the new guy's supposed to get the shit job, remember?" Johnston shrugged. "But fine. I think I'd rather go after the alligator-man than look at three dead little girls."

Several uniforms escorted Dales and Johnston into the fairgrounds proper, while Lambert took Mulder down a trail that led from the parking lot to the beach below.

"How many paths are there that lead from this area down?"

"Just two—one from this side and one from the other. We had men on both of them since we started looking for the missing kids. No one's come up or down that we didn't know about, and no one went by carrying three bodies."

"So how did the bodies get onto the beach?"

Lambert shook his head. "No idea."

The morning fog still hadn't burned off, and the day was cold, with a strong enough breeze to muss up Mulder's hair. What the breeze might be doing to any evidence at the crime scene he wasn't sure, but the smell of the ocean was nice—until they got closer to the bodies.

The nearer they got, the more he could smell sewage, and by the time they were at the scene, the area stank.

The bodies were still being photographed. They were in a hole that looked about four feet deep, piled on top of each other, and had sand all over them. "Were they buried in the sand?" he asked Lambert. "Or just left in this hole?"

"In the hole."

"How long ago?"

"ME isn't positive, but put the time of death between midnight and four a.m."

"And there were police in the area at that time?"

"Yes. We've had the entire area searched and had men stationed at intervals along the beach, as well as throughout the fairgrounds area."

"What distance were the intervals?"

"About a hundred yards apart, give or take."

"And no one saw someone dig a four by five hole and toss three girls into it?"

"No," Lambert said snidely. "Because if someone *had*, we'd have shot and killed the bastard. And then read him his rights."

"No argument," Mulder said mildly. He stepped away from Lambert and studied the ground around the girls' impromptu grave.

The breeze was moving the sand around a bit, and despite the care being given, the CSI team's footprints were smudging the area. However,

Mulder saw some marks in the sand that weren't made by shoes or breeze. They looked like claw marks.

He waved the team's photographer over and had him take shots of the marks. Then he put his hand against them. "Why are you doing that?" Lambert asked.

"Testing a theory." Dales' theory, but still. The scratches didn't look made by human hands—they were more animalistic. If he took the leap, a giant alligator should be able to dig a deep hole quickly. Alligators had short legs, but they were powerful, and this alligator probably had longer limbs anyway. And if said alligator timed it just right, it would be too dark for human eyes to notice, especially since the police hadn't had a man stationed every two feet down here on the beach.

But the alligator had to come from somewhere, and it wasn't down either path. Mulder was willing to credit the Vista Buena police with the ability to spot a giant alligator dragging or carrying three dead or dying girls down a path they were standing on, even in the dark.

Mulder looked around and tried to see the scene without all the LEOs there, to see it how it might have been before they got here and found the grave. He was rewarded by spotting something else that wasn't right.

Part of the sand looked more pressed down than other parts, as if something heavy had been dragged along this area. The pressed sand was about two feet wide, but it wasn't a straight line, it was more serpentine. And there were indentations on either side of the compacted sand, a set of five and a set of four on each side. He had the photographer take pictures of this, as well, ignoring Lambert's muttering about the FBI's ability to waste time.

The compacted sand led to the edge of where the police had cordoned off the crime scene. Mulder followed the packed sand leading away from the scene, Lambert following him. In a short time he was rewarded by finding a large drainage pipe that emptied out onto some rocks—it was well hidden by two sand dunes. The sand trail began near this. "Has anyone investigated that?" he nodded towards the pipe.

"Sent a couple uniforms in it last night and again this morning. It's the sewage overflow pipe."

"Really? You let raw sewage overflow right onto the beach here?"

"It's there for flooding," Lambert snapped. "My men followed it back, there's a locked gate. The perp didn't come through this way."

"It's large enough for a man to walk in, so long as he was stooped over."
Or for an alligator to crawl through on his belly.

"You want to take a look? Be my guest." Lambert turned and stalked off.

"Touchy." Mulder pulled out his flashlight, which he'd had the fore-
sight to put in his coat pocket, and his gun. He didn't have the high
caliber rounds Dales had suggested, but if he went off to get a bigger gun
the alligator-man could escape.

Why he believed in the alligator-man now Mulder couldn't say.
Possibly it was the strength of Dale's belief. But he lost nothing by
checking this out, and they might lose everything if he didn't.

VISTA BUENA COUNTY FAIRGROUNDS, FREAK SHOW TENT

Dales had taken a .357 and a .44 Magnum from the arsenal provided
by the Vista Buena Police Department. He'd considered taking one of the
hunting rifles the local police had provided, but they were going to have
to go down into the sewers, and as tempting as a rifle was, reality said
that he'd have a better chance with a handgun.

Johnston had opted for a 30-30 rifle and a .44 Magnum. They both
had a lot of extra ammunition. And a lot of backup—they were taking a
dozen policemen with them. This time, Sewers wasn't going to escape.

As it had been in Bailey's Crossing all those years ago, Dales found the
Malligator's exhibit located right on top of the sewer manhole. What was
different was that no one in this circus seemed to know who Sewers was.
And, even though the tent and its setup looked the same as the one from
1963, no one had heard of Emilio Zartec, either.

The party line seemed to be that they didn't possess an alligator-man,
no one knew of Allan G. Sewers or the Malligator or anyone matching
his description working with the circus, and that a patron with four children had turned into a monster, attacked his kids, and dragged them off
into the darkness.

The cotton candy vendor confirmed that he'd sold four cotton candies
to the "father" for his three girls and a boy. Other witnesses, including some
of the circus freaks themselves, confirmed seeing the man turn into a giant
alligator, though some said he'd turned into Godzilla with a longer snout.

The fact that this event had happened in the daylight didn't matter—the Freak Show tent was dark, with only its exhibits lit, and not too well. The police had searched the tent and the sewers but found nothing. This didn't surprise Dales in the least.

"Remember," he told Johnston and the policemen coming with them as they headed down, "if he's in the form I expect him to be in, he's going to be hard to shoot fatally. One shot probably won't do it. Focus on getting the boy away from him. He needs the boy for some reason. If we can save the child, maybe we stop this cycle from ever happening again."

"It's a maze," Johnston said as Dales joined him and their police escort inside the sewer tunnel. "We're right in the heart of a stinking maze. Pun definitely intended."

Sure enough, there were seven options for where to go. They divided into teams of two, Dales and Johnston staying together, and headed off on the hunt.

VISTA BUENA SEWER SYSTEM SPILLWAY

There was no evidence that proved anyone—man or alligator—had come down this pipe. However, there was no evidence that one of the police force had been in here, either. Mulder sloshed through some dirty water as he made his way to the locked grate about a hundred yards in. His flashlight showed nothing untoward in the water.

His nose had shut down by the time he reached the iron grate. It was a typical latticed covering, there to still allow water to go out, and to keep anyone, kids in particular, from getting into the sewer system. The gaps in the lattice were big enough to stick a man's arm through, but not big enough for anyone's head.

He rattled the grate. It seemed secure. However, closer examination showed that while there was a lock on it, that lock was on the inside—and it showed signs of activity. The grate and the lock were both rusty, but parts of the lock looked like some of the rust had been scraped off recently. And the lock itself looked odd, as if it had been mangled and then shoved back into its right shape.

Mulder slid his arm in and pushed the body of the lock down. The lock opened. He put it in his pocket, then flipped the latch open and moved the grate as quietly as he could.

Mulder left the grate ajar—in case Lambert decided to be a cop and follow him, why make it hard on his backup? And if Mulder needed a fast exit, why make it harder on himself?

Another hundred yards or so in, the spillway connected to the main sewer tunnels. He had a choice of going left or right. Mulder listened. There were faint sounds coming from both ends. Could be the alligator, the boy, or Dales and Johnston. He was pretty sure Dales would be in the sewers by now, hunting.

Mulder shone his flashlight around the pipe. The alligator-man had come through this way, meaning there should be some trace of him in here, showing Mulder which way to go.

Diligence was rewarded—there was a small reddish smear just above the waterline going to the right. Mulder went that way, keeping his flashlight on the waterline. He was rewarded again by spotting another reddish smear. One of the girls had lived long enough to try to leave a trail using her own blood. He went on.

VISTA BUENA SEWER SYSTEM

Jason ran. He had no idea where he was going, but out of Gator's horrible nest was a good start.

He felt funny, though. As if he couldn't run as fast as before and yet, at the same time, like he could run faster if he could just get his legs to work right. Everything looked weird, too. Colors were different, and his point of view seemed wrong.

His sense of smell was off, too. Instead of this place smelling horrible, now it smelled safe, comforting, and normal.

The sewer system was a maze—every kid was taught that in school, so they wouldn't be stupid enough to come down here for kicks or to do drugs. But Jason didn't feel lost. He could smell something, something that smelled right. He headed for that smell.

Mulder almost missed the smaller tunnel offshoot. If he hadn't been following the blood trail he *would* have missed it.

He followed this smaller tunnel, gun out and ready. But he reached the end of it without running into anyone else.

There was what looked like a foul nest made here, and the blood-soaked rags indicated this was probably where the girls had been mutilated. But what was on the small box that served as a table was what interested Mulder the most.

There was a small pyre with some odd herbs smoldering in a small set of teeth that looked like they could be from a baby alligator. In front of this were small figurines that looked homemade or at least badly crafted—larger and smaller alligator-ish things, three sort-of females, and one horrible looking human-alligator face.

Mulder pulled out his handkerchief and put all of the figurines into his outer coat pocket, kicking himself for not having an evidence bag on hand. He emptied his cigarettes into his pants pocket and poured the smoldering herbs into the empty carton, then pocketed this and the teeth as well. The bloody rags he left for forensics to recover.

He went back through this smaller tunnel then considered his options. There had been plenty of pipes to go down as he'd traveled here. But he hadn't spotted anything. He turned away from the blood trail and went down the so-far unexplored section of this pipe.

As he came to a T-intersection, Mulder heard something off to the left—water sloshing and the sound of grunting. He moved that way quickly.

Dales couldn't hear the police anymore, which meant that he and Johnston were likely farther from them. Hopefully this meant they were on the right trail. They were in a very wide section of the sewer. It reminded Dales of the sewer in Bailey's Crossing now—walkways on either side, sewer water running down the middle.

No sooner wished for than granted—they rounded a corner to see an alligator running towards them in the water. It wasn't as large as Dales remembered. In fact, it looked young.

Johnston aimed and fired, but Dales knocked his hand away and the bullet ricocheted harmlessly. "No! I think it's the boy!"

The alligator skidded to a stop and looked around, clearly panicked. Of course, a young alligator was still more of a challenge than not. Dales wondered if he'd done the right thing.

A roar from behind him said possibly he had. He spun as a much larger alligator that also looked something like a man, slammed into both Dales and Johnston.

As Dales flew across to the other side and his hip slammed into the tunnel wall in an extremely painful way, he watched as the larger alligator picked up the smaller one.

"Kill the big one!" he shouted to Johnston, who'd gotten to his feet, rifle in hand.

The Malligator roared, but before anything else happened, Mulder's voice came from behind the gators. "Stop! I have your totems and I'll destroy them if you don't give yourself up."

The Malligator spun around, growling. Johnston took his shot.

Mulder held up the alligator teeth. He shone his flashlight into the larger alligator's face—the eyes were wrong, like a combination of human and reptile, the wrong parts of both. The younger alligator was thrashing in the larger one's hold.

Both of them looked like they were alligator-people, and Mulder was willing to bet that the smaller one was the missing boy. But before he could say or do anything else, a shot rang out.

It hit, but the big alligator had thick hide, and if the shot penetrated, it didn't do any real damage.

The same couldn't be said for the alligator. He slammed his gigantic tail into Johnston, who went flying towards Mulder. Johnston hit the concrete with a sickening thud.

Mulder ran to him. Johnston's head was bleeding profusely and his lower body was at a bad angle to the rest of him. "Guess I…blew it, Spooky," he gasped out.

Mulder grabbed his hand and thought about what Samanda had said. "It's okay, Clayface. We'll get you help, just hang on."

Johnston's expression changed—he looked incredibly happy. "Always…wanted my partner to be…my best friend." He sighed and then his eyes went glassy.

Mulder felt for a pulse, then, finding none, gently closed Johnston's eyes. He turned to see the giant alligator's back turned to him. That meant he was after Dales. Like hell was Mulder going to allow this monster to kill Dales, the man he respected, the same way he'd killed his partner.

Guns weren't going to work, though. That had been proved in 1963. "I'm destroying them all, now!" he thundered, as he slammed the alligator teeth onto the concrete by his feet.

The Malligator spun around and roared. Mulder ground the teeth under his foot, as he dropped the three female figurines onto the ground and jumped up and down on them. "All gone, you bastard! I'm going to make sure your Voodoo never works again!"

The smaller alligator wriggled out of the larger's grasp and ran towards Mulder faster than he thought should have been possible. For a moment he considered shooting, but the smaller alligator was on him too quickly.

But it didn't attack. Instead, it ate the remains of the teeth and figurines. And started looking a little more human than reptilian.

Dales was shooting at the Malligator, forcing it to pay attention to him, as Mulder pulled the rest of the bizarre voodoo implements out of his pocket and smashed them to pieces, and the smaller alligator ate them up. As they did this, the Malligator also looked less like a reptile and more like a man.

They finished and the small alligator now matched the description of the missing boy. And the larger alligator matched the description of the man who'd kidnapped the kids. And, as he bore down on Dales, Mulder heard the roar of a gun and saw a hole tear through Sewers, who fell backwards from the force of the shot.

Mulder grabbed the kid, who started barfing into the sewer water, and ran to make sure Sewers was as dead as Johnston. Then he went to Dales.

"You okay, sir?"

Dales nodded. "Think I'm going to need a new hip, but otherwise, I'm better than poor Clay."

Mulder swallowed. "Yeah." He looked at the boy. "Jason Winger?"

The kid nodded then started to cry as he went to Dales and hugged him. "Thanks for not letting the other man kill me."

Dales patted the boy's back as the sounds of their backup filtered down the tunnels. "It's okay now, son. It's all over." He looked at Mulder.

"You believe now?"

Mulder managed a smile. "Yes, sir, I do."

WASHINGTON, D.C.
DECEMBER 1990

"Good job on this one, Mulder," ASAC Carter said. "I'm sorry we lost Johnston, though. He was a good man. Giving him a hero's memorial, not that there's anyone to appreciate it."

"No?" Mulder asked.

"No family left."

Mulder cleared his throat. "Ah, he was my, uh, friend, sir. If there's something that I can do…"

Carter shrugged. "You can keep his medal, if it means anything to you."

Mulder nodded. "Thank you, sir. It does."

"How's your consultant holding up?"

"Mister Dales will have to walk with a cane, but otherwise, he's good, sir, thank you for asking."

Carter shot him a rare smile. "Once a Special Agent, Mulder, always a Special Agent. Remember that."

VISTA BUENA, CALIFORNIA
DECEMBER 1991

Jason went down to the sewers and waited. He'd done the right thing, of that he was sure. By ingesting then regurgitating the magic into the same water Gator had been floating in, the magic should still be able to work. And that meant that, tonight, his new father would come back. And then, they'd go away and hunt together. Forever.

THE END

CLAIR DE LUNE

By David Benton and W.D. Gagliani

In memory of Charles L. Grant

SOMEWHERE SOUTH OF OTTAWA, CANADA
4th OCTOBER, 1994, 5:45 p.m.

The rental Ford's windshield wipers fought to sweep away the
onslaught of wet heavy snowflakes, as Special Agent Fox Mulder
wove his way cautiously south of Ottawa. They had just been
diverted off the 416 due to snow accumulation, and now he realized that
had been a mistake. Perth was off to their right, somewhere. His passengers watched the increasingly white landscape unfolding with obvious
trepidation.

It was the kind of blizzard that kills all school and business activities
and grounds all flights, and indeed their direct flight to Washington,
D.C., had been one of the first on the board to flip from On Time to
Cancelled. It was the kind of once a season blizzard that causes the
closure of even the main highways, so S.A. Mulder had elected to test the
conditions on a more rural route.

But it wasn't going well, not at all.

Visibility on the darkening road was limited to only what the car's
underpowered headlights illuminated, and even that had taken on the
look of a fuzzy television screen tuned between stations, the image
blotted out by the streaming white specks. And the lines on the road —
for that matter everything else — were rapidly vanishing beneath a thick
blanket of fresh white snow.

Now Mulder was navigating by pure instinct.

"We should have waited until tomorrow and taken a flight," Special
Agent Dana Scully said from the navigator's seat while straining to see
past the windshield. "It would have made more sense, Mulder."

"What, and miss all of this?" Mulder could have been talking about the storm, but he'd smirked and motioned toward the seat behind them, where the extradited prisoner they were escorting, one Carlo DesMarais, sat handcuffed and ranting. He hadn't stopped since they'd slid him, hands manacled behind his back, into the seat.

"Please, you have to let me go!" Carlo yelled now, after a short respite from his previous outburst.

"You're not running out of steam back there, are you?" Mulder asked. "I missed the sound of your mellifluous voice. It's the only thing keeping me alert, and therefore keeping us alive." He winked sideways at Scully, who frowned.

"You don't understand," their prisoner pleaded, struggling against his handcuffs. "I keep telling you, this is the wrong time to move me. You *have* to wait until next week."

"Sorry, pal, the wheels of justice turn slowly enough as it is. No point making it worse. You decided to sing, and now the rehearsal is over. Time for you to shine on stage. Or in the witness box." Mulder turned briefly to Scully. "Before he knows it our guest is going to be lounging in some Club Fed, proud to have helped bring down the likes of Jean-Paul the Scud and his gang of greasy gunsels."

Scully smiled mirthlessly. Mulder could wear on you, not much less than their talkative charge. But he was a good driver to have in whiteouts. You learn things like that about your partner.

Carlo wailed, his words a jumble of Spanish, French and some sort of patois neither agent recognized.

"What are you raving about, Carlo?" Mulder said, his eyes finding the crazy man's in the mirror and meeting them for a brief moment. "I mean, isn't it late to complain? This is your show. You decided to take the government's deal and talk."

The diminutive thug stuttered. "B-b-but... I told them I wanted some time, a few days, a w-w-week. To p-p-prepare. I-i-it's a full moon!"

Mulder chuckled. "Looks way overcast to me. I don't think we'll be seeing the moon tonight."

"You don't n-n-need to see it! I'm t-t-telling you, you're in t-t-terrible danger! You have t-t-to turn around now, or l-l-let me go!"

"Calm down, DesMarais," Scully said, her hand loosening her parka over where her Sig P228 sat snug in its holster. "The only thing we're in danger of is getting stuck in this storm before we get you back to the States so you can testify. We're trained and prepared for this kind of situation. And armed, too, keep in mind." She half-turned to glare at the curled-up witness, who was trying to find a comfortable position despite his handcuff situation.

"Your g-g-guns won't help you!" the prisoner blurted, his high-pitched voice changing to a near-growl.

"Well, they surely won't help us shovel our way out of here if this snow keeps piling up," Mulder agreed, sighing. "Scully, we may need to find a place to hole up for the night."

"Now you say that?" said Scully, raising a finely-sculpted and well-used eyebrow.

"Yeah, well… I had to try. Syracuse is just south of the tip of Lake Ontario, on 81. If they're not socked in, we could have been on a flight to D.C. in a few hours. Doesn't look good now, though."

As the car crept forward through the rising snow cover, a sign materialized on the right side of the road. There were words, and an arrow pointed crookedly downward.

"Serendipity, I think," Mulder said with his usual sideways smirk. "Can you make it out?"

"Not exactly, but I can read the flashing *Vacancy* part," Scully answered. "Looks like a motel must be somewhere under all this snow."

"See, my unerring sense of direction leads us out of danger yet again," he said.

"Just drive, Mulder, before the wheels freeze up and we become tomorrow's archeological find like the wooly mammoth."

"Scully, you're starting to sound like me."

"God forbid," Scully muttered, but she was smiling.

Their passenger seemed to be snoring. Then Mulder realized he wasn't asleep at all — Carlo was praying under his breath, presumably a stream of muttered supplications.

"Make sure you get one of those in there for the heat to work in this dump," Mulder said.

Slowly nosing off the main road onto an even worse offshoot, Mulder guided them toward what seemed the entrance of the empty parking lot, the light Ford Tempo fishtailing as its tires struggled and slipped in the ever-deepening powder. The wipers barely moved any of it and he had to hunch and squint to see through the tiny aperture left on the windshield. Around them, the near-whiteout seemed to worsen, whipping the snow pellets into a frenzy.

Finally Mulder pulled up in front of the building's main door.

"See, the Bates Motel's been waiting for us."

The place was a typical Fifties design, an L-shaped one-story building with the office at one end of the short wing and individual room doors facing out onto the snow-clogged lot, larger windows set beside them. Most of the sign's letters were burned out, which was why Scully couldn't read it, but the green vacancy sign's Morse-code blinking had served as a welcome beacon. It was a sad and desolate place but at the moment it might as well have been a resort, as it would provide the shelter they needed, if nothing more.

Scully fought to open the door, snow and wind whipping inside as she got out. She turned back to Mulder: "You guys keep each other company," she shouted before closing the door and restoring quiet. She headed for the motel's entrance.

Mulder kept the engine running, drumming his fingers on the wheel. Carlo muttered his unintelligible prayers.

Maybe they were curses. Mulder couldn't tell.

Scully trudged through what by now had to be eight inches of wet, sludgy snow, tugged open the glass door, and stepped inside the retro light-paneled lobby.

No, it wasn't retro, she realized as she glanced around. It had never been updated from the day the building was erected. Weak strip lighting gave everything the pallor of terminal illness.

She stomped the mess from her completely inappropriate shoes and brushed clinging flakes from her shoulders, then aimed for the front desk across the empty room. She checked her surroundings, her training taking over, and spotted all the doors and windows. It was second nature. Although the lights were on and the heat seemed to be working, there was no one behind the counter. The door in the rear was ajar, a dim light on somewhere behind it.

She rang the bell, cursing Mulder for his usual disregard of just about everything that would have made the most sense.

"P-p-please. You *have* to l-l-let me go," Carlo DesMarais said from the rear seat, trying to calm his stutter.

"Why, what's going to happen if we don't?" Mulder didn't remember the guy stuttering so much before, but then they hadn't heard him speak much. All they had to do was transport him, not make a new buddy. Still, the little guy did seem highly perturbed.

And that kind of thing always piqued Mulder's curiosity.

"B-b-bad things. Bad things are g-g-going to happen if you don't let me go. You d-d-don't understand. Your lives are in d-danger. And the lives of everyone here are in d—"

Mulder jumped in. "Well, Carlo, if we were to let you go, then my *job* would be in danger. And I take my job very seriously, some of the time."

"You g-got to believe me. I don't want to b-b-be responsible for what's gonna happen here tonight. You need to let me g-g-go."

Mulder tried again. "What's going to happen, Carlo?"

"You — you wouldn't b-b-believe me if I told you!"

"I'm a pretty open-minded guy, Carlo. Why don't you try me?" He knew they called him "Spooky" Mulder back at Quantico, and word had gotten around the D.C. office, too. It had a lot to do with his office having been relegated to a far corner of the dusty basement. And being assigned Scully to babysit him. He was *too* open-minded.

"It's a full moon t-t-tonight and if you don't let me go p-people are gonna d-d-die! That's what's g-gonna happen! So take off these — *hand-cuffs*... and let's go back or... or let me go!"

Mulder glanced at the door, where Scully had disappeared too long ago. Still nothing. "Tell me more, Carlo... there must be a line in there."

Inside the motel lobby, Special Agent Scully was getting impatient.

"Hello?" she called out. She was half ready to walk around the counter and help herself to a couple sets of the room keys that hung from a double row of dust-encrusted hooks on the wall, when a middle-aged man with uncombed thinning hair finally emerged from the doorway.

"Hello? Hello?" the man said while adjusting his stained paisley shirt. His glasses were askew. *Literally caught napping*, Scully thought. Mulder would have blamed some faceless conspiracy or spy cell. He always looked for the most difficult and less likely reasons for everything.

That was the key to her job, in a way.

"Hello," she said, trying to keep her natural impatience out of her tone. "It's great that you're open."

"I wasn't expecting anybody tonight with the storm and all. But I left the sign on just in case, eh?" Now he was adjusting his glasses. Scully nodded graciously, thinking of the mostly illegible no-tell motel sign, and forced herself to smile. His Canadian lilt was obvious.

"So, what can I do ya for?" the clerk, maybe owner, asked. He took a better look at his customer through the straightened glasses. Winked.

"Two rooms please, as close to the end as possible," Scully said, ignoring the wink. "One night." She slid her Bureau credit card across the desk.

"Terrible weather out there. Haven't had a storm like this in I don't know *how* long." The man talked while processing the card, squinting at her. She might have been the best thing he'd seen in a long time. "American FBI, eh? What brings you out on a night like tonight?"

"Business."

He hesitated, waiting for a more detailed response but none was forthcoming. Finally he handed Scully a form and receipt. "If you could just sign here," he said, sniffing a little at her slight, and then he turned to retrieve the keys. "Last two rooms down that other wing, on the right."

"Thanks."

He nodded, looking over his glasses. "You got it, little lady." *Wink.*

Shivering and not only from the cold, Scully returned to the idling car and climbed into the passenger seat.

"We missed you," Mulder quipped. "Had a nice talk, we did. Didn't we, Carlo? He still thinks he's saving our lives if we consider releasing him. Even tried to bribe me with some ill-gotten gains."

Carlo was in muttered prayer mode again.

"Last two rooms on the end," said Scully, blankly. She pointed.

Nothing had been plowed, nor did it look as if it would be anytime soon.

The tires spun for several long moments before finding a slight grip on the slickly-covered pavement. Slowly, Mulder pulled the car up to their rooms. "Honey, we're home."

Once the agents were out of the Ford, Scully unholstered her pistol while Mulder muscled DesMarais out of the back. Their prisoner struggled, his hands gesticulating behind his back.

"Let me g-g-go!" he shouted, wriggling his whole body and almost escaping Mulder's grip. Scully targeted him from the far side of the car, her hand steady even in the whipping wind.

"We *can* take you in with a bullet wound. Assistant Director Skinner gave us the green light. As long as you are still able to talk, we're okay with damaged."

The small witness was trembling as if suffering an epileptic seizure, but they'd been told he was cleared medically.

Mulder slammed DesMarais down on the car trunk. His feet slipped as the agent kicked them apart. "Take it easy," Mulder barked. "We don't want this to be any harder than it has to be."

The shivering prisoner suddenly more malleable, Scully lowered her gun and opened the door to one of the rooms, waiting as her partner wrestled DesMarais inside and tossed him sack-like onto the sagging bed. Still outside, she looked around once more and saw the manager's disembodied face across the lot, staring at them from the behind the lobby door. She considered flashing her badge, but then followed them inside instead.

"Please, I'm b-b-begging you, for your own g-g-good, let me go!" yelled Carlo from his new fetal position. Suddenly nervous, Scully trained her gun on him again.

"Sorry, Charlie, no can do," said Mulder.

Walking to the head of the bed, Agent Fox Mulder gripped the headboard and shook it to make sure it was secure. It was a rank of steel bars, and bolted to the floor. Then he dragged DesMarais closer, unlocked one of the prisoner's wrists and quickly latched it to a steel bedpost. Then he leapt up out of the way before DesMarais could reach him with his free hand.

"No! Please, you don't understand!" Carlo shrieked. He wasn't trying to grab Mulder—he was supplicating.

Mulder ignored him and turned to Scully. "That should hold him no matter what's supposed to happen..."

Carlo DesMarais was still crying and yelling incoherently when Mulder escorted Scully out of the room and into the cold of the blizzard again, closing and locking the door behind them.

"Aren't we going to stay and stand guard?" Scully asked as she took the room key.

"Yes, we will. I just need to get away from him. We can take turns staying awake, but from next door. I don't want to listen to him all night. And where's he gonna go?" The wind whipped some of his voice away as an exclamation point, but it couldn't cover up the nervous quality in his tone.

Scully paused, lips pursed, looking at Mulder questioningly.

"He'll be all right," Mulder assured her. "If he doesn't grow fangs." He stood and stared out into the white heart of the blizzard for about a minute, then turned back and waved Scully ahead of him.

They entered the second motel room and Mulder switched on the light, shrugged off his parka, then stepped into the washroom. He leaned over the grimy sink, and splashed cold water on his face.

Scully observed all this without comment. But then she asked, "Do you really think it's safe to leave him in there alone?"

"I couldn't stand another minute more of his yelling and carrying on. I mean, if you're going to turn into a werewolf just do it, don't go on and on about it." He dropped into a threadbare armchair.

Scully sighed. She should have seen this coming. "Mulder, you can't be serious. You can't really believe that man in there is a werewolf, a man who turns into a hairy monster when the moon is full. *Please* tell me you don't believe it." She paused, waiting, but he said nothing.

Then her eyes widened. "And don't tell me *Spooky* Mulder volunteered us for this jaunt just because he was curious about something in the transcripts of his interrogations. Please don't tell me!"

Mulder smiled crookedly. "Are you forgetting the origins of our little enterprise here?"

"What are you talking about?" She'd shucked her parka, and now she tried giving herself a neck massage, but gave up and just rocked her head, waiting for a snap that would bring relief. Then she pulled over the rickety desk chair and sank gratefully into it with a groan.

Mulder stared at her white turtleneck sweater for a second, then settled into the lecturer's tone he often preferred. "It was 1946, and FBI director J. Edgar Hoover came face to face with something he could not explain. If you open Case File number one and read between the lines, it'll be obvious that he and his trusted agents were faced with exactly that—a man they realized could indeed morph into a *Canis lupus*."

"Mulder, that's what happens when *you* read between the lines." She shook her head, her neck just as stiff as it had been. Lack of sleep was beginning to show on her pale features. "Give them more credit than that. They found perfectly rational explanations for what happened."

"Yeah, it was rational to admit something strange was going on when the human tracks switched to paw prints and back again. We saw that once, too, Scully," Mulder continued. "Remember that case in Montana? The reservation, the rancher's son, then the rancher himself? The time gap between the groups of murders... ring any bells?"

She chuckled. Sometimes her partner was *so* predictable. She could almost read the report she would have to doctor for Skinner.

Not the first time, and certainly not the last.

It was her job, after all, to officially debunk his wild theories.

But Mulder went on, undaunted as usual, "Look, the ancient Greeks called it *lycanthropy*, the Normans had the *garwalf*, the Italians call him *uomo-lupo*, literally *man-wolf*, and our friends up here in French Canada call it the *loup-garou*. You can't ignore the spread of a legend across cultures."

"No, but you *can* ignore it when it's more likely a mental illness that makes people *believe* they can turn into wolves—"

"Or any other animal," Mulder said.

"A *mental illness*, Mulder, that makes people think and believe they can turn into all sorts of animals is still a mental illness. Something that looks like something is not automatically the other thing."

"Scully, that's weak and you know it. You disappoint me."

She smiled. "Let's go with your theory, then. It's too bad you didn't bring any silver bullets with you."

"Believe me, if I'd heard this guy's ranting before we left, I would have."

"Where would you have bought silver bullets, Mulder? Your local sporting goods shop?"

He made a face halfway between patient and irritated. "What makes you think I would have had to *buy* some?"

"You already have some? Wait a minute — Mulder, don't tell me you've *made* silver bullets!"

He shrugged. "I'm a big fan of preparedness. Big Scout thing, being prepared."

"You were a Boy Scout?"

"No, but I read things."

Scully shook her head in exasperation. She checked her watch. "Speaking of preparedness, if the roads are plowed sometime tonight we may be able to get an early start. We'd better get some sleep. I'll take the first watch."

"Okay, Scully, and I'll go give him a bathroom break. Unless you'd like to..."

She held up a hand. "Say no more, he's all yours!"

"I hope he's off the Larry Talbot routine. I love *Abbott and Costello Meet Frankenstein*, but this is getting ridiculous."

NEAR PERTH, OTTAWA
12:17 a.m. EASTERN TIME

Something woke Mulder from restless sleep. The heater really did not work very well, so they'd kept on their parkas. His rustled as he rolled onto his side. Dismayed, he realized this was supposed to have been his watch shift.

"Scully, you awake?"

"Well, one of us had to be, Mulder."

"I was just resting my eyes..."

Scully was about to make a wry comment when Mulder sat up straight, cutting her off with the suddenness of his movement. "Shhhhh... Do you hear that?"

The sound of distant baleful howling filtered through the window again as if in response.

"I've been listening to it the last five minutes," she said. "Coyotes, I think."

Mulder listened as the chorus of howls and yelps multiplied.

"That's not coyotes," he said.

"Well, I guess it could be wolves," she said, hesitantly. "We're north enough."

"Wolves," he began. "You know what that could mean..."

Then a crash cut off his next words, and a second crash followed rapidly after the first.

It sounded like furniture suddenly being tossed and bodies being thrashed.

And it came from next door...

Screaming, turning into a hideous gurgle. Another scream.

Also from next door.

The agents locked eyes for a long second in the dim light of the one glowing desk lamp, then scrambled for their weapons and tumbled simultaneously toward the door.

Glass was breaking with dramatic abandon in the other room, a crash and tinkling that briefly overrode even the wild wailing of the wind.

Then there was another blood-curdling scream, but it was clipped off.

Gun in hand, Mulder reached the door first and threw it open, falling back as a blast of wind and snow washed over him. He dived into the wicked weather, Scully close behind.

Outside the snow whirled through the white landscape, thrust by the wildly wailing wind. No more sounds came from next door.

That sudden silence was unnerving. Mulder trampled through where snow had drifted like sand into a pyramid shape immediately outside their room. He scanned the area for movement, looking for anything that might explain the commotion. To his immediate left he could see the swath of light shining not from Carlo DesMarais's door, but from the shattered window that had been set next to it. Mulder side-stepped to stand almost in front of the jagged hole. Blood painted the remaining glass shards.

And outside of their prisoner's room splashes of crimson stained the broken snowdrift and the path of large prints that led away from it.

"Carlo!" he called out. There was no response. "Scully, Carlo's gone! He's loose!"

Scully was so close behind him that she stumbled into him when he abruptly stopped again, fumbling to fit the key into the door lock.

"Carlo, are you in there?" Mulder called out, but he knew there would be no answer.

I should have listened to my gut, he thought.

The moon was up there, somewhere behind the snow clouds. He imagined it was full.

"I should have known, Scully!" he shouted in frustration. "I had it, and I let it get away! I should have—"

"You can't blame yourself, Mulder!" Scully's eyes were awake now, but her hands were shivering.

Mulder swung around and entered the room, his Sig leading the way. Scully was right behind him at a crouch, her own sidearm scanning the remaining space.

The bed was awash in blood. A pool of it was already soaking into the mattress near the headboard and in the depression left by Carlo's body where Mulder had thrown him a few hours before. A path of splatters led from the headboard toward the window.

But Carlo himself was nowhere to be seen.

Something rested in the center of the pillow. The agents stepped closer, their breath ragged.

There, on the spreading crimson stain, was Carlo's still-cuffed hand, its fingers curled obscenely.

It had been chewed off just above the wrist.

"God, Mulder, looks like he mauled off his own hand to get away!" Scully's voice was full of shock.

"I told you—" Mulder began.

Somewhere outside the room, but not far away at all, the agents both heard the growling of a dog — *or was it a wolf?* — echoing through the milky white environment.

Mulder spun around, Scully following closely, and they retraced their steps out the door, this time staring at the series of blood splatters marking the path from the shattered window out the open door into the storm. Lampposts had come on with nightfall, throwing anemic light in globular shapes that did nothing to dispel the whiteout. Indeed, the lights probably worsened its effects on visibility.

Mulder pointed at the splatters.

Like Hansel and Gretel following a trail of bloody breadcrumbs, he thought.

"Come on!" he called out to Scully, but she was already on his heels, all thought of cold forgotten in the heat of the chase.

The tracks seemed somewhat round in nature, perfectly compatible with the kind of disturbance in fresh snow Mulder figured a wolf's paws might make. He saved his lecture for later.

They followed the trail of disturbed snow, they themselves struggling in the deepening layer. A second trail of tracks from across the lot joined the first at an angle. The agents pulled up at the far end of the empty parking lot, light globes glowing with surreal intensity above them.

"Scully, look."

"I see it." She hefted her gun again. "Mulder, what is it?"

Just a few yards away on the white expanse of blanketed pavement, something lay steaming in a pile on a swirly snowdrift. One of the bloody trails of prints led right to it.

They approached warily, guns up and ready.

Mulder thought his heart would burst.

They hunched over what at first looked like ragged clothing.

There, on the ruined beauty of the snow, lay DesMarais's body, fat white flakes melting as they landed on his still-warm corpse.

His *butchered* corpse.

Carlo's neck had been ripped through clear down to the spine and his head was missing. His belly had been torn open, loops of his intestines scooped out and strewn in a wide circle around his torso. Protruding jagged ribs indicated where his heart had been sloppily removed. Around him, more bloody imprints were already filling with snow. They were paw prints. And the sets of tracks left by three — or maybe four — apparently large animals led directly into the stand of tall pines guarding the motel's perimeter like sentries.

There was no helping Carlo, so Mulder and Scully half-heartedly followed the tracks to the trees. One set of tracks seemingly changed from animal to human and back in a distance of several yards.

Like a playful au revoir *message.*

The agents stared at each other, not knowing what to say. They realized they were still shivering as the blizzard continued its frenzy around them.

"What about the manager?" Scully said, staring along the other trail toward the front door of the main office.

Now they could see that it, too, was a splintered ruin.

Indeed, the elderly man was in the same shape as Carlo DesMarais, as they determined after trudging back across the lot. They stood over his mutilated body.

"I guess Carlo wasn't the werewolf after all," Mulder muttered.

In the distance, howling again broke the eerie silence.

Scully glanced at him, and at the old man who'd leered at her. She felt numb.

5:35 a.m. EASTERN TIME

Mulder handed off the messy crime scene to the swarm of efficient Mounties summoned by their call, relief flooding through his tired system. He shook hands with their team leader and promised to coordinate reports.

It was dawn, and the blizzard was over. Most of the tracks had been obliterated or simply covered by new snow. The agents swept their car clean and minutes later turned onto the newly plowed road. Inspector Reynard gave them the word that the main highway was open again. They tried calling the D.C. bureau office, but their cell phones were dead.

"No signal out here in the sticks," Mulder said as he flipped the phone shut. "It'll be nice if these things ever get the coverage we need."

His foot hit the brake hard and the car's rear end slewed as they came to a stop at an angle.

A dog — a very large, black dog — stared at them from where he had suddenly appeared between snow banks left by the plow. Or was it a wolf? Definitely too large to be a coyote—its eyes appeared green in the brilliant white of the background. Still staring into the car, it walked slowly across the road. Mulder held the brake pushed down and only when the animal had disappeared did he realize that he was in danger of putting the pedal through the floor.

He shook his head, glanced at Scully, who studiedly avoided his gaze.

They drove in silence a while, many things better left unsaid.

Finally Mulder cracked. "What are we going to tell Skinner?"

Scully shrugged. She'd wondered the same. "That Carlo won't be testifying against his old gang because they tracked us somehow and got to him while we slept?"

"I really read the whole thing wrong, didn't I?" Mulder mused.

Scully almost shrugged again, but caught herself. She said nothing.

"At least he tried to warn us," Mulder pointed out as he turned cautiously onto the 416 again and set the car on its way to the border.

"There is that," Scully agreed. "Yes there is."

THE END

IT'S ALL IN THE EYES

By Heather Graham

PURGATORY PASS, ESSEX COUNTY, MASSACHUSETTS
30th OCTOBER, 2009, 1:00 a.m.

keletons hung from the rafters along with images of classic movie monsters. Witches rode on broomsticks and as Hannah Barton entered the giant warehouse store, a motion-activated ghost went flying over her head. The shelves on the walls were packed to the gills with smaller versions of monstrous creatures, tombstones, diseased rats, little green men, alien blobs, and all kinds of scary decorations.

She didn't think much about the creatures—most of which were incredibly expensive. Most of what they sold at Mayfield's Monsters and Mayhem Emporium were movie replicas of horror creations that were done through companies approved by those who own the motion pictures that had spawned them and they were wonderfully crafted. Of course, no one needed a license to create some of the magnificent ghosts, witches, vampires, and just plain creepy looking corpses, clowns, dolls, and other decorations they carried. Still, they were all top notch.

She walked down to the aisle that carried their corpse dolls, notebook in her hand. She was there—after working hours, mind you—because one Caitlin Corpse had been returned the night before. A few of her fellow co-workers—Randy Smith and Roberta Blake—were behind her. They were taking their time, doing this more or less out of a sense of duty. And extra pay.

But Hannah wanted to rise to the more elite ranks in the Mayfield's Monsters and Mayhem hierarchy, so she was here alone, forging ahead. She would do the bulk of the work—even the record keeping and reporting. Going above and beyond meant that she might one day get to

297

go on the buying trips and head out to some of the studios where the creations were conceived and constructed.

That's because Matthew Mayfield was a total aficionado of the genre. He wanted to believe that the aliens had long come and landed, that the dead rose as zombies, and that ghosts and creatures lay hidden just beneath the earth's surface everywhere. She rather figured that he was like her—he just loved all that was eerie and creepy. But she also liked to believe she was his pet—she could rise in the ranks to become management.

Not that it was bad working here even as a peon—she loved it. Since she'd been a little kid, she'd loved all that was creepy and chilled the flesh, the old stuff—Poe and Lovecraft, Shelley, Stoker, you name it—and more contemporary writers such as Steven King and Peter Straub, Matheson and more. She loved old Hammer films and every new horror, sci-fi, fantasy film or game to hit the market. And when things here went on sale when the season was over, she and the other employees got first dibs. It wasn't a bad job at all—and she could rise within the ranks.

If that meant taking time after work to take a look at the rest of their Caitlin Corpse dolls—when most of the rest of the staff was wearily calling it quits—she didn't mind.

Caitlin Corpse was in high demand—it was almost Halloween.

Caitlin Corpse—when her "on" switch had been flicked—was motion activated. She was truly dreadful looking and life-sized. Hannah knew that a top model had actually been hired so that Caitlin could start out as a truly beautiful young woman—but once the model had been cast, the fright fabricators had set to her with a relish. Her flesh was a gray that truly seemed to speak of death and decay and the grave. Her cheeks were sucked out; her teeth had been filed. The eyes had been enlarged and blood had been made to drip from a ring around her neck, from her eyes, and from her ears. She wore a dress that was consumed by spider webs. She was usually set behind a door and when that door opened, she would reach out—as if she were about to embrace anyone entering with her skeletal fingers and gruesome nails and, certainly, scare that person half to death.

Caitlin cost a lot—and yet the manufacturer had received so many orders for her that Caitlin would soon have a whole clan. They were now creating family and friends to join her—Carly Corpse, Conar Copse,

Cathy Corpse, Mama Corpse, Grandpa Corpse, and more were in the works. Hannah had seen the sales ads for Grandma Corpse—although she wasn't going to be out until next year.

Hannah suddenly stopped walking, staring ahead. There were only two big windows in the store, and those were at the far rear. They looked out over the old Anglican church and the graveyard that were part of the New England charm of the area—especially at Halloween. But, for some reason, seeing the rise of cherubs and angels, vaults and mausoleums, aged and lichen covered, caught her breath. There seemed to be an eerie light that had settled over the church and graveyard. The moon, she told herself. It would be full soon—just in time for Halloween.

As she stood there, she jumped, caught by a noise. One of the ghosts had flown over her head again.

"Hey!" she called back. Randy and Roberta should have been closer behind her. She gave herself a mental shake—she couldn't let them see that the creatures had unnerved her. They'd laugh—or worse. They'd tell everyone else.

She made a point of looking away from the graveyard. But it seemed a noise was coming from the back, something like... wind and cold whistling as if it were coming through.

It *was* coming through, she realized. She had been attracted to the windows and the light beyond because something was wrong. There was a crack in one of the windows.

"Randy, Roberta! Where are you guys?" she demanded, making herself walk to the back to check it out.

It wasn't just a crack. Part of the window had been crashed in—there were glass fragments all over the floor.

Did that mean that there was someone in the warehouse with her— someone who wasn't Roberta or Randy?

She looked out the window and stood frozen in fear for a minute. It looked as if a bomb had gone off in the graveyard—she realized that tombstones were askew and scattered, praying angels lay broken on their sides...

Corpses littered the ground.

She fumbled in the pocket of her skirt for her cell phone as she backed away.

She backed right into one of the Caitlin Corpse dolls. The shop had three of them, all identical. They were all five-six, with spider-web-infested-hair, all wearing the same ragged, lacy, spider-webbed dress. They were beyond gruesome with their filed teeth and ripped up faces. And their eyes. They bulged in shadowed circles—with blood dripping from the tear ducts. She'd never noticed any difference in the eyes before, but tonight...

One of the dolls had blue eyes, the second had eyes that were a smoky gray. The third—the one she'd backed into—had yellow, snake-like eyes. The pupils were vertical, not round. And it seemed to stare at her—really stare at her—like a snake, ready to strike.

She was going crazy because she'd back into it. She shouldn't have backed into it. It should have been against the wall!

She thought she heard something and quickly looked at a row of evil clown dolls that were next to a row of creepy Victorian dolls. They were the most normal—which somehow made them the creepiest. That was it; she was scaring herself. It had almost sounded like a chattering, as if the creatures in the place were speaking to one another in a strange language.

It was just rustling; the heat was on. Motors were going on and off...

The dolls weren't talking—or laughing.

They just sat on the shelf, as decorations. Scary things to make up a cool Halloween atmosphere for a party or a haunted house or hay ride.

Yes, that's what they were, what they were...

She turned and was in the arms of the Caitlin Corpse doll.

And she froze.

It was moving; it was holding her... it was...

Evil eyes gleamed into hers, the laughing sound grew louder...

She fought hard for sanity.

Well, of course, the doll moved. She was here to make sure that they all were moving properly. The one had been returned because it had hugged a guest at a party—and hugged him so tightly that he had bruises and cuts.

And this one was hugging her and hugging her...

And looking at her with those evil eyes.

It seemed as if they had all taken a step forward.

It was late. Everyone was gone.

Throw it off! Fight it!

She was just unnerved and being ridiculous. But the dolls were just about her size. It was as if she was facing three evil... creatures.

Living creatures.

Okay. She worked with monsters, but...

Then the one blinked. Blinked with the snake-like eyes.

It blinked. It wasn't supposed to blink!

She heard laughter and tried to fight the hard arms of the mechanical creature.

It sounded as if laughter had come from the clown dolls.

The clown dolls were doing nothing, and yet...

The sound of laughter seemed to echo throughout the vast corridors and shadows of the room.

The arms were tightening around her, the bony, decaying arms...

And the snake-like eyes blinked again. Just as the rotting lips twisted twisted into a smile.

Hannah screamed, struggling, and fighting those arms—nothing but the instinct to survive driving her mind.

Her fight was to no avail. The Caitlin Corpse doll twirled its skeletal fingers into her hair and ripped her back so hard that she fell.

Stunned and flat on the ground, she looked up. The doll was bent over her. The chattering, the sound like laughter, seemed to grow...

She screamed and screamed...

But the eyes just came closer and closer...

ALL HALLOW'S EVE
6:30 a.m.

When Dana Scully arrived at the scene, there were people everywhere. Fox Mulder had arrived before she had; he was speaking with a young woman who trembled so vehemently that Dana could see her across the room.

She took a quick moment to survey the situation before Mulder saw her and before the local police detective in charge could approach her and skew her first impressions.

First, it was difficult to tell what was real. So many distorted, bleeding, evilly grinning, or disarticulated creatures were spread through the room that she had to look twice to find the corpses.

There were two of them, the bodies of a young man and a young woman. They were standing in the midst of two full-sized corpse dolls, a skeletal body with a pumpkin head. She was glad to see that no one had touched the bodies as of yet; she would be able to view them first in situ.

As she started to make her way across the room, the detective in charge waylaid her. He was a big man, tall and hefty, and she liked him immediately. Maybe it was his size; he didn't feel the need to be puffed out or macho, despite seeming a little puzzled that she had managed to come as far as she had. "Ma'am, this is a crime scene, I'm afraid. I'm so sorry, you shouldn't have been able to get past the tape at the front."

She flashed her badge. "Scully, sir. FBI. And I'm also a medical examiner. May I?" She indicated the bodies that were posed against the wall as if they were one with the Halloween creatures."

"You may," he told her. "Detective Ben Fuller out of Boston. And I'm here to follow you—this is the damnedest thing I've ever seen. You've just come across the top of the heap here. I have no problem whatsoever with the FBI taking the lead, though my men will be happy to assist in any way you so choose."

"I appreciate that, Detective Fuller. What did you mean? There are more—dead?" she asked.

Fuller scrunched up his face. "Thousands of them really—but maybe fifty or so that matter."

"Fifty?"

Mulder's call had been brief; he had only told her about two murders.

"Not fresh, mind you. And they're strewn all over the cemetery," Fuller told her. "Out back—the adjoining property belongs to the Anglican Church—since the end of the 1600s. The surrounding acreage is a graveyard. Crypts were broken into—there's a massive hole where the catacombs that were—still are—part of the church. You'll have to see it, ma'—"

Fuller broke off. He was about to call her ma'am.

"Agent Scully."

Dana looked around. Fox was still talking to the young woman who was shaking so fervently.

"Our one witness," Fuller said.

"She saw it all—she knows who did this, all of this?" Dana asked.

Fuller shook his head and scrunched his face in aggravated disgust. "Crazy as a loon—or guilty as all hell. She says the dolls did it."

"The dolls?" Dana repeated, frowning.

"To be specific, the Caitlin Corpse dolls," Fuller said. "Your partner is humoring her, I imagine, trying to find something that's truth there in her story."

Dana was torn then between heading straight to the dead or straight to the attractive young woman shivering so fiercely as she spoke to Mulder.

Mulder, she knew, was listening intently. He wasn't humoring the girl.

Dana didn't have to ask Fuller to go on; he was a good cop and continued with, "Hannah Barton. She's the one who dialed 911, hysterical. She was entangled in a heap of the other dolls, screaming that they were all coming to life, that she needed help. To be fair to the woman, a clown puppet was hanging there in the dark and she must have walked right to it and gotten entangled in the strings. She was really wrapped up and I don't see any way she could have gotten up. Nor can I see how she could have done that to herself. I was going to send her straight to the psych ward but your partner wanted to talk to her. By all reports, and through her boss—Matthew Mayfield, who owns the place, she was a hard-working, level-headed girl—until tonight."

"Mayfield was here?"

"No, he'd gone home for the night. We got him out after the 911 call."

"Where is he now?"

"Outside, sitting on a grave stone—and waiting for us in case we have more questions."

"Thanks, Detective," Dana said. "I'll take a look at the corpses and then join my partner and take a look at the graveyard destruction. As soon as I can, then, I'll appreciate a lead on the autopsies, I'll just need you to direct me to the morgue."

"Yes, ma'—Agent Scully. Make your way through the—creature crunch here on the floor."

Fuller led her through the piles of dolls, pumpkins, puppets, evil clowns, and so on that were strewed along the floor.

As they walked, she looked to the rear of the place. Glass was broken down at the windows that over-looked the graveyard. Through what remained of the windows she could see the massive and bizarre destruction of angels and cherubs, mausoleums and tombstones.

"No one heard all this?" she asked Fuller.

"No one," Fuller said. "But then again, the nearest neighbor—other than the graveyard of the real dead—is a gymnasium down the hill. When this places closes for the night—unless it's Christmas Eve—there's nothing going on here. Perfect place for perfect quiet—or a near perfect crime."

Dana paused in front of the two young people who had been killed. He had been skinny—possibly somewhat geeky looking in life. He'd been hung on hooks in the wall so that he looked like a puppet—awkwardly akimbo, like a Halloween decoration himself. The girl had her mouth opened in a huge O. While autopsy would reveal far more detail, it didn't take a medical degree to ascertain cause of death—they'd both had their throats ripped out.

"Have you found the murder weapon?" asked Dana.

Fuller made a face. "Yeah, we found it." He winced. "Take a look at the doll next to the corpse."

Dana did so. The nails on the skeletal fingers on the rotting and skeletal hands were crusted in blood; real blood ran down most of her gruesome apparel.

Just as real blood soaked and covered the clothing of the two who had been killed.

It did indeed look as if the doll had committed murder.

Hannah Barton needed to get to a hospital; Fox knew it, Hannah knew it, and the EMT who stood by them knew it. But Fox wanted to listen, just as much as Hannah wanted to talk.

"I don't know why I'm alive," Hannah repeated. Fox couldn't begin to count just how many times the girl had said the words. She was a pretty thing with long blond hair and enormous blue eyes, shaking like the wind. It didn't appear that she'd been really hurt—other than the fact that her wrists were chaffed and she seemed to have acquired a few bangs and bruises. "She started with me—she started with me. I thought

Caitlin would kill me!"

He knew she was referring to one of the creepy dolls on display. He had seen where her two co-workers had been hung with their throats ripped out—he'd seen the fabricated hands and nails on the doll and that, indeed, the doll had been used as a murder weapon.

But while he knew the police were not discounting Hannah as a suspect, he wasn't in the least convinced she could be guilty in any way—there wasn't a speck of blood on the young woman.

"Take a deep breath one more time," he said softly. Fox could see that Dana Scully was coming across the room. He lowered his head for a minute, hiding a little smile. After years of skirting around one another, they both knew that come what may, they were partners in far more than seeking the truth. He also knew that Dana would see this as a matter-of-fact event—no matter how bizarre. Murderers—sick, psycho murderers, quite possibly—had determined to kill two young people and destroy a Halloween shop, an Anglican church, and a graveyard.

They didn't need to look to the skies. There were people on earth demented enough to perform such atrocities.

And yet...

The good thing was that—while she might be skeptical as all hell—Dana betrayed nothing with her expression. She was grave when Fox introduced her as Agent Scully to Hannah Barton. She spoke softly and calmly, telling Hannah she was sorry—she knew she'd already told her story—but did she mind doing so one more time.

Hannah didn't mind.

"We were trying to find out why one of the dolls had been faulty," she explained. "I was coming here with Randy and Roberta—"

Hannah paused for a minute, a catch in her voice, tears forming in her eyes once again, "because we volunteered. I wanted to be Miss Johnny on the spot, you know, get a raise, impress Matthew Mayfield and the other bosses, and make my way in the company. So I was ahead, in front. And I came down here... saw the broken window. When I turned, getting out my cell phone..."

Her voice trailed off again.

"You ran right into the Caitlin Corpse doll," Mulder continued for her, looking over at Dana.

"It had come to life!" Hannah whispered.

"It does move—it's basically an automated figure, right?" Dana said, looking back at Mulder.

Hannah nodded. "Yes, you see, that was it, that's why we were here. One was returned; the people said that the doll was broken, that it 'embraced' a guest and they had to rip it off of the person. So we were going to test them all, and see that they were working right. But then there was the broken window, and when I backed away..." She stopped speaking again and looked back at the place where the Caitlin Corpse dolls hung with her dead friends and she shuddered and started to sob again. Nearby, the EMT made an irritated noise; he wanted to take the young woman to a hospital. Mulder lifted a hand to him; it would be just a minute more.

"And then?" Dana asked quietly.

"She was holding me—one of the Caitlins—was holding me. She had put her arms around me and the whole place seemed to be alive. The evil clowns and the skeletons, witches—ghosts! They were all chattering and laughing and the Caitlin had... snake eyes. She looked at me with snake eyes and squeezed me and then..."

"And then I thought I was dead," Hannah said flatly, suddenly deflated, not shivering, not crying, just staring ahead as if all her emotion had been drained from her. "She squeezed me... I thought I was dead. But, I woke up... all entangled, and the creatures were everywhere and I could—I could smell the blood—that tinny, terrible smell of blood. And I dialed 911."

She looked at Dana, and Dana knew, that as far as the girl was concerned, she had the truth, the absolute truth. Whatever had happened in here, Hannah Barton believed beyond all sense that she had been attacked and nearly killed by a doll.

Mulder nodded to the EMT tech who came over and began speaking to the girl and then guiding her toward the emergency vehicle that waited outside.

"You saw the bodies?" Mulder asked.

"Yes. And you know, of course, that I'm going to do thorough autopsies."

Something that was almost a smile touched his lips. "I expect no less from you, you know."

He was talking about a lot more than the autopsies. She was his anchor; he was her imagination. She nodded in acknowledgment. They were good together in many ways.

"You been outside yet?"

"No."

"Shall we then?" she asked.

He nodded. They made their way carefully through the debris of gruesome "decorative" creatures and around the police markers to the back of the store. Giant double doors led to the back.

Nothing really separated the properties—Mayfield's Monsters and Mayhem had a thatch of mown lawn directly behind the back receiving doors that ran straight into the overgrown, tree laden, grass tufted grave-yard.

The Mausoleum and vault doors seemed to be opened throughout the graveyard; massive holes were dug everywhere.

Graves—disturbed to the point it looked as if an army of crazed moles had been at it all night.

Bodies, in various stages of decomposition—from the freshly embalmed to heaps of disconnected bones—were strewn about haphaz-ardly.

"This would have taken all night—dozens of people. Or more!" Dana murmured.

"It had to have happened quickly," Mulder told her. "The place cleared out of customers at midnight. The bosses were gone within thirty minutes. Hannah Barton and her friends—the dead, Randy and Roberta—were left behind. This all happened in less than an hour."

Something seemed to be moving beneath a corpse that lay just outside the grated steel door—now hanging on its hinges—that had led to a family mausoleum.

"Mulder," Dana said, hurrying toward the body.

He was quick to see what she was talking about—and he followed her, reaching the body before her. He hunkered down—as he did so, he was quickly thrown backwards as *something* leapt from the ground.

It was black—that was all she could really catch. It looked as if it were a nutria or large rodent, or... like a very large, incredibly fat, black snake.

It was gone before either could really see it, burrowing into a bush.

Mulder immediately went after it. Dana ran after him. "Fox, stop! You don't know what it is, the creature could be rabid!"

He didn't stop—but neither did he catch the creature. He thrashed through the bushes where it disappeared. He searched beneath and around a number of the corpses strewn about. But there was nothing.

"What the hell was that, Dana?" he demanded.

"An animal, Mulder. There are animals all around. It was—something."

"Something—what?" he asked her. "Have you ever seen anything like it? The damned thing appeared to be a giant slug!"

"If it was a giant slug, Mulder, it didn't do this. Forget it. Look around you. A giant slug didn't do this!"

He stood straight, staring into the distance. She shook her head at him slightly. "Mulder, I always go the distance with you—you know that. But focus. Look around you."

He started walking. "Mulder!"

"I'm investigating," he told her, looking back and then pointing across to the church. There were two men there—one, fifty or so, white-haired, and wearing the collar that denoted him as an Episcopal priest. Another man was next to him, perhaps ten years or so younger, dark-haired and gesturing wildly as he spoke to the priest.

"A good father and our Mr. Mayfield, I believe," Mulder said.

She nodded and followed along behind him.

As they approached the men Mulder held up his FBI identification. "Mr. Mayfield, Father. I'm Agent Fox Mulder and this is my associate, Agent Dana Scully."

"Father Timothy," the priest said, rising. They'd been sitting on a very old tomb. Time had weathered away most of the words, but Dana judged it to be of the Revolutionary War era. It had somehow been ignored in the mass destruction.

The other man rose, too. Dana noted that his fingernails were dirty.

Had the man been digging in the earth? But could one man have done all this?

"Matthew Mayfield," he said.

"I'm sorry for the loss of your employees, Mr. Mayfield," Dana said.

He nodded, distracted. Then he looked at her oddly. "I knew they were coming," he said.

Fox glanced at her. She winced.

"They? Who?" Mulder asked him.

"I don't know," Mayfield said. "But—I heard them. Before. They all said that I was crazy—that I'd lived with my creatures too long."

Dana nodded, trying to appear like Mulder—patient and willing to listen to whatever.

"Please, Mr. Mayfield, go on," she said.

He took a deep breath. He didn't answer. Father Timothy stepped in. "Mr. Mayfield is a deacon at the church. He was doing some maintenance duties down in the crypts last week. He heard talking. He found one of the old tombs had been broken into." He took a breath and shrugged. "I'm afraid the youth of America can be destructive and ridiculous when it comes to the Halloween season. However, they'd tried to steal one of the corpses. We found it—a pile of dust, really—near the broken stone. We put it back."

Mayfield shook his head. "Father Timothy is afraid they're going to lock me up. But..."

"Please," Mulder told him. "We discount nothing. Anything you have to say just might matter—we need your help."

"A few days before that—I heard a boom. And there was suddenly a burst of light in the graveyard. I called Father Timothy. The next day, we found a huge patch of burned out grass in the middle of the graveyard."

"Kids again," Father Timothy said quietly.

Mayfield stared at him and sucked in his breath, looking at Mulder and Scully. He let out his breath.

"Aliens," he said.

Father Timothy lowered his head and shook it, as if he were afraid that Mayfield had just signed his name and crossed the T's in getting himself committed to a mental ward.

"Aliens?" Mulder said. She was glad he had spoken—she would have allowed doubt to creep into the word.

"I really would have noticed little green men," Father Timothy murmured.

Mayfield shook his head vehemently and seemed pained when he looked at Father Timothy. "Why does everyone assume little green men? Why even assume that they have eyes and ears and stand erect? How the hell would we begin to know what an alien—with intelligence—might look like? They could be way smarter than us—but not even have brains that begin to resemble ours?"

"Mr. Mayfield, do you have any known enemies? Perhaps someone who loathes your place as anti-religious, or perhaps, even, someone who wants to be your competition?" Dana asked.

"The only problem we usually have is with the high school and college kids," Father Timothy said. "Matthew is known for miles around—people come here to shop from as far away as New York City."

"I've had no offers on the store," Mayfield said. "And God help me, to the best of my knowledge, I have no enemies. I love what I do. It's fun, it's creative, I meet movie producers, I travel... I have great people working for me. And now..." He paused, obviously hurt by the loss of Randy and Roberta.

His emotion seemed honest.

"They come at night," he said suddenly.

"Pardon?" Dana asked.

"I—I didn't know what I was seeing. But I know this. They come at night."

"They—who?" Mulder asked carefully.

"The aliens. Or the creatures. I've seen them when I've been leaving sometimes, late at night. Something—something that scurries in the ground. But sometimes, too, they stop and look at you."

"You've seen them look at you?" Dana asked.

He nodded gravely. "You can tell... they have strange eyes—the kind that glow. It's in their eyes—they're like snake eyes."

Dana closed her eyes and looked down for a minute.

Little green men that weren't little green men. This man was feeding into Mulder's theories that they didn't always really know what they were looking for. Feeding into the bizarre—the X factor of all that they did.

There were two dead young people, and that was the reality.

"I'm going to perform the autopsies, Mulder. Mr. Mayfield, Father, thank you so much."

She turned and walked across the graveyard, heading back in. She had to sidestep broken and disjointed corpses and shattered stone, marble and cement.

That was real. The destruction was real.

She hoped that Mulder understood he really had to find who had done this—and who had killed the two young people inside.

Four hours later, with Dr. Forbes, the local medical examiner working in tandem with her, Dana finished the autopsies. Detective Fuller had stood through the entire procedures, quiet, listening, taking notes.

"To summarize, no apparent drug or alcohol use, though it will take some time before all the lab reports are in," Dr. Forbes said, glancing at Dana. "Unless my colleague here has an objection, we'll be stating that death was due to exsanguinations from the throats being violently severed. Due to the, er, violence and unusual circumstances of these deaths, lab reports have been rushed, and the blood on the nails of the Caitlin Corpse doll does match with that of the victims. Somehow, the perpetrator used the doll to kill these people."

"So, you're saying that the killer got behind the doll, most likely, and then used the hands and the nails to—to nearly behead these young people?" Fuller asked.

"Roberta suffered from juvenile diabetes," Dana said.

Fuller dismissed that.

"And Randy would have suffered some difficulty in the years to come; his heart was enlarged," she told him.

"Certainly, none of that matters now," Fuller told her. "They died because their throats were torn out—and the murder weapon was the nails on the dolls."

"That's what we're theorizing, yes," Dana said. "The nails of the doll were definitely the murder weapon. How, exactly, the murders were committed, we're still surmising."

Fuller shook his head. "Some really insane son of a bitch."

"One?" Dana asked. "Detective, I believe there had to be more than one person involved."

Fuller gave off a sound like a snort. "A horde of aliens—as Mayfield suggests. Let me tell you—he's at the top of my suspect list."

"Has the man ever done anything to suggest that he's mentally unbalanced—or that he might be capable of such violence?" Dana asked.

"Done anything..." Fuller said thoughtfully. "No. But he lives and breathes those freak things! Costumes, creatures... it's easy to see where he might have gone bizarre and off the deep end. Yeah, my money is on him."

Dana didn't say anything other than, "Well, I do believe that we will continue to investigate." She didn't add that she was damned glad that she and Mulder, the FBI, had been given lead in the case. While it might well be that Mayfield was certifiably insane and involved, she didn't believe in assumptions and convictions without facts.

She peeled off her gloves and thanked Dr. Forbes and his assistants, who would sew Y incisions on the body now that the procedures were complete. As she did so, Fox Mulder arrived at the autopsy room at last.

He was, she noticed, dusty and covered in spider webs.

Real ones.

"Hey, Mulder, you need some good notes, I've got them," Fuller said.

Mulder refused to take offense. He nodded. Dana resisted the temptation to dust off his shoulders; he looked as if he'd been crawling around in the catacombs.

It was Mulder—he probably had been. And he wanted her away from Fuller and anyone else before he discussed what he was doing.

"Detective Fuller, thank you for your dedicated attention," Scully said, and hurried out with Mulder.

She'd driven her own car to the morgue; he suggested she leave it and drive with him.

"Back to the hotel—where you can shower and change?" she suggested.

He glanced her way and shook his head. "It's going to be getting dark soon," he said.

"And?"

"We're going to wait at the church—and watch."

She lowered her head and groaned. "I believe they intend to have detectives watching the grounds and the shop tonight. To the best of my knowledge, Miss Hannah Barton remains at the hospital—under sedation. They've brought in a number of high school and college boys they've had trouble with in the past. Fuller told me that they asked Matthew Mayfield to remain at the station. He's not under arrest, they're being very polite to the man, but Fuller is convinced he's involved."

Mulder didn't answer.

"Mulder?"

"He's innocent of anything but observation," Mulder said.

"And you know this because?"

He looked over at her quickly as he drove. "Slime."

She groaned. "Slime, Mulder—really?"

"Just listen to me for a minute, will you? Yes, I know I'm going to sound as crazy as Mayfield, but just listen."

"All right."

They had a ways to drive—at least twenty minutes. The morgue for the area was on the outskirts of Boston and while the rush hour traffic was down, they had a little ways to go.

"Go ahead," she told him.

"What if Mayfield is right?"

"About aliens landing? The light in the graveyard—the burned grass? Father Timothy said that they'd had trouble with kids and young adults—like the ones they're questioning at the station—before. Kids get crazy around Halloween. You know that."

"Crazy and destructive. They have school clubs, hazing, things to prove. They drink, they get into sex and drugs. But they don't become murderers."

It was Dana's turn to be silent.

"Scully, I went into the catacombs of the church," he told her.

She nodded, looking at him. She'd expected as much.

"All right, what it appeared to be is that… I believe that there is an alien intelligence at work here. They aren't little green men. They don't have brains like ours, but they are highly involved—just differently."

"Slime—so you're suggesting highly evolved slugs?"

"They wouldn't be slugs—they would just appear like slugs to us."

"They change what they are—like chameleons?"

He hesitated. "This is all theory."

"Thank God."

"They can inhabit other bodies," he said quietly. "They landed in the graveyard. They tried the dead. The dead didn't work. The dead happened to be by Mayfield's Monsters and Mayhem. They tried the creatures—the things in the store. They didn't work either."

"I'll play along. So, they needed someone living," Dana said.

Mulder nodded thoughtfully.

"No!"

He looked over at her and she quickly continued, "They needed something living? They found Hannah Barton and they tied her up and then killed her friends? That doesn't make sense."

"It does if they were afraid, if they could control the dead or the dolls—but only for a few minutes."

"And why would that be?"

"They need the strength of the host they've taken. I don't believe they meant to kill."

"Wait—you want me to believe that body-stealing aliens arrived in a grave yard—and realized that they couldn't inhabit and utilize the bodies of the dead—and then tried the shop—trying to inhabit and utilize the bodies of a bunch of dolls and puppets—and then finally found live bodies?"

Mulder looked at Scully. "You've got a better theory?"

She stared back at him. "Yes. Someone came and ripped all the bodies out of the ground and tore up the cemetery. They got into the shop. They used the Caitlin Corpse doll to attack Hannah, and then realized that some idiot fabricated the doll with nails sharp enough to kill—to slit a human throat. They killed Randy and Roberta—they didn't get to Hannah once they'd figured out how to kill and that they needed to—or be caught, perhaps—because she dialed 911 and the police came so quickly."

"I went down into the catacombs. I broke open the stone that had replaced the one that been broken by mischief-makers according to Father Timothy. I looked at the remains—Dana, there was a weird slime all over it."

"It could be anything," she told him.

Mulder looked at her, shaking his head in that way that sometimes deeply aggravated her.

Mulder believed with his whole heart that aliens had come to earth. Of course. It all went back to his sister. But for Dana belief was much more of a challenge. She believed in Mulder, but that wasn't the same as sharing his beliefs. Her relationship with the man was so complex. They'd investigated the absurd so many times, and often, the investigations had revealed the totally absurd. And yet…

"So, let's test our theories," he continued. "It will be dark just about when we get to the church and the cemetery. We'll wait—and watch."

She didn't argue with him; she thought they should be at the police station, questioning the boys. But, they could continue along that line of investigation in the morning.

Yellow crime tape glistened oddly in the rising moonlight. Little had been done to set the graveyard to rights; Dana wasn't surprised. Police photographers were busy all day. Crime scene people set markers about. It was a monumental task.

And two young people were dead. The investigation had to be thorough.

There were two patrol cars stationed in front of the store and two in front of the church. She saw uniformed men at the gates to the cemetery.

Mulder flashed his badge and they headed on into the church.

It was a lovely old church; engraving on a plaque over the door denoted that it had been built in 1714 to replace an earlier structure. The windows were stained glass, the altar held a gorgeous silver cross, and old stone stairs behind the altar led down to the crypts beneath, while doors to the side led, Dana believed, to the small rectory alongside.

As she entered with Mulder, Father Timothy came out of the door to the rectory.

"Thank you for coming tonight," he said. "I couldn't leave. My faith should keep me strong, but I didn't want to be alone."

"I'm not sure what we're watching for, but we're glad to be here with you, Father," Dana said.

"Come, come this way. I'll make tea," he said.

They followed him through the church to the rectory.

"You live here?" Dana asked him.

"Yes."

"And you didn't hear the big boom that Mayfield heard? You didn't see a flash of light?"

He hesitated and winced slightly. "Anything could have happened. I've been diagnosed with cancer. I've had some treatments—I don't sleep well, though they say I may make it. At any rate, I take pills to sleep. A complete invasion could be going on—and I wouldn't awaken."

He made them tea. They sat in a cozy little Victorian style parlor and sipped it. And waited.

Suddenly, Mulder said, "Cancer?"

"Yes."

Dana looked at Mulder. It seemed rude and cruel to push the point.

But, to her surprise, he stood and pulled out his cell phone. He'd called Fuller, she realized. "Can you find out for me if Hannah Barton and Randy and Roberta suffered from any ailments? Yes, even if one of them had a common cold."

"Roberta had juvenile diabetes and—" Scully lowered her head. She didn't want to add fuel to Mulder's feelings.

But there was no choice. She never hid the truth—even when it did feed his fantasies.

"Never mind on the other two—can you check into Miss Barton's health issues for me? Thank you," Mulder said, and hung up.

Father Timothy looked at Mulder with wary amusement. "You—you didn't buy into Matthew Mayfield's words, did you?"

"I just follow every path my mind takes, Father," Mulder told him.

He'd barely spoken when they all started; a creaking sound, distant and yet clear, startled them all.

"It came from the church," Mulder said.

"It's—it's the gate," Father Timothy said. "The gate to the crypt."

Mulder and Scully both rose, drawing their weapons.

The priest saw the guns and cried out. "You can't do that, this is a church!"

"God will understand that we don't want to end like Roberta and Randy," Mulder told him.

Father Timothy didn't argue that.

They moved through the rectory doorway and slipped behind the altar. Mulder hurried down the old stone steps first with Dana close behind him.

Father Timothy followed her.

"Light, we'll need light!" he called.

Dana paused to accept one of the candles he handed her; his fingers trembled as he lit it. She wanted to rush after Mulder but she waited for the priest to gather his own candle. They were altar candles at least— large, and casting a nice glow of illumination.

She couldn't cup her flame and manage the Glock at the same time so she moved carefully to keep her candle lit.

When they reached the crypt, the dampness, the smell of decay, seemed to wrap around her.

Anything could slither here, she thought.

Then she stopped. Mulder was standing just before the centuries-old gate to the tombs, staring in.

She realized that there was a man there.

Matthew Mayfield.

She came closer to Mulder, lifting her candle so that the glow fell into the crypts—and cast some illumination on Mayfield.

"Mr. Mayfield, what are you doing here?" Mulder asked.

Mayfield turned and looked at him and smiled. "I need it open—but it is open. You opened the portal."

Dana couldn't help it; something in the way he spoke sent a shiver down her spine. The portal?

This was a church. The portal… to what?

Father Timothy let out a shriek and she quickly spun around. There was something in the crypt with them.

Something black and scurrying, like a large rodent. Something black and slithery… like an extremely fat snake!

It let out some kind of an ear-splitting sound—and seemed to rise like a bloated bird and aim directly for Father Timothy.

She fired—killing it in midair.

It fell to the ground, shrieking—and disassembling into a mass of…

Slime.

There were more of them. And they all intended to attack. There was no time to wonder about what they were…

Or if communication was possible.

She fired on one, and another. Mulder was firing as well.

Father Timothy was huddled down on the ground, shaking.

Then, she and Mulder spun around and looked at one another. They were partners; they judged their safety. The things seemed to be gone.

Not just dead. Gone.

But then, another sound—horrific, high, ear-piercing—tore through the room. This time it was no black creature aiming at her. It was Mayfield.

They hadn't paid attention to him, and now, he was pitching himself at Scully.

She hadn't expected him; she lowered her weapon. She had no time to raise it before he was on top of her, staring down at her. Her candle went flying into the shadows of the crypt, and then its glow was gone and all that remained was the faint light from Father Timothy's candle.

She saw the man above her, with his powerful, death-grip upon her, crushing her.

And she saw his eyes. They were snake eyes, vertically slit, and gold except for those slits. These eyes were purely evil, filled with hatred.

He opened his mouth… and there was something black inside of it, something black with eyes that were the same. Snake eyes, evil eyes, eyes of hate and loathing and…

She screamed. And as she did, Mayfield was ripped from her. She saw that he was on Mulder, grappling him down with a strength unlike anything she'd ever seen.

She groped for her Glock, cast somewhere on the ground when she fell.

Before she could find it, Mayfield threw Mulder off. Mulder crashed against the wall and fell.

Mayfield was coming back for her.

She fired and caught his arm, but it didn't stop him. He was back on her, his fingers around her throat, his mouth opening…

His eyes. His terrible eyes on her.

She struggled, and they went down. She couldn't look away. Something was in him, something dark and fetid and evil and he meant to release it on her.

Just when she thought she couldn't breathe anymore, when she would die or worse, Mayfield was torn away.

She heard an explosion.

As she gasped for breath, she managed to roll. Father Timothy was praying, words tumbled from his mouth. His candle illuminated the space they were in on the ground of the crypt.

She saw that Mayfield was prone just inches from her and Mulder was crawling over to her.

Mayfield was dead.

His eyes were open. He stared at her.

He stared at her with eyes that were an ordinary brown, with ordinary pupils.

"Scully, Scully, Dana… talk to me!"

She looked at Mulder. Smiled and touched his face.

Searched out his eyes.

"I'm all right," she told him.

The next morning, it was determined that the case was closed. The world would assume that Matthew Mayfield had played with creepy monsters so long that he had become one himself.

By morning's light, Dana wasn't even really sure what she'd seen herself.

Father Timothy thought that Mayfield had been possessed by the devil.

She knew that Mulder believed what Mayfield had told them. That a ship had come, crash-landed perhaps, and burned the hole in the graveyard. The creatures had known that to survive, they needed to inhabit living bodies.

They had tried.

They had needed healthy bodies.

First, they'd tried to inhabit the dead.

Then, they'd found Mayfield, and they'd tried for more, but despite whatever their intelligence, they'd tried to inhabit fabricated creatures.

They'd learned they needed the living, and the healthy.

By the time things were straightened out and she and Mulder were driving away, Dana didn't know what she thought.

They'd been told to take a few days.

"Where do you want to go?" Mulder asked her.

Dana looked out the window at the fall decorations that seemed to cover the countryside. Scarecrows stood tall in fields, pumpkins were everywhere, dangling skeletons hung from trees and white billowing ghosts seemed to be everywhere.

"Anywhere," she murmured.

"Anywhere?"

"Anywhere they don't celebrate Halloween," she told him.

Their eyes met. They would never really agree on what had happened. They wouldn't be good partners if they did. He needed her to be skeptical.

He reached over and found her hand and squeezed it.

"I do have them digging up and searching that graveyard and the church, you know."

"That's fine. Where are we going?"

"Somewhere that doesn't celebrate Halloween," he assured her, and he gave his attention to his driving. She realized that they were headed to the airport. No doubt, Mulder would have a great place for them to go next.

Before they were called out again. She smiled and caught his glance in the rearview mirror.

He had great eyes. There was so much in the eyes. Human eyes.

She was the skeptical one. And yet she knew what the invaders had never realized.

It was all in the eyes.

THE END

THE HOUSE ON HICKORY HILL

By Max Allan Collins

BANEWICH, MASSACHUSETTS
29th DECEMBER, 1997, 4:15 a.m.

On a crisp afternoon in mid-November in quaint, seemingly idyllic Banewich, Massachusetts, sixth-grader Heather Creed—walking home from school—found herself at the mercy of a handful of sadistic male classmates.

The boys tagged along after the blonde, blue-eyed, cherubic child, teasing the "new kid" at school for being stuck up and a teacher's pet.

Straight-A student Heather was a pleasant, if somewhat withdrawn, girl whose primly pretty Laura Ashley attire set her apart from the baggy, rumpled apparel of her schoolmates, particularly these boys.

They began to taunt her about the "haunted house" she lived in, an ancient barn remodeled into a modern home looming up ahead on Hickory Hill.

"They used to hang witches there," a freckle-faced boy said. "Perfect for a little witch like you!"

A pig-nosed boy piled on, saying, "There's monsters and murderers up there! They're gonna kill you in your sleep!"

Heather walked on, chin high, apparently impervious.

"You know what they do to *witches!*" a buck-toothed bully said, and then the boys were pitching pebbles and twigs at the girl, "stoning" her. This too got no reaction.

But when they pitched harder, stinging Heather's flesh, she whirled on them.

"*Stop it!*" she shouted, taking the bullies aback. "*Stop it right now!*"

Her sweet features were fierce now, a vein trembling in her forehead.

The red-haired boy clutched his throat and tumbled into a pile of leaves, his friends gathering around his thrashing form. "Help me— I...I...can't *breathe!*"

Concerned, Heather rushed to him—and the boy bolted upright, laughing at her, hurling leaves in her face. His friends began laughing hysterically as the girl ran off, crying.

"It'd be quicker on a *broomstick*, 'Carrie'!" the redhead shouted down the street.

Drying her eyes, Heather climbed the driveway up Hickory Hill in the shadow of the barn-like structure, thinking about how much she hated living in Banewich, in this awful house. She had a vague sense that it would not be forever—her father, Arthur Creed, was writing a book about the house and the "bad things" that had happened there, none of which he'd shared with his daughter.

Not that her mother, Alice, had been any more forthcoming about the house's history than Daddy. And as for her teenage stepsister, Charity, well, Heather and her didn't get along at all. If Charity knew anything about the house, she'd never said. The teenager almost never spoke a word to Heather.

Entering the kitchen through the back door, Heather decided not to say anything about the humiliation she'd just experienced from the bullies.

Instead she merely said to her mother, who was shucking corn at the counter, "I'm hearing things at school about this house."

Her mother—slender, lovely and as blonde as Heather—said, "Oh?"

"Stuff about witches and murderers and...what *did* happen here, Mommy? What makes it a place Daddy wants to write about?"

"Honey, this is just a house like any other. It has an unusual history and that makes it a good subject for your father." She ripped stiff green away from golden sweet corn. "Just ignore them. It's superstitious nonsense."

Later, at supper, Heather looked for an opening to bring up the house's history, but the atmosphere at the table couldn't have been more tense if this *was* a haunted house.

Right now Charity—currently grounded and denied driving privileges—was asking in a phony voice, sweeter than the corn, that these restrictions be lifted.

"I've got my grades up, and I haven't had any problems at school all week." Heather's attractive brown-haired stepsister smiled in desperation. "My counselor says I'm really starting to fit in. Call and ask her!"

"No," her father said, cutting his meat loaf and spearing a piece into the gravy of the mashed potatoes. He was a dark-haired rugged man who looked more like a carpenter than a writer. "You'll serve your complete sentence. As far as I'm concerned, I was lenient."

Heather had no idea what Charity had done, but suspected it had to do with a boy. The child tuned out of the ugly argument that followed, ending with the teen storming away from the table.

Charity and Daddy hadn't gotten along at all well since the move to Banewich. But Heather always found her father easy to talk to, and when he came in to her third-floor bedroom to say goodnight, she blurted out to him what she'd been going through at school.

Her father, sitting on the edge of her bed, said, "Sweetheart, something bad *did* happen in this house, a long time ago."

"What?"

"It's not the kind of bedtime story that suits a young girl. All you need to know is that a house is a house—just a structure...wood, cement, plaster. A building doesn't have any memory of the things that happened inside it, bad or good."

But later Heather overheard her father in the hallway, saying to her mother, "If I'd known this stupid town was so steeped in all this superstitious bullshit, I'd never have come here."

"Once your book is written," her mother said, "and the publicity runs its course, we can move anywhere we want."

"Too bad—'cause I really do love this stupid place." Her father chuckled. "And don't tell anybody, Alice, but I haven't seen a single sign of 'evil' since we got here."

"Not counting Charity, of course," her mother said.

With her parents' uneasy laughter lingering in her ears, Heather took a long time to go to sleep, sounds and shadows amplifying in her child's imagination into disturbing thoughts and images. Finally she dropped off, but—deep into the night—loud creaking noises roused her.

Heather sat up, rubbed her eyes, got out of bed and went out into the hallway...

...*where the walls seemed to bulge and throb, as if the house was breathing!*

Wide-eyed with wonder and fright, the child moved down the hallway, floorboards beneath her feet rippling. At the end of the hall, by the stairs that would take her down to her parents' room on the second floor, the wall was streaky—dripping, oozing, with a glimmering red liquid...*blood?*

With a frightened little yelp, Heather turned and ran in the other direction, toward the only other source of help she could think of: her older sister, whose room was also on the third floor.

But Charity's bedroom was empty, covers thrown back, furnishings toppled, the entire room in disarray. Had a struggle taken place?

On the rumpled bed was a sheet of typing paper pasted with letters cut from magazines and newspapers: HALF MILLION FOR CHARITY! NO COPS! NO FBI!

The signature, however, was not cut-and-paste, but a red scrawl—apparently in still damp blood: *Clayton Geech.*

Heather hurried to get her parents, moving so fast that she almost doesn't notice that the wall that had dripped blood was now clean and dry.

WASHINGTON, D.C.
TUESDAY, 1:45 p.m.

The next afternoon, Fox Mulder was making a presentation to his partner Dana Scully in the cramped X-Files office in the basement of FBI HQ in Washington, D.C. The lights were dim, a slide show about to begin.

"You've heard of Arthur Creed," Mulder said.

"Anybody who ever bought a paperback at an airport has," Scully said. "True-crime specialist, wrote the first Ted Bundy book. But he's been off the bestseller lists for several years."

"Which is why he moved in here."

With a click, Mulder displayed a dramatically lit picture of the house on Hickory Hill.

Scully nodded. "Ostensibly to write a book exploring the history of the house. Mulder, Creed moving into this infamous place is a blatant publicity stunt—*People* magazine and *Entertainment Tonight* have already covered it."

"I didn't know you had such cultured tastes in your reading and viewing habits, Scully."

"Considering *your* reading and viewing tastes, Mulder, I wouldn't—"

"Do you remember the history of the house?"

"Only vaguely."

"Were you aware there's already an X-File opened on the 'House on Hickory Hill'?"

"No...but I think I'm about to find out."

Mulder continued his slide show.

Some twenty years ago, a family had remodeled the hundreds-of-years-old barn into a lovely home with every modern convenience. In the fall of 1979, around midnight, the father—clergyman Clayton Geech—inexplicably murdered his wife, thirteen year-old daughter and young son. Found innocent by reason of insanity, the clergyman lapsed into catatonia, interrupted only by his final act, in the State Hospital for the Criminally Insane: cutting his throat with a shard from a water glass, leaving a note scrawled in his own blood, indicating he'd committed this foul act to protect his loved ones from evil.

"In the intervening years," Mulder told his partner, "no family has lasted in the house longer than six months—mysterious sounds in the night, bleeding walls, insect and vermin infestation, unexplained 'accidents,' have chased every occupant out."

"That much I remember from the article," Scully said. "The house hadn't been lived in for over ten years, enabling Creed to pick it up for a song."

Mulder switched on the lights. "And Creed's career has already turned around—he's received a half-million dollar advance from his publisher on the work-in-progress."

"*The Banewich Terror*," Scully says, "yes, I remember them talking about it on TV. Mulder, first, this is an obvious publicity stunt from a writer trying to jump-start his career by taking advantage of the public's interest in this clichéd 'haunted house' nonsense. Second, the only crimes involved here are a decades-old, *solved* murder case, and maybe some sort of fraud—"

"This isn't just an old X-File, Scully—it's a fresh kidnapping."

She frowned. "Who's been taken?"

"Charity Creed—seventeen." Mulder went to his desk and flipped open that Scully-cited issue of a popular celebrity magazine to the article on Creed. He pointed out the pretty teenage brunette in a smiling family portrait.

Then Mulder filled Scully in on the details of the kidnapping, and showed her a fax of the cut-and-paste ransom note.

"The kidnapper is demanding exactly the amount of Creed's book advance," Scully noted.

"That signature, by the way, is in blood."

"Mulder, most kidnappers don't sign their names..."

"Recognize it?"

"...Yes."

Clayton Geech—the long-dead clergyman who killed his family in that house back in '79.

"That matches Geech's blood type, by the way," Mulder said, pointing to the signature.

"Does it match anyone else's blood type in the house?" Scully asked. "The kidnapped girl, for example? We may have a runaway here, trying to raise some money for a new life."

"It's type AB Negative—which matches nobody in the Creed household."

"Type AB Negative is rare, Mulder, but not *that* rare... and I presume Clayton Geech's signature is available in reproductions of that suicide note in numerous true-crime books and magazine articles."

"That doesn't explain why our handwriting experts say it's a perfect match for the late reverend."

"Mulder, we don't usually work kidnapping cases. That's specialized task-force work...."

"Skinner has already approved our participation. We'll be investigating while the kidnap team from the Boston office carries out the operation at the Creed house—actually, they're already doing that."

Though the ransom note had advised not calling the authorities, and specifically mentioned not contacting the FBI, that's exactly what Creed had done, last night.

"There's been no communication from the kidnapper since the initial ransom note," Mulder said.

"If we can crack this thing before any ransom exchange goes down," Scully said, fully on board now, "maybe we can save a girl's life."

"It's worth trying, don't you think?"

RURAL MASSACHUSETTS
TUESDAY, 6:45 p.m.

A plane ride to Massachusetts later, the two agents were tooling in their rental vehicle through the lovely fall landscapes of New England.

"This is something of a homecoming for you," Scully pointed out.

Mulder, driving, said, "I wasn't raised in this part of Massachusetts."

She smiled, just a little. "I'm surprised. Isn't this witch country?"

"Scully, anyone with roots in 17th century Massachusetts could have any number of witches hanging from the family tree."

"Surely you don't think there was anything truly paranormal about the Salem 'witches'?"

Mulder shrugged. "Who knows what really happened back in 1692? The only documentary evidence available is legal records of the day, which do include testimony of paranormal activity."

Scully couldn't let him get away with this. "Mulder, the 'witchcraft outbreak' in Massachusetts was a textbook example of massive clinical hysteria, acerbated by a power-hungry clergy, and the spiteful pranks of bored adolescents, gotten out of hand."

"Or not."

By now, dusk settling, Mulder and Scully were in Banewich, where the town square revealed a picture-book community reveling in its notorious past, a tourist destination with historic homes turned into museums and storefront windows replete with conical hat-wearing, broomstick-riding witches.

"A shame we missed Halloween," Scully said wryly.

"I have a hunch every day in Banewich is Halloween," her partner noted.

From its hilltop at the outskirts of Banewich, the Creed residence seemed to dominate the landscape. But as they moved up the driveway to the notorious house, the agents were struck by the modern look of the home—despite its barn-like configuration, the large dwelling did not fit any caricature notion of a haunted house.

The atmosphere within the House on Hickory Hill was one of charged, electric, barely controlled hysteria, not helped at all by Thomas Hertel, the Yuppie FBI officer leading the operation, who was immediately confrontational.

"You're here at my sufferance," Hertel said, his blond, blandly boyish features managing a scowl. "I know all about you two, and have no desire to share an investigation with the Bureau's resident Ghostbusters."

"We're just here to lend investigative support," Scully said. "We won't get in your way."

"Yeah," Mulder said, "you guys will be doing the important work— manning the phones, keeping the reporters away, watching the yard."

Hertel glared at Mulder, who just beamed back at him innocently.

Keeping her voice low, Scully asked, "Agent Hertel, can I assume you're exploring the possibility that Mr. Creed himself may have staged this kidnapping?"

"Why would he do that?"

"To hype his book into the next *Amityville Horror*."

This had clearly not occurred to the Special Agent in Charge, who said brusquely, "We'll be exploring all possibilities."

"I assure you," a commanding voice said from behind them, "that I had *nothing* to do with my daughter's kidnapping."

Scully and Mulder turned toward a glowering Arthur Creed, his roughly handsome features stark in a face turned white with rage.

Holding up a peacekeeping hand, Mulder asked, "I believe you, sir. Might we have a word?"

With a gesture to Scully that told her to stay behind, Mulder and Creed found a corner.

"I'm sorry about that, Mr. Creed," Mulder said.

He sighed. "No...I am. That woman is right to raise the possibility. You people have to explore every angle. And whatever's happening, I'm essentially to blame."

"Oh?"

He shook his head glumly. "Bringing my family into this evil house."

"Have you witnessed any of these previously reported paranormal activities, since moving in?"

"That's the irony of it, Agent Mulder. Just hours before my daughter was kidnapped, I'd remarked to Alice how this house hadn't lived up to its nasty reputation."

Creed said that his wife—who had been urging him for some time to get away from Manhattan and move to a small town—had been behind him one hundred percent, in the move.

"Alice has been terrific," Creed said. "Understanding, forgiving...even after all my bad investments and poor career decisions put us in a position of having to go bargain-hunting for a place to live."

Creed explained that Alice—the writer's second wife, his first wife having died of cancer—found the house on the market, noted its odd history, and suggested the notion of both the move and the book to her husband.

Elsewhere in the house, Scully was talking to Mrs. Creed, who tearfully revealed that her stepdaughter, Charity, the only child of Creed and his late first wife, had a troubled background of drugs and rebellion, and openly despised this small town she's been "stuck" in.

"But even with all her problems," Alice Creed said, with a crinkly smile, "Charity always accepted me as her mother—at least till we moved here."

"That marked a change?"

Alice nodded. "Charity loved living in Manhattan, Agent Scully...but she was running with a 'druggie' crowd, and that was one of the reasons we got away from the city. And with my other daughter, Heather, soon to come into *her* teenage years, too...can you blame me for wanting to get away from that terrible place?"

"I take it Charity blamed you for the family relocating to Banewich."

"Oh yes," Alice said, sniffling. "She's become very hostile...but I love her, Agent Scully, couldn't love her more if she were my own."

"Mrs. Creed. This is difficult, but I have to ask. Could Charity be behind this? Could this be something she staged herself?"

"I wish I could tell you I think she's capable of that, because it would mean she's unharmed...but my instinct is that Charity is still a good person, down underneath all the typical teenage disobedience."

"Mrs. Creed, do you think my partner and I might talk to your younger daughter, alone?"

In her bedroom, sitting at her computer desk, the twelve-year-old told Scully and Mulder of finding the ransom note in her sister's "messed up" room; but there is something stilted about the telling.

"Did you see anything else that night?" Mulder asked the girl. "Anything strange, or out of the ordinary?"

"I...I don't think so."

"You don't *think* so? But *maybe* you did?"

"Well...I didn't tell anybody."

"Tell us, Heather."

"I think I must've dreamed it."

Scully asked, "What did you dream, dear?"

And the child told them of the bulging walls, the rippling floor, and the blood on the wall by the stairs.

Gently, Mulder asked, "Did you dream this, or did it happen? Think carefully now."

"I *thought* it happened...but I *must've* dreamed or maybe imagined it. Maybe because my friends were making fun of me, before."

She told them about the after-school taunting.

And how she'd always hated growing up in Manhattan, that she'd often daydreamed of living in a rural environment, spending time in the school library paging through picture books, leafing through *Better Homes and Gardens* on rainy weekends.

"I thought moving to Banewich would be a dream come true," Heather said. "And it is—a *bad* one."

Next Mulder and Scully had a look at Charity's bedroom, no longer in disarray, the crime lab specialists having long since finished with the crime scene. Methodically they went through Charity's belongings, talking as they did.

"You know, Mulder, Heather's analysis of what happened is probably correct: she heard stories about the strange house and her imagination plugged in familiar haunting elements from books and movies."

"I might buy that, if she'd experienced those things *after* finding her sister missing."

"But don't you see, Mulder—when Heather discovered that her sister was missing, she snapped out of it. She didn't see a bleeding wall anymore—just a white one."

After they'd completed their search of the teenage girl's things, Scully said, "You know what's missing, here?"

"A Harley?" Mulder asked with a smirk, nodding around a room conspicuous with the accouterments of the daughter of a well-off family: computer, CD player and CDs, scads of clothes and shoes.

"Charity's *personal* life," Scully said. "No letters, no diary, no photos..."

"You've got something, Scully," Mulder said, frowning, moving to the dresser mirror. "You can see where photos were taped, and removed..."

"Something else has been removed," Scully said, noting the empty space in an array of pop star posters. She found the gray-and-yellow corner of a poster otherwise torn away. "You think Charity stopped to take some things with her?" "Meaning she either staged this or was in on it?"

Scully nodded. "Kidnappers don't usually give their victims time to gather mementos."

"There's another possibility."

"Such as?"

Mulder indicated the dresser mirror. "The *kidnapper* was in those missing photos."

After mulling that a moment, Scully said, "Maybe her parents can tell us what that poster was and who was in those photos."

Moments later, Alice and Arthur Creed were standing just inside their missing daughter's room, both shaking their heads.

"You'd be surprised how seldom either of us was in here," Alice said. "Charity demands her privacy, and we've always tried to respect that."

Scully asked, "Does Charity have a steady boyfriend?"

The parents looked at each other and shrugged, then Alice said, "Not that we know of."

Mulder asked, "How about a potential stalker among *would-be* boyfriends?"

The Creeds shook their heads.

Midnight approached. Arthur Creed's study was now the nerve center of the FBI's operation, and from there, agents would attend the phones round-the-clock. The large, modern, but rustic-walled house provided enough guest quarters for the FBI to maintain their presence, in residence, with both Mulder and Scully in guest rooms just off the kitchen.

Mulder stayed up reading, determined to look into the history of the house. Creed gave Mulder permission to look at the author's manuscript-in-progress. It seemed that the hill the house and—before that—the barn was built on had indeed been the site where witches had been hanged in the Salem era. Rather than a gallows, the trees on Hickory Hill itself had been used for the hangings.

Finally putting the manuscript aside, Mulder was about to drift off to sleep when he heard what seemed to be the sound of an intruder.

Cautiously, he followed the sounds to find Scully in the kitchen, raiding the refrigerator.

"My stomach was growling at me," Scully said mildly embarrassed, "and I figured I better feed it before it bit me."

"I could eat something."

As they sat at the kitchen table having a pajama-clad snack, Scully seemed sympathetic to Mulder's intense interest in this investigation, invoking memories, as it did, of the abduction of his sister.

"Heather's a sweet child, but very sheltered," Scully pointed out. "It's no wonder the other kids give her a rough time, her mother sending her to school dressed like that."

"Dressed how?"

"Like Martha Stewart's little girl."

"Well, Heather's not a little girl, or anyway won't be much longer....You know, Scully, in a way this is really quite typical—poltergeist activity often surrounds an adolescent female approaching puberty."

"You're not saying *Heather* caused the manifestations herself? What, and the kidnapping, too?"

"Maybe the kidnapping and the manifestations aren't interrelated...other than a general aura of evil lending itself to both. Don't you feel a certain...creepiness in this place?"

"No. Just an occasional draft."

Mulder gestured up toward Heather's room. "That girl could be the vehicle, the vessel, for the spirit of some lower entity that hasn't moved onto the next plane of existence."

Scully sighed. "'Lower entity.' Somebody *dead*, you mean? What, Clayton Geech is hanging around, possessing or...channeling himself through that adolescent girl?"

"Spiritualists believe that a spirit who hasn't come to terms with his or her violent traumatic death can—"

"If that girl caused the walls to bulge or bleed or whatever—and that's a very big 'if,' Mulder—it's a natural mechanism of the mind."

Mulder grinned. "Are you admitting the existence of psychokenesis?"

She shrugged. "The ability to move objects with the mind is recognized by science, just not yet explained. Telepathy, too–if that girl has telepathic abilities, she could be misinterpreting 'data' she's receiving as the sounds of a 'haunted house.'"

"You mean she might be like a receiver picking up strange signals from this station and that one."

"Perhaps. But in any case, I don't think Clayton Geech possessed that girl, who then kidnapped her own sister. Do you?"

Brought back to earth, Mulder admitted, "No."

As if expressing its own opinion on the subject, the house interrupted their table talk with an array of strange sounds, moanings, creakings....

"Let's check this out," Mulder said.

But Scully was already on her feet. The agents returned to their rooms for guns and flashlights, then prowled the house, peeking into rooms. Everyone seemed peacefully asleep, including Hertel and other slumbering agents. On the third floor, Mulder lingered, studying the sleeping form of young Heather.

"If that kid is generating these poltergeist phenomenon," Mulder whispered, joining Scully in the hallway, "she's doing it in her sleep—and a restful sleep at that."

Scully, wrapped in a robe now, said, "Every old house makes unexplained noises in the middle of the night."

"Yeah," Mulder said drawing out the word, "but...do the walls bleed?"

And down at the other end of the hall, blood streamed down in scarlet trails, like the ceiling had a leeching wound.

Carefully, they approached it—wet to the touch! The sticky substance even had the coppery scent of blood....

"I'll be right back," Scully said, an eyebrow arched.

"I'll keep it covered," Mulder said, gun still in hand.

But as soon as Scully disappeared, so did the blood—not all at once, rather seeming to soak into the wood, as if the house were siphoning the liquid back within itself. Even the stickiness on Mulder's fingers evaporated.

And when Scully returned with a small vial to take a sample, Mulder was touching a now dry, clean wall.

BANEWICH, MASSACHUSETTS
WEDNESDAY, 9:45 a.m.

The next morning, as the two agents drove into Banewich, Scully reminded Mulder that there was no proof of what they'd seen last night.

"It was dark," she said. "Moonlight was streaming in. After what we'd been discussing, we were in a suggestive state."

"You *know* what we saw, Scully," Mulder said irritably.

"I know we saw something, but what? That house may *look* new, but strip away the remodeling and you have a very old structure, in a region where they've had heavy precipitation all year."

"That was rainwater? We saw rainwater."

"Mulder, behind those walls is ancient barn wood, painted red probably, with who-knows-what in the paint, and the absorption of years of insecticides and other farm chemicals. The coppery smell could come from copper pipes. Plus, we don't know what building compounds, past and/or present—adhesives, wallpaper paste, insulation—might have combined to—"

"Turn into blood?"

"I'll scrape a few wood shavings off that wall and send them in for analysis, if that will perk you up."

He gave her a tiny smile. "I feel perky already."

"But we'll keep this to ourselves. There's no need to upset the Creeds any further...and discussing this with Agent Hertel isn't necessary, as any paranormal activity that *might* exist in this house seems quite apart from the kidnapping."

"Scully, I don't mind keeping Hertel out of the loop, or the Creeds...but how can we know what we witnessed last night doesn't in fact relate to the kidnapping? Young Heather saw the same things we did, the night Charity was taken."

"How on earth could it relate?"

Mulder gave her a boyish grin. "Who said anything about 'on earth'?"

"Please. I suppose Clayton Geech returned from the dead and kidnapped that girl."

"Well, he did sign the note. Anyway, if you were coming back from the dead after thirty years, don't you think you could use half a million bucks walkin'-around money?"

First stop for the agents was Banewich High, where friends and teachers substantiated Charity's wild nature. From several of the girl's peers—she seemed not to have had any really close friends—they heard that Charity had been seeing an "older boy" who attended the local community college, one Cliff Dain. According to one girl, Charity met Dain in New York last summer.

At Banewich Community College, a college administrator talked openly to the agents, telling them that Dain—a would-be rock musician—had been recently expelled, and was suspected of selling drugs.

"We don't have a current address on him," the middle-aged male administrator said, checking on a computer monitor, "but I can give you a previous address—that of his parents in Malden, near Boston."

"He didn't have a New York address?" Mulder asked the administrator.

"No. According to his transcript, he was a Massachusetts boy."

In a college corridor, Scully and Mulder stood and discussed their next move, Mulder suggesting a drive down to Malden to look for Dain. Listening, Scully noticed a yellow-and-gray poster on a bulletin board.

"Mulder, take a look at this..."

The poster advertised Coven—an area heavy metal band—making an appearance at a Banewich bar.

"Glad to see you taking an interest in the local culture, Scully."

She pointed to the lower right corner of the poster. "This is the poster that somebody ripped from Charity's bedroom wall."

"So it is....You think one of these jokers is Cliff Dain?"

"Well, there's a booking address. Shouldn't be too hard to find out."

BANEWICH, MASSACHUSETTS
WEDNESDAY, 1:23 a.m.

In a rundown farmhouse in the country on the edge of the woods, a band was practicing—classic heavy metal with Satanic-themed lyrics. The agents walked to the front door, but their knocking was either unheeded or unheard, so Mulder went over to a living room window with a view on the band and held up his FBI I.D.

Soon Cliff Dain was at the door. The agents and their sullen host talked on the porch, away from the rest of the band.

"Yeah, I date Charity." Smoking, Cliff was beefily handsome, early twenties, with long hair and a well-tended beard; he wore a leather vest and jeans. "She's a lot of fun. Why, is she in trouble or something?"

"Why?" Scully asked. "Would you expect her to be?"

The musician grinned. "Well, she is kinda 'out there.' Particularly, for Banewich...for all the witchy trappings, y'know, it's still just another conservative little jerkwater."

Mulder smiled. "Like Malden?"

"Yeah, but worse. Listen, is she okay?"

"You met her in New York last summer, right?" Scully asked. "Were you living there?"

"No, the band did some gigs in Soho. Is she okay or not?"

"When did you see her last?" Mulder asked.

"It's been two weeks, at least. She's been grounded."

Mulder smirked. "You know they're young when their parents can still ground 'em, huh, Cliff?"

Dain's frown mingled irritation and concern. "What's going on, anyway?"

Scully filled him in about the kidnapping.

"Oh god," Dain says, apparently surprised, and now only the concern was left. "Oh God...."

The rocker slumped to a seat on the porch steps, seemingly shaken by the news.

Mulder asked, "Where were you last night, Cliff?"

"What, am I a suspect?"

"Depends on where you were last night."

But Scully already knew. "Your band was playing at a bar in Banewich, right?"

Both Dain and Mulder were surprised by this.

"Yeah, that's right," Dain said, and nodded toward the house. "You can ask the guys."

Dain said he was with his band members until at least three a.m. The agents asked a few more questions, until finally Dain said, "Listen, I want to help you people out, but I'm kinda in the middle of a rehearsal, here."

"We'll need to talk again, Mr. Dain," Scully said, "in more depth."

"I'm not going anywhere."

"That's right," Mulder said.

As they walked to their car, Scully said, "He did seem upset."

"Not enough to call off band practice. How'd you know our boy Cliff had a gig last night?"

"Maybe I'm psychic, Mulder," she said, not revealing what she had noticed that her partner hadn't: that the poster at the college had been advertising last night's appearance.

Back at the House on Hickory Hill, Mulder and Scully brought Agent Hertel up to speed.

"You're right, Agent Scully," Hertel said, his hostility on hold. "We need to interview Dain and his band members in depth. I can arrange to do that at the Banewich police station with back-up from local law enforcement."

Mulder took Scully aside. "You mind handling this? Looks like you'll have plenty of help."

"If you like. Why, Mulder, you have another angle?"

"Yeah. There's a suspect we've been neglecting."

"Who?"

"Clayton Geech."

"Mulder...."

BANEWICH, MASSACHUSETTS
WEDNESDAY, 2:23 a.m.

At the Banewich library, utilizing microfilmed newspapers, Mulder researched the original murders in the house, turning up an interesting anomaly. The clergyman was charged only with the murder of his wife, not that of his slain children. Noting the name of the county attorney who prosecuted the case—Gerald Allison—Mulder went to a phone book and found the man listed.

"Jerry's been retired for many years now," the attorney's wife said to Mulder over the phone. "But if you'd like to talk to him, he's doing volunteer work this afternoon, over at the historical society."

That proved to be housed in the Banewich Witch Museum, a two-storied many-gabled mansion that seemed a more likely candidate for being haunted than the Creeds' modernized barn.

Mulder presented his credentials to the retired attorney, an elderly, dignified gentleman in a three-piece suit, explaining in confidence that he was investigating a kidnapping.

Allison appeared happy to help, and filled Mulder in on many additional details about the original murders, though expressing some confusion as to why those murders might have a bearing on the kidnapping of the Creed girl.

Mulder said, "The ransom note was signed 'Clayton Geech.'"

"Ah, but Clayton Geech is long dead."

"Well, his signature's alive and well, or anyway a reasonable facsimile thereof—in blood, yet."

"That's just some sociopath's sick joke."

They were seated in an austere chamber, with plain dark wood and long wooden tables, where centuries ago witches had been tried.

"You know, Agent Mulder, the misguided men in this room believed that evil existed....And I can say, as a former judge myself, that however foolish they were about how they went about it, they were correct in that belief."

"Maybe they were evil themselves."

"Perhaps. But evil does exist. And Clayton Geech was infected with it. I saw the bodies of his family myself...I *still* see them, after all these years."

"Why wasn't Geech charged with *all* the murders?"

"Wasn't he?"

"Not according to the *Banewich Bugle*."

"Well, it's been so many years...I don't remember."

"Mr. Allison, with all due respect, sir, if the sight of those slain children has lingered in your memory all these years, surely you remember whether or not you prosecuted Geech for their murders."

Allison bristled. "With all due respect to *you*, Agent Mulder, as a former county attorney, and a current taxpayer, I'd like to see you get the hell out of this library and go down some more productive avenue. You've got a child to find, don't you?"

Mulder's cell phone chirped and he excused himself.

Scully said, "I'm at Dain's farmhouse with Hertel and the local law."

"The boys still rehearsing?"

"Not exactly. The house is empty—not only has Coven flown the coop, they've taken their instruments, amplifiers, the works, with them. No sign of Dain, or any of his things. He's cleared out. Skipped."

BANEWICH, MASSACHUSETTS
WEDNESDAY, 4:17 a.m.

Back at the house on Hickory Hill, Mulder and Scully were discussing with Hertel the probability of Dain's involvement when the phone rang.

Creed, as was the case whenever any call came in, answered it.

And finally, after many false alarms, this was the real thing: an anonymous, electronically distorted male voice with the details for the ransom drop, to be made by Creed himself that very night in a park in Boston.

"How will we make the exchange?" Creed asked.

"No exchange," the voice said, as Mulder, Scully and Hertel listen in. "First I get the money. When I'm safe and away and it's been counted, I'll release her."

The phone clicked dead.

"First," Hertel said to a wide-eyed Creed, "get it out of your head right now that you'll be delivering this ransom yourself, *whatever* the kidnapper demands."

"But surely we have to comply with—"

"Mulder here is approximately your build and coloration, so he'll be delivering the money."

After some further heated discussion, Creed acquiesced.

Mulder gave the SAIC an innocent smile. "See? Sometimes having a Ghostbuster around comes in handy."

BOSTON, MASSACHUSETTS
WEDNESDAY, 8:27 p.m.

Boston Common was fifty central acres downtown, where—starting at midnight—Mulder was sent hopscotching from one phone booth to another on the surrounding streets—Tremont, Park, Beacon, Charles, Boylston—until at last, in the darkness of the park, he saw a brawny jogger in a ski mask and hooded sweatshirt headed his way.

Like a relay runner, the figure held out his hand, not breaking his stride, and Mulder passed the briefcase of money.

Mulder watched as the figure jogged off, briefcase of money in hand; after a few beats, he followed, cutting around behind some bushes...

...and almost stumbling over a corpse of someone he'd never met but immediately recognized: *Charity Creed.*

The girl showed no signs of violence, and might have been curled up sleeping—if she'd had a pulse.

Pinned to her t-shirt was another cut-and-paste note—signed again by the long-dead clergyman, in blood, saying, TOLD YOU NO AUTHORITIES.

Whipping out his cell phone, already on the run, Mulder reported the dire news to Scully, waiting in an FBI unmarked van on Tremont. But as he came from around the bushes, the jogger was no longer in sight.

Though the FBI swarmed in on the park, they had lost their man. Apparently the jogger made his way into the nearby district of bars and restaurants and blended in.

A thorough search of the park took most of the night, the only result of which was the discovery of the hooded parka, ski mask and the now empty briefcase (which had been bugged), abandoned in a thicket.

BANEWICH, MASSACHUSETTS
THURSDAY, 8:46 a.m.

The aftermath of the tragedy found Arthur Creed rebuking himself for bringing the FBI in. In his study, their frustrated host faced Mulder, Scully and Hertel and said, "I intend to move my family—what is *left* of it—out of this cursed place as soon as possible."

For now, no one argued with him. Later they would reason with him to stay put as long as the investigation continued. But at the moment, both Creed and Alice were clearly devastated. Mrs. Creed had to be sedated, while the author himself just sat there holding onto his surviving younger daughter like a life preserver. The child remained mute, in a kind of blank near catatonia.

Finally, mercifully, the family members went off to bed, in shock and sorrow.

Privately, Mulder asked Scully, "Do you still believe Creed himself could be involved in this?"

"Filicide is rare, but it does happen."

"Like AB Negative blood. Scully, the man was blubbering like a baby."

"That could be guilt as well as sorrow...or psychosis, for that matter."

"Scully..."

"Who knows? Maybe he's just a good actor. Creed's done all sorts of personal appearances, after all."

Though they would stay the night, Hertel's FBI team was already packing up. The SAIC tells the X-File agents that homicide specialists from the Boston field office will be taking over the investigation tomorrow, no longer working out of the Creed home.

"There's real concern from the bureau," Hertel said, "that the FBI will be blamed for this."

Scully nodded gravely. "It's already all over the media."

"The two of you are to stay on here at the house," Hertel instructed them, "to provide some continuity."

"That's fine," Mulder said, "but we prefer to be actually involved in the investigation—"

"This isn't optional. It comes straight from the Assistant Director."

"But if we're to stay," Mulder insisted, "we'll need the Creeds' permission..."

"If anyone can swing it, you can, Agent Mulder," Hertel said. "Creed seems to like and trust you. Make it happen."

Alone with Scully, Mulder said, "This is punishment duty. Babysitting duty."

"Yes, but at least we haven't been pulled off the case entirely, which is what I expected."

Mulder grunted a laugh. "I guess I hadn't thought of it that way. What this really means is we can use our assigned duty to—"

"Keep investigating," Scully said with that slight smile of hers that said so much.

BANEWICH, MASSACHUSETTS
FRIDAY, 7:14 a.m.

Early the next morning—while Scully went off to Banewich General to perform the autopsy on Charity Creed—Mulder remained at the House on Hickory Hill, where he helped Hertel's men load up their gear. Young Heather wandered out into the yard and Mulder went over to talk to the waif-like child, her expression blankly haunted.

"I don't feel very sad yet," the child said. "Am I a bad person, for not feeling sad?"

"No. Not at all. It probably just doesn't seem real, yet."

"Charity was mean to me, and I said mean things to her, too."

"She isn't mad at you, Heather."

"Are you sure?"

"Yes."

"Do you think she's in heaven?"

Mulder swallowed—that wasn't his belief system, but there was a child who needed comforting. "Sure she is."

"Good. I was afraid she might be in hell."

Mulder could find nothing to say to that.

In the house, he found Creed at the kitchen table, Alice preparing breakfast, in a rote, zombie-like manner. Mulder explained to Creed about the changing of the FBI guard from kidnap specialists to homicide, making clear that the FBI presence in their home will be minimized.

"Minimized how, Agent Mulder?"

"Well, with your consent, Agent Scully and I will stay. To provide some continuity, and protection."

Suddenly Mrs. Creed, who had been rather submissive through all of this, spun to shake a spatula at Mulder like a weapon.

"You people caused Charity's death! I want all of you FBI bastards out of this house. *All* of you!"

Mulder excused himself, leaving the husband and wife alone, and went back out into the yard, to report Mrs. Creed's reluctance to Hertel. Mulder's cell phone rang before he could.

"Mulder, it's me," Scully said. The snapping of her taking off a latex glove told him she was calling from the hospital morgue. "Can you talk?"

"Yes."

"Charity Creed, cause of death? Heroin overdose."

"*What?* Are you telling me that kid was a heroin addict?"

"That's just it, Mulder—I'm not. She has no needle 'tracks,' no indicators of addiction whatsoever."

"From what we heard at the high school," Mulder said, pacing in the yard, "it's doubtful Charity was ever into anything but pot and pills."

"If Cliff Dain was a dealer," Scully said, "he'd have access to the harder stuff."

"So now you think *Dain's* our man? Hertel already agrees. 'Wanted for questioning' has escalated into a full-scale APB."

"As well it should, Mulder. Flight's an admission of guilt."

"Yeah, I agree, of course… but Dain made more sense as Charity's accomplice, running off with his girl friend, after scamming her parents out of that money. Why would he kill her?"

"Maybe they quarreled, maybe Charity got cold feet. Or perhaps he didn't love her. He could have been just using her. Didn't you ever hear of a man using a woman, Mulder, to further his own ends?"

"Is that a scientific theory, Scully?"

"One of the more easily proven ones."

BANEWICH, MASSACHUSETTS
FRIDAY, 3:54 p.m.

The rest of the day remained tense, as the clock ticked, with Mulder and Scully all too aware that murder cases grow colder by the second. The morning had an inexorable feel to Mulder: Hertel's unit moving out; Creed convincing his wife to allow Mulder and Scully to stay on; the two agents meeting the homicide team from the Boston field office and briefing them at the Banewich hotel out of which the team would work; and several reported sightings of Cliff Dain that proved to be false alarms.

Finally, Scully received information from D.C. pertaining to the wood shavings she'd sent in for analysis.

"No traces of blood, Mulder," she told him, "AB Negative or otherwise...but the lab did turn up certain organic traces...proteins, lipids, carbohydrates, plus some inorganic salts."

Mulder snapped his fingers. "That could explain what we saw, Scully."
"How?"

"The bleeding wall may have been an ectoplasmic manifestation."

Scully goggled at him. "Ectoplasm? Mulder, you've outdone yourself. Do I have to say it?"

"What, that ectoplasm is a palpable protoplasm extruded from bodily orifices, conveying paranormal messages or images?"

"Actually, Mulder, I was thinking more along the lines of cheesecloth, netting, dough or paste treated with phosphorescent paint. Parlor tricks by phony mediums."

He grinned at her. "As opposed to legitimate mediums? Scully, that lab report indicates a biological compound with exactly the composition you'd expect of ectoplasm. You're not arguing with science, are you?"

"Science denies the existence of ectoplasm, Mulder."

"Maybe you'll get a chance to prove otherwise. That would be sweet: Dana Scully receiving the Nobel Prize for substantiating the existence of ectoplasm."

That night, Mulder again awoke in the wee hours, hearing strange sounds. This time it wasn't Scully rummaging for a late night snack. Moving through the dark house with his flashlight, Mulder entered the living room, where the walls of the house were throbbing, bulging, as if a living, breathing thing!

He rushed to Scully's room and knocked, hard.

"Scully, I need you!"

Cracking the door, she looked out at him, sleepily wry as she tied herself into a robe. "This is a little sudden, isn't it?"

Filling her in along the way, Mulder dragged her into the living room, where moments before the walls had protruded and palpitated.

Now—nothing.

"I suppose you also have a frog that sings," Scully said.

"I *saw* it. Just like we both saw those walls oozing red."

"Mulder, you were half-awake, in a dark house, with a mind filled with ectoplasm."

"I know what I saw."

She swallowed. "If you say you saw bulging walls, I believe you saw bulging walls."

"Thank you."

"But suppose this house *is* a focal point of some sort of paranormal activity? That's not why we're here. Bulging walls don't pertain to the death of that young woman."

"How do we know that? You're usually not much for coincidences, Scully. I think these walls hold the secret. Maybe they're trying to...speak to us."

Scully looked at her partner, sensing his frustration, knowing that the abduction and murder of the girl resonated with his own personal loss.

"I think you've been put through two long, harrowing days." She touched his arm, gently. "Get some sleep, Mulder."

BANEWICH, MASSACHUSETTS
SATURDAY, 6:46 a.m.

Just after dawn, Mulder awoke to the sound of rapping at his bedroom door. He quickly answered it and found a distraught, horror-struck Creed.

"Now *Heather's* been kidnapped!" The big man's voice was trembling, his face a mask of agony. "Right under your damn noses! Come *see* what you've done!"

In the child's bedroom, Mulder and Scully took in a nearly identical crime scene right down to the cut-and-paste ransom note with that now-familiar signature-in-blood: SECOND CHANCE. NO COPS, NO FBI THIS TIME, MAYBE YOU GET THIS ONE BACK.

Creed's voice was soft now, yet threatening. "I want you two out of here."

Scully said, "Yes, of course, until the crime scene techs—"

"*No!* Out of here. Alice doesn't know about the second kidnapping and I want to tell her myself. *By* myself. I want you to leave, and keep the FBI and any authorities away from this house. This time I'm going to pay the ransom and act alone."

"Mr. Creed," Mulder said gently, "kidnapping is a federal crime. Sir, you don't have the option of turning us away—but I can help you minimize the intrusion."

It took five minutes to convince him, but finally Creed agreed, and went off to deliver this latest awful news to his wife.

Using the speaker phone in Creed's study, Mulder called Skinner, bringing the assistant director up to speed.

"We'll respect Mr. Creed's wishes," Skinner said, "and leave you and Scully as the family's only FBI contacts. But I'll inform Hertel, and get his team back in—at a distance."

"That's wise, sir," Scully told Skinner. "The kidnapper may be watching the house; there was a definite awareness of our role, here."

They could hear the frown in Skinner's voice. "I thought the kidnapper was I.D.ed as Clifford Dain."

Mulder said, "He's just one suspect, sir."

"Do you have another?"

Scully and Mulder traded looks, her eyes widening. Would Mulder tell Skinner that he suspected the late Clayton Geech? Or maybe the house itself?

"We're still developing that, sir," Mulder said, to Scully's obvious relief, and the phone conversation ended.

Scully prowled the study anxiously, saying, "Mulder, haven't you been troubled by the ease with which both these kidnappings were accomplished? The second time circumventing FBI presence? No one, none of us, heard or saw anyone in the house. It's as if...don't say it."

"A ghost did it? We *did* hear something last night, after all, or at least I did."

"And *saw* something." Scully headed out of the study. "Let's have a look at those walls that bulged."

Mulder followed Scully to the living room. She knocked on the walls, listening for hollow places.

"Heather saw and heard strange things the night of the first kidnapping," Mulder pointed out.

"Yes. Suppose those 'paranormal' activities were staged as distractions..."

"While the kidnappings were taking place?"

Scully nodded. "Maybe when this house was remodeled, and new walls dropped, space was left behind, for storage, or passageways, for access to wiring..."

"You mean, perhaps the walls bulged because someone was moving behind them?"

"Maybe. Or an accomplice putting on a show. And maybe there are ways in and out of this house we don't know about."

"Well, I know who *would* know."

"Who's that, Mulder?"

"The man who had the house remodeled—Clayton Geech."

Quickly they went to Creed, who told the agents that there were no plans, no architectural drawings of the home: do-it-yourselfer Geech had done his own remodeling.

Mulder drove into Banewich, seeking further information on this subject, while Scully stayed at the house with the Creeds, waiting for the phone to ring. Mrs. Creed was not happy with Scully's presence but kept to herself. Her husband was busy arranging for ransom money—Scully listened in as the author spoke with his publisher on the phone, arranging a further $500,000 advance on *The Banewich Terror*.

When he hung up, Creed said to Scully, with weary, even tragic resignation, "Now I have to *write* the goddamned thing."

"Oh, but you'll be back on the bestseller list," his wife said to him bitterly.

BANEWICH, MASSACHUSETTS
SATURDAY, 11:16 a.m.

In Banewich, Mulder easily located the real estate agent who sold the
Hickory Hill house to Creed.

Seated across his desk from Mulder, the agent, who seemed near
retirement age, confirmed Creed's story that Geech did his own remodeling, and that no plans existed.

"We did do a survey once, of the exterior and interior of the house," the
real estate agent said, "just to come up with specs for our listing...and,
funny thing—the outside of the house and the inside don't quite match
up."

"How do you mean?"

"A number of the walls in that house are unusually deep."

"Deep enough for passageways?"

"Deep enough for *rooms*, in some cases. I have pictures on file, of the
house on Hickory Hill, if you'd like me to point some things out specifically."

"Please do."

The agent did, and as they dug into the real-estate equivalent of an X-
File, Mulder said, "The other families who owned that house over the
years, those who moved out, reporting strange occurrences...did any of
them have children?"

"Why, I believe so. I believe *all* of them did...I can check on that for you."

And in every instance of so-called poltergeist activity, a girl either about
to, or just entering, puberty had been living in the Hickory Hill house.

Revitalized by this new information, Mulder again sought out retired
county attorney Gerald Allison, at the man's home this time, impressing
upon him the urgency of the situation.

"One girl is dead," Mulder said to Allison. "Another girl is in the
murderer's hands."

Allison wore a haunted expression. "I told you before, Agent Mulder:
Clayton Geech is long buried."

"So is the *truth* in this matter. You need to tell me what you know, sir.
You may have been a judge, and a fine one, in your day...but right now,
you're no judge of what's pertinent in this case."

It took no further coaxing. The retired county attorney admitted that,
although they'd been discovered drugged and near death, the two chil-

dren of the clergyman had actually survived; it had been decided to protect them from their father's terrible deed.

"They were sent to a distant relative of their murdered mother," Allison said, "to be raised out from under the shadow of their father's sins."

"But his sins didn't include killing his children."

"No. We thought it better to lead the public to believe the children were...gone, so they could start over somewhere else, fresh, out from under that dark cloud."

BANEWICH, MASSACHUSETTS
SATURDAY, 1:42 p.m.

Back at the house on Hickory Hill, Mulder went to Creed's office to sort back through the research materials on the history of the original crime. He studied a photo of the clergyman's daughter. She was a sweet-looking young teenager, possibly thirteen.

Then Mulder joined Scully with the Creeds by the phone. No call had come in.

Alice Creed turned a withering gaze on both FBI agents.

"Until they're gone," she said to her husband, "we don't have a prayer of getting Heather back."

She began to berate Creed further for allowing the agents to stay, and finally Mulder held up a hand.

He said to the couple, "This is something the two of you need to discuss....Scully, let's step outside for a moment."

"But Mulder," Scully said, knowing that leaving the phone unattended was a serious breach of procedure, "what if the kidnapper calls...?"

"If that happens," Mulder said to the Creeds, "we'll be just outside. One of you come get us, right away."

As a beautiful sunset painted the quaint little town of Banewich below, a frustrated Scully said, "What's the idea of leaving our post?"

Mulder showed Scully the photo of the clergyman's daughter. "Remind you of anyone?"

"No...I don't think so."

"Look harder. Could that be Alice Creed, as a child?"

Scully almost gasped as she too caught the resemblance.

"What does this mean, Mulder?"

"It *may* mean Alice Creed orchestrated these kidnappings."

The seeming absurdity of that brought an incredulous smile to Scully's face. "And killed her own *daughter*?"

"She didn't kill her daughter: Charity was a difficult girl and the offspring of Creed's *other* wife."

"But, Mulder, what about Cliff Dain? If he wasn't guilty, why would he flee?"

"What's so unusual about a drug-dealing dropout heading for the hills when the cops want to talk to him? Or maybe they're in on it together, could be Cliff's into milfs."

Scully rolled her eyes.

Mulder raised a forefinger. "One thing's certain, Scully...Alice said it herself: Creed's not going to get a ransom call tonight...not with *us* still around."

"Do you think Alice would harm her *real* daughter?"

Mulder shook his head. "I don't think so. I mean, she pampers her, shelters her...but who knows what some parents will do to their kids these days. Anyway, I think I know where to find Heather. But we have to wait to look for her."

Scully frowned. "Where do you think she is, Mulder?"

"In there," he said, nodding toward the big house. "Somewhere in there...."

And Scully turned her narrowing eyes to the barn-like structure while a chill breeze ruffled the barren branches of the hanging trees around them.

BANEWICH, MASSACHUSETTS
SUNDAY, 2:34 a.m.

The phone did not ring throughout the long evening.

Deep into the night, after the Creeds had finally gone to bed, Mulder and Scully with their flashlights went prowling through the huge house—every room, including the large finished basement, every nook and cranny of the garage. Finally, utilizing a crowbar, and knowledge that a real estate agent has shared with him, Mulder carefully pried loose a wallboard...

...and he and Scully soon found themselves wandering through passageways, flashlight beams beams slicing the darkness as they moved down hidden hallways that existed between walls and ancient barn wood. Finally a passageway opened into a dark, attic-like room, where off to one side they found a trunk.

An airhole-punched trunk.

Inside was Heather, in what was apparently a drug-induced sleep.

Scully knew at once that the child needed to be taken to a hospital. Mulder cradled the unconscious girl, looking at her with longing concern, and Scully—gun in hand—escorted them from the house. Gently Mulder put the child in the backseat of their rental car and dispatched Scully off into the night, with the Banewich emergency room her destination.

As she drove off, Scully watched Mulder go back inside, silently wishing him Godspeed, and headed down Hickory Hill. As she paused momentarily at the driveway's mouth, a hysterical-looking disheveled figure staggered in front of the car.

Cliff Dain!

BANEWICH, MASSACHUSETTS
SUNDAY, 3:48 a.m.

Mulder, in the meantime, had gone back inside the house to deal with the Creeds, unsure whether Arthur Creed and his wife were in this together. Mulder found Creed sleeping fitfully, his wife not beside him in the rumpled bed.

Mulder shook him awake. "Where's your wife?"

Groggily, he said, "What...?" He looked at the empty place beside him. "Alice? Uh...I...I don't know."

Then Creed's eyes widened and he cried out as a carving-knife slashed down past Mulder, sinking deep into the writer's chest.

Creed tumbled back in bed, bleeding, barely conscious; Mulder wheeled, gun in hand, but Alice Creed's withdrawn blade slashed through his sleeve into his arm, causing him to drop his nine millimeter.

Mulder—seeing the knife poised to swing down on him—threw a fist into the woman's stomach, doubling her over. The knife flew from her hand and skittered under a dresser. Mulder dove for his weapon, but Alice grabbed him by his bleeding arm and tossed him against the wall, with shocking strength.

Then she was on him, choking him, her grip vice-like, her face contorted with rage and dementia, pushing him back against the wall—*a wall that oozed red.*

Alice, seeing the bleeding wall, recoiled in horror, and Mulder knew at once that the woman feared this house, feared these manifestations, and he used her hesitation to shove her off and away from him.

Mulder scrambled for his nine millimeter, but a shaken Alice, eyes wide with walls that bled and bulged, kicked it from his hand and fled frantically from the bedroom.

After retrieving his Smith and Wesson, Mulder followed her into the hallway, where the walls throbbed and pulsed and leeched scarlet. The floor too was bulging, making it hard for either of them to keep their balance. Creaks and groans seemed amplified now, like the moans of some huge creature, echoing eerily; doors were opening and slamming themselves, windows flying open, then shut, as if the house were a living thing having a nervous breakdown.

Astounded though Mulder was, it was Alice Creed who was really freaking out, and no wonder—*the house seemed to be attacking her!*

Mulder struggled for his footing and then pursued her, yelling for her to stop, which she ignored. She started down the stairs and to her shock, and Mulder's, the steps seemed to fold up into a smooth, slick surface, as in a funhouse, and she lost her balance and went tumbling, toppling down, landing hard.

When Mulder followed, however, the stairs returned to their natural state, allowing him to go quickly down after her. The house seemed to be settling down, but Alice hadn't: she had gone to a closet where she was pulling down a shotgun from a shelf. She leveled the weapon at Mulder, and he fired at her, or rather tried to. The hard fall to the floor upstairs jammed his weapon!

Triumphantly, Alice trained the twin eyes of the shotgun on him, fingers on twin triggers, and was about to fire when she was sucked back into the closet, with sudden, inexorable force, like a vacuum cleaner picking up a gum drop.

The door slammed.

And the sound of the shotgun firing within the closet was like a terrible belch from the depths of the place.

Tentatively, Mulder went to the closet, opened the door...

...and, wincing, saw what was left of Alice after both barrels of the shotgun had gone off in her face at close range.

Around him, the house was still.

Then his cell phone trilled and Mulder about jumped out of his skin.

"Mulder," Scully's voice said, "it's me....Are you all right?"

"Better than Alice Creed." He was already moving back up the now normal stairs. "She just ate two barrels of a shotgun, after she stuck a knife in her husband....Send an ambulance over."

BANEWICH, MASSACHUSETTS
SUNDAY, 6:47 a.m.

At the hospital, Mulder met up with Scully, who reported that the child was fine, and personally patched up her partner's slashed arm, telling him that Arthur Creed would also survive.

Then Mulder spent a tender moment with Heather, comforting her, sparing her for now of the news of her mother's death, as the girl seemed to have no realization that her mother kidnapped her.

Mulder rejoined Scully in the hall, where she escorted him into a room where another patient recuperated: Cliff Dain.

"He had a rather interesting story to tell," she said. "He hitched a ride with me here."

Dain, sedated in his hospital bed now, had told Scully (who now told Mulder) that Alice Creed was his sister...and his mother.

Over coffee in a waiting area, Scully gave her partner the rest of Dain's story.

Cliff and Alice had grown up together sharing the secret that they were "the evil" their father, Clayton Geech, had hoped to eradicate years before on that other night in the house on Hickory Hill. Alice had been the victim of her father's incest; and Cliff had been the offspring. Alice's mother had not known that her daughter's teenage pregnancy was Alice's father's doing, having been led to believe a local boy had done the deed. It was the discovery of Cliff's real paternity that had led to the violence of that terrible night long ago.

In the hallway, Mulder said to Scully, "I don't think his daughter's pregnancy was the only evil that drove Clayton Geech to his mad act."

"No?"

"Alice had just entered puberty. Poltergeist manifestations had probably begun—let's use your theory and say it's some as yet uncharted natural mechanism of the mind that Alice generated—manifestations that seemed a sign to the preacher that the evil must be wiped out."

"The evil being his little girl."

"Yes, and his entire contaminated family. And by the way, every subsequent outbreak of manifestations in that house occurred when a young teenage girl was living there."

"Well," Scully sighed, "the teenage girl that was Alice Creed grew into a full-fledged textbook sociopath—able to convincingly play the role of devoted wife and mother. She sought out a rich husband and, when his fortunes began to fail, put this scheme in motion, with the help of her son...er, brother..."

"Forget it, Scully—it's Banewich town. So... is Cliff a sociopath, too?"

"I don't believe so—although I think, with a little research, we'll find an interesting array of antisocial behavior on his part, over the years, culminating with his participation in the plot to return to the house where it all began...Alice manipulating Arthur Creed into doing a book on the subject, with Cliff's job to get close to Charity Creed. I would imagine Cliff was told the kidnappings were simply designed to help hype Arthur's book into a surefire bestseller."

"But Cliff wasn't counting on Charity being murdered."

She shook her head. "No. That went well beyond his capabilities. He drugged the girl, at his mother's bidding, not realizing he was giving her an overdose...and when he learned what he'd done, he freaked out. Now he's cooperating completely. Turned the ransom money over and was hoping for immunity, if he testified against his sister. Mother."

"He'll have to cut a different deal now. Where's he been hiding?"

"In the house...those passageways we found."

"Actually, Scully, *you* figured that out. I can't take any credit...but I don't agree with you that Alice was motivated solely by greed."

"Why else would she come back to that house?"

"Maybe something compelled her. Something in that house drew her back. Called her home."

Scully didn't bother controlling her smirk. "Well, I could accept a subconscious desire on Alice's part, to confront her demons. But why bring her young daughter into harm's way? Alice doted on Heather, loved the child—or at least she did as much as any sociopath is able to love anybody else."

"That house seems to be a conduit for troubled young girls. Maybe it called out to both of them."

With a lift of her eyebrows, Scully said, "Might I suggest you leave that notion out of your report? Anyway, the biggest surprise to me, Mulder, is Alice Creed killing herself. That's the one thing a self-absorbed sociopath is generally incapable of."

Mulder shook his head. "Alice Creed didn't kill herself."

Scully frowned. "Well, she certainly did. She looked down those shotgun barrels and fired."

"Scully, the house killed her."

Scully arched an eyebrow. "The *evil* house, you mean?"

"I don't think that house is evil, or ever was. In fact, I'll wager the next bargain-hunting family'll find it blessedly free of bleeding, bulging walls...even if they have a teenaged daughter."

"And what makes you think that?"

"The evil that was haunting that house is gone."

That was all too vague and elliptical for Scully, who demanded, "What *happened* back there, Mulder? What really happened while I was rushing Heather to the hospital?"

Mulder, who knew there was absolutely no way to convince his partner of what he saw and experienced, popped a sunflower seed.

"Scully, you had to be there."

THE END

TIME AND TIDE

By Gayle Lynds and John C. Sheldon

PORTLAND, MAINE
12th JANUARY, 2000, 9:20 a.m.

t was dangerous going. Three teenagers climbed over the slippery
rocks along the shore of Great Diamond Island, one of the Casco Bay
islands near Portland, Maine. The tide had deposited slime on the
rocks, and a fall would hurt. But the more risky terrain they put behind
them, the more likely they could escape detection while smoking the
dope they'd bought at the ferry terminal. Their names were Carole,
Jackie, and Allen, and they were celebrating their high school graduation.

Ahead stood a tall bluff, at the base of which lay a stretch of sand.
After crabwalking over the final few yards of rocks, the teenagers crossed
the beach to the base of the cliff. Where the beach met the high water
mark of the sea stood some bushes that hid their view of the water and,
more importantly, the view from the water.

Chuckling with relish at their isolation, they sat facing each other.
Jackie pulled out her stash, Allen the papers, and all began rolling joints.
Then they shared a book of matches, inhaled, and awaited pleasure.

Several minutes later, with one joint behind them, Allen stood and
stretched his arms over his head. He was of medium height, with curly
black hair down to his collar and the upper arms—exposed because he'd
rolled up his sleeves—of a bodybuilder. As long as he and his family had
summered on the island, he'd never had the incentive to visit this spot.
He took a few steps toward the water, turned around and glanced up the
cliff. There he spotted what looked like two large slits, each about twenty
feet above his head and the same distance apart.

"Hey, come check this out," he said to his friends.

Jackie and Carole were soon standing beside him. The girls were a Mutt and Jeff pair: Jackie was the tallest of the three and thin. She wore her brown hair in a ponytail. Carole was the shortest and slightly heavy-set, with long, elegant red hair in a braid down the middle of her back.

Allen pointed up to the slits he'd discovered. They appeared of equal size, about three feet high and a couple of feet wide. The outside perimeter of each was rough, as if the opening had been harshly chiseled out, but on the inside each had a window.

"One of them's open. Let's find out what's inside," Carole said, high and adventuresome.

"You're not going to climb up there," Allen said, chuckling and shaking his head.

That was a dare to an unathletic-looking 18-year-old who wanted to impress her male companion. "Watch this." She started up the rocky face. A minute or two later she reached the open window, gazed inside, and turned to her friends below: "There's a living room or something, and nobody's here." She checked back inside again, and then shimmied in through the window.

The others gawked.

"Good God, she did it," Jackie said.

"I didn't think she could," Allen agreed.

A moment later, Carole stuck out her head. "Come on up. This is cool."

"We shouldn't," Jackie began.

"Don't be a jerk," Carole said. "C'mon."

Thus goaded, Jackie climbed, followed by Allen. Soon all three stood inside the room. The place was about 20 feet square and smelled dank like a cave. Rusted rebar showed through the cement ceiling, which was stained with water splotches. The walls also appeared to be concrete—it was hard to tell because the only light in the place came from the windows, which were too deep and narrow to illuminate the sides clearly. There was a bed, slept in and not made, two chairs at a table, a lamp on the table, and a kitchen area against a sidewall. An unlit passageway opened on the side of the room away from the windows.

"This must have been a bunker or something, from when there was a fort here," said Allen.

The three knew a military post—Fort McKinley—had occupied the easterly end of the island during wartime, although they weren't sure which war or when. It had been abandoned for as long as they could remember.

"This place creeps me out," Jackie said.

"Holy shit, look at this!" Carole said. She was staring down through the glass of the other window—the unopened one on the left side of the room.

The others joined her. There, just beyond the bushes that had protected them from view, was a flat seabed. Two skeletons lay partially embedded in the sand, one ribs-up, the other on its right side.

"What the " said Jackie. Puzzled, she returned to the window through which they had entered. "Look down here!"

Carole and Allen joined her.

"High tide," Carole said. "Nothing but water."

They went back to the second window: The tide remained low and the skeletons were still there. Carole grabbed the crank and opened the casement window. She lifted herself onto the sill to get a better view.

Suddenly there was a grating sound behind them, the noise of a heavy door dragging across concrete as it was being opened.

"Shit, someone's coming!" Jackie said.

"Follow me," Carole said in a low voice. In the window, she pivoted on her backside and swiftly climbed down.

Jackie jumped up onto the sill and followed. As soon as she'd cleared the window, Allen started through.

"Hey, *wait*, don't go out there!" a man's voice shouted.

If Allen needed any more incentive to hurry, that provided it. He skinned his knees as he clambered down the bluff. At the bottom, he took off with his friends across the beach and through the bushes to the exposed seabed.

Before them lay the skeleton on its back, ribs bare and white. They slowed to gape at the ominous sight.

"Gross," Jackie said.

"Wonder where it came from, and how long it's been here," Allen said.

Carole gazed at the other skeleton, several yards toward the sea. "Look at that." She pointed to a swirl of sand rising out of its rib cage, growing taller and wider. Its shape was vaguely cylindrical, a greyish golden twisting column. Spinning over the skeleton, it slowly bobbed up and down.

"What the hell is it?" Jackie said.

"Maybe a little gust of wind or something?" Carole offered.

"But there's no wind here." Allen wet an index finger and stuck it in the air, to confirm the point. "And how come there's no sound?"

Carole giggled nervously. "It looks like something out of a Mr. Clean TV commercial."

Then she gasped. The shape rushed toward. Jackie shrieked but her voice was abruptly cut off as the vortex of sand consumed her.

"Jackie!" Carole screamed.

But Jackie had vanished. Not moving from the spot, the thing whirled and bobbed and still made no sound, just as it had when they'd first seen it—as if it were indifferent to its sudden prisoner.

Allen grabbed Carole's hand and pulled violently: "C'mon, we gotta get away!"

Their eyes wide with terror, they ran across the flats. Then, after about 50 yards, they looked back. The whirling thing had disappeared, but where Jackie had been lay a skeleton. A third skeleton.

"Oh, my God," Allen breathed.

Carole burst into tears.

They ran again, their feet pounding as they rounded a bend in the shoreline where the fort side of the island ended and the westerly, civilian part began.

Ten minutes earlier, Ed Gorman had been driving his golf cart back from the island's pier, where he'd picked up some freight from the Casco Bay Lines ferry. Golf carts were standard transportation on the island, where motor vehicles were generally prohibited.

He stopped at a large iron door hanging on hinges set in a formidable, rectangular, concrete structure that extended out from a hill. He jumped out of the cart, unlocked the door, and pushed on it; the heavy thing reluctantly scraped across the concrete floor, its iron panels enhancing the noise like the sounding board of a piano.

When it was far enough open, Gorman grabbed his packages from the golf cart and carried them inside, where a tunnel led to a chamber that was serving as his temporary residence. The boxes were bulky but

Gorman was a muscular six-footer and handled them easily. Nothing seemed amiss until he entered the chamber. There was movement at the left window: a young man was dropping from view.

"Hey, don't go out there, come back!" Gorman ran to the window. "Come back!"

But three young people—the boy and two girls—were running down the sandy bank, through some bushes, and out onto the sand flats.

Then they stopped and looked down at something in the sand. Beyond them, Gorman noticed movement, a rising, twisting something pulling sand up inside it. At first he thought it was a waterspout, but there was no indication of a wind around it, and it wasn't funnel-shaped. It rose and settled, as if floating on gentle waves. Parts of it sometimes expanded, sometimes contracted. Except for the eeriness of the thing, it was comical—a six-foot-tall, cucumber-shaped, twirling thing on a slow-motion pogo stick.

It remained over the same spot for about fifteen seconds, and then charged one of the girls and she disappeared inside it. The other two kids took off running. A few moments after the tube or whatever it was had swallowed the girl, it vanished—or evaporated, or just apparently stopped existing. Where it had been lay a skeleton, ribs up. That's when Gorman noticed two other skeletons lying in the sand nearby—apparently the things the kids had stopped to look at.

Gorman grabbed his phone and dialed Fox Mulder. "We've got a problem. At least one kid, and I think two more, broke into the chamber." He described the spinning thing that had attacked one of them. "I don't know what happened to her," he continued, "but I'd better go down there and find out. At the least, if that's her skeleton I should bring part of it back for DNA analysis."

"Do you know who the kids are?" Mulder asked.

"No, I haven't looked at the security camera's tape yet. But they ran toward the other end of the island, and it shouldn't be hard to find them. It's not like there's a huge population here."

"Do it. Let me know."

Gorman ended the call, hurried to the far end of the tunnel where he'd stashed a ladder, carried it back, and slid it out the same window the young man had gone through. Climbing down, he crossed the beach to the bushes. The two kids were gone, but when he had time, he could follow their footprints in the sand.

First, he needed some bone for the DNA test. Walking to the new skeleton, he was about to kneel down when he noticed the whirling thing was back. He reversed direction, sprinted to the ladder, and shot back up to the room. But the moment he got through the window, his legs collapsed and he fell to the floor. It took him a while to realize his strength had abandoned him. Uncertain whether he could stand, he crawled to a nearby chair, hiked himself up, and called Mulder.

"I couldn't retrieve any bone, and I can't go after the two other kids. Don't ask me to explain what's going on. Get here ASAP."

Carole and Allen ran up some steps, around a beach cabin, and flopped down behind tall blueberry bushes. Carole was crying so much she could barely breathe, and panting so hard she could barely weep. Covered with sweat, Allen sat with his elbows on his knees and his head in his hands, staring at the ground.

Between sobs, Carole managed to ask, "What are we going to do?"

"I don't know," said Allen, who hadn't moved. He shook his head slowly. "I don't know, I don't know."

Carole broke down again, and this time it got to Allen. Tears fell from his cheeks.

Several minutes passed; they said nothing.

Finally, impatience overcame his grief: "This isn't getting us anywhere. Let's go to my camp—Dad will help." He offered his hand to Carole and pulled her to her feet.

By "camp" Allen meant his family's summer cabin, one of many at this end of the island, where the military had never laid claim. They hurried to the nearest road—barely more than a wide dirt path.

As they passed an old hydrant, Carole stopped. "Oh, my God!" She pointed to a human skeleton face down several feet off the road. "Not here, too?"

Allen took two steps toward it and discovered a second skeleton beyond it, at the bottom of a dip in the terrain.

Without a word he returned to Carole. "Come on, fast!"

On the straight line Allen took, his family's cabin was about a quarter of a mile away through woods and across a field of tall grass. Neither of them saw anything else unusual—until they came around Allen's front porch. There on the ground lay another skeleton.

"No!" Allen ran up to it. "Oh no, no, *NO!*" he screamed in anguish. He turned around with his hands covering his face.

At that moment Carole noticed some leaves begin to swirl above the skeleton.

"Allen!" she yelled. "Here comes another one!" She pushed him toward the porch, up the steps, and inside the camp. She slammed the door and locked it, and then closed and locked the window next to it. The whirling thing grew and spun, bobbing up and down just like the one that had taken Jackie.

Carole retreated to the middle of the cabin's main room—kitchen and living areas combined—watching through the window as the thing twirled and continued to expand, picking up more leaves, twigs, and grit. Once again, it made no noise, and there was no wind to or from it that disturbed the grasses and bushes in its vicinity. It had no color and emitted no light; but for the vegetation and dirt it picked up, it would have been invisible. It raised itself onto the porch—how, Carole couldn't tell—and hovered just outside the front door.

Then it started moving along the porch, across the front of the building, first to one end and then to the other. It seemed to be looking—"looking," though it had no eyes—for an entrance into the cabin. Perhaps it was "smelling" the trace of its prey?

Allen was kneeling on the floor, sobbing.

Carole grabbed him by the shoulders and shook him. "C'mon, Allen, you've gotta help."

The vortex was crossing back to the far end of the porch and, suddenly, was off the porch and starting along one side of the building.

"Oh, god," Carole cried. She locked the window on that side and ran into the bedroom in the left rear corner. The single window there, on the back wall, was shut; she locked it. She rushed to the bathroom, and then to the other bedroom, and then back to the main room, securing every window she found.

Carole's frantic activity broke through Allen's anguish, and by the time she reached the window over the kitchen sink he looked up. He noticed the curtains at the window and frowned—he didn't recognize them. He peered at the other side of the room; a sofa stood under the windows—not against the back wall, where it always had been. It was upholstered with a flowery print he'd never seen. On the wall above where the sofa used to be was a picture of a lobster boat, not of the Portland Head lighthouse he himself had hung.

"Carole, this isn't my house. I mean, it's in the right place, it looks the same outside, the kitchen sink is where it's supposed to be—but it's different." He stood and went into one of the bedrooms and quickly returned. "My baseball glove and fishing pole are missing, and there's a bunch of books I've never seen."

Carole said nothing. She was staring at the thing outside, which was back on the front porch by one of the windows.

Allen went into the other bedroom and returned with a revolver. "Guess what I found!" He strode to the window where the thing was "watching" them and yelled obscenities at it. That had no visible effect so he checked to see if the gun was loaded.

Carole intervened. "What are you going to do, shoot it through a window? And put a hole in the glass so maybe it can suck itself inside? You can't shoot wind and leaves."

Allen shook his head at her. "Dammit, Carole, you got any ideas?"

He looked back outside and aimed the gun. "You know who that son of a bitch reminds me of? Vice Principal Barton. Everywhere I went in school, there was Mr. Barton, watching me, waiting for me to screw up so he could screw me." He bellowed through the window: "I'd love to shoot you now, you prick!"

Carole grabbed his arm and pushed it down. "You can't, and you know it."

Allen turned and hollered at Carole. "So what am I supposed to *do*?"

"How in hell do I know?" she yelled back at him. They stood looking at each other, breathing hard. Then Carole put her hands on his shoulders—to calm them both. "But it looks as though Mr. Barton can't get inside. I think we're safe for now, and it's getting dark out. Maybe it'll be gone in the morning."

"What if it *never* leaves?"

"I'd rather die in here than let it eat me alive."

THURSDAY, 11:45 a.m.

At midmorning the next day Fox Mulder and Dana Scully were among a small crowd of people disembarking from the Casco Bay Lines ferry onto the Great Diamond pier. It was perfect summer weather; a front had come through the night before, leaving the sky clear and the air cool. There was a light breeze.

They were dressed casually. Mulder wore jeans, a tee-shirt that said "Maine is Cool" over the drawing of a moose, and running shoes. Scully wore long khaki pants, a polo shirt, tennis sneakers, and a baseball cap that covered much but not all of her auburn hair. Mulder had vacationed in Maine as a child but hadn't been back since, and had never visited this island. Scully had never been to Maine and knew so little about it that she'd mistaken the moose on Mulder's shirt for an elk.

The pier bisected a small harbor at the southwesterly tip of the island. A couple of sailboats were moored on one side, and a lobster boat on the other. An official-looking powerboat, with MAINE FISHERIES AND WILDLIFE lettered on the side of its pilothouse, was tied to the pier. Next to the boat a man in green fatigues with a pistol on his hip was bending over a dog, adjusting its harness.

Scully stopped beside him. "Mind if I ask what the dog's for?"

The man straightened up. "She's a tracker; we've got a report of some kids gone missing. It'd help us if you'd keep an eye out. Teenagers, two girls and a boy." He reached into a backpack lying next to him. "Here's a flyer with their pictures."

"Of course," Scully said, and hurried to catch up to Mulder.

"Did you hear that?" she asked him. "Three kids missing. Probably the ones Ed Gorman told you about."

Mulder nodded somberly and kept up his pace.

Some of the crowd drove off in golf carts that had been left in a parking area; Mulder and Scully continued on with the rest, walking along a dirt road. As they reached other roads, forking off toward a variety of homes and summer cottages, the crowd dwindled. Finally Mulder and Scully were alone, and they kept going east another fifteen minutes toward old Fort McKinley.

"Pretty island," Scully remarked.

"Yeah, but kind of bipolar," Mulder answered with a chuckle. "All fishing and sailing and summer fun at that end"—gesturing with his thumb over his shoulder—"and up ahead nothing but the business of war."

"Do you know the history of this place?" Scully asked.

"Yeah. Portland used to be a strategic military site because it's America's closest deep-water harbor to Europe—an ideal launching point for convoys. All the rocky islands in Casco Bay were good places from which to defend the harbor, so many of them were fortified. Starting during the Spanish American war, army engineers built artillery emplacements and bunkers, and barracks and mess halls and the usual stuff you find on military bases. They also built underground facilities and joined them together with tunnels."

Mulder paused to pick up a stone and hurl it at a tree. He missed.

"Not a pitcher, I see," said Scully. "Better try out for first."

They walked again, and Mulder continued: "By the end of the Second World War, the fort was obsolete, so the army withdrew all their personnel, removed their weaponry and machinery, and abandoned the entire place."

"Okay," said Scully, "so what's happened since then?"

"*Nada.* It's been a ghost town—up until recently. Somebody bought it from the government, and he's trying to turn it into a destination resort."

They'd reached the fort's entrance. It was marked by an open, rusted iron gate. Beyond the gate was an assembly of brick buildings—over a dozen in all—circling a quarter-mile-long parade ground.

"That building," Mulder said as he pointed to an enormous structure straight ahead, "was the barracks for a company of 100 men. There are four more like it. The buildings on the other side of the parade ground were one- and two-family quarters for the officers. It's all a big condo project now."

They soon reached the first barracks. Workmen were repairing its front porch and installing windows; the rest of the buildings were boarded up. If the fort wasn't a ghost town, it was close. However, the parade ground looked good: a pleasant, recently mowed grassy space big enough for several football fields. The agents crossed it and then, following Ed Gorman's directions, headed down another dirt road.

Mulder continued the story. "The new owner found the bunker we're going to behind a heap of rubble. At first he thought of marketing it as a residence because it had two windows with a nice view of the harbor. But then he discovered that what should have been the same view looked different depending on which window you looked out of, and he got spooked."

"He should have," Scully said. "I've seen the pictures, and it's *real* spooky."

Mulder nodded. "That discovery led to some phone calls that led to me. So I sent Gorman here to take notes and photos of what he saw through the windows, and to guard the place. I've already told you what happened yesterday."

They had reached an iron door hanging on hinges set in concrete walls—just as Gorman had described. Mulder rapped on it. Nobody responded. He pounded on it. At last there was the sound of a bolt disengaging. The door slowly opened inward.

There stood a man about 80 years old: wrinkled face, sunken cheeks, a flap of skin hanging loosely under his chin, forearms thin and hands mottled. The man gazed at Mulder, and then at Scully, but didn't say anything.

Mulder stared back. "Have we met?"

"Yup." The man gazed at the ground.

Mulder frowned. "I'm sorry, but I don't remember. Is Ed Gorman here?"

"Yup." The man raised his eyes to meet Mulder's stare. "I'm him."

"You're Ed?" The person before Mulder and Scully looked nothing like the robust ex-army major Mulder had sent here six weeks earlier. "What happened?"

The man frowned, as if pondering the question, and then said, "I came back." He turned and shuffled down the tunnel.

Mulder and Scully exchanged shocked glances and followed.

Once he reached the chamber, Gorman flopped into an armchair. Mulder pulled up a wood stool. "What do you mean, you came back?" he asked, concerned.

Gorman picked up the coffee cup from the table beside him. "I was doing what you told me to do, taking pictures and keeping a log. And nobody got in or out unless I let them, except for yesterday—those kids."

"Has there been any sign of them?" Scully drew up a chair.

"Not that I know of. Haven't seen the swirly thing either."

"Tell us about that," she said. "Could it be a natural phenomenon?"

Gorman snorted. "You kidding?" He put the cup back on the table. "You ever use a kitchen blender?" Before either of the agents could answer, he continued, "Imagine you fill it with clear water and turn it on. Except for the bubbles you don't see anything. Now add rice or something that doesn't dissolve and turn it on slow. You see the stuff whirling around. Now hit the pulse button a couple of times and see how the stuff goes up and down. Except for the fact that there wasn't any glass holding the sand in, that's what the damn thing looked like. Oh—there wasn't any sound from it that I could hear, either."

"What did it do?" Scully asked.

"First it was swirling and kind of springing up and down, and it looked goofy, and all of a sudden, in no more than a couple of seconds, it moved to where the girl was and"—he paused and shrugged—"it disappeared her. She just vanished inside it. A few seconds later—ten, maybe fifteen—it vanished itself. Gone, *poof*! Where it had been, and the girl had been, was a skeleton."

They were silent.

Scully changed the subject. "So, what have we got, besides that kitchen blender thing? Three missing young people—that's what the warden on the pier said." She pulled the flyer out of her pocket and handed it to Gorman. "Are these the kids and, if so, can you tell us which one died?"

Gorman studied the pictures for a moment. "I think these are the kids, although they didn't exactly pose for the security camera. Their relative heights are right, and the boy had black hair. It was the tallest one who got it and these were probably the other two." He gave the document back to Scully. "I couldn't get down that ladder again to follow them even if I tried. All I can say is they ran toward the civilian end of the island."

"Okay," Mulder said, "so we've got to recover a bone from the skeleton Ed says the kitchen blender left behind, if only to nail down biochemically whether it's the girl."

"The analysis might explain what killed her, too," Scully said.

Mulder slapped the flyer he was holding with the back of his fingers.

"In any event, we've got to find these kids before the same thing happens to them. If it hasn't already."

"And before the State Police and the Coast Guard are called in," Scully said.

"Right. So there's nobody else here to do it except," Mulder stared at Scully, "you and me."

"How are you going accomplish that without having whatever happened to the girl, or to me, happen to you?" asked Gorman.

"Good question." Mulder rose from his chair and went to the window on the right side of the room. "If I've got this correct, the three kids came in through this window here," and he patted the windowsill.

"That's what the tape shows," Gorman said. "And they went out the left one."

Scully joined Mulder at the window. "When's high tide supposed to be?" she asked.

Gorman pulled a tide chart out of the drawer of the table by his elbow. "It ought to be about half tide now; it'll be full in about 3 hours."

"That's a good approximation of the tide out this window," she said. "But," and she crossed to the left window, "it's high tide out through this one, so this one must be doing the distorting."

Mulder followed her to the left window and peered out. "I agree." He studied the beach below. "So I've got a theory. Suppose I were to go out through the window on the right—to avoid any confusion, let's call it the Good window, since it hasn't hurt anyone. If I come back in through the same window, nothing's going to change. At least, nothing happened to the kids when they came in that way. But if I go out the other one—call it the Bad window because it hurt Ed—I'd wind up in the same place but at a different time, or different era, or different *something*. Whatever weirdness is going on here, you have to be inside, and then either look through or go through the Bad window," and he pointed to the left one, "to encounter it. And if you come back through the Bad window, you're locked into the time, or era, of whatever's out there. That'd explain what happened to you, Ed."

Scully spoke up: "So you're suggesting it's a time warp? If so, the difference in time between in here, right now, and on the other side of the Bad window, is the same number of years that got added to Ed's age when he came back through?"

"Yeah," Mulder said. "You put it better than I could."

"So, let's guess that Ed aged about forty years when he came back through the window—sorry Ed, but that's what it looks like. So it must be, what, 2035 out there," she said as she pointed to the Bad window.

Mulder nodded. "I think so."

"So your theory is that if we go out the Bad window after the kids, we can still get back in here safely, in *our* era, if we climb up the ladder and enter through the *Good* window."

"Or through the door at the other end of the tunnel."

"Neat theory, supported by dangerous assumptions," Gorman said.

"Anyone have a better idea?" Mulder said.

There was an uneasy pause. Finally, Mulder rubbed his hands together. "So, time for an experiment. Any volunteers?"

Gorman gave his head a firm shake: "No way! Once is enough."

Scully stared at Mulder. "Yeah, I'm looking at him."

Mulder shrugged, unsurprised. "Okay. Give me a hand, Scully."

They pulled the ladder into the room. The ladder didn't appear to change. Then they slid it out the Good window and lowered it. Giving Scully a fingers-crossed sign, Mulder climbed over the sill and onto the ladder.

He looked back at Scully and grinned. "Made it." Then he climbed back onto the sill and jumped down to the floor of the bunker, where he stood, poking himself with his fingers. "See anything different?" he asked Scully.

"Well, your looks haven't improved, if that's what you mean," she said with a straight face. "Otherwise, no."

"Right." Mulder returned to the Good window. "Chapter Two. Watch for me out the Bad window." He went out onto the ladder, climbed down, picked it up and moved it to the other one. He climbed it and peered inside, and there was Scully.

"What do you see?" he asked.

"The tide's high, the sky isn't as clear, and your looks still haven't improved," she said.

Mulder nodded and, pivoting on the ladder, gazed down at the water. "From my point of view, right now, it's not high tide. And there are no skeletons."

"You're not coming in through that window!" Gorman was the army major again, giving a command.

Mulder shook his head and mouthed "no." Then he descended the ladder and returned it to the Good window. Walking out onto the exposed seabed flats, he waited to see whether the blender, as Gorman had called it, would appear. After a full minute nothing happened, so he climbed back up into the bunker through the Good window. Facing Scully and Gorman, he raised his arms, palms up, like a preacher giving them a blessing. "Presto, nooo change-o."

"Congratulations, Houdini. What's next?" Scully asked.

"We go get the two kids." "Wrong, Houdini. You go out the Bad window and come back in

the Good one and we see what happens."

Mulder paused, pondering, and then said, "No, if we go out the Good window we'll never locate them—we know that. If we go out the other one we can—or at least we have a chance. If we find them, we'll be able to help them thereafter, even if none of us can get back to now. So we find the kids first. *After* that we test my theory."

"Terrific," Scully said. "You better be right."

"So help me with the ladder again, please."

They repeated the ladder process in reverse and slid it out the Bad window.

Once it was in place Mulder gazed at Scully and then tilted his head toward the ladder. "Dare ya."

She pointed at Mulder and then swept her finger in the same direction. "Age before beauty."

THURSDAY, 5:10 a.m.

As dawn began to break, Carole and Allen sat leaning against each other, back-to-back, in the middle of the cabin's main room. They'd assumed that position the night before: By watching in opposite directions, their mutually dependent back support placed each on immediate notice if the other fell asleep and slumped over. Not that either had felt like sleeping, but the tactic had worked a couple of times.

The evening before, Allen had flipped on the front porch light and the spotlights that illuminated the four outside corners of the cabin so Carole and he could keep their enemy in view. Barton, as they had named it, continued to patrol the circumference of the cabin, appearing at one window, then withdrawing from the light, then reappearing at another. Because none of the windows rattled, it apparently did not attempt to enter. But it wanted them; it would wait.

Now in the morning light, Barton had apparently picked up more leaves because it looked less like a soup than a stew, but at least it was no larger.

Since they couldn't go anywhere, Allen and Carole ate canned fruit they found in the cupboard. Once they'd finished, they both chose books from the bedroom, but soon found they couldn't concentrate. So they rummaged around until they found a checkerboard set, set it in the middle of the rug, and started playing. They didn't speak, and after a short while the checkers ceased to distract them, too. Without a word, they simply stopped playing.

After a while Carole bent her neck back and said to the ceiling, "How long is this gonna take?"

"How long can we take this, is what you mean," Allen answered.

Standing, he went to the window. Barton was still there. He noticed clouds gathering in the western sky. "I think we might get a thunderstorm. Maybe the son of a bitch will get hit by lightning."

Carole stared at him, shaking her head. "I need something to do—*something* other than sit here and wait for I don't know what."

Allen threw up his hands. He had no answer. They were trapped, frustrated and frightened. The menace outside was as patient and pitiless as a tiger lurking in the jungle.

When Mulder reached the bottom of the ladder, he turned to the ocean, scanning for whatever it was that had consumed the one girl and chased Gorman back up to the bunker. Nothing had appeared by the time Scully made it to the bottom.

"Wait here," he told her. He walked toward the ocean, pushed through the bushes, and stood with the water lapping over his Pumas.

"What are you doing?" Scully called.

"Just want to see if anything happens." He stood there a while longer. "I'm guessing I'm not close enough to a skeleton, or maybe the blender thing doesn't like water." He beckoned Scully to follow him in the direction Gorman said the surviving kids had run.

Because the tide was high, they had to work their way along the rocks that lined the shoreline until they were able to climb up to the woods above. Sunlight filtered down through the tall oaks. From there they kept the ocean to their right and headed off. A half-mile later, they emerged onto a grassy hilltop that sloped gradually down to a couple of cabins and, ultimately, to the western end of the island. Beyond was Casco Bay and, beyond that, the City of Portland. A light breeze ruffled their hair and the sun was still out, but dark clouds were building above the city.

They stopped, surveying the pleasant view.

After a few moments, Scully asked, "What do you notice, Mulder?"

"Nothing."

"That's right, nothing. No boats, no voices, no artificial sounds of any sort, none of the activity we saw when we were on the ferry, or on the island after we got here."

"Eerie," he acknowledged.

They watched and listened—in vain.

After a while, Mulder said, "Let's head down there." He pointed in the direction of a cabin that sat in the fork of a road. "Maybe we'll find someone."

When they reached the cabin, they mounted the porch. Mulder knocked on the door. No response.

"Hello!" he called. "Anyone home?"

Again, silence.

There was another building a short way up the road's right fork. As they walked toward it, they spotted a human rib cage lying in a bush.

Mulder stuck his arm out to stop Scully. "Damn," he said.

They nervously glanced around. The breeze turned leaves in the surrounding trees, but nothing else moved.

"Maybe the reason we haven't seen anyone is because no one's left alive," Scully said. "You're thinking the same thing, aren't you?"

Mulder nodded. "Remember what Ed told us. It was when he and the kids stood over a skeleton that the blender thing arose. Let's move away."

They hurried to the far side of the road and were continuing toward another home when they heard a low rumble of thunder.

"Storm's coming," Scully observed.

At the next cabin, the front door was ajar.

Scully climbed the steps and pushed it open. "Hello!"

Receiving no answer, she stepped into a kitchen. Through a side window she noticed an outside light shining from a nearby camp. She went to the window, and saw more than the light. There was a commotion, a windy disturbance of some sort.

"Mulder, come in here," she called in a low voice. As he joined her, she asked, "Think that's one of those blender things?"

"Gotta be," he replied. As they watched, the thing spun, narrowing as it rose and expanding as it fell. "I'd guess it's hovering over a skeleton."

"Maybe, but remember, it's predatory," Scully said, "so there could be someone inside that building."

Lightning flashed across the darkening sky, followed shortly by thunder, louder than before. Moments later the wind gusted. The spinning thing stayed where it was, apparently unaffected by the wind.

"This'll be a test of my theory," said Mulder.

Scully looked at him. "What theory?"

"That it dislikes water. Remember after we climbed down the ladder and I stood at the ocean's edge, but nothing appeared?"

"Yeah, but maybe that's because there's only one of them, and it was busy here."

The rain started with a few heavy drops, and then fell steadily. Still the thing bounced and spun, but it was more transparent now—it contained less detritus.

"Is the thing diminishing, or is the rain just obscuring it?" Scully wondered.

"A little of both, I think," replied Mulder.

The rain increased and fell in sheets; frequent bursts of wind drove it laterally. The spinning thing faded, and faded more, and finally disappeared.

"It's now or never," Mulder said. "If we're going to find out who's in that cabin, it better be now."

Scully nodded. "Whatcha waiting for?"

They ran out the door, up the short hill to the camp with the light on, and jumped onto the porch. Both were drenched.

"I'll watch for our blender friend," Mulder said.

Scully banged on the door. "Anyone here?"

A teenage girl came to the window in the door.

"Open up, the thing's gone!" Scully said.

Mulder and Scully ran to the kitchen area, where they shook their arms and stamped water out of their clothes onto the linoleum.

"Who are *you*?" Allen asked.

"Tell you in a minute," Scully said, still stomping.

"Well, whoever you are, we're *real* glad to see you," Carole added.

When the agents finished de-soaking themselves, Scully pulled the soggy flyer out of her pocket and handed it to Carole. "This you?"

Carole and Allen peered at the paper.

"Yeah. Where did you get this?" Carole asked.

"How'd you find us?" Allen wanted to know.

Mulder ignored the questions. "Is there anyone else around here?"

"Not that we've found," Allen said.

"Unless you count Mr. Barton as a person," added Carole, feeling relieved enough to attempt humor.

"Who's Mr. Barton?" Scully asked.

"Some weird cyclone thing that wants to eat us," Allen answered.

Scully nodded. "We saw it from the cabin over there," pointing to where they'd come.

"But who are " A brilliant flash and an immediate crack of thunder interrupted her. " are you, and how'd you get here?" Carole asked, stammering.

"We'll fill you in about everything, but first we've got to get out of here before your Mr. Barton comes back." Mulder headed for the door.

"What about the lightning? Will it be safe?" Carole worried.

"I think the risk's worth it, given the alternative," Scully answered.

Allen grabbed Carole's hand. "Baby, we're *going*."

"Hold on a minute." Mulder opened the door and checked outside. Then he headed left, circling the cabin. The rain continued heavily, and the wind continued to gust. Back at the door, and dripping wet again, he said, "We're okay for the moment. Show us the quickest way back to that bunker you were in yesterday."

With Allen in the lead, they moved quickly to another dirt road. In places, it was a slippery paste of sand and mud.

As they passed through the forest, Scully explained who she and Mulder were, the bunker and the window, their interest in the kids, and how they proposed to return to the "present." Mulder stayed behind them and kept watch to the rear.

This was the same road the agents had used when they'd first come to the island, but now they were rushing so fast that they covered the distance between the civilian end and the fort in half the time. It was a tiring pace. When they reached the fort's gate, they paused to rest. Lightning still flashed and thunder boomed, but the rain was slackening.

It was then that Mulder noticed the gate was no longer rusty. It glistened—not only from the rain, but also from new black paint. He looked up the road. The first thing that caught his eye was a white window box bearing bright, red flowers on one of the barracks buildings.

He pointed to the window box, and asked Carole and Allen, "Have you ever seen that before?"

They were as surprised as he was. "That place doesn't have flowers— it's a dump," said Carole.

Mulder urged them on, and they hurried into the fort.

When they reached the parade ground, no workmen were present and none of the buildings was boarded up—all were in immaculate condition. Golf carts and bicycles stood here and there. But there were no people.

"Look at this place!" Carole exclaimed, gesturing around. "This is crazy!"

"What should it look like?" Mulder asked.

"A bunch of rundown buildings," she answered.

"It's like at my house, everything has changed," Allen said.

"Thanks to that window you went through," said Scully.

"Keep up with me," Mulder said.

They jogged across the parade ground. By the time they reached the road at the other end, the rain was a drizzle and the wind had died. The bunker was still a half mile away.

When they finally arrived at where the tunnel entrance should be, there was no iron door and no concrete structure upon which to hang it. Apparently, the place had been leveled. Instead, there was an octagonal gazebo, painted yellow with green trim, large enough for a small band. Several chairs stood in a semi-circle on its floor; two more had blown over. The area around the gazebo was a lawn, as if for an audience to sit on. The grass was high; nobody had mowed it in weeks.

Mulder climbed the steps and stood on the floor of the gazebo, searching for a trap door. "Look underneath, see if there's any opening under here," he told the others.

Scully and Allen dropped to their hands and knees and peered through the wooden cribbing.

"Nothing but flat, bare ground," Scully called from her crawling position, and they both stood.

Mulder addressed them all: "Okay, we're down to one option: We have to get to the bluff where the windows are. Show us how, kids."

Allen nodded. "This way."

They followed him into the woods and down an incline. By then the sun was shining on the calming sea. The four started across the rocks lining the shore, but the rain had so slickened the irregular surfaces that they had to help each other—Allen holding Carole's hand, and Mulder, Scully's. Progress was slow.

"Damn," Scully exclaimed after about ten yards, as her foot slid and jammed between rocks. "*Damn!*" she said again, in pain.

"Give me a hand," Mulder said to Allen. Allen kneeled down and pulled up the rock that was trapping Scully's ankle, while Mulder steadied her until she could regain her footing. But her ankle was bruised and moving over the rocks had become impossible.

"Let's try it down there," Mulder said, indicating the flats, now exposed by the tide that had been receding since they'd first left the bunker

"No chance!" she replied. "You kidding?"

The flats were not all the lowering tide had exposed. Ahead, two of the three skeletons were visible again. Scully's objection caused Carole to look up, and as soon as she saw the skeletons she sobbed, covering her mouth with her hand. Allen reached for her and urged her forward.

"We'll stay close to the shore and away from those things," Mulder said.

He helped Scully limp her way to and across the sandy flats, through the bushes and up the beach to the bluff, where Carole—tears still brimming—and Allen stood waiting. Nothing had arisen from the skeletons.

"Watch for Mr. Barton," Mulder told the women. To Allen, he said, "You guys came out that window, correct?" He pointed at the Bad window, below which the ladder still stood.

"Yeah, although there wasn't any ladder there," Allen replied.

"Understood. Give me a hand." Allen helped Mulder reposition the ladder beneath the other window.

"Okay, Scully, now *you're* the guinea pig. Head on up, and after you're inside tell us if anything happened to you." To the kids he said, "Help Scully up the ladder. After she assures you she's okay, go through the window yourselves. Otherwise, stay here."

"What are you going to do?" Scully asked, worried.

"Barton-watch."

"Your goddam theory had better be right. If I die I'll never forgive you."

"Don't. Die, that is."

Mulder moved to the side of the ladder and turned so that his back was to the cliff. He surveyed the flats. "If and when everyone's inside, let me know. If I understand how the windows operate, you'll have to tell me through the Bad window. The left one," he added for the kids' sake.

He waited, his hand on the ladder.

Moments later, from Scully: "It worked, I'm okay, c'mon up."

In less than a minute he heard Allen from above: "We all made it."

Relieved, Mulder walked to the shoreline. Then he realized he'd forgotten something: "Which one's your friend's skeleton?" he yelled over his shoulder.

"The closest one to you, just to your left," Allen replied.

That put it about 15 yards away. Mulder took a deep breath, ran to the skeleton, and wrenched at a finger bone.

"Watch out!" Allen yelled. "It's coming back!"

Mulder kept trying to work the bone loose but the sinews were too tight.

"You gotta move!" Allen bellowed.

Mulder looked up. The swirly thing was now about as tall as a grown man. He shuddered with fear. Giving up on the finger bone, he put a foot on the skeleton's shoulder, grabbed the upper arm, and simultaneously yanked and twisted. The arm came free.

The vortex was now eight feet tall. It towered, bobbing.

Sweating, Mulder sprinted across the flats and the beach.

"Here it comes!" someone yelled. "It's chasing you!"

Carrying the arm in one hand, Mulder grabbed the ladder with the other. He went to step on the bottom rung, but his foot slipped.

"Damn," he swore. At that moment he felt like he'd been thrust in an incinerator. The worst of the heat was coming from behind. He was broiling and baking at the same time. He tried to force himself up the ladder, but his legs would not move. His fingers slid off the rung. He couldn't breathe. The heat was unbearable.

Cold water drenched him. Suddenly his legs worked. He scrambled up the ladder as if the hounds of hell were chasing him and dove through the window. His right foot caught the frame of the window. He twisted in mid-air and landed on the floor on his left shoulder. The hideous thing he had been carrying flew across the room.

"Nice entrance," Scully said. She limped forward to help him up.

"Thanks." Mulder stood, scrutinizing Allen, Carole, and Scully. They appeared normal. Gorman was standing behind them, an old man, solemn.

"Everyone okay?" Mulder asked.

All nodded.

"Who did the water," he asked.

"Me," Allen said.

"After we got up here, I asked Allen to fill a pail," Scully explained.

"I was going to dump it on you to get the thing to leave you alone," Allen said. "But it was so fast, instead of hitting just you I hit you both at the same time."

"Lucky for everyone," Scully added

"Thanks," Mulder said. "It was like being inside a torch. Now I know what it felt like to be Joan of Arc." With his fingers, he swept water off his forehead. "Well, we were right, weren't we? Twice. The Good window worked. And Mr. Barton doesn't like water."

"If it's the same Mr. Barton," Scully added. "There might be a whole family of them."

Mulder looked out the Good window and saw an ordinary tugboat towing a barge. It was close to high tide. He went to the other window.

The tide was lower and the same two skeletons were lying in the exposed sea bottom.

Meanwhile Scully had scooped up the bones. As she put them in a box Gorman handed her, she said, "Mulder, we've got to get these kids home and call off the search. What are we gonna tell their parents, and this girl's parents"—she raised the box—"about what happened?"

"How can we tell them anything?" Mulder replied. "First of all, we don't *know* what happened. Mr. Barton, the skeletons, the sudden change in the fort. None of it makes sense."

"I know. No way in hell anyone's gonna believe us," Scully replied. "We need a cover story."

Ed Gorman spoke up: "How about they got stranded on Cow Island overnight?" The agents looked puzzled, so he explained: "Cow Island is about two acres of rock and bushes just to the north of here. It's uninhabited."

Scully nodded. She gestured at the kids: "You caught a ride over there with a friend and he promised he'd come back to pick you up, but he didn't. So you had to wait to catch a passing boat and that didn't happen until today. Does that work?"

"I guess so," Carole said. "But what about Jackie?"

"She wanted to get back last night so she started swimming, and you haven't seen her since," suggested Mulder.

"Not good," Allen said. "She didn't like to swim, and she hated cold water."

"Look," said Mulder. "It doesn't have to be the best story in the world. We'll figure out some way for the FBI to take jurisdiction. We'll conduct an official investigation, and she'll simply have gone missing." He looked at Scully. "We'll figure out the details later.

"But it's not true," Carole said. "I'm sorry, but it's all a big lie!"

"You're right, Carole," Mulder agreed. "But think about your Mr. Barton out there. What's 'true' about that?"

Scully joined in. "What choice do we have? We can't just say nothing, because everyone will know *something* happened. And if we tell the 'truth' "—she mimed quotation marks with her fingers—"we'll all get labeled as crazies."

Mulder nodded. "Or maybe panic everyone else. It's not that we like lying. Sometimes—not often, but sometimes—the truth has to be contained, as if it were anthrax, or a deadly virus. This is one of those times. Do you see what I mean?"

"Here's some reassurance," Scully added. "Mulder will make a full and honest report and file it with our office. But they won't make it public."

Carole looked at Allen and then back at Scully. "Is this what they mean about government conspiracies?"

Smiling, Scully nodded. "Yup, you're dead center in the middle of a big, fat government conspiracy. But when you're on the inside, it doesn't look so evil, does it. Because"—she shrugged—"what else can we do?"

Allen was nodding. "If we ever tried to explain what really happened I can see our faces staring out at us from those tabloids in the super-market checkout lines."

Carole frowned. Then, hesitantly: "I guess so."

Mulder turned to Gorman. "Speaking of containment, Ed, do we have any masons on our staff?"

"Yes, we've got a special detail that just finished a project in Council Bluffs."

"Get them up here as fast as you can. I want that left window bricked up—no, don't use brick, use granite. Two courses thick. You stay here till it's done, and then we'll work on permanent plans—including what to do for you. If you want to try going back through the window to reverse your aging, we need to know before they get here."

"Okay, I'll think on it." Gorman tottered to the phone.

"Let's get some tape to wrap that box up tight," Mulder told Scully. "We'll come back to pick it up after we get the wardens to call off the search and we've talked to the parents. If it's okay with you, I'll take these guys to theirs. You're gentler than I am. I'd be grateful if you'd talk to Jackie's. And we'll need some DNA from them for comparison."

Scully nodded grimly. "Of course."

He walked over to Carole and put his arm around her. "We'll work on your cover story on the way." Then, to Allen. "C'mon, let's go home."

MONDAY, 2:45 p.m.

Six weeks later, a tall man in his fifties, wearing a suit and a fedora and carrying a brief case, walked past the barracks buildings. He was a gray, unremarkable man. The workmen who were installing front steps and painting a front door paid no attention to him.

He crossed the parade ground and followed the road to the iron door. A large, new padlock hung from a hasp welded to the front. He pulled some keys from his pants pocket, selected one, unlocked and removed the padlock, and pushed the door inward. From his attaché case he took out a flashlight, shone it down the tunnel, and entered, following its beam.

When he reached the chamber, he aimed the light at the right window, which was covered with a curtain. Then he aimed it at the left window—or where the window had been. From bottom to top, the space was filled with granite paving blocks mortared into place. He crossed the room to inspect the construction closely.

He shone his flashlight on two of the stones and lightly, slowly, ran his finger along the joint between them. After a moment, tiny grains of mortar trickled down, like crystals of salt from a reluctant saltshaker, barely visible to the naked eye.

He delicately stroked the mortar between two other stones, higher up. Minute particles started falling from that intersection—one or two specks at a time, perceptible only to someone watching closely, some so small they floated down the face of the masonry.

He ran his finger along all the other joints, caressing them.

When he'd finished, he turned around, and the flashlight's beam revealed a tall wooden stool nearby. He pulled it up and sat before the new stonework. Securing the flashlight against his chest with his upper arm, he put his hands into the pockets of his suit jacket. From one pocket he pulled a cigarette, from the other a lighter. He lit the cigarette and inhaled, watching as tiny grains of particulate drifted, with increasing frequency, down through the beam of light.

Ever so slightly, he smiled.

THE END

STATUES

By Kevin J. Anderson

FURNACE CREEK
DEATH VALLEY NATIONAL PARK
11th MAY, 1995, 10:16 a.m.

The blazing sun washed across a rugged landscape of brown, tan, copper, ochre—like a watercolor painted with molten precious metals. Ragged mountains rose from the valley floor, and a razor-straight road sliced across the desert, a place of recreational vehicles and gawking tourists in a valley where old pioneers had seen only death.

A red Jeep roared along the shimmering road, like a spot of blood flying in a spatter pattern from a murder weapon. The wheels kissed the gravel shoulder and kicked up a spray of rocks before the driver regained control, barely avoiding a rollover.

The Jeep hurtled toward a cluster of civilization at the vanishing point on the other side of the valley, a splash of unexpected green in the desert. Furnace Creek: a campground, gift shop, gas station, and world-class resort facilities in startling contrast to the rest of Death Valley. Golfers in colorful shirts and plaid shorts stood on the well-watered greens and paused mid-swing to watch the oncoming Jeep.

The driver struck the knot of town, dodging pedestrians and a "luxury coach" tour bus. More of a projectile than a vehicle, the Jeep raced beneath an arch spanning the highway—FURNACE CREEK RANCH, complete with a saloon, general store, steakhouse, boardwalk, and decorative hitching posts.

The Jeep smashed into a split-rail fence in front of the saloon and lurched to a stop. The engine gasped, and the radiator exploded with steam. Spectators rushed to help, while others just stared; a few even took photos to memorialize the event for their family vacation scrapbook.

The driver's door popped open with a loud creak, and he wrenched himself out of the smashed vehicle. He moved stiffly, dazed, and hauled himself into a brittle standing position. The man swayed, then lurched forward with a stiff-legged gait, like the Tin Woodsman from *The Wizard of Oz*. He turned his head, but his face was chalky, his expression unnatural and frozen. He couldn't speak.

A Park Service ranger hurried out of the nearby Visitor Center. The driver took two lurching steps toward the ranger, as if hoping for rescue, heaved a loud gasp, then fell forward like a toppled tree. His clothes, hands, face, even his hair were caked with glittering mineral deposits as if he had been sprayed with wet flour and sand that had dried hard in the sun.

The ranger squatted next to the fallen man, who lay motionless as if petrified. He grabbed the driver's shoulders, listened for respiration.

"Why is he so white?" asked a potbellied man in a t-shirt that said *I Survived Death Valley*.

The ranger touched the fallen man's wrist, looking for a pulse, then he tried to lift the arm, but it was stiff, like a statue. When he touched the victim's cheek, there was no resilience whatsoever to the skin. The eyes were open and staring—and solid chalky white.

The ranger said, "He's… *turned to stone.*"

FBI HEADQUARTERS
WASHINGTON, D.C.
MONDAY, 4:52 p.m.

The Medusa mask was hideous, the hair a tangle of fanged snakes, a face that would have been the sure-fire winner in a "Psycho Ex-Girlfriend" photo contest. From behind the mouth slit, he said, "Hi, Scully."

Standing in Mulder's office, Agent Scully put her hands on her hips, not the least bit scared. He pulled the mask away so she could see his wry smile. "It's a Medusa mask. You never know what might be useful." He set the mask on the clutter of his desk. "It's research for a new case. According to Greek legend, a glance from Medusa could turn people to stone. This is said to be an exact representation."

"And how would any sculptor manage to get a good look without turning to stone himself?"

Mulder wasn't deterred by logical conundrums. "Stories about creatures that can turn humans to stone appear in many cultures—Medusa, the basilisk, the cockatrice."

Scully said, "The legends probably originated from people finding fossils. It was their attempt to explain how living creatures could have turned to stone. In fossilization, minerals gradually replace organic matter over a very long period, leaving a stone copy of the original creature."

He could barely contain his smile, since she had asked exactly the right questions. "Yes, the process is supposed to take centuries. Normally."

Scully waited. They had played this game many times before.

Mulder showed her a photo he had printed out. She looked at the white petrified man sprawled on the ground at the Furnace Creek Ranch. "This man fossilized instantaneously—in front of dozens of witnesses."

She frowned at the photo. "Mulder, that's impossible."

"The victim was a freelance prospector for a mineral reclamation company out in the Mojave Desert. According to initial reports from the medical examiner, he has mineralized all the way down to the bone." He took the photo back and slid it into its folder and added it to his open briefcase. "Now do you see why I'm interested? We need to find out where this man went and what he discovered. They're holding the body for us to examine. Travel papers already filed." He hurried her out of the office. "We're heading out to Death Valley. I already packed sunscreen."

PENDRAGON GALLERY
LOS ANGELES, CALIFORNIA
MONDAY, 8:07 p.m.

Two waiters strolled through the high-end gallery, holding silver trays with hors d'oeuvres. An audience of aloof men and women in formal attire, dressed to kill or dressed to be uncomfortable, sipped champagne and admired the display. *Bernard Lumke, Exclusive Sculpture Exhibition.*

Patrons gathered around a motionless crowd of lifelike, yet disturbing, sculptures: lumpy human figures that sparkled in the harsh fluorescent light, as if fashioned out of clay and mixed with alkaline salts: eight human figures, and one contorted stone coyote. A sculpture of a screaming man pressed stone hands to his head. Another figure had curled up into a fetal position and lay on the floor. One looked like a bearded prospector from a previous century.

Travis Ashton, well-known art critic— at least in his own mind— worked for two independent freebie newspapers that paid for his columns in copies. He studied the statues as he chatted up a plump young woman wearing a lot of pearls. He stroked his trendy goatee. "I've been part of the LA art scene for years, and I've never seen anything like this." He paced around the statue of the screaming man, looking at the realistic expression on his face, the gaping mouth, the stone eyes. "So *primal*, so eerie, it reminds me of Edvard Munch's *The Scream*. But it's an original take."

"Oh, I love it. Bernard Lumke is this week's genius." The woman didn't seem to be flirting with Ashton, but he could always hope. Maybe she had heard of him from his columns. "A splendid display of talent, although not something I'd like in my own yard."

Ashton forced himself not to roll his eyes. "I don't think these were meant to be displayed outside in anyone's yard." What was she looking for? Pink flamingos? He bent to regard the suffering stone coyote, wondering how that particular piece fit with the rest of the exhibition. He hadn't discovered the underlying theme of the exhibition. But, since the young woman was looking at him, he nodded knowingly, as if he understood perfectly well.

"Lumke lives out in a ghost town in the Mojave somewhere. He's a recluse," Ashton explained to the young woman, trying to impress her and hoping she hadn't read the same brochure on the front reception desk. "His technique is unlike anything the art world has ever seen, and he refuses to tell anyone how he does it."

He turned to eye the next statue as much as he was eyeing the woman with too many pearls. No wedding ring, and she had come alone. "I'm going to try to arrange an interview with him," he announced. "Even if I have to drive all the way out to Death Valley." An exclusive profile like that would get Ashton a cover in an arts magazine, maybe even one that paid.

"I'm sorry, Mr. Ashton, but my client sees no one—especially not critics."

He turned to see a slender, dark-skinned woman with extravagant cornrowed hair. She was stunning—so stunning in fact, that he forgot about the plump young woman, who wandered off to look at the statue of a hunched-over man who appeared to be retching. "In fact, sometimes he won't even see me... not that I'm keen to visit Frustration Corners any more than he's keen to come to LA." She extended her hand. "I'm Kendra Pendra, and I represent Mr. Lumke's work. As you can see, our working relationship is solid as a rock." She smiled, but only slightly.

Ashton returned her warm laughter, hoping to work his way into Pendra's good graces. The connection could prove valuable. "When an artist is in such demand, he can afford to be eccentric," he said. "It enhances the mystique."

He doubted she would give him contact information or make any sort of recommendation, but Ashton could figure it out himself. Frustration Corners? It might not be more than a flyspeck on a map. Population... what, twelve? It couldn't be too difficult to find the sculptor.

FURNACE CREEK URGENT CARE/MEDICAL CENTER
DEATH VALLEY NATIONAL PARK
TUESDAY, 11:03 a.m.

Scully parked the rental car in front of the limited Medical Center in Furnace Creek. To reach Death Valley, they had flown from Washington D.C. into Las Vegas, then driven the desert highways. Scully wasn't a reckless driver, but the straight roads and the shimmering desert lulled her into believing that 90 mph was the new 60.

The medical facility wasn't large enough to qualify as a hospital; it served primarily as a trauma center for "stupid tourist injuries"—heatstroke, dehydration, broken bones or sprained ankles from reckless hiking. She doubted this place would have the facilities necessary for performing a full autopsy. The body might have to be moved to a more sophisticated lab in Las Vegas.

As they walked up to the entrance, she asked, "Are you sure this isn't some kind of hoax, Mulder?"

He had a spring in his step, eager to look at the man who had supposedly turned to stone. "Like the Cardiff Giant? In 1869, a farmer in New York claimed to have dug up a petrified prehistoric man ten feet tall. It was exhibited to great crowds, caused quite a sensation—until it was revealed to be a sophisticated fake. A decade before that, a California newspaper published a letter claiming that a prospector in the Sierra Nevada mountains had turned to stone after he drank liquid found inside a geode. The letter turned out to be bogus, too." He sounded disappointed as he held the door open for her and they entered the air-conditioned facility. "This victim, though, turned to stone in front of a group of witnesses, including a park ranger."

A harried looking man with leathery skin, liver-spotted scalp, and eyebrows like toothbrushes, hurried forward to meet them. Mulder's black jacket and slacks, white shirt, black tie, and Scully's professional business attire, made them stand out among the usual tourists.

"Agents Mulder and Scully? I'm the county's medical examiner, Bryce Adams. We kept the body for your inspection, per Agent Mulder's request. I have paperwork to complete, and I hope you two can help me fill in the blanks. I'm really stumped on this one."

Scully followed him down the hall, all business. "Do you have a morgue?"

"Don't need one in this case." Adams pushed open a set of swinging doors. "You can inspect the victim right here."

Scully frowned. "No morgue, in this heat? I hope you didn't just keep the body out in the open. Deterioration would have—"

Adams cut her off. "Don't worry. As you can see, there's no need for refrigeration." Inside the examining room, a figure lay on a gurney, stiff and frozen, arms bent and upstretched, back arched. It looked as if it had been carved from a block of stone, the expression frozen at the point of death.

Scully moved forward, fascinated, with Mulder close beside her. She bent over the man's head and pulled on a pair of latex gloves so she could touch the skin. "It feels hard, like cement. It's as if his entire body spontaneously *calcified*. All the flesh mineralized."

From a stainless steel instrument table, Adams picked up a white, caked rectangle, a wallet surrounded by chipped remnants of cloth. "His clothes, his skin, everything was petrified, but we chiseled his wallet free. This, in addition to his vehicle records, identified him as Wilson Beatty, a freelance prospector working for a mineral concern in Tirona, California. Dry Sea Resource Works. A couple of hours from here."

She reached out to hold the victim's splayed, stone fingers, his grasping hand. "It's like... petrified wood." She tried to flex the fingers. "The palm is hard and immovable, the muscles frozen, entirely brittle—"

The stone hand cracked at the wrist, then snapped off. Scully was left holding the broken-off limb, and she looked at the jagged wrist stump to see etch marks of the bones, the blood vessels, everything solid stone.

"Yesterday, this man was moving. People watched him step out of his Jeep alive, and he collapsed in front of a crowd." Adams sounded more curious than horrified. "And now he's solid stone."

Scully looked at Mulder, holding the broken stone hand. "Mulder, we've got to find out what happened here. If he was contaminated somehow, and if other people were exposed . . ."

"Right, Scully," Mulder said. "No sightseeing until tomorrow at least."

DRY SEA RESOURCE WORKS
TIRONA, CALIFORNIA
WEDNESDAY, 3:17 p.m.

The industrial town of Tirona was a festering boil on the landscape, built on the edge of a dry lakebed where the main industry was strip-mining chemical deposits left over when the inland sea evaporated. Railroad tracks ran along one side of the highway, gracing a rundown company town of trailer parks, gas stations, and dreary houses.

Rough mountains butted up against the sparkling white lakebed. A large factory rested on the flat expanse, complete with belching smoke stacks and chain link fences. Giant extractor machinery crawled along the alkaline flats, ripping up the top layers of powdered chemicals.

"Lovely place, Mulder," Scully said, as he drove into town. "Death Valley is a garden spot by comparison."

He headed toward the fenced gate of the large chemical plant. "Let's not drink the water."

A big metal sign identified the place as Dry Sea Resource Works, with a cheerful logo and the slogan "Chemicals Are Our Best Friends" right next to *No Trespassing* and *Do Not Enter* signs. He stopped at the guard kiosk in front of the chain-link gate and rolled down his window. "We're here to see Mr. Hancock."

The guard checked on his clipboard, scowled. Their business attire and professional appearance made them look like aliens to him in this heat.

"We have an appointment," Scully added.

The guard found their name, checked it off on his clipboard, and gave them a pass for the dashboard of their car. "As long as you're not one of those *Save the Desert!* protesters." He snorted. "Look around you—we're already way past saving."

Once past the guard shack, Mulder drove toward a ramshackle complex of trailers that formed an administration building. The temporary buildings had obviously been there a very long time.

"Let's see what Beatty's supervisor can tell us," Scully said, "but he didn't actually work in Tirona. He was a mineral rights scout who ranged far and wide across BLM lands and unclaimed territory."

Mulder parked the car. "Then we need to find out exactly where he went looking. He must have kept a log."

A desiccated-looking receptionist let them into the offices of Mr. Hancock, the company supervisor, who greeted them with a smile and a well-lotioned hand. He looked far too young for the position; Mulder doubted the man would last long out here. Everyone else on site seemed to be dusty, dried up, and old beyond their years.

"Mr. Beatty's death was quite shocking to us, Agents Mulder and Scully. I'm happy to help however I can. We don't know how to explain it."

"We'll need some information, sir," Scully said. "It's important that we find out where Mr. Beatty explored and what he might have encountered."

Hancock already had a manila folder ready for them. "Wilson was an independent sort, wandered all over the desert and took samples. But he always kept good records—an important part of the job. You know how many stories there are about lost mines and fabulous veins of gold that nobody can find again? Or big uranium strikes."

"Uranium?" Scully said.

"Different times. There was quite a boom in the 1950s, but now all those spots are marked as environmental hazards. Fortunately, there'll always be a good market for dry chemicals such as potash and borax. One hundred percent natural, deposited by Nature herself." He smiled. "When the ancient seas evaporated, rich layers of minerals filled the area... some lying right out in the open, like the dry lakebed here, but Mr. Beatty was always hunting for more obscure deposits. Something special."

Mulder slid the medical examiner's photo of Beatty's petrified body lying on an examination table, arms akimbo, like a scarecrow made of stone. "Looks like he found something special, Mr. Hancock. Agent Scully and I will try to retrace his path, if you can provide us with his records."

Hancock nodded, all smiles. "Wilson covered a lot of miles around the area—California, Nevada. Borders aren't very clear out in the wilderness. Wilson often logged time on the old Jeep roads, exploring possible valuable deposits."

"He made his way to Furnace Creek," Scully said. "He must have been inside Death Valley National Park."

Hancock shrugged. "Technically, he wasn't supposed to be inside the park boundaries, but he could've driven a long way to get to Furnace Creek. There aren't many medical facilities around. If he felt the fossilization coming on and made a beeline . . ."

Hancock directed them to a large map on the office wall, which was studded with red stickpins. "This shows all of Wilson's primary stops. In order to secure the mineral rights in unexploited regions, we need to have exact documentation, after which we file all the appropriate forms." The supervisor's brow furrowed, and he surreptitiously plucked one of the map pins just inside the boundary of Death Valley National Park and moved it back across the border. "Of course we're careful to remain outside all protected areas as the law requires."

DEATH VALLEY NATIONAL PARK
THURSDAY, 10:14 a.m.

The next morning, in the passenger seat, Scully unfolded the maps Mr. Hancock had given them, looking at all the off-road places Wilson Beatty had explored and logged.

Mulder had worked long into the night to consolidate the data points, marking 23 spots with a yellow highlighter. "These are the general areas where missing persons have been reported over the past several years. I think we may have found Death Valley's version of the Bermuda Triangle. A place called Frustration Corners. And Beatty explored that area, too."

"I wouldn't put too much stock in the missing persons reports, Mulder. It's called Death Valley for a reason. A huge park that gets over a million visitors each year, and a lot of them do careless things." She flipped through the folders, seeing nothing unusual. "Families on vacation come out to see the scenery and they're totally unprepared for the desert back country. People get lost out here and are never found. There's no mystery... it's just human error."

"That might explain most of them," Mulder said, "but probably not all."

Now they drove off into the desert, following "roads" that were little more than gray dotted lines on the map. And a tiny dot. "Frustration Corners. Is that a real town?"

"Probably not much of one," Mulder said as he took his turn driving. "The only notable resident area, maybe the only resident, is an artist—a sculptor, actually—named Bernard Lumke. Probably the only person in fifty miles. Artistic solitude. Inspiration—and cheap rent. If Wilson Beatty was prospecting out here, maybe they crossed paths. It's worth checking out."

He turned down an unmarked road, bouncing around potholes, attempting to dodge rocks and often failing. "Not much traffic out here."

"Or much pavement either."

They toiled past abandoned metal shacks, switchbacking past mining ruins and rusty and indefinable equipment. Steel cables sprawled like dead snakes across the rocks. They came upon empty trailers, abandoned homes—a dusty dump that was more of a ghost town than an active metropolis. A skeletal old windmill hung motionless in the sunlight as if hoping for a breeze. A shotgun-pocked sign announced that they had arrived in Frustration Corners. The utter silence was matched only by the intense heat.

Leaving the car parked in the ghost town, they walked among the creaking rusted buildings, finding the lone cabin that appeared to be inhabited; at least the windows were unbroken. On stilts at roof level, a large white plastic water tank stood tall enough to provide water pressure, filled by an occasional truck.

In front of the home was a bizarre garden of oddball sculptures constructed of scrap metal, old glass bottles, broken mirrors, automotive parts, telephone pole insulators, pieces held together by chains or rusty hinges. Mulder winced.

Scully frowned. "No wonder he hides his work out here in the middle of nowhere—where it belongs."

Among the odd junk contraptions, though, they discovered a different kind of statue, a lumpy human figure like a weathered old medicine man. Its feet were just stumps, as if it had been chiseled from a larger platform and propped in the middle of the sculpture garden.

Mulder leaned closer to the odd statue that looked entirely out of place among the kitschy junk sculptures. "Doesn't this remind you of something we just saw?"

The door to one of the old barns flung open and a man strode out, carrying a shotgun. "Who the hell are you and what are you doing out here? This is private property."

Scully froze. No time to reach for her weapon. "I thought this was a town. It's on the map."

"A private town."

"You must be Bernard Lumke," Mulder said. "We're big fans of your work."

Scully slowly reached into her jacket pocket and pulled out her badge. "We are Federal Agents, sir, investigating the death of a man who may have passed through here. He worked for a mineral exploitation company as a prospector and explorer."

Lumke advanced, still holding the shotgun. "Lots of prospectors came through here over the centuries, but I don't care about any of them. Just want to be left alone to do my work." He glanced at the Rube-Goldberg junk sculptures. "Unless you've come to buy?"

"Sorry, no room in my apartment," Mulder said.

"The man's name was Wilson Beatty. He worked for the Dry Sea Resource Works." Scully cautiously slid her business card into a gap in one of the rusty sculptures. "Please give us a call if you remember anything."

Mulder added, "Or if you get phone service."

Lumke's shotgun didn't waver the entire time it took them to return to their car and climb inside. "He doesn't seem to be much of a welcoming committee," Scully said as they cautiously descended the steep road out of town. "What does he do out here?"

"He's got my curiosity piqued." Mulder was actually smiling. "Lumke's agent operates out of Los Angeles, and she may be more willing to answer questions. Maybe we should find out more about him. He's known for his unusual statues." He raised his eyebrows, then grabbed the wheel again as they hit a pothole. "It's only a few hours drive, and we have unlimited miles on the rental car."

She looked out at the bleak, yet dramatic, desert scenery. "All right, I'd love to get out of this heat." She reached forward and turned the car's air conditioning up to MAX.

PENDRAGON GALLERY, LOS ANGELES
THURSDAY, 4:05 p.m.

Surrounded by vibrant skyscrapers instead of collapsing rusty buildings, Scully listened to the traffic on the streets, glad to be back in civilization again. They arrived at a small boutique art gallery, open for the day's business. A sign in the window still advertised the Lumke exhibition from three days before.

The Pendragon Gallery had no customers, and a slender well-dressed woman with lavishly cornrowed hair came forward wearing a smooth, professional smile. Scully pulled out her badge and identified herself. "Ms. Pendra, we'd like to ask a few questions about your client, Bernard Lumke. And how he makes those unusual statues."

The woman's face stiffened, as if it had turned into a statue. Long thin braids dangled around her face. "I'm afraid information about my client is confidential. He's a private person."

Mulder said, "We've noticed. We visited him in person earlier this morning."

Pendra's eyes widened. "Then you know more than I do. I've never even been to his studio up in Frustration Corners."

"Calling it a studio might be an… exaggeration," Scully said.

Mulder brought out the dossier of missing persons reports and spread them on one of the empty tables in the gallery. He arranged photographs, faxes, then unfolded the large map on which he had meticulously combined Wilson Beatty's explorations with the Last Seen reports. "Quite a few people have disappeared in the vicinity of Frustration Corners."

Pendra frowned at the map. "Bernard delivers his statues to the gallery, and I pay him whenever a piece sells. I'd be happy to show you his work, but I have little other interaction with him." She led them into the main room of the gallery. "He's been pestering me to exhibit his found-material sculptures, but I have no interest in those."

"I doubt anybody would," Mulder said. "We've seen them ourselves."

Several of the lumpy statues remained on display—the screaming man, the coyote, the figure bent over retching, the old-time prospector. Pendra seemed impressed with the work, but Scully couldn't imagine why anyone would own one of the odd monstrosities.

"You won't find similar work anywhere. Many of Bernard's pieces have sold to private collectors, but this selection shows the depths of his genius." Pendra handed them each a brochure. "And a price list, of course."

Mulder said, "I prefer lawn gnomes."

Scully refolded the brochure. "With prices like these... Mr. Lumke must be a very successful artist. He could afford a mansion in the hills. Why does he live out in the desert?"

"Bernard has all the amenities he needs, and he draws inspiration from the desert. Death Valley gives him all the raw material for his work."

Mulder studied a statue of a man wearing street clothes, but the details were obscured by white alkaline cement. He frowned when he looked at the statue's face, then went to his dossier of missing persons reports. He pulled out one of the sheets with a blurry faxed photo and held it up to the statue. "See any resemblance?"

Pendra chuckled. "You have an impressive imagination, Agent Mulder."

"Yes I do, but I also wonder . . ." He reached out to tap the stone forearm. "Why is this statue wearing a wristwatch?"

"Bernard's fixation with details has gained him critical acclaim."

Mulder removed the rental car keys and used the sharp end to chip at the statue's wristwatch. Pendra yelped. "Stop! That's a priceless work of art."

One sharp crack broke away the caked residue to reveal a real wristwatch with a crystal face under the stone. It was still ticking.

"Not a priceless work of art, Ms. Pendra," Scully said. "It's just a cheap Timex. But it is real... and so is the arm under it."

Pendra stared in horror, but Mulder couldn't tell if she was more shocked by the damage to the sculpture, or the suggestion that it was composed of an actual body.

He held up the photo of the missing person. "This statue—and I presume all of them—are human beings turned to stone. With a little digging and comparison, I suspect we can match all of Mr. Lumke's statues with these missing persons reports."

Pendra's mouth opened, closed, then opened again, like a fish in search of a hook. "Are you saying that Bernard Lumke is a serial killer?"

"We don't know how the petrification happens, Ms. Pendra," Scully said. "I'm taking these statues into evidence. I'll know more after I perform a detailed analysis."

Pendra pushed her way forward, indignant and still disbelieving. "*Analysis?* These are works of art. I can't let you—"

Mulder blocked her from coming closer, and as the woman struggled, he bumped the statue not entirely by accident. It crashed to the floor and shattered. Bones protruded from concrete-like skin, and even the head broke open like a thunder-egg, exposing crystallized lumps of brain.

Pendra reeled backward and put both of her hands against her face in an expression of complete horror, which was also a reasonable copy of *The Scream.*

FRUSTRATION CORNERS
DEATH VALLEY NATIONAL PARK
THURSDAY, 4:28 p.m.

Travis Ashton drove his Volvo up the rugged road on the edge of Death Valley as he made his way to a place called Frustration Corners. During the exhibition, the gallery owner agent had let slip that Bernard Lumke lived way out here, and if Ashton showed up on his doorstep, how could the man turn down an interview request?

Dust covered his windshield and the wipers did little to clear it. The washer fluid turned the smear of dust into a smear of mud, which made the task of dodging rocks and potholes even more difficult. He finally arrived at the ramshackle cluster of abandoned buildings, rusted mining equipment, a windmill—and a garden of artistic disappointments, scrap metal sculptures welded and painted with far more kitsch than charm. How could the artist who created the visceral sculptures on display at the Pendragon Gallery be the same person who had slapped together this trash?

He sighed. That was something he'd find out in the interview, an exclusive—inside the mind of one of the art world's hottest new discoveries.

Ashton stepped away from his car and shaded his eyes against the pounding sunlight. "Hello?" He listened for any noise, looked for any sign of habitation. A raven swooped overhead, scolding him. "Mr. Lumke! I'm an art critic from LA. Your agent, Kendra Pendra sent me here. She gave me your address." Not quite true, but it sounded legitimate.

He frowned at a bright pink Kokopelli made of cast iron and kitchen implements; another junk sculpture was a cute robot with an equally cute robot dog. Awful stuff! Then he saw the lumpy sculpture of a Native American medicine man—now that was the right stuff! So strikingly different from the tepid crap in the rest of the sculpture garden.

Lumke strode out of a less-dilapidated-looking home, one with glass in the windows and a big white water tank at roof level. "A critic? That's supposed to impress me?"

Ashton blurted out, "I respect your privacy, Mr. Lumke, so I've come alone. Nobody knows I'm here. I want to do an exclusive interview with you about your marvelous statues."

The sculptor remained cautious. "So you're not with those other two? From this morning?"

"What other two?" Ashton's pulse raced, and he stroked his goatee, concerned. Had someone else scooped him? "Did you talk to a different publication?"

Lumke brushed the thought aside. "Nevermind. I sent them away. I don't normally give interviews, but if you came alone..."

Ashton handed over his business card and kept talking, breathless. "Your excellent exhibition at the Pendragon Gallery drew a lot of attention. I'd present a very positive profile, and we could increase your exposure dramatically. Could I see your studio, get a glimpse of your technique?"

Lumke narrowed his close-set eyes. "I don't have a... traditional studio. I create my sculptures in concert with nature itself." He cast his gaze around the silent ghost town, then glanced at the rugged mountains dotted with caves and old mine shafts. "Maybe it is time I gave an exclusive interview. It's your lucky day, Mr. Ashton."

Ashton brightened. "Then it was worth the long drive from LA!"

Lumke drove his own 4x4 on a rugged jeep road up to a crack in the side of the rockfall. Ashton found the drive terrifying, but his excitement to see the unusual studio outweighed his fear.

Lumke stopped at the base of a slope of loose rock that led up to the narrow crack of a cave opening. He began to climb, expecting the critic to follow. "I've showed very few people. I draw all my inspiration from inside this cave. It's the genesis of every statue I've ever made."

Ashton was panting, dusty, sweating from the climb, but he was intrigued. "Your studio's inside the mountain? It doesn't look like a mine-shaft. Is it a natural opening?"

"Natural... and unnatural. I discovered it while exploring side canyons." He indicated complex petroglyphs on the rocks around the opening. "But the Shoshone found it long before I did." He gestured the critic inside as he switched on a powerful flashlight to illuminate the path ahead.

Ashton smiled. "This is exciting."

"Yes, it is," said Lumke. The two men worked their way deeper into the cave, and Lumke kept the flashlight directed toward their feet so they could pick their way around the fallen rocks, ducking under lumpy stone protrusions, leaving the window of daylight far behind them. Dust pattered down, and even their footsteps seemed to make the cave unstable.

Ashton sounded nervous as pebbles trickled down. "How much farther?"

"We're almost to the stream, and then you'll see marvels like you've never imagined."

Finally they emerged into a larger room that the single flashlight could not illuminate; the sounds of a stream trickling across the stone seemed refreshing. The cave air was cool and humid, strikingly different from the desert outside, with a sour alkaline smell. Lumke directed the flashlight down toward the flowing water that had sliced a channel across the cave floor.

"This is my special place. The Shoshone considered this grotto holy—I'm sure that's what the petroglyphs mean. You have to taste the water. It's like drinking liquid electricity."

Ashton's shadowed face showed concern. "Drink... the water? Wouldn't it be alkaline? I don't want to—"

"Purified and filtered through all this rock? It's the blood of the muse, you've never experienced anything like it. Fresh, pristine, cold... magical." Lumke hardened his voice. "And it's important background for your interview. If you're not willing..."

"All right." Ashton bent down to his knees, dipped his hands and scooped up a handful of water. He sipped, then slurped. "Tastes chalky, lots of dissolved minerals." He stood, wiped his wet hands on his pants. "Can we have more light so I can see where we are?"

"I've installed battery lanterns, connected with cords. Now I can show you everything you need to see." Lumke found a switch, and lanterns illuminated a giant grotto, filled with stalactites, stalagmites, and glittering crystals that grew out of the ceiling. The stream flowed across the floor and poured through a crack into unseen chambers below. "This is my real statue gallery."

Ashton suddenly realized that many of the thick, shadowy stalagmites rising from the floor were *human-shaped*, people covered with layers and layers of deposited stone, as if someone had poured hardening wax on top of them. Some had been there so long their arms or legs were barely discernible, while others looked fresh. Ashton noticed fresh gashes in the cave floor, where Lumke had chopped out the existing statues.

"Nature is the sculptor."

Ashton stared at the display and tried to form questions, but he was breathing heavily. He clutched his throat, wiped his mouth, and swallowed, but it felt as if his chest had filled with gravel. "My mouth... tastes like sand." He shook his head, raised a hand and tried to flex his fingers. "My arms and legs. I can barely move."

"It's the water," Lumke said, matter-of-fact. "Simple contact with the skin is sufficient, but that takes so much longer. Now that you've actually swallowed the water, the internal process should go fairly quickly. You'll be part of my next exhibition."

Ashton tried to turn, already stiffening in place. He couldn't lift his leg. "What have you done to me?"

Lumke just smiled and stood watching. "I always hated critics."

———————

FRUSTRATION CORNERS
DEATH VALLEY NATIONAL PARK
FRIDAY, 10:58 a.m.

Driving back to Death Valley the next day, this time prepared to confront the reclusive sculptor, Mulder wound the rental car up the road to Frustration Corners. Whether or not he had done it purposefully,

Lumke knew what caused the fossilization of the victims, and they needed to learn what it was.

When the two agents reached the ghost town, Mulder looked at the dilapidated buildings. "I could get used to this place, Scully." He parked in front of the bizarre junk-sculpture garden with the kitschy metal contraptions. "Or maybe not." He saw a dusty but relatively new Volvo partially hidden behind a big rusty shack, a vehicle he had not noticed before.

Scully emerged with her weapon already drawn. "I hope he gives us a warmer welcome than he did last time." Mulder followed, also drawing his Sig Sauer.

Kendra Pendra had been taken in for questioning in LA, and FBI teams were rounding up all of Lumke's statues that had previously been sold to private collectors. Once the art connoisseurs learned that the life-like sculptures came complete with a real human body inside, few would object to having them removed.

Scully raised her pistol, looking toward the lone inhabited house with its water tank. "Federal agents, Mr. Lumke. You're wanted for questioning in several murders."

The sculptor must have seen and heard them drive up. A moment later, the man emerged from his ramshackle house, holding his hands up and looking alarmed. "Don't shoot! I haven't done anything wrong—I'm just an artist. I'm no murderer."

Mulder said, "Sir, we know you're connected with at least eight missing persons who disappeared in this area."

Lumke wore an innocent and baffled expression that wasn't entirely convincing. "Eight missing persons? That's more people than I see in a year!"

"Their bodies were found inside the statues you exhibited at the Pendragon Gallery," Scully said. "We have a warrant for your arrest."

The sculptor was aghast. "You're saying those statues are *real people*? My God!" He swallowed hard, looked nervous and terrified. "I thought they were natural formations. I find them in a cave nearby."

Mulder nodded toward the lumpy Shoshone statue, which looked so out of place among the kitschy junk sculptures. "*Natural* formations?"

Still holding her handgun, Scully looked at her partner. "We need to see the source of the petrification process, Mulder. And we have to make sure no one else is exposed, like Wilson Beatty."

Lumke seemed overly earnest and cooperative. "I can show you if you don't believe me. It's only a mile away." Ignoring the weapons pointed toward him, the sculptor rolled open the corrugated garage door of an adjacent shed to reveal a 4x4 off-road vehicle. "I'll drive. That rental car of yours won't make it a tenth of a mile up the road we're going. Come on, you can see for yourselves. I haven't killed anybody."

The two agents kept their weapons handy while Lumke drove in low gear, grinding up a steep road that didn't look like a road at all. Mulder thought the eccentric artist routine was just an act, and he remained guarded. Through the passenger window, Scully peered over the edge of an impressive drop-off. The wheels seemed only inches from the precipice.

"Nobody else knows this route." Lumke sounded cheerful, chatty, as if desperate to demonstrate complete cooperation. When even the hint of a road petered out, he ground the 4x4 to a halt and engaged the parking brake. "We'll have to go on foot from here." He glanced at the agents' professional attire. "You might get a little dusty."

Mulder climbed out to stand on the rocks. "Don't worry, these are my hiking clothes."

Scully was tense, keeping her hand on her weapon. "Show us the source of the statues, Mr. Lumke."

They climbed up the steep talus and scree to reach a gash in the mountainside—not an old mine shaft, but a cave. Mulder was intrigued by the petroglyphs around the opening. "I recognize some of these. They're warning symbols."

"The Shoshone called this a sacred place," Lumke said. "When their great medicine men grew too old, they would come to this cave and give up their lives to *become* part of the mountains. Other people must have found it over the years, too. It's a natural wonder. I'll show you the grotto, and you can decide for yourselves." He strode inside, expecting them to follow. "Careful—I don't think the rock is terribly stable."

Scully frowned, but Mulder lowered his voice. "We have to see." He entered the cave, calling out. "Wait for us—we've got very good flashlights."

They entered the dusty, cool passageway, their lights splashing bright pools on the narrow confines. The rock looked loose and crumbly, crusted over with powdery white residue. Several confusing side passages branched off in various dead ends, but the artist led the way. "I promise, it'll be worth it. You've never seen anything like this."

They wound their way through the labyrinth, following Lumke, alert for any treachery. When the cave opened into a large grotto filled with the sound of running water, Lumke sounded boyishly excited. "The first time I stumbled in here, I thought it was a cave of wonders, like in *Aladdin*." He found a switch on the wall and illuminated several electric lanterns he had set in place.

As light flooded the grotto, Mulder and Scully saw a stone floor studded with lumpy stone figures. Human figures. Animal figures. Mulder shone his flashlight on a cluster of lumps on the ceiling, like rock protrusions.

Bats, fossilized in place.

At the back wall of the grotto, a human hand protruded from the flowing mass of travertine, as if grasping for escape. Another figure had been in the cave so long it looked as if a truckload of molten wax had poured on top of him.

But one statue was fresh and white, obviously new—a young man with a goatee. His hands were clutching his throat, frozen in place. Scully inspected the statue. "Total replacement of body tissue with mineralized deposits."

Mulder bent over the stream in the center of the cavern, sniffing. "You can smell the chemicals."

Scully touched the statue of the young man, rubbed her fingertips together. "The water in this cave must have a highly unusual combination of dissolved salts and minerals. A mixture that has a natural affinity for organic material—a very strong affinity. Like a seed crystal suspended in a saturated solution, these dissolved minerals turn skin and muscle into stone."

Mulder stood at the edge of the stream. "Mr. Lumke, you've been here numerous times, but you haven't been exposed."

Water trickled from the stalactites above. A large drop splashed on Lumke's shoulder, and he looked at it in alarm, frantically brushing the droplet away. "I've been careful."

"And why didn't you report this as soon as you discovered the grotto?" Scully asked. "These 'statues' are obviously *people*."

"I thought they were human fossils at first, works of art made by the mountains themselves. So I removed one from the cave and showed it to Ms. Pendra, just as a curiosity. I was trying to get her to set up an exhibition for my found-material sculptures, but she wasn't interested. When she saw the fossil statues, though, she got excited. In fact, the fossil statues were all anybody wanted." He shook his head. "I sold one immediately, then two more. I was trying to form an artistic career. I couldn't tell her I had just *found* them, could I?"

Scully stood with Mulder beside the stream, sniffing the alkaline water in the air.

Lumke continued, "The popularity took me by surprise. After struggling for so many years, I couldn't turn down avid buyers, and the demand grew so great that I had to create more statues." In the eerie half-light of the electric lanterns, his smile became strange. "For that, I needed more raw material."

He lunged forward as Mulder and Scully both whirled to raise their weapons, but he wasn't trying to subdue them—just knock them off balance. Like a charging linebacker, the sculptor rammed into the two agents and shoved them backward.

Mulder staggered, his shoes slipping on the cave floor. Scully grabbed him for balance, but they both tumbled into the running stream. It was only three feet deep, but their clothes were soaked. Mulder even got a mouthful of the water and he spat it out, gasping.

As they scrambled out of the slick streambed, Lumke ran to the edge of the grotto and doused the electric lanterns, so that only the uncertain flashlight beams played havoc through the gallery.

Mulder fired his Sig Sauer at the sculptor's receding flashlight beam, but the bullet ricocheted off a stalactite. Dust trickled down from cracks in the ceiling. Scully also fired her weapon, a loud boom, but Lumke was retreating, abandoning them. He fled, dodging up the steep path, ducking the ceiling boulders. He shouted back at them, "It's only a matter of time—you've already touched the cave water."

Wet and annoyed, Mulder recovered and made sure Scully was all right. At least his flashlight still worked, even though the electric lanterns had been doused. "Lumke knows the way out of here, but we can find the path, I think." He wanted to get out of the cave before the sculptor got to his 4x4 and drove off, stranding them in the desert.

"Mulder, the water… " Scully said, and there was a dry rasp in her voice.

He could already feel a tingle on his skin as he ran after the suspect. His suit jacket and slacks felt stiff. His legs creaked as he ran. "Let's get out of here."

Scully was gasping. "We have to wash this off of us. We need clean water."

He didn't remind her that they were in the middle of Death Valley, and clean water would not be easy to find. "How long do we have?"

"No idea what the reaction rate is. Wilson Beatty drove all the way to Furnace Creek. We'd better run."

But the cave was like a maze. Mulder didn't remember the exact way out, but they worked their way through the main passageway, trying to follow flickers from Lumke's light. Dust and stones trickled down from the ceiling; the resounding echoes from their gunshots had disturbed the cave's delicate equilibrium.

They climbed over boulders and turned past a side passage. Ahead, Mulder spotted a glint of Lumke's receding flashlight, but the sculptor disappeared, maybe ducking into a hiding place.

"If the petrification has started, he knows he can just wait us out," Scully said. "The mineral contaminants—"

"We're not going to just wait." Mulder tugged on her arm as he led them through winding cracks that looked familiar. "Switch off your flashlight. Maybe we can see daylight ahead."

They both did so, groping along; they heard more stones pattering down, a deep grumble as the rocks resettled. Mulder worried they might be buried in a cave-in sooner than they were fossilized.

Larger rocks crumbled from the ceiling, loose boulders from the tight walls sloughing down, disturbed by the increasing tremors.

Scully was gasping, and Mulder's chest felt heavy, like cement.

Finally, they pushed their way around a tight dog leg, relieved to see a slice of sunlight ahead. He worried that Lumke was waiting to ambush them—but they emerged into the dry, open air finding only emptiness, no sign of the murderous sculptor.

And his 4x4 parked on the rocky trail.

"He must still be hiding in the cave," Scully said. "He knows we have weapons, and he's confident we'll turn to stone before we catch him."

"We'll get him later—first I want to get us to fresh water." Mulder tried to brush himself off, but cave dust covered them. "Remind me never to take up spelunking as a hobby." He pulled off his jacket and threw it aside, but the mineralized water had already soaked through his shirt and pants. He felt his skin tightening, his joints seizing up. Or maybe he was just imagining it.

Reeling, exhausted, uncoordinated like two stiffening marionettes, they staggered down the rocks toward the vehicle. Mulder heard rocks and small avalanches continue to fall in the unstable cave behind them, but he was intent on getting back to Frustration Corners, Lumke's home—in hopes of finding indoor plumbing.

Together, they reached the 4x4 and slumped against it, sure that they would make it now...

Bernard Lumke had ducked into a side passage and watched the two doomed agents stagger past. They would turn to stone before long, and he only had to wait—and avoid being shot. If he had gone out into the open, they might have seen him, fired on him. Better just to lie low. His pulse was racing.

From the side alcove, he watched them pick their way upward and out into the light. Well, if they became statues in the open, it would be a lot easier to move them. For his next exhibition.

Moving cautiously ahead, he heard the shift and grumble of the unstable cave walls and ceiling. The loud gunfire had caused enough tremors to start a domino effect. He had not anticipated how fragile the cave was.

As he made his way out of the side passage, scrambling toward the entrance, the rocks continued to fall. One struck his shoulder, and he ducked. Discarding caution, he pushed ahead as more boulders slid down, blocking the entrance.

Shouting, he raised his hands to ward off the rocks but the debris kept coming down.

Mulder and Scully staggered across the rocky landscape, one step, then another. The blazing sun pounded down. "Honest, Scully, I thought *you* knew how to hotwire a car..."

Scully kept going, determined. "If we don't wash off soon… we'll become part of the landscape."

Mulder managed to raise his stiffening arms, which were caked with a whitish residue. He was visibly getting grayer, turning to stone. He tried to sound defiant. "I will not become a lawn ornament."

Scully touched her face, pressed her hardening cheek. "Skin… losing plasticity… Crystalizing." She looked at her trembling hand, bent her fingers but could not straighten them again. "Muscle control increasingly difficult."

Mulder grabbed her arm and pulled her forward. "Come on." He looked up and finally saw the ramshackle town of Frustration Corners, the collapsed buildings, the rusty equipment. "That's not a mirage."

They staggered among the collapsed shacks and into Bernard Lumke's weird sculpture garden of junk contraptions. As they struggled to keep moving, Mulder couldn't help but think of the photos he'd seen of Wilson Beatty, just before he collapsed in front of the Furnace Creek Ranch.

He spotted the water supply tank mounted to the roof of Lumke's home. With a stiffening arm and shaking hand, he raised his Sig Sauer and fired off three shots, puncturing the wall of the cistern. Warm water gushed out like transparent blood.

Scully lurched under the downpour. "Quick, Mulder—any longer and our tissues won't be able to recover." The two stood under the gush of water, which drenched them, rinsed them. Mulder knew they would still need extensive IVs and complete cleansing for a full recovery, but right now just the stream of tepid water felt absolutely wonderful.

"It's not professional for two partners to take a shower together," Mulder said, already feeling the residue wash away. "This time I'll make an exception."

They stood under the pouring water, scrubbing, rinsing, recovering, until the cistern was completely drained.

Bernard Lumke tried to claw his way through the rockfall, but the cave entrance was entirely sealed. His flashlight battery was weak now, and in the dim light, his bloodied hands were starting to look chalky.

It would have been better just to die in the avalanche.

When he made his way along familiar passageways to the grotto, he turned on his battery-powered lanterns, which lit up the eerie display of the fossilized damned. Water from the stalactites dripped down, splashing into the stream of deadly concentrated minerals.

The statues—both the ancient relics and his recent victims—surrounded him as darkness closed in. Tainted water continued to trickle around him, on him. Lumke swallowed hard in his dry throat. He was already very thirsty.

When the battery lanterns finally went out, he shouted, "Help me!"

But the darkness returned, giving him no answer. He heard only the continuously dripping water and the silence of stones, and he discovered that he could no longer move—at all.

THE END

AUTHOR BIOS

TIM LEBBON is a *New York Times* best-selling horror and fantasy writer from South Wales. He's had almost 30 novels published to date, as well as dozens of novellas and hundreds of short stories. His most recent releases include the apocalyptic *Coldbrook*, *Alien: Out of the Shadows*, *Into the Void: Dawn of the Jedi* (*Star Wars*), and the Toxic City trilogy from Pyr in the USA. Future novels include *The Silence* (Titan UK/USA) and the thriller *Endure*. He has won four British Fantasy Awards, a Bram Stoker Award, and a Scribe Award, and has been a finalist for World Fantasy, International Horror Guild, and Shirley Jackson Awards. Works in development for screen include *Pay the Ghost* (starring Nicolas Cage), children's spooky animated film *My Haunted House*, his script *Playtime* (written with Stephen Volk), and *Exorcising Angels* (with Simon Clark). Find out more about Tim at his website timlebbon.net.

PETER CLINES grew up in the Stephen King fallout zone of Maine and—fuelled by a love of comic books, *Star Wars*, and Saturday morning cartoons—started writing science fiction and dark fantasy stories at the age of eight. He is the author of the upcoming novel *The Fold*; the best-selling superheroes-vs-zombies *Ex-Heroes* series (including the upcoming *Ex-Isle*); the acclaimed, genre-twisting *14*; numerous short stories; countless articles about the film and television industry; and an as-yet undiscovered Dead Sea Scroll. He currently lives and writes somewhere in southern California.

AARON ROSENBERG is an award-winning, #1 best-selling novelist, children's book author, and game designer. His novels include the best-selling DuckBob series (consisting of *No Small Bills, Too Small for Tall,* and the forthcoming *Three Small Coinkydinks*), the Dread Remora space-opera series and, with David Niall Wilson, the O.C.L.T. occult thriller series. His tie-in work contains novels for *Star Trek, Warhammer, WarCraft,* and *Eureka.* He has written children's books, including the original series *Pete and Penny's Pizza Puzzles,* the award-winning *Bandslam: The Junior Novel,* and the #1 best-selling *42: The Jackie Robinson Story.* Aaron has also written educational books on a variety of topics and over seventy roleplaying games, such as the original games *Asylum, Spookshow,* and *Chosen,* work for White Wolf, Wizards of the Coast, Fantasy Flight, Pinnacle, and many others, and both the Origins Award-winning *Gamemastering Secrets* and the Gold ENnie-winning *Lure of the Lich Lord.* He is the co-creator of the ReDeus series, and one of the founders of Crazy 8 Press. Aaron lives in New York with his family. You can follow him online at gryphonrose.com, on Facebook at facebook.com/gryphonrose, and on Twitter @gryphonrose.

PAUL CRILLEY is a Scotsman living in South Africa. He wrote *The Invisible Order* series for Egmont USA, *The Adventures of Tweed & Nightingale* for PYR, and the award-winning detective novels *The Abraxis Wren Chronicles* for Wizards of the Coast. Paul also writes computer games, comics, and television scripts. He worked on the Bioware/Lucasarts MMO *Star Wars: The Old Republic* and adapted his *Eberron* detective duo Abraxis Wren and Torin for comic publishers IDW. He recently planned out and wrote three issues of their six-issue comic crossover series, *X-Files: Conspiracy.*

STEFAN PETRUCHA has written over 20 novels and hundreds of graphic novels. His work has sold over a million copies worldwide. He also teaches online classes through the University of Massachusetts. Born in the Bronx, he spent his formative years moving between the big city and the suburbs, both of which made him prefer escapism. A fan of comic books, science fiction and horror since learning to read, in high school and college he added a love for all sorts of literary work, eventually learning that the very best fiction always brings you back to reality, so, really, there's no way out. Much more on him and whatever madness he's currently perpetrating can be had at petrucha.com.

BRIAN KEENE writes novels, comic books, short fiction, and occasional journalism for money. He is the author of over 40 books, mostly in the horror, crime, and dark fantasy genres. His 2003 novel, *The Rising*, is often credited (along with Robert Kirkman's *The Walking Dead* comic and Danny Boyle's *28 Days Later* film) with inspiring pop culture's current interest in zombies. Keene's novels have been translated into German, Spanish, Polish, Italian, French, Taiwanese, and many more. In addition to his own original work, Keene has written for media properties such as *Doctor Who, Hellboy, Masters of the Universe,* and *Superman.*

KEITH R. A. DECANDIDO has written fiction in more than two dozen different media universes, ranging from other TV shows (*Star Trek, Doctor Who, Supernatural, Stargate SG-1,* and many more) to movies (*Serenity, Resident Evil, Big Hero 6, Cars*) to games (*World of Warcraft, Dungeons & Dragons, Command & Conquer, StarCraft*), and lots more. He also has written plenty of fiction in his own universes: the "Precinct" series of fantasy police procedurals, starting with *Dragon Precinct* and continuing through several novels and short stories; and a series of urban fantasy stories set in Key West, Florida that have appeared in *Buzzy Mag,* the collection *Ragnarok and Roll,* and the anthologies *Tales from the House Band Volumes 1 & 2, Bad-Ass Faeries: It's Elemental,* and *Out of Tune.* Recent and upcoming work includes *Star Trek: The Klingon Art of War, Sleepy Hollow: Children of the Revolution,* the novelization of *Big Hero 6,* the short story collection *Without a License,* the graphic novel *Icarus,* and "Time Keeps on Slippin'" in *Stargate SG-1/Atlantis: Far Horizons.* Keith is also a veteran podcaster, a second-degree black belt in karate, a rabid baseball fan—oh yeah, and he also helped run two small *X-Files* fan conventions in New Jersey in the mid-1990s. Because he's that much of a dork. Find out less at his web site at DeCandido.net.

RAY GARTON has been writing novels, novellas, short stories, and essays for more than 30 years. His work spans the genres of horror, crime, suspense, and even comedy. His titles include *Live Girls, Ravenous, The Loveliest Dead, Sex and Violence in Hollywood, Meds,* and most recently, *Frankenstorm.* His short stories have appeared in magazines and anthologies, and have been collected in books like *Methods of Madness, Pieces of Hate,* and *Slivers of Bone.* He has been nominated for the Bram Stoker Award and, in 2006, received the Grand Master of Horror Award. He lives in northern California with his wife, where he is currently at work on several projects, including a new novel. Visit his website at RayGartonOnline.com.

TIM DEAL is a writer, editor, a Bram Stoker Award Finalist, and an adjunct professor of writing and liberal arts. He's currently working with the U.S. Army and the State Department in providing security training and support in the Middle East. He has three kids, two dogs, and one wife (for now).

GINI KOCH writes the best-selling fast, fresh and funny Alien/Katherine "Kitty" Katt series for DAW Books, the Necropolis Enforcement Files series, and the Martian Alliance Chronicles series for Musa Publishing. As G.J. Koch she writes the *Alexander Outland* series and she's made the most of multiple personality disorder by writing in a variety of genres under a variety of other pen names as well, including Anita Ensal, Jemma Chase, A.E. Stanton, and J.C. Koch. Please buy her books — her meds don't come free. Her work *Touched by an Alien* (Alien Series #1) was named as one of Booklist's Top Ten Adult SF Novels of 2010. *Alien in the House* (Alien Series #7) won the RT Book Reviews Reviewer's Choice Award as the Best Futuristic Romance of 2013. The Alien/ Katherine "Kitty" Katt books are consistent Barnes & Noble and Ingram's bestsellers.

W.D. GAGLIANI is the author of the novels *Wolf's Trap, Wolf's Gambit, Wolf's Bluff, Wolf's Edge, Wolf's Cut, Wolf's Blind* (upcoming), and *Savage Nights. Wolf's Trap* was a finalist for the Bram Stoker Award in 2004. He has published fiction and nonfiction in numerous anthologies and publications such as *Robert Bloch's Psychos, Undead Tales, More Monsters From Memphis, The Midnighters Club*. His book reviews and nonfiction have been included in, among others, *The Milwaukee Journal Sentinel, Chizine, HorrorWorld, Cemetery Dance, Hellnotes, Science Fiction Chronicle, The Scream Factory, The Writer* magazine, and the books *Thrillers: 100 Must Reads, They Bite,* and *On Writing Horror*. **DAVID BENTON** has worn many hats: warehouse worker, landscaper, printing press operator, cheese maker, brick layer, and janitor. As a musician, he is the bass player for Milwaukee band Chief and tour bassist with the heavy metal novelty act Beatallica. The team of Gagliani & Benton has published fiction in venues such as *SNAFU: An Anthology of Military Horror, SNAFU: Wolves at the Door, Dark Passions: Hot Blood 13, Zippered Flesh 2, Masters of Unreality* (Germany), *Malpractice: An Anthology of Bedside Terror, Splatterpunk Zine,* and *Dead Lines,* along with the Kindle Worlds *Vampire Diaries* tie-in "Voracious in Vegas." Some of their collaborations are available in the collection *Mysteries & Mayhem*. Find them both on Facebook: facebook.com/wdgagliani and facebook.com/david.benton.7509. W.D. Gagliani can also be found at wdgagliani.com and on Twitter at @WDGagliani.

HEATHER GRAHAM is the International, *NYT* and *USA Today* best-selling author of over two hundred novels, novellas, and stories. The founder of Slushpile Productions, she hosts numerous venues with dinner theater and author rock bands for various children's charities. Heather Graham and the Slushpile also have a number of recordings available on iTunes and other venues. Creepy-crawly-scary things have long intrigued her. She has written horror, suspense, romance, historical fiction, and Christmas family fare. Find her on Facebook or at theoriginalheathergraham.com. She sincerely hopes you enjoy her entry here as she is an avid *X-Files* fan!

MAX ALLAN COLLINS is the author of the Shamus-winning Nathan Heller historical thrillers (*Ask Not*) and the graphic novel *Road to Perdition*, basis for the Academy Award-winning film. His TV tie-ins include *CSI* and *Criminal Minds*, and his movie novels include *Saving Private Ryan* and *The X-Files: I Want to Believe*. His innovative '70s series, *Quarry*, has been revived by Hard Case Crime (*Quarry's Choice*) and he has completed eight posthumous Mickey Spillane novels (*King of the Weeds*).

GAYLE LYNDS is the *New York Times* best-selling Queen of Espionage. Her recent novel, *The Book of Spies*, was named one of the five best thrillers of 2011 by *Library Journal*. Her novel *Masquerade* is among *Publishers Weekly's* Top Ten Spy Novels of All Time. She is a member of the Association for Former Intelligence Officers and the co-founder (with David Morrell) of International Thriller Writers. Gayle interested **JOHN C. SHELDON** in fiction after they married in 2011. John, a former Maine state judge and Visiting Scholar to Harvard Law School, had published frequently in legal journals. He now prefers writing fiction because "you can blow things up and grease people." They live together on fourteen wooded acres outside Portland, Maine.

KEVIN J. ANDERSON has published 125 books, more than 50 of which have been national or international best sellers. He has written three *X-Files* novels and numerous novels in the *Star Wars* and *Dune* universes, as well as a unique steampunk fantasy novel, *Clockwork Angels*, based on the concept album by legendary rock group Rush. His original works include the Saga of Seven Suns series, the Terra Incognita fantasy trilogy, the Saga of Shadows trilogy, and his humorous horror series featuring Dan Shamble, Zombie PI. He has edited numerous anthologies, including the *Five by Five* and *Blood Lite* series. Anderson and his wife Rebecca Moesta are the publishers of WordFire Press. Wordfirepress.com.